D0772944

AGOAK

The Legacy of Agaguk

Yves Thériault has had a number of books translated
into English including:

Agaguk (McGraw-Hill Ryerson)
Ashini (Harvest House)
N'Tsuk (Harvest House)
Ways of the Flesh (Gage)

AGOAK
The Legacy of Agaguk

Yves Thériault
Translated by John David Allan

McGraw-Hill Ryerson Limited

Toronto Montréal New York St. Louis San Francisco
Auckland Beirut Bogotá Düsseldorf Johannesburg Lisbon
London Lucerne Madrid Mexico New Delhi Panama
Paris San Juan São Paulo Singapore Sydney Tokyo

AGOAK
The Legacy of Agaguk

Canadian Cataloguing in Publication Data

Thériault, Yves, date
  [Agoak. English]
  Agoak

Translation of Agoak.
Sequel to Agaguk.

ISBN 0-07-082947-0 bd
ISBN 0-07-082934-9 pa

I. Title. II. Title: Agoak. English.

PS8539.H43A6513   C843'.5'4   C78-001636-X
PQ3919.T4A6513

1 2 3 4 5 6 7 8 9 10 D 8 7 6 5 4 3 2 1 0 9

Printed and bound in Canada

CONTENTS

PART ONE
THE ESKIMOS

CHAPTER I

When he had come of age, tested his mettle and set his sights on certain goals, Agoak donned the three-piece suit which people in Povungnituk said he wore so well, withdrew a good portion of his savings from the Caisse Populaire and left for Frobisher Bay, his future home. A bush plane belonging to a pilot friend took him as far as Fort Chimo. From there he travelled on the Nordair 737 which serves Frobisher Bay. Agoak arrived at his destination and had the Nanook taxi take him to the big building in the centre of town, a building taller than he might have imagined. He had been told at the airport it was the nerve centre of Frobisher, incorporating the hotel and related facilities, the shops, the bank and other key public meeting points of this Arctic settlement, whose very size suddenly alarmed Agoak a little. As his taxi travelled along the gravel road, he noticed numerous fuel-storage tanks of an imposing size, a baffling quantity of different antennas and a reddish-brown building marked Telesat. Here at last was one landmark he knew about — the place where all those aerial pulsations from the Anik satellite ended up. He also spotted the school and the offices of both the federal and territorial governments. A little dazed with having taken in so many sights so quickly, Agoak finally entered the hotel. He hadn't reserved a room, but it was the off-season. Summer was over and the approaching winter had begun to leave morning frosts and a chill in the air, portents of the misery to come, even if it was still more imagined than real.

Agoak was promptly given a room on the third floor of the six-floor hotel. He was dressed like a White and carefully groomed, and his English left nothing to be desired. Where doors were opened to Agoak, an Eskimo travelling by dog-team and reeking of seal and rancid fish might well have been turned away. Agoak's stay in Moosonee, and his two study trips to Montreal and Toronto respectively, had taught him much about relations between Whites and Eskimos, as well as about the differences between the norms of the South and those of the North. He had a fairly stoical approach to his dealings with the Whites, such as they were, having learned to appreciate that everyone's personal development must move through trying and often unpredictable stages. As an Eskimo, he was in fact rather surprised at having been welcomed so warmly, a turn of events he attributed to his manner of dressing and the attention he paid to being neat, well-groomed and articulate in English. He was not unaware, however, of the way a full-blooded Inuk, a repository of the ancient traditions, could be treated on occasion. He had seen this for himself, even in Povungnituk, where Eskimo life was much less altered than it was here, or at Fort Chimo, or again, as he had been told, at Inuvik, far away to the west across the Top of the World.

In the spirit of his grandfather Agaguk (this grandfather who now seemed so remote!), Agoak was anxious to explore the new territory for himself. After freshening up in his room, shaving and preening as much as he thought necessary, he headed off on foot into the fresh, windy weather. He had begun by strolling around inside the hotel and shopping complex. Once outside he surveyed Frobisher itself down to the ground, doing perfect justice to his heritage. He looked over the town's amenities, put his nose to the wind and came very close to examining the ground for tracks, all in order to acquire a gut awareness of what this new world held in store for him, the pleasant surprises as well as the dangers.

The next day, satisfied that he had found a wavelength he could tune in to, Agoak began looking for work. He had devoted a whole day to locating the points of interest, the residential areas, the stores, business firms and the offices of the various governments. He knew where to find the hospital, the bars, the restaurants, the cafés, the local branch of the Bay and various other facilities. He had toured the different neighborhoods of the town and sized up some of their basic differences.

He was aware he didn't know everything about Frobisher, but he had learned enough to form a clear overall picture. He could live well in this place, and even prosper in it. Since returning to Povungnituk from his study trips, he had worked as a bookkeeper for the Eskimo Art Co-operative, and on several occasions had filled in for staff at the Caisse Populaire when they were on leave or holidays, or had taken ill. With this experience behind him, he turned up for an appointment at the Frobisher bank. He had not always been well-received elsewhere, but this time he hit it off with the manager. They got right down to business and two days later he began work as a teller, to become the virtually heaven-sent replacement for an employee who had grown weary of the Arctic and fled to the South without even collecting his final pay cheque.

Although he had just settled in, Agoak could already boast that he had cleared the first hurdle. Had old Agaguk not always secured his survival by first checking the lay of the land? Then, and only then, did he select a site for his dwelling. Agoak would follow his example.

Now, however, it was no longer a simple question, as it was in the old days for Agaguk, of wandering across the tundra until a location was found which accorded with the usual demands of the weather and the basic needs of life. For an Inuk immigrating to a town, other standards, those of the Whites, of civilization, of progress, created demands of another sort. Having been hired at the bank made Agoak eligible for a dwelling. However, the search for a roof had to be made through a particular agency. After making inquiries, Agoak learned he would have to meet the local officer in charge of accommodation. He was a man with problems and was constantly being bombarded by requests for shelter. He had at his disposal only a small housing quota, which could not be increased without the grudging approval of the Government of the Territories and its apathetic bureaucrats. They had the last say on the town council's expansion projects and more often than not withheld approval. Over a two day period, therefore, Agoak was forced to shunt back and forth from one bureaucrat to another, and start his laborious explanations from scratch each time. As might have been expected, he was immediately offered accommodations — in the form of a simple two-room apartment — in one of the buildings designed for new residents such as him. But Agoak knew he could claim for a house and it was to a house that he intended to bring Judith. Unfortunately, he was not yet married to the girl, so that administratively speaking, she did not exist. Otherwise she would have to be considered his common-law wife, and in the strict and puritanical outlook of the bureaucrats, this was unthinkable. In extreme cases, involving low-class Inuit laborers, such liaisons might be tolerated, but a bank teller was on a level with the White Man and, this being the case, it was essential that everything be in order, or as the expression had it — *legal and proper*.

"She must be your wife," the bureaucrat declared.

"She will be," said Agoak. "When I come back with her to take possession of my house."

"Of the house that will be allocated to you," the bureaucrat said, correcting him.

"Fine, as you wish. But when she gets here, we'll have been married in Povungnituk."

Finally, with less than good grace, they told Agoak, "Houses are in short supply and we don't want to find ourselves having to evict you. Sign this document."

It was a sworn statement that Judith and Agoak would not return unless they were legally married and had in their possession official testimony confirming this beyond any shadow of a doubt.

Once that was done, the bureaucrats went into a huddle and discussed in a half whisper whether Agoak should be tucked away in the White section or in the Eskimo village of Ikaluit. It was Agoak himself who cut short their discussions.

"I'm looking forward to working with Whites," he said, "but all the same I'd rather live in Ikaluit."

There were disapproving looks, but Agoak paid no attention. During his walking tours through Frobisher he had taken note of the freedom of movement enjoyed by the Inuit. They were allowed to go practically anywhere and, on the whole, to enjoy a degree of freedom Agoak had never witnessed before. He was aware that by moving into the Ikaluit neighborhood he might incur certain problems, but his idea of making the transition into White society involved a long, slow process, one which had begun for him quite some time ago. He was sixteen when, as a brilliant pupil at school, with little taste for hunting expeditions or meals of raw seal-meat or frozen fish, he had earned the right to complete his studies in Moosonee. Once there, however, and faced with the prospect of going to Toronto to take a university degree, he had hesitated, equivocated, weighed the alternatives and finally made his way back to Povungnituk. This was not necessarily the end of the matter, but for the time being there was Judith, whom he missed terribly. It had occurred to him to pluck her out of her present environment, bring her to Toronto with him and leave the Eskimo world behind them once and for all. But how could the two of them hope to survive in what was reputed to be such a hostile environment? Fearing the consequences of what he thought might be a rash undertaking, he had chosen to return, in the anticipation that there might be other paths to follow. And so he found work at the Co-operative, at the same time promising Judith that with prudence, foresight and diligence, he might manage to take her away with him one day.

Agoak spent much of that evening pondering his fate. With a cup of coffee on the table beside his armchair, he sat in his hotel room and passed his life in review. What struck him most of all was the felt presence of his primitive background. He conjured up childhood days when life was much as it was described in the ancient stories told by the old people. Naturally Agoak had not been born in an igloo; he had been raised in one of the prefabricated houses provided free for the Eskimos. His childhood home was an inelegant structure, a mere box, whose only saving grace seemed to be that it shut out the cold a little better than the traditional igloo. But there were three other children younger than Agoak in the house, with all the attendant noise, commotion and lack of privacy. Comforts which were now fairly commonplace had not always been available. Then one day electricity and propane gas had suddenly appeared, along with the snowmobile, which virtually replaced the dog-sled for winter travel. But the house was still small and they crowded together in it as best they could, and while the igloo seemed far off in the past, their present situation had little to commend it in the way of physical comfort. Agoak's father, whose talents as a sculptor quickly gained attention, earned a fairly good living at the Art Co-op, and the family allowance cheques from Ottawa helped too; but this only allowed them to escape abject poverty and nothing more. Agoak had long since resolved to realize his dreams and go elsewhere, go where an Inuk had the best prospects.

"One day I'll leave," Agoak had often said to Judith

Judith, her face contorted and her eyes full of pain, would look away nervously. Usually she would say nothing, though occasionally she would mutter, "You'll never come back."

"I will come back, I promise."

Then she would begin to cry to herself.

Down through the ages, the Eskimo woman has played the role of the drudge, the slave, the subjugated but uncomplaining female. She has always been patient and resigned and since any thought of revolt would have made no sense in the community of people to which she belonged, in the end she experienced no feelings of real frustration. For one thing, she had no meaningful points of comparison. Eskimos who came into contact with Indians discovered living conditions pretty much the same as their own, except for those connected with the rigors of the climate. As for the women, they lived in the same subservience, and it was a matter of incontestable fact that in the old days, Agaguk's wife Iriook would never have seen this situation as cause for revolt.

Later on, everything changed. The Whites arrived and there was something new to contend with: women who were more independent, men who were more heedful. In those days the first contact with the Whites was a revelation for Iriook. For her, and others like her, nothing could be the same again. The seeds of revolt had been sown, with a minimum of fuss and flourish. Little by little the Eskimo woman learned to hold her own, to stop obeying her alleged master in so servile a fashion, and set about her work with less feeling of constraint or obligation. Life was hard, for her as well as her man, but she accepted this and gradually won more privileges, including a more equitable division of labor — this time in her favor.

The trouble was that some of the old attitudes were not so easily dispelled, nor was the Eskimo woman so easily liberated. Often times, even when in the right, she would choose to give in. Thus, Judith, though emancipated, educated and fairly uninhibited, tended to be meek and submissive with Agoak. Was this perhaps the form her love for him had taken? Perhaps she had unconsciously fashioned her behavior after the sort of white woman who, in her anxiety over the stability of a relationship, chooses to be submissive, at least as long as things remain uncertain. Agoak spoke of leaving and Judith could only cry.

In the end it was her only defence, a wholly instinctive and unreasoned way of taking refuge which she resorted to without knowing exactly why. With Agoak gone what would be left for her? A family of alcoholics who were drunk practically every night, fought among themselves at the slightest provocation and upset the whole village with the racket they made, while Judith's mother, an Eskimo of the old traditions, nursing the baby, closed her eyes and hummed quietly in a hoarse voice. . . . Was this her legacy, her future?

"I'll come back for you, I promise."

But Judith kept crying. Could she ever tell Agoak that her Uncle Josi had raped her one day? That her own father was always slipping his hand into her pants and fingering her while he asked: "Is it wet? Is it wet?" in the raspy voice of the incurable alcoholic.

She would have liked to leave as well, to get away from this houseful of whining brats, confirmed drunkards, hateful quarrels and perpetual poverty. All the different kinds of social insurance payments they received were barely enough to keep the men in alcohol. She was fairly well educated, but had no practical training, no trade, no skills. Thrown back on her resources, she had managed to get work as a domestic with some of the white residents of Povungnituk. Once, she had been hired at the Bay warehouse, because she was as strong and fit as a man. It was there that her uncle, taking advantage of an idle moment, had caught her by surprise and raped her on a pile of flour sacks. After this episode, which was fortunately never repeated, Judith was able to get herself hired in an English household. It was a job with little future, nothing to build ambitions on. But she had finally been noticed by Agoak, whom she had admired from afar ever since their school days. They saw each other once, then again, and little by little a bond developed between them and grew. Today they had progressed to the point of pondering their future together.

"I'll come back for you, I promise!" Agoak kept saying.

In Frobisher, going back was just what was on his mind. He was quite confident he could assimilate the banking routine quickly. There would be nothing too difficult or trying about his job, and the salary was more than sufficient. Even with the increased living costs and Judith to support, he would live well and be able to save some money. With his mind at ease, he could at last begin thinking about the much-promised journey back to Povungnituk to fetch Judith. Even if she did break down and cry this time, it was likely to be for reasons of sheer relief.

He already had a departure date in mind. Since it was now the beginning of August, there were only a few short weeks to wait until the Labor Day holiday in early September, when Agoak would have the time to make good on his promise. With the help of his savings, which he had hardly touched in these early days of his new life, he had gone ahead and reserved a charter plane, a solid Beaver transport, to take him to his beloved Judith.

Agoak's dream was a fine one and had been a long time in the making. For three years he had toiled to the limit of his talents, talents which, though raw at first, had gradually become more developed, more flexible, more marketable. In effect, he had had to start his education all over again from scratch, because what he had been taught in Moosonee was nothing more than a kind of key for the future. Little attention had been paid to the mysteries this key might one day unlock. Fortunately, when it came to penetrating the mysteries of modern accounting, he had the resources of a quick, bright mind to fall back on. The result was that after three years, he had acquired a self-confidence and a facility in handling problems which now gave him access to a position of responsibility. He was convinced that at the bank he would bring this same serene self-assurance to tasks no one yet dreamed him capable of. For only he was aware of the fact that he had undertaken a correspondence course in data processing and successfully mastered its intricacies, so that if the bank were ever linked up to a computer, he would not only be perfectly capable of operating the terminal but also of setting up the files and transferring the data into them.

It was infinitely more than anyone in that part of the country might have expected from a mere Eskimo. Agoak knew this and had cunningly revealed nothing more at the interview than his accounting experience, which in itself was enough to get the job. One day he would be in a position to surprise the right person by displaying an expertise which had gone entirely unsuspected among his colleagues. Even Judith was not privy to the secret. As far as she was concerned, his rather disconcerting lack of availability several evenings a week had something to do with his studies, but just what kind of studies they were he had never revealed . . . any more than he had explained the reason for his stays in Montreal and Toronto, where he had gone for the purpose of logging twenty hours on a computer terminal and gaining practical experience as an operator.

He treasured his secret and it became for him a source of strength, like some vital wellspring. He had told the bank about nothing more than his basic skills and these had been found perfectly satisfactory. With what he held in reserve, any number of possibilities were open to him. As an Inuk descended from the age-old bands who had roamed the Arctic and managed to survive and reproduce, he was going to make his mark with characteristic poise and careful planning — but for once other than by hunting seal or bringing down the great white bear!

Yes, Agaguk seemed remote indeed, as did his world of icy misery and near-savagery!

CHAPTER II

Agoak was finally allocated a house in the Ikaluit area, which was inhabited almost exclusively by Eskimos. He had had the option of taking a house in Apex Hill, the point of highest elevation in the region, but there were few Eskimos living there. Agoak stuck to his original decision to live with Judith in Ikaluit, without being fully aware himself just how significant his gesture was.

The situation was paradoxical, as he knew perfectly well. Here he was, an Inuk with computer training and a qualified accountant, who chose to dress and eat like the Whites, who had long since abandoned Eskimo ways of thinking, here he was rejecting an opportunity to live among these same Whites, to enjoy their standard of living and many of the same amenities, all because of an instinctive decision which was as spontaneous as it was unfathomable. He had opted for a house which was definitely less luxurious – if one can speak of luxury in Frobisher — and of dubious construction, with its plywood walls, hemispheric roof and facilities which though adequate were more rudimentary than those of the houses in Apex Hill or the apartments in the town-centre complex. In fact, it was little better than a cabin, but Agoak felt somewhere inside that this was the choice he had to make.

Agoak had resolved while very young to extricate himself once and for all from the primitive conditions in which most of his people still lived. He had studied hard and applied all his intellectual resources to freeing himself from the grip of tradition. Not that he had ever felt any contempt for his ancestors. Although he had little sympathy for his grandfather Agaguk's primitive ways, he had nothing but admiration for his determined efforts to build a worthwhile life on his own terms. He had no less admiration for his grandmother Iriook, since he recognized in her a unique quality which had allowed her to challenge nefarious and age-old customs, to the point of actually transforming Agaguk into a man sensitive to the most complex of human emotions. That was something he did not intend to forget.

But he was also aware of the dramatic changes which had gone on all around him. In Povungnituk he saw what Father Ricard's patient work as a social worker had achieved: a primitive people once barely capable of managing their own domestic affairs were suddenly taking on the formation of co-operatives, improving the quality of their lives and organizing the marketing of their sculptures, the product of an age-old art-form at once utilitarian and mythological. These ancient hunters of the whale, stalkers of the seal, "eaters of raw flesh" looked down upon by the Indians of the woodlands, had become administrators, officers of the Caisse Populaire, radio operators and, in keeping with the main local sources of livelihood, merchants and businessmen. It was still a far cry from the level of progress attained in Frobisher Bay, and Agoak was well aware of the fact, yet they were already very different from the igloo-dwellers who killed baby girls at birth and ate their own dogs in times of famine. Seeing an Eskimo from Povungnituk talking with perfect ease to a Co-op representative in Quebec City by HF radio, made one forget that less than a few decades before, this man's father thought nothing of eating a raw seal liver dripping with blood.

And yet Agoak, who had just cleared the last hurdle and might soon be enjoying all the benefits of life in the South, suddenly felt hesitant. He was proud and happy to have accomplished so much, but he was also worried that his forward motion had picked up so much momentum that he seemed prepared to abandon all the heroic generations in one sweeping gesture. This was why he had steered his course towards Ikaluit and decided to make it his base of operations in Frobisher.

What would Judith's reaction be? He would have to wait and see. Agoak had kept her in mind to some extent in making his choice. He had stalked around Frobisher and observed the behavior of the Eskimos who lived there. He had also noted the attitude of the Whites to the Inuit, as much as he could at least, and it was so different from Povungnituk, there was such an abyss between the situations in the two places, that he had been concerned not to make the transition too difficult for Judith.

This did not mean that racist attitudes were unknown in Povungnituk. In the final analysis the Whites are too powerful, and too unpredictable in their attitudes to the Eskimos, for the white inhabitants of POV (as it is known to the locals) to treat the native population in a uniformly forbearing way. Some even evince overt hostility. Judith had not therefore been able to avoid the occasional humiliating experience, but she had one thing in her favor: she lived among her own people, who were in the majority, she felt supported and sustained, and the damage done was usually not very serious. But in Frobisher, far from her loved ones, from familiar faces, from the familiar human and physical geography, how would she react to white hostility? Could she survive psychologically in a white community, cut off from daily contact with an Inuit community?

Agoak had often discussed the problems of race with Father Ricard. Ever since his stay in Toronto, where he had witnessed a kind of paternalistic and condescending racism, which is the hardest to contend with, Agoak had become aware of how difficult it was for an Inuk to find self-fulfilment in the Arctic. His discussions with Father Ricard had been fruitful and he had often tried to take them up again with Judith, in her own terms. Though she was intelligent and showed a surprising degree of adaptability, she was wracked with anxiety. She was afraid. She had once said to Agoak, "Aren't you afraid of venturing too far?"

The remark took him by surprise.

"I didn't know there were limits."

"Maybe there are."

"What do you mean?"

"You're moving into the White Man's world. Until now you've been able to set your own pace. But what if the Whites decided you'd gone far enough?"

"It's a free country, I'm a respectable citizen, I pay my taxes like everybody else, what reason could they have for deciding that?"

"I don't know, it's just a gut feeling I have."

Agoak did not attempt to pursue the point, but he had been left with a feeling of panic. For some time now, he had sensed the workings of powerful instincts in Judith. Far more than he, she seemed to have retained the sixth sense which for eons had been the Inuk's most valuable weapon and which explained better than any other single fact his near-miraculous ability to survive through tens of thousands of years in a climate which could only be described as cruel, destructive, implacable and relentless. Nevertheless, through living by his wits and with the help of the igloo, the harpoon, the dog-sled, clothing which warms with layers of air, fat to combat the cold, huge quantities of animal protein and direction finding by the stars, he had managed to survive and even multiply. As a result, he had no real need of the sophisticated tools the Whites brought with them when they first arrived. Naturally he did not hesitate to take advantage of them, especially metal goods, firearms, traps and, later on, snowmobiles. But he could have carried on as before, equipped with only the traditional resources, and probably survived longer than the Whites — and perhaps much better as well. Anyone familiar with the Arctic knows the construction problems caused by the permafrost, the year-round freeze-up of the soil which starts just below the surface and goes down 500 metres and more. He also knows that no tent, no temporary shelter of any kind, could ever match the igloo, which is quick to build, solid, comfortable, made from material which is available everywhere in unlimited quantities, costs nothing and can be left behind without the slightest regret, since at the next stopping point another one can be erected with just as little fuss. It was by placing unquestioning faith in instincts totally unknown to the White man that the Eskimo conquered the Arctic and managed to survive in it.

Judith, then, still possessed instincts which Agoak felt much less strongly. Having noticed this about her, he had found reason to be uneasy with her powers of perception. Though he may have been confident of success, of being able to blaze a trail for himself and go much further in life than the average Inuk, he still felt vague stirrings in his heart, stirrings which he would not even acknowledge, and it was as much to protect Judith as to prevent being uprooted himself that he had so unhesitatingly chosen to live in Ikaluit.

It was perhaps for these same reasons that he had avoided any premature discussions of his ambitions and plans. It was best that Judith learn her role as an assimilated, or near-assimilated, Eskimo woman, very gradually. And it was incumbent upon Agoak that he measure out the stages of this process with care and guide Judith along them wisely and patiently, for he was creating a life which she had never experienced before, or even dreamed of, and which she was certain to find baffling. Pursuing this apprenticeship in the midst of women of her own race and outlook was a more promising approach than flinging her into the hustle and bustle of Frobisher, where the rhythm of life was so very different from that in Povungnituk.

Saturday came and Agoak was finally free to take stock of all that had happened in this short time. He had left Povungnituk the Saturday before, in the early morning. He had slept in Chimo and spent Sunday there exploring the local resources, which disappointed him. On Monday he had boarded the Nordair flight and arrived in Frobisher Bay that same evening. And now, with the first week behind him, he had a job and a house, and a date was set for the charter flight on which he would go to POV to fetch Judith. That was a lot of water under the bridge; the first step, a giant step, had been taken, and Agoak was astonished that everything had fallen into place so easily.

This was the first free time he had had to himself since starting work, and during the night he had made a close examination of what he found around him. The house was scarcely better than the one he had had in Povungnituk, but it was better equipped. Bright and early, Agoak had gone on foot to the Bay to buy provisions, come back by taxi with all he had purchased and filled the refrigerator and cupboards. Then he had returned to the store, this time to get some furniture, a bed, a table and straight-back chairs, two armchairs, and a few lamps, as well as dishes, cutlery, and pots and pans.

By noon, having managed to locate a van to transport all his purchases instead of waiting for a store delivery, which would have meant postponing until the following week, Agoak found himself in a house equipped with all the necessities. There was even a little Japanese-made color TV sitting proudly on its gilt metal stand. With the Anik satellite now carrying broadcast signals as far north as compasses would function, the TV set would be their window on the world.

By evening, Agoak was well-ensconced in one of his new armchairs digesting the dinner he had prepared for himself in the sparkling white kitchen with the red curtains, using the propane gas cooker, which he continued to marvel at. It was a hefty appliance, worked by a number of buttons, with gauges, four burners and a big oven. Agoak had only seen two like it before, one at the home of the Hudson's Bay manager in POV, the other at the home of the Catholic missionary. And now he had one of his very own! Only yesterday he had been a mere bookkeeper; he had had nothing but his dreams. With one sweeping gesture, his whole life had taken on a new dimension. Was this not how it had been for Agaguk? In different circumstances, of course, determined by a primitive existence long since vanished, but similar in its basic form to what was happening today. When the old people told stories of an evening, they talked of how Agaguk had fled the village, how he had found a place to live of his own, then later returned to fetch Iriook, whom he took as his woman. They pooled their meagre resources and went to settle on the deserted tundra, toiling for decades to survive and bear children. And how Iriook, his woman, had managed to impart civilized ways to Agaguk, a new outlook which up to that point had been completely alien to him. . . .

Was the course Agoak had set for himself, which had brought him here and led him to a new home, and which tomorrow would take him back to Povungnituk to get Judith Nooluk, was it so different? He had almost everything to offer this girl who was about to embark on a great journey with him, like Agaguk and Iriook before them.

CHAPTER III

Agoak discovered a whole new world at the bank as well. The manager was an anglophone White who had come all the way to the high Arctic harboring certain anxieties, although these had subsided with time, as he himself admitted, and he now seemed perfectly well-adjusted to the somewhat peculiar local problems of living, relating to people and conducting bank business. On the whole, banking transactions here are not all that different from those carried out in the South, apart from exceptional cases at least. But it is in connection with just such cases that there exist both problems and a sense of excitement, which together make banking in the Arctic unique. A loan to a seal hunter whose annual catch is virtually guaranteed has little in common with the kinds of loans usually extended in Montreal, Three Rivers or Kingston. It was a little unsettling to be dealing on a daily basis with Inuit who, having scarcely moved out of the Stone Age, seemed to navigate through credit transfers and term financing arrangements with as much self-assurance as they navigate kayaks through the treacherous waters and world-record tides of Frobisher Bay. Early in his tenure, the manager had had to muster an unusual degree of adaptability in order to cope with this unusual situation. It had not been easy for him, as he hinted to Agoak on the very first day.

"I intend to leave you with some pretty sizable responsibilities. I express myself poorly in Eskimo and I don't understand it very well either. You'll be doing the talking for me." He made it clear that he would play out a lot of rope to his new employee: it was up to him to see he did not hang himself with it.

Agoak was moved by this comment, and troubled too. He was comfortable enough with the intricacies of the banking business.

15

Perhaps he had begun in a special state of grace, with a calling. At the Caisse Populaire in POV, whose business involved more than just handling deposit accounts, he had quickly come to grips with the routines and procedures, and after his first few hours in a chartered bank he had seized on the similarities between the two systems, even though their respective terminologies differed in some ways.

At first the manager's remarks scared him a little, until he had examined their implications and came away not with a feeling of despair but with a carefully measured sense of anticipation. He was going to be given responsibilities in connection with the Eskimo clients, be made a kind of deacon for purposes of the financial rituals involved. He could scarcely have wished for more. From that day forward, he wore a broad smile of satisfaction. At the counter he was voluble and easy-going with the Inuit clients. He served them in their own language, and whenever he was presented with professional problems by his fellow Inuit, he broached them not only with the interests of the firm in mind, as was to be expected, but also, and to an equal extent, with the interests of the Eskimo in mind. He did not treat the Inuk like an anonymous file number but rather like a human being who had lived, as his ancestors had lived, in conditions of a difficulty the White Man had never known, and would never be capable of understanding. Agoak had been entrusted with duties which, within limits imposed by banking practice, would allow him to treat the Inuit with a kind of understanding they had seldom encountered before.

It was more than Agoak could have hoped for. It had occurred to him that in the long run he might arrive at a position of responsibility such as this; but he had never imagined that events would develop so quickly. He had even resigned himself to spending much longer actually looking for a job and had only vaguely expected to get taken on at the bank. Landing up there with so little effort seemed to him a sort of miracle. He had thought it much more likely that upon his arrival in Frobisher he would start by doing unskilled labor or servicing utilidors.* He had been assured that as an Eskimo with fluency in both Inuktitut and English, as well as a halting knowledge of French, he would have no trouble finding a job — though just what kind of job had not been specified. He had more readily

---

* Insulated tubes sitting above ground and enclosing water and sewage pipes, which service Northern settlements built on permafrost.

imagined himself working with his hands than being accepted straightaway as an employee of the bank. He had obviously had a stroke of luck walking in at the right moment. He would now do everything in his power to make sure he did not disappoint his superiors: he would devote himself to this job body and soul. It had become of paramount importance to him that he exemplify what an Eskimo could be when he put his mind to it and when others responded by placing their confidence in him. Agoak had a dream and in it he envisaged the development of close human and material commitments between the Inuit and the bank, commitments which he would initiate and one day, perhaps, orchestrate.

Agoak was walking on air. He harked back to his studies and the day when, conscious of the talent for mathematical reasoning he had always shown in his classes, he had decided to pursue this advantage as far as possible. Today, even though he regretted not having continued on into university, he realized that his expertise, which would be enriched by future practical experience at the bank and elsewhere, could take him further than an Eskimo had ever gone before.

All of this was enough to create a surge of euphoria in the pit of his stomach. Soon the urgent desire to share his high spirits with Judith became practically his only reason for living. He impatiently checked each day off the calendar until the Labor Day weekend, feeling beside himself at having to wait so long.

Finally the fated Saturday came, bringing with it the journey by chartered Beaver and the beginnings of the second phase of this adventure of a lifetime. Thus far, all the winning cards were in hand and a sunny future was on the horizon.

CHAPTER IV

Judith had now been in Frobisher two months. The snow, the ice, the bitter cold would be around until well into June, but the oil-fired central heating warmed the house nicely. Water simmered on the stove for much of the day, ready for making tea when needed. Judith had taken the time to hang some cheery, colorful pictures on the otherwise drab walls. Practically all day long a cassette recorder played quiet music which Judith listened to blissfully as she sewed or knitted.

One evening Agoak said, "If you want to get a job somewhere, you can."

Judith shook her head and smiled.

"Why?" she asked.

"As something for you to do, for your own enjoyment."

Judith, who had become his wife (for Agoak had quietly submitted to the regulation and got Father Ricard to marry them before they returned to Frobisher), got out of her armchair and snuggled up next to Agoak.

"Do we need the money?"

"No, not at all."

She kissed his neck, cooed, then took a thoughtful tone.

"I've got all I need here."

She pointed around the room, stopping as her finger reached the door.

"There's no drunkard coming in at all hours. The sounds a man makes don't scare me anymore."

"I know."

"Agoak, if you want me to work, I'll go and find a job."

"You're under no pressure."

"I'll certainly have a job one of these days, but I'd rather wait."
"As you like."

She climbed onto him, hot and quivering, and Agoak felt his own flesh swell, his penis ache with the urge to burst free. He took gentle hold of Judith, helped her to her feet, stood up himself and showed her the hard muscle which seemed as though it would rip open his pants.

Judith uttered a series of long, quiet groans in the back of her throat, pressed herself against him and moved her buttocks back and forth against Agoak's crotch. Then she spun around abruptly and threw herself against him in one movement, grinding her hips frantically as she cried, "Me too, me too . . ."

He led her into the bedroom and began to undress her feverishly. Beside Agoak's fairly trim frame, Judith seemed thick-set, almost chubby. Her hard breasts with their dark, swollen nipples were naked now and they excited Agoak, who began by softly caressing the very tips, pinching them and rubbing them with his palms. He then swallowed them voraciously, sucking them for all the pleasure they held, while his hands fondled the firm masses of flesh. Judith grimaced and rolled her eyes, as her hips moved back and forth in response to every throb in her vulva and vagina. Agoak quickly undid the fasteners of Judith's pants, which fell to the ground, and she lent a hand by pulling them off altogether. Then, while Agoak was getting his clothes off, Judith threw herself on the bed and rolled around on it fondling her breasts, her stomach, her vulva, moaning all the while.

After Agoak had tasted all her juices and brought on a series of orgasms by playing his tongue over Judith's vulva, he penetrated her at last and both let out long, gut-wrenching cries which became a single howl of pleasure when his sperm exploded into the woman's orgasm.

After two months, and a very gradual start, they had made considerable progress in their love-making. It was in this house, which they had moved into as man and wife, that their first act of love had taken place. Previously, in all the time they had spent together, they had restricted themselves to furtive kisses and fondling of breasts, although on one more auspicious occasion, Judith had slipped her hand into Agoak's pants and briefly caressed his penis, causing him to ejaculate. This so aroused Judith that even with so little stimulation, she was soon in the splendid throes of her first orgasm.

The great joy they shared that evening marked a turning point in

their relationship. Agoak had been patient, gentle and understanding.

On a previous evening, the evening of their arrival in Frobisher, the
long-awaited mutual exploration of their bodies was about to take the
form of an attempt at penetration when Judith said, "You're hurting
me. . . . I was all messed up by my uncle, go easy."

Agoak withdrew immediately. Later on, after long kisses and much
fondling of her breasts, Agoak gently explored her vulva, and short of
actually inserting his finger managed to summon an ardent response
from Judith's clitoris with his skillful manipulations. For Agoak as
much as for Judith, this was part of an initiation into sexual
techniques which neither of them had reached by any natural
progression. Both had read a number of sex manuals recommended
— and in some cases actually provided — by a government nurse who
happened to be travelling through their area; sometimes, when they
were able to find a little peace and quiet, they would read them
together. They were therefore applying from memory caresses learned
beforehand, caresses fondly hoped for but till then unrealized.

"I'll be patient," said Agoak the evening he had tried to enter her.
"We've got our whole lives in front of us."

Judith in her gratitude had then attended to Agoak's pleasure. At
first she had only caressed his penis with her hands. Later, over the
days and weeks of their apprenticeship, as Agoak had inspired
orgasm with his lips and tongue, so too Judith took to bringing the
fleshy penis to her mouth and quickly learned how to trigger an
ejaculation.

They tried penetration, which was still painful for a while, then
became easier as their attempts continued. To finish with they would
come back to their caressing, their oral love-making, in a state of
greater and greater abandon. The soaking wet sheets and sweating
bodies bore witness to the intensity of their passion. Every evening the
house rang with their cries. Then there was a kind of slack period
when they both seemed to need to recover their composure and
contented themselves with affectionate gestures and terse conversations, Eskimo style. Agoak would relate the highlights of his busy
day, while Judith talked about the more limited demands made on
her as a housewife who lived alone, without children, in a house
which was relatively easy to maintain.

When they began to talk of the future, the tone changed a little.
"You know," said Agoak, "I'm gaining ground every day at the
bank."

"What do you mean?"

"I'm taking on more and more responsibilities."

"The bank lets you?"

"I wouldn't take them on if it didn't."

"Will you become manager some day?"

That was a weighty question; Agoak thought it over before answering.

"One day, yes, I might."

"When the English leaves?"

"Or I'm posted somewhere else."

That evening the wind was strong, unpredictable, close to the ground. The walls of the house trembled occasionally in the impertinent gusts.

"Somewhere else?"

"Yes."

"With the Inuit, like here?"

"Perhaps."

"What do you mean — perhaps?"

"It might be farther away."

"In the South?"

"Yes."

"With the Whites?"

There was so much despair in Judith's voice that Agoak felt a sudden reluctance to continue.

He got up and switched on their color TV. It was eight o'clock Monday evening and in Frobisher it was time to watch the adventures of *Cannon.* Judith methodically laid her knitting to one side and said to Agoak, "We'll need to talk more about this."

Then, with her man beside her, she became engrossed in the action on the screen.

Two days later, they finally reached their ultimate erotic goal and then every evening for a good week they did their best to recreate what they had discovered — a completely fulfilling experience, an absolute and utter sense of mutual abandon. For the moment Agoak's obsession with future plans were forgotten. Their sexual destiny had taken them so far, and they were capable of attaining such extraordinary heights of pleasure, that nothing else seemed to matter.

Often in the course of the day Agoak was forced to do violence to his feelings in order to recover some measure of lost concentration. But his other dreams, his personal dreams of career and future, were not forgotten completely. As sexual experimentation lost its novelty, its urgency, the day in fact came when Agoak's daydreaming turned sharply away from conjugal bliss to the more distant future. The day also came, after a certain amount of procrastination, when Judith decided to pay a little less attention to the life of pleasure and begin pondering the remarks made by her husband on the subject of work.

An old Eskimo woman who lived nearby had developed an interest in Judith from the moment the young woman had moved into the Ikaluit house. She said her name was Kuksuk and that she was a grandmother who lived alone on an old-age pension and a pension granted her as the widow of an Inuk who had long worked at utilidor maintenance and garbage collection. Kuksuk knew that some day soon she would be sent to the golden-age home people talked about, which housed Inuit past their prime. In earlier times, tribal law required that these old people be left to die, for they were just so many useless mouths to feed and had to be eliminated. They could choose the means of death, but they could not postpone it. An igloo was built for the old person and he was left in it without fire, lamp or provisions to die alone of cold and starvation. This was the iron law of tradition. Today, this ancient and barbaric custom has been superseded and old people are crammed into dull, lifeless buildings — which happen to be well heated and stocked with food. But there is more than one way to die of starvation. Before long Kuksuk would be taken from her home and forced to finish her days as best she could in an institution built to house the useless members of society.

She had communicated all this to Judith with the short, pithy sentences of an old Inuk not much given to verbosity. She was a remnant of the ancient tribes, all wizened and toothless. One day long ago her husband had brought her to Frobisher, where he had immediately found work. The woman Kuksuk could have been had since reached old age, and in a particularly distasteful manner, as she pointed out.

"I live like a White woman. I lived in an igloo, then here," she continued. "I loved the igloo. I was young and strong."

She flexed her arm muscles.

"I kept strong because I worked hard."

Judith had heard other old women tell the story of their youth. The work they did was usually taxing, work fit for beasts of burden. There were not only the daily chores in the igloo, which in themselves were not too demanding. The man often needed help outdoors as well, which meant strapping the children on to the sled and carrying the baby in the hood of the anorak, running along on snowshoes, helping the dogs pull their load, as well as watching out for seal, like a man, shooting like a man too, and no mercy if the shot was wide of the mark, confronting polar bears, and if by chance a kill was made, gutting, skinning and butchering the seal or the walrus or the caribou or the one-ton polar bear. Horrendous tasks which could overwhelm and exhaust even young men in their prime, and which the women faced unflinchingly.

"But I stayed strong," concluded Kuksuk.

She feigned a desperate look and rocked from side to side whining, "Ha-Ya-Ha-Yah, look at me."

She touched the leathery skin on her naked, emaciated arms, which stuck out of the openings in her sweater. She took off the sweater to reveal her breasts, droopy, flaccid sacks which had lost all their flesh and turned a horrible brownish color, with nipples shrivelled up like raisins. She uncovered Judith's firm breasts and fondled and caressed them as she sighed with admiration.

"I was once like you," she said, "beautiful and solid. But I live in this White man's house and look at me. It makes me sad."

"But why?" asked Judith. "You're comfortable there."

"I'm dying. You're dying too."

"I don't understand," said Judith.

"When I went with my husband," continued Kuksuk, "I was alive. He came here, he worked, but he worked alone. I was left in this house. I began to die. And time finishes you off."

"But I'm happy," said Judith.

"Can you work with him, at his bank, and share his tasks? And while you're at home, what do you do with your arms, your muscles, your strength?"

This was the longest sentence Kuksuk had ever uttered in Judith's presence. The young woman was nonplussed. She looked at this unsightly creature with her slobbery mouth, who chewed tobacco and spat where she liked: she had lived life to the full, but was much the worse for it now. Would Judith also be emaciated and decrepit like this one day?

Judith could not get Kuksuk's words out of her mind. She knew perfectly well she could not lend Agoak a helping hand at the bank. She could not, in her ignorance, even discuss his work with him in the evening. Being alone in the house and still childless, she could say all there was to say about her working day, such as it was, in no time at all. She could hardly dwell for long on the fact that she had made the bed, mopped, dusted, done some dishes and put dinner on to cook, especially in a house where everything practically ran itself, with central heating, hot running water and even snow removal taken care of.

What to do about all this? Perhaps Kuksuk was right. Perhaps this kind of progress was just another way to a slow death.

One morning Judith could contain herself no longer and instead of letting her visit to Kuksuk revolve around the usual cups of tea and humdrum conversation, she arrived at the old woman's home determined to seek out advice. She came straight to the point.

"Agoak wants much more out of life," she said.

"Here?"

"Not necessarily. He talks of going somewhere else."

"To where the Whites are, in the big cities of the South?"

"Yes, I suppose so."

"I've seen pictures, the ones that move."

"Films and television."

"Yes. I've seen all that. It's very shiny and very dry. There doesn't seem to be any wind or any snow."

"They have snow in the South too."

"But it's all soft and sticky. Suastsiok has been there. When he came back he told us all about it. He was sick. The air down there looks clear, but it's dirty, there's something invisible in it that eats away your stomach."

"I know," said Judith. "Agoak went to Toronto and he said the snow was dirty."

"The air too."

"Yes, the air too."

"You see?"

"I know," said Judith sadly.

"He wants to go there?"

"Agoak says there's no limit to what he can do. He might even be manager of a bank some day."

"And will you be with him?"

"Yes."

"Somewhere where there's nothing but Whites?"

"Probably."

"There are Whites here too," said the old woman. "They're big and strong, their houses are tall and bright. They go up and down the streets in their cars and snowmobiles, and their planes make a big racket as they pass over our heads. But we Inuit are strong in numbers.

The Whites had to give us houses, they greet us in the street, they let us go anywhere, they don't make life too difficult for us, our children go to their schools. Here everything is fine."

"And?"

"But what is there in the South?"

"Whites, like here."

"And that's all there is — Whites!" said Kuksuk in a contemptuous tone. She spat out a brown gob of tobacco juice and punctuated her gesture with an Eskimo expletive.

"E-E-E-Ea."

Then she took her head in her hands and swayed around as she moaned, "Ah-ya . . . why does Agoak have an *agiortok** in his head? A man who listens to an evil spirit is doomed."

Suddenly the old woman broke into a smile. She stretched her hands out in front of her, palms forward, "An Inuk always remains an Inuk," she said. "You must not forget that. He should remember that too."

More upset than ever, Judith returned home and spent what seemed to her a very long day.

That evening, after dinner, she led Agoak to the sofa, sat him down and snuggled up next to him.

"Talk to me," she said.

Agoak looked surprised. Judith's request was not unusual in itself, but there was a tone in her voice which was. Agoak seemed in a quandary, wondering what was up.

"Talk to me," Judith repeated.

"Do you have something to say to me?" asked Agoak.

She shrugged her shoulders, "I just want to hear your voice," she said.

Agoak smiled.

"I get the feeling you have something on your mind," he said quietly.

Judith bit her lip, thought for a moment, then suddenly made a resolve. She gestured around the room, indicating the furniture, the TV set . . .

"Where's all this leading, Agoak?"

He looked at her with an inscrutable expression.

"What are you driving at?"

Judith threw up both hands in a vaguely imploring gesture, "Agoak, you've talked about going to live in other places."

---

* Evil spirit.

"Yes."

"Of maybe leaving."

"Ah, I see, and you're frightened by the prospect?"

She hesitated, then shook her head, "Not really frightened, but ..."

"But . . .?"

"But going to live with the Whites?"

"Wherever it's necessary," said Agoak, who then asked, "Have you been seeing a lot of old Kuksuk?"

"Not every day."

"No?"

"No."

"But you've been seeing her."

"Yes."

"You have talks with her."

"Yes."

"You've told her I want to leave?"

"I've said you mentioned it, yes."

"I've talked about it as a possibility. Did you explain that?"

"Not . . . not really."

Agoak was patient. He put his arm around her shoulders.

"Kuksuk is old," he said. "Sometimes old people are wise and it's worth pausing over what they have to say about things. At other times, it's not."

"You don't think she's always wise?"

"When it comes to the modern world, the one we live in, the world of the Whites, even our own, a woman like Kuksuk understands nothing."

"Some of what she says is true."

"Oh?"

"That the snow in Toronto is dirty. You told me that yourself."

"Yes."

"The air's dirty too and eats away your stomach."

Agoak got up. He stood in front of Judith and talked very quietly in a patient, understanding tone, the way he had talked to her before in her time of distress, in Povungnituk, when she had been overcome by feelings of panic.

"You spend too much time alone. The only company you've found is with an old woman who wants to destroy you. I should've known something like this would happen."

He paced up and down the room, then found his words, "I think you should find a job outside the house."

"What about our meals?"

"We'll manage. Being all alone is putting ideas in your head."

Judith lowered her eyes and murmured, "You want me to work?"

Agoak began to say something, but caught himself.

"Will you need the money I earn?" Judith continued.

Agoak had never revealed the amount of his weekly salary to Judith, in the belief it could not be of any interest to his wife. She took no part in the financial management of the household and depended on him for everything.

He nodded: he had a trick up his sleeve. He just might have found a solution to Judith's lonely anxieties, a way to force her to move in step with him along the roads he wished to travel. He was in effect telling a lie by not letting Judith know that his salary was quite sufficient and that she could just as well stay home. But if she did, it would only be to worry herself sick with fear and delusions.

"Yes, I will need it."

Judith nervously took hold of Agoak's arm, "Is it too expensive living here?"

"No, no, you don't understand."

"But you just said it would help if I was earning a salary."

"We could save more, have a better life, go out more often."

"I like being at home with you when you're not at work."

"We should get out and meet people, make friends."

"I don't need to meet people and I don't want any friends."

"But I have to get to know some people and move around more in Frobisher, for my work. Having friends is important."

Judith looked away, then shrugged her shoulders, "Fine, I'll go and work if you say so."

"Yes, I'm saying so."

"But I don't have an education like you. Where am I going to find work?"

"Do you remember eating with me in the hotel coffee shop?"

"Yes."

"Yesterday I heard them saying they were looking for one or two girls to wait on tables. You could do that."

"When we were there the place was full of girls serving. Have they all disappeared?"

"They were students earning money before heading back to the South."

They went to bed early that evening and there was little love-making. Agoak fell asleep quickly but Judith lay awake for a good while staring into the dark. Agoak was certainly right: it was best she found something to busy herself with. It wasn't good for her to be idle. But could Agoak appreciate the great peace, the relief Judith felt at having been rescued from her family at last? Naturally she still had anxious moments, but that could never compare to the brawling, the carousing, the obscenities, the beatings, the crying fits which never seemed to cease, which were the stuff of her daily life in Povungnituk. At last she was in a secure, peaceful environment surrounded by her own things. She had been wrong to get so upset and especially to bring Agoak into it. Suddenly, in the silence of the night with nothing outside but the distant and barely perceptible buzzing of snowmobiles, Judith had a horrible thought. In a flurry of panic she woke Agoak from a sound sleep. He came to in a daze, his heart beating wildly.

"What is it?"

"What if I'm working, Agoak, and I have a child one day, what will I do?"

"You'll stay home with him, of course."

Judith smiled happily in the dark. She felt reassured. She had also stumbled on an unexpectedly rapid solution to her dilemma.

"Agoak," she murmured, "make me a child . . ."

He chuckled softly and made affectionate noises, then undressed Judith by feel, got undressed himself and let his fingers, hands and mouth roam over his wife's body, causing the tension to build up in her muscles and nerves while Judith did the same thing to Agoak's body. Soon the sheet was soaking wet, and Judith's desperate moans prompted the final union, the knotting of their flesh in a last contorsive spasm, the ultimate cry of completion. She then fell into a deep sleep, with her belly full of sperm, while Agoak, who had collapsed against her, fell into a deep sleep devoid of thoughts or dreams.

In Judith's moist, intimate recesses a minute creature made its way in the direction of the waiting ovum. The next day it would reach its goal, effect its penetration, so that in due course a child would be born to Judith.

CHAPTER V

Agoak secured Judith the job he had talked about without her having to lift a finger. The people who ran the hotel were customers of the bank. Agoak knew them and often had occasion to talk with the manager of the coffee shop on his breaks. They knew Judith by sight and they respected Agoak. Since Judith was attractive, well-groomed and polite, they willingly agreed to make her a waitress, despite her lack of any practical experience in that line of work. Agoak assured them that his Judith was bright and resourceful, that she learned quickly and would create no problems for them. The very next morning she was at her post by seven o'clock. And since she had been unable to serve Agoak his usual breakfast at the house, she served it to him instead at the coffee shop. This was to become a regular routine for them every weekday for some time to come.

"You'll see," said Judith to her husband with a giggle, "Sunday mornings when I don't have to be at work, I'll make a breakfast fit for a king and bring it to you in bed."

Agoak had not been wrong in recommending Judith to the people at the hotel. By Friday, after barely five days, she had become a waitress the manager could describe as one of the nicest and most able he had ever hired.

"If only she was a bit less shy . . .," he said.

"As far as I can tell," said Agoak, "that's something that'll never change. She's always been that way and always will be."

"Listen, I'm not making that a condition," added the manager, "I'm quite happy with her as she is."

At the house that evening, Agoak was touched when he saw how happy Judith was.

"You were right," she said, "you were right, Agoak. I enjoy my work, I feel good there. People are so nice to me."

31

"Even the Whites?" asked Agoak a little pointedly.

"Yes, even the Whites." Then, embarrassed at having to admit it, she added, "Especially the Whites."

Life went on, but now everything had changed. Judith was up early in the morning in order to rush off to work. Agoak slept a little longer, got up at his appointed time, made himself a coffee which he drank as he washed up, then around eight o'clock arrived at the coffee shop, where it was Judith's privilege to serve him. At noon Agoak came in for a light meal, served him of course by Judith. She finished at three o'clock, returned home and fixed dinner for Agoak, who was off work at five. Two or three evenings a week they went to a movie or to the bowling alley, or got together with people at one of the recreational centres.

Then, one Sunday evening, they opened their door to their first guests, a white couple, an employee of the Territorial government and his wife.

It was a relaxed, pleasant evening. The wife was a regular at the coffee shop and already knew Judith. The husband had often had dealings with Agoak at the bank and they had got to know each other, man to man. By the time their guests left, around midnight, the beginnings of a friendship were already evident. They saw one another again the following Sunday, at the home of the white couple, in Apex Hill. Their relationship followed its natural course, each couple, from one time to the next, discovering in the other certain affinities and mutual sympathies. Like Agoak, the other man was ambitious, and his career was already well under way. Like Judith, his wife worked outside the home, as an employee of the telephone company, and since both of them served the public, they had a shared experience which brought them closer together.

Later on, an Eskimo couple came and joined the four of them. The other Eskimo, like Agoak, had a substantial education and spoke perfect English, as did his wife. Nochasak worked at the airport. A little older than his new-found friends, he had a son in Toronto who was already a pilot. His son's dream was one day to take command of the Nordair jet which flew the regular service to Montreal. When he had logged enough hours working as a co-pilot for a smaller airline and became eligible for a job with Nordair, he intended to do everything within his power to get himself hired. Meanwhile, he was taking night courses in order to learn about all the different guidance systems and was getting practical training on some of the systems in use in Canadian and American airports.

Judith listened dreamily as her Eskimo guests talked about their child's future. And as their other friend talked nonchalantly about plans that were many years in the future — all to a chorus of agreement from his wife. Yes, they too would have children. And he explained what he wanted for them.

"We'll return to the South and they'll go to the best schools, no matter what. I'd like my son to be a doctor some day, or an engineer . . ."

Everybody had their say. Nochasak had another son and two daughters.

"I'm saving my money," he said. "When the time comes, we'll be able to send them off to study anything, anywhere, even if it costs thousands and thousands of dollars."

"I want my children to have the best in life," said Judith with a dreamy look in her eyes.

"But what do you want them to become?" asked Nochasak's wife. "What is the best in life anyway?"

"Whatever they choose to be, on their own."

"Children still need some guidance," interjected the White woman.

"They'll choose their own fate," replied Judith.

"And what if they chose to remain igloo Eskimos all their lives?" asked Nochasak abruptly.

"If that made them happy," replied Judith, "more power to them."

Sensing that she had ventured onto thin ice, she blushed deeply and got up with an awkward motion, making a sort of pirouette.

"Let's move to the table," she exclaimed. "I'll make some coffee and I've got a cake I baked myself. Come on!"

Life had certainly changed for Judith and Agoak. Judith, for her part, had not been back to see Kuksuk for weeks. The old woman and her forecasts of gloom and doom were now the furthest thing from Judith's mind. She had virtually forgotten all that had been said and she realized she was no longer in the grip of the same paralyzing fear. She still had an occasional pang when she left work and went into the bank for a moment to say hello to her husband, which she would do if he wasn't too busy. Whenever she saw him in his handsome ready-made suit, with a nice shirt and a well-knotted tie, she felt a little shudder. It seemed to her that this man bore no resemblance to the Agoak she had known in Povungnituk. In fact it seemed to her that he even bore little resemblance to an Eskimo any more. Something subtle, intangible, made him seem more and more like a White.

On one occasion Judith left in a hurry and tossed off some remark about being late, which was nothing more than a convenient excuse invented on the spur of the moment. She went home and took a while to calm down. Then she began to think to herself how crazy it was for her to act that way. The two of them were happy, and what she took to be a White man's demeanor in Agoak was simply a manifestation of his success, his happiness, of the satisfaction he derived from doing his job well, from being respected and admired.

When Agoak arrived back at the end of the day, dinner was on the table. It was good, for it had been prepared with love, and Judith, who had finally calmed down, had nothing but a pretty smile and kind words for her man.

Two weeks went by and one afternoon, just after Judith got home, Kuksuk came knocking on her door.

"You don't come," she said, "so I come."

"I'm working now," Judith replied, "so I'm not here during the day anymore."

"I know. You work for the Whites, you work with the Whites."

"Yes."

"And you invite Whites over here."

"I also invite Nochasak!"

"Some Inuit are more white than the Whites. They're traitors, they don't deserve to live!"

The old woman was slobbering and staring aggressively at Judith with her rheumy eyes.

"Why are you looking at me like that? Why are you saying these things?"

"Are you becoming White too?"

Judith lost her patience at that point.

"If Agoak was here he'd throw you out!"

"Who's Agoak?"

"You know perfectly well!"

"You mean the man who sleeps in your bed every night?"

"Don't talk like that!"

Judith could imagine what the old woman was about to say and had no desire to hear it.

"That man's no Inuk," said Kuksuk in a falsetto voice, "he's a White. You sleep with a White, you'll have a White man's children."

"Shut up!" Judith yelled. "I don't want to hear any more!"

Just then Agoak came in and spotted the old woman, hunched over, leaning on her cane, a skeletal and sinister figure.

He took Kuksuk by the arm and led her gently outside, then all the way to her own door two houses away, while she yelled at him in a voice trembling with rage, "Let go of me, you dirty White! You're no Inuk! Agiortok! Traitor! Liar!"

When he got back, Agoak collapsed in an armchair and remained silent for a while. Judith was leaning against the wall by a window sobbing hysterically, unable to collect herself, her stomach knotted with pain.

Finally, through her tears she said, "Why do people think you're a traitor?"

"People?"

"Kuksuk."

"People are one thing — the ravings of a crazy old woman, that's something else."

"She may be old, but she's not crazy."

"So you're prepared to listen to her, are you?"

"No, in fact I was in the middle of telling her that if you were here, you'd throw her out."

"But now you're all upset and defending her."

Judith extended her hands and with an imploring look said, "Agoak, help me, I don't understand anything anymore!" Agoak sighed and shook his head slowly, "What is it you don't understand? We're comfortable here, aren't we? We're happy, aren't we? We have a good life, you like your work. . . . Do you like your work?"

"Yes, of course."

"We have some close friends, we go out, we talk with people, we socialize, we belong in this town. . . ."

"Do we really belong in it?"

"Has anyone ever insulted you or even given you the cold shoulder?"

"No."

"Do our friends respect you?"

"Yes."

"People in Frobisher, your boss, the customers, the other waitresses, don't they all respect you?"

"Yes, yes!"

"Same thing for me at the bank. Don't you find that an important consideration? Is that how things were in Povungnituk?"

"No, not always."

"Add up all the Whites there are. Six times, ten times, a hundred times more than there were in POV, and we're living well, we're relaxed, happy, fulfilled."

"But what about in the South?"

"It's not so different."

"I've heard there's discrimination."

"There is. There is everywhere. Even here, if you looked hard enough you'd find it. But it's directed mainly against Inuit who don't know how to behave, who can't hold their liquor, who are lazy or dishonest. It's the same in the South. Is that the kind of Inuit we are?"

"No."

"We're punctual, responsible, we work hard. Look at Nochasak. He's the same way. He has grown children who are doing well in the South. Don't you find that encouraging?"

Judith had stopped answering. Her head was lowered in a reflective pose.

"Am I right about all this, Judith?" asked Agoak.

"Kuksuk kept shouting you were a traitor."

Agoak burst out laughing, "Are you still worried about what she said?"

Judith walked slowly over to the window, her face impassive, her shoulders thrust back. Suddenly she seemed to stiffen, gave a wave of the hand and called over Agoak in a peremptory tone, "Come here."

Agoak walked over to her side. Judith pointed through the window.

"Look," she said.

The scene was a familiar one: an Eskimo, his wife (who was carrying a baby in her hood) and two older children, were leading two sleds, each of which was pulled along by a team of six dogs. They had come south-east, ultimately no doubt from the Brevoort Islands on the inland arm of the Cumberland Sea, now that the ice was setting in again. They were all in snowshoes, adults and children, the sleds were heavily laden and everyone was doing his best to urge on the dogs, who were unaccustomed to built-up areas and were becoming more and more skittish as the group advanced.

Agoak and Judith contemplated the scene in silence.

"They've had a long journey," said Agoak finally.

"Yes," said Judith, "I guess they've come to trade some skins and get some provisions. Now, do those children look sturdy?"

"What are you driving at?"

She pointed to the man.

"You aren't like him anymore."

"Obviously I'm not."

"You haven't been for a long time."

"I know."

"How many like him are left?"

"Oh, I don't know, a few thousand."

"And what do they have, compared to what you have?"

"If they live near a town, like this one, or some other good-sized settlement, they'll have access to a variety of provisions, they'll have medical care and the government's help in surviving. And if they live right in the settlement or town, their children will go to school."

"A white school?"

"Of course."

"Of course, because there aren't any others."

She frowned.

"Do *you* help them?" she asked.

"At the bank? When I can, but it's not easy. They're always on the move, especially if they live on the islands or further up, towards Clyde or near the Cumberland Sea."

"And apart from the bank?"

"I don't see what you mean."

"When you put on your three-piece suit from the Bay, or walk around in your synthetic fur coat and snowmobile boots with the yellow trim, what are you doing for them?"

"What do you expect me to do? The social welfare agencies and the RCMP look after them. What can I do all by myself?"

"Don't you feel you're betraying them? Aren't you a traitor?"

Agoak, flushed with anger, was almost shouting.

"Because I don't live like them, like a savage?"

Judith shrugged her shoulders, walked pensively around the kitchen, then decided to put on her boots and annuak.

"Are you going out?" asked Agoak.

"Yes. Dinner's on the stove. You can just help yourself. You're a White, so you shouldn't have any trouble playing housewife!"

"Are you going to Kuksuk's?"

Judith brushed off the question with a sweep of her chin and walked out.

Through the glass in the door Agoak could see her heading for the hotel complex and the coffee shop. He assumed she was going to have a coffee and talk with people there. He walked back into the centre of the room and stood there for a while staring into space. Then he got out a cup, poured himself some tea and sat down at the table. He drank the scalding beverage in small, careful sips.

They had just experienced their first quarrel. But was it really a quarrel? Agoak did not entirely understand what Judith was getting at. He failed to understand her reasoning. His own behavior seemed perfectly rational to him. He had freely chosen to better his lot, to escape the bonds of the primitive life, and Judith had known that all along. He recalled that she had often given him encouragement and consoled him when things weren't going as he wished.

She had seemed very pleased about his coming to Frobisher and happy about going back with him. Now she seemed to have reversed her position. What did she want? Did she actually want him to revert to the traditional Eskimo life again? Did she have any idea of the work that entailed for her, the unrelenting hardships, which meant spending most of the day just trying to survive? Wasn't she happy working in clean surroundings, prettily dressed in her fetching uniform, her sleek hair piled up in a bun, all the while surrounded by smiles and pleasant manners? Would she rather brave the fury of the Arctic, choosing a miserable existence instead of a comfortable, well-organized one? Here there was the magic of electricity and central heating, and thanks to the utilidors, which were impervious to the worst cold, the most inclement weather, there was also running water and sewage disposal. Life was good in this house, as it was in the big complex in the centre of town. Did she want to jettison all that, along with their whole future, the chance to get ahead, the exciting possibilities open to both them and their children? . . . It was a logic Agoak simply couldn't understand. Why, after moving so far along the road to success, should he now shift into reverse? And what was behind this business of helping his fellow Eskimos? The best way to help was to prove to the Whites through his own achievements that an Inuk could go far in life and do so with grace and skill, if given half a chance. Even the Inuk he had just seen leading the dog-sleds — could he not, given the opportunity, realize his potential just as well as Agoak? And his children too, perhaps even more so than he.

But first you had to feel strongly about leaving this land of ice and snow and unspeakable cold. You had to look beyond the horizon, towards the land of milk and honey. You had to use your brain and your powers of reasoning for some purpose other than overcoming a thousand and one dangers just to secure a miserable bit of raw meat or fish or frozen whale blubber, which was often too tough to chew . . . all this in order to stave off the threat of death, until the day might come when there was nothing left of the Inuk and his family but a few frozen corpses lost forever somewhere on the icy Arctic wastes.

It seemed to Agoak to be tempting fate, to say nothing of good fortune, to deprive oneself of such an agreeable opportunity to gain access to a better life and a better world, and to excel in ways few would think possible for an Inuk.

In the old days, the endless winter nights in the igloos were often spent improvising long epic songs which gave an immortality of sorts to the many Inuit deemed to be the bravest, most skillful hunters and fishermen, the elite of the miraculous harpoon. Was it not within the realm of possibility that, at some future time, they would be singing the praises of other skills, of other successes, of other achievements? They had sung Agaguk's praises. Now they could sing Agoak's as well, if for different reasons.

The more Agoak pondered all this, the less able he was to understand what might be troubling Judith. He had imagined that being alone in the house was putting misguided ideas into her head; he had therefore persuaded her to take a job. Judith had plunged enthusiastically into her work. She seemed relaxed and happy and was living her life to the full. Yet it had needed nothing more than a spiteful visit from old Kuksuk and the inopportune arrival of a family of primitive Eskimos in order for the same anxieties suddenly to take hold of Judith again. Did it take so little to upset everything? Were yesterday's fears and misgivings still that close to the surface?

And to top it all off, she had actually criticized him for the way he dressed!

Agoak really had no idea any more what to think about this strange turn of events. Judith was apparently angry as she left the house earlier. But had he confused anger with distress? Was it spite or sorrow that had her so upset? Or both? Agoak's entire education, after all, had been based on figures, and a mind trained in this way often has little grasp of the subtleties of human behavior. What he was confronted with now was no mere problem of financial accounting, but one of emotional and, it might be said, even sociological accounting. Naturally he was aware of the sort of intolerant reception he might encounter at a later stage in his career. But he had calculated the risks which might be in store with an almost mathematical precision. He realized that he had a most effective weapon in his calm, confident mastery of certain skills and that his skills could only grow with time. Provided he consolidated them and made good use of them, what had he to fear? He could not understand why Judith seemed incapable of using what she had learned in order to grasp something he thought was perfectly logical. What did it matter if they did set out for the cities in the South? He would have more to distinguish him than his brown skin and flat features: he would also have his invaluable experience and acknowledged expertise.

Agoak, lost in his thoughts, had not kept track of the time. The minutes had been ticking away, however, and when he finally glanced at the clock, he was surprised to see it was already nine and that Judith was still not back. Outside it was a peaceful evening, and the lights from centre-town sparkled in the snow piled up in front of the house. Agoak wondered what to do: there wasn't a sign of Judith. Should he be getting worried about her? Should he make the first move? She was unlikely to be encountering any trouble, that much he knew. At the same time, he was curious to know where she was. In the end he knew very little of what went on in her head. How could he expect to predict her actions? It occurred to him that she might have done something rash. But what? Judith was introverted. She had never shown herself capable of violence or even an angry outburst. Today she had probably reached the limits of any selfish streak she might have. Was she capable of anything worse? Agoak had trouble believing so. And yet, the thought suddenly struck him — did he really know his wife? He made up his mind. It took only a moment for him to dress; he left the house and headed at a brisk pace towards the imposing silhouette of the hotel building.

Agoak did not have to look for long. Judith was sitting in the coffee shop with an Inuit couple and their two children. He recognized them immediately as the family they had seen passing by the house with their dog-sleds as they arrived from somewhere far away.

Judith spotted Agoak and got up without waiting for him to reach their table. She dressed in the twinkling of an eye and walked straight over to her husband. He was barely as far as the cash register when Judith accosted him. The Eskimo couple watched the scene impassively from three tables away.

"I'm ready to leave," said Judith.

Agoak started to walk towards the other couple, but Judith took him by the arm and pushed him gently through the entrance-way.

"Come on," she said, "we're going home."

Once outside, Agoak stopped. He shook his head slowly.

"I don't understand," he said.

"What?"

"Don't you want me to talk to your new friends? Who are they? Where are they from?"

Judith shrugged her shoulders and walked off quickly in the direction of the house. Agoak tried to keep up with her, but she managed to stay several steps ahead of him. Judith got back first and didn't stop until she reached the kitchen table.

"Well, are you going to answer me?" asked Agoak.

He got undressed slowly. Judith just stood there with her outdoor clothes on, staring defiantly at her husband.

"Why should I?"

"Because I believe I asked you a perfectly legitimate question."

"Really?"

"Yes, Judith. Back there it seemed as if you didn't want me to talk to your friends."

"Maybe I didn't."

"Why?"

"Maybe they wouldn't have understood you."

"I'm an Inuk, like them. I speak Inuktitut, like them. You know that perfectly well."

"Yes, I know that, but there's more to it than just language. . . ."

"What, for example?"

"What you say with the language, what you talk about."

"Am I supposed to be worried about that?"

"Yes."

"You'd better explain yourself."

"They're Inuit, those people, real Inuit. There weren't any like them even in Povungnituk."

"I spotted them right away. . . ."

"Real Inuit?"

"Yes."

"That's what you said, is it?"

"Yes."

"So I'm not a real Inuk then?" asked Agoak calmly.

"No, not like they are."

"And I wouldn't have understood them?"

"Worse still, they wouldn't have understood you."

"Oh really?"

"They have the same word for living as you, but it doesn't mean the same thing for them."

"You're talking nonsense!"

"No. For you, living means being a White. For them, it means being an Inuk. That's how big the difference is."

"Did they talk about themselves?"

"Yes."

"About the misery, the occasional famine, the cold, the back-breaking work, the endless journeys on snowshoes?"

"Yes."

"About how savage an existence it is!"

"No!"

"Are you going to stand there and deny it? Look around you. Do you think they don't envy you? If that woman saw your house, do you think she'd be happy to return to her igloo?"

"She doesn't want to have anything to do with my house."

"Is that what she told you?"

"Yes."

"So you'd like to live like them, would you?"

"I'm not sure."

"You're not serious!"

"All I'm saying is I'm not sure."

"And this woman told you she wanted nothing to do with your house? She actually said that?"

"Yes!"

"I presume they live in an igloo."

"And in a tent during the summer."

"I'll ask you once more: would you like to live like them, wandering from one place to another according to how good the hunting is, bringing up children without any chance to go to school?"

Judith lowered her head and fell silent. Agoak had never seen such an expression of consternation on her face. He was about to walk over and take her in his arms when she darted away, taking off her anorak as she went. She went into the bedroom without uttering a sound. Agoak stood motionless, rooted to the spot. He heard her in the darkened room taking off her boots, undressing and, then when everything was quiet, going to bed. He sat down in an armchair, lit a cigarette and waited till she fell asleep. Only later did he realize he hadn't eaten and that supper was simmering on the stove. He went and shut off the burner, then sat down again. It was past midnight when he finally went to bed himself.

In the middle of the night, something woke him up which he couldn't identify at first. After a moment he realized Judith was crying. He came to and turned towards her. In a voice broken by sobs, she said, "Agoak, I think I'm going crazy. I don't know what I'm saying anymore. Forgive me. You're good and I love you."

"Go to sleep," breathed Agoak, "get some rest."

He held her tightly in his arms. In the warmth of his embrace she was soon asleep.

In the morning, which had come up grey with a thick, enveloping snowfall, Agoak could not help but think that something serious had happened the night before, something which would affect them both for a long time to come. Yet he was still unable to discern what the cause, or the implications, of this experience might be. However, since Judith was all smiles when he came in to the coffee shop for his breakfast, he decided to respond in kind and smiled back.

CHAPTER VI

Strangely enough, Judith seemed to return to her old ways in the weeks that followed. There were a few days when the atmosphere was awkward, if not really tense, when she had fewer smiles to offer and was more withdrawn than usual, but Agoak had decided not to let on about anything, to be as attentive and concerned as ever and in particular to let nothing, whether by word or deed, whether sympathetic or impatient, act as a reminder of the exchange they had had, which Agoak now thought of as a moment of madness. And yet, he should have seen it coming. Judith had never really been enthusiastic about their new life. He had long known that his wife feared the White man's world. He had never imagined that she would react so strongly, but it was better, in any case, to let things lie for the moment and just wait. Judith had to do some thinking on her own. The night of their argument she had actually asked Agoak to forgive her. She had acknowledged her distress and tacitly confessed to being in the wrong. It wasn't much to go on, yet it was reassuring, for here was proof that Judith was grappling with the problem. It was even possible that the smiles and the return to a happy sex life, full of untold heights of pleasure, might signify a return to common sense. Agoak, in any case, clung to this hope in order to drive out the unpleasant memories — without, however, putting more stock by it than was called for. He was beginning to understand how certain men could find women complicated and unpredictable, not to say unstable. Was Agoak up against a real change of heart or nothing more than irrational behavior? He concluded that only time would tell and that meanwhile it was best to keep quiet on the subject.

It was also best that they live as normally as possible. If Judith was willing to carry on with her daily duties, as though nothing had happened, fine, that was tolerable. And one day perhaps the bubble would break. For the time being, his work at the bank demanded all of Agoak's energies. Judith, too, had her responsibilities. She had to work hard, but her tips were good and the bank account she had opened on her husband's advice was growing steadily.

Once or twice she had asked Agoak, "Do you need money? I've already saved several hundred dollars of my own, which you can have if you like."

But Agoak declined.

"I might need it one of these days, but everything's fine for the moment. Keep saving, you're off to a good start."

As their respective tasks took on unforeseen dimensions, they gave more and more of themselves. They continued to receive people at home and make new friends. Their free time was now taken up with a variety of activities, bowling, social get-togethers, shows, snowmobile excursions into the surrounding countryside. If Kuksuk were to have come back to Agoak's she would find the door closed. She and Judith had had no new confrontations; nor had she and Agoak, an even less likely eventuality. This was perhaps the one thing that was guaranteed to keep the couple on good terms. Other Inuit who lived the traditional life turned up in Frobisher from time to time, and Agoak would see the odd one come in to the bank to do business or the coffee shop to have a bite to eat. He and Judith might meet up with some on a Saturday or Sunday, but nothing untoward happened when they did. Judith carried on as if she had not even seen them and she said nothing more about the family she had talked with in the coffee shop. Agoak, of course, kept mum. A truce was therefore established which, in Agoak's estimation, might be either long- or short-lived. Or even permanent, who could say?

Thus the weeks went by, without any reminder of the near-disaster they had lived through. One morning as he arrived at work an hour before the doors of the bank opened, Agoak was called to the manager's office.

There was nothing unusual about this, for the day often began with a review and assessment of the previous day's business. Agoak therefore walked into his boss's office feeling quite relaxed. However, the man behind the desk had a long face. Agoak stood watching him in silence. Whenever he had seen this expression before, it always signalled serious trouble. Yet Agoak was quite confident he had done nothing irregular. In the preceding few days, in fact, business had been so routine, predictable and easy to handle, that the manager was more likely to be suffering from boredom than anxiety.

"Sit down," he said to Agoak, pointing to the chair in front of him. Feeling easy in his mind yet a little concerned, Agoak sat down.

"I've got some unpleasant news for you."

Agoak broke into a cold sweat.

"It's something I just hadn't anticipated for the near future. Believe me, I didn't hire you knowing this would happen. I expected I'd be breaking you into the work here, then if necessary, sending you off for further training. . . . Anyway, things have turned out differently, much to my regret. You're one of the best employees I've had in a long time."

Agoak sat motionless, his mouth dry. He suddenly realized he was about to be dismissed. With some difficulty he managed to ask, "What . . . what's going on?"

The manager sighed and threw up his hands.

"I've known for two days now and haven't been able to get around to telling you. We'll soon be linked up to a computer at the head office in Montreal. They can do it now with the Anik satellite. . . . Wait a minute, you seem to find this funny."

Agoak was leaning forward and chuckling to himself.

"You're laughing? I'm giving you your notice and you're laughing?"

"Tell me," said Agoak, "did they describe the system to you?"

"What system?"

"I doubt very much it's COBOL. Given the way our data is organized here, I wonder what it might be. Emulator? And what kind of operating system is that likely to be? 1400? DOS/VS, DL/I, CICS/VS? Didn't they give you any details?"

"I haven't the faintest idea what you're talking about."

"They didn't even tell you what computer language we'll be using? I might be able to figure out the operating system from that."

Agoak's astonished boss looked at him with his mouth open and his eyes as wide as saucers.

"Do you know about computers?"

"Of course."

"But you never let on."

"Let's just say I wanted to be able to surprise you one of these days."

"But where did you learn? Surely not at the Povungnituk Co-op."

"No. I took a correspondence course, then gave myself some time off to go to Montreal and Toronto in order to get practical experience on a terminal, with key-punching and the different job-control languages currently in use."

"You know all about that?"

"Of course."

"You mean if we had a terminal here, you could operate it?"

"Yes. And transfer our files to the central processor and access any data that was needed."

Agoak had never seen his boss so moved. Here he was, the cool, contained English-Canadian of good background, so non-plussed he was unable to contain himself. He got up, paced around the room, rubbed his hands together, laughed and finally walked over and touched Agoak on the shoulder.

"You're sure you know what you're talking about?"

He had hardly been able to believe his ears.

"Of course I am."

"All this stuff about operating systems and accessing . . . how does it go? . . ."

"Accessing data."

"Anyway, all this computer business is pretty much of a mystery to me. I was convinced I'd have to get someone in, I'd have to ask head office to send me a man."

With a burst of enthusiasm he exclaimed, "That's the best damned joke I've heard yet. I have the man right here. I had him all the time!"

The manager had never been so exuberant about anything.

"I'd never have believed it!" he said. "Not in a million years!"

Agoak was overcome by his boss's infectious good spirits and he too was now laughing and briskly rubbing his hands together.

"You should have told me," said the manager. "Why didn't you tell me, in fact?"

"I was waiting for the right moment," replied Agoak. "Like this one."

The manager opened the cupboard near his desk and took out a bottle and two glasses.

"We must drink to that. This calls for a celebration."

"I'm sorry," said Agoak, "but it's too early in the morning, I couldn't."

"A computer expert!" exclaimed the manager. "And sober as a judge to boot. I must be doing something right!"

Agoak recovered his composure and asked, "When might you know what operating system and language are involved? I'm going to have to do a little brushing up, at least a few hours' worth, especially if they're using a Honeywell 58, since I never had much chance to familiarize myself with it."

"I've got an idea," said the manager. "I'll fill in for you at the counter when we open, while you make yourself comfortable here and telephone the data-processing unit at the head office in Montreal."

"Maybe that would be the easiest way to go about it."

"You can tell them all they need to know about the amount of space we have here, the electric current and I don't know what all else."

"Okay."

"Go ahead and call them. It's ten o'clock and time for us to open, but you just take as long as you need."

Alone now, Agoak pulled a pad of paper towards him and began dialing the Montreal number. Seeing how happy his boss had been to learn he was not going to lose his teller, warmed Agoak's heart. He had always felt appreciated at the bank, but in the steady rhythm of his day-to-day work, Agoak's conversations with his superior were always couched in the impersonal language of the banker. For the first time ever, his boss had gone beyond simple approval and given free rein to emotions Agoak had not thought him capable of. He had also underlined more explicitly and categorically than he had ever done before just how much he valued his employee.

Agoak was flabbergasted. He hadn't anticipated all this in his wildest dreams. Although he had long felt ready to participate fully in North American life, he had not, until this morning, had any tangible proof of his eligibility. Now that he had such proof, he felt capable of climbing to dizzying heights of success.

A voice answered in Montreal.

"Hello," said Agoak in a calm, self-assured tone. "Give me the head of data-processing, please."

That morning Agoak skipped his break and didn't go to the coffee shop until his usual lunch-time. The place was so jammed that the waitresses were barely keeping up with the orders. But there must have been something unusual written on his face, because Judith managed to get over to him almost immediately.

"I'll just have something light today," he said.

"I won't be able to serve you right away. Do you mind waiting a little while?"

"Okay, but . . ."

Judith leaned over and said: "I came over to find out if there was something going on. You look like a different person!"

"No, there's nothing going on."

She turned on her heel and went to look after some customers by the window who were clamoring for service. But she looked back at

Agoak twice, as if she were genuinely puzzled by what she had seen.

Agoak had made a resolution on his way to lunch. The fact was that throughout this memorable morning he had been haunted by the question of Judith's possible reaction. Six months earlier Agoak would have announced the good news without a second thought. But ever since the onset of Judith's strange behavior in the past few weeks, she had said enough (more than enough!) about her real feelings to serve, if not exactly as a basis for discussion, certainly as a warning to Agoak. What he had to tell Judith would certainly not strike the same responsive chord in her as it had in his boss. There was suddenly something inexorable about Agoak's ambition to explore new worlds. How would Judith react? In Agoak's estimation, the gossip that would soon be circulating about him among his wife's friends, from one end to another of this isolated little town, would serve to soften the initial blow, and Agoak would therefore have an easier time explaining himself.

But it had not occurred to him that so much would show on his face. Should he tell Judith everything that evening? And look for some sort of miracle in the meantime? But what exactly would he say to Judith if no excuse came along before closing?

Agoak got his miracle, even if it was less than earth-shaking and fairly predictable. At four o'clock that afternoon, the manager called Agoak into his office again.

"I've been talking to Montreal myself," he said. "They sounded pretty pleased with what you seem to know about computers. I asked for and got you a raise, effective next pay day."

The amount involved was substantial, in fact surprising. Agoak could now boast that he was comfortably within the White man's salary range. He no longer had to think of himself as a man of color, who was paid a pittance and treated condescendingly. This was the piece of news he could report unhesitatingly to Judith that very evening, and which he could rely on to explain the expression he had been wearing at lunch-time.

He soon discovered, however, that he was not the only one bearing good tidings. No sooner had he made Judith aware of his success at the office than she announced in turn, "I've had some news today myself. I didn't talk to you about it before because I wanted to be sure. The hospital telephoned me this afternoon with my test results."

"What test results?"

"They were positive. I'm pregnant!"

It was a strange evening. Agoak had been bowled over by the news of Judith's pregnancy. It was too much for one day. Too much sheer joy. Their cup was filled to overflowing, a new day had dawned in their lives and they now had entirely too much good fortune to contend with. He almost wanted to go and bang his head against the wall or pinch himself, to be sure he wasn't dreaming. It hardly seemed possible that all this could sweep over them at once, like a beneficent tide, a great wave of happiness. He sat smiling in his armchair with his hands folded together on his lap, his ears buzzing, his heart racing and his brain full of sweet music.

"I'd like to telephone my friends and tell them the news," said Judith at one point.

Agoak sat up with a start. A professionally ingrained prudence suddenly came to the fore.

"About my raise?"

"No," said Judith, in a reproving tone. "It's up to you to say what you want about that. I was talking about the little fellow I'm carrying inside me."

"Of course," said Agoak, relieved. "Tell anybody you like. And speaking of the little fellow, keep in mind that it could just as well be a little girl."

Judith giggled in an uncharacteristically mischievous tone.

"Or both, Agoak," she said, "and maybe even more. Can't you just see me having three or four babies all at once?"

"Stop!" exclaimed Agoak. "I'd need a raise three times bigger than what I got. I mean can you see us with four cradles lined up in the bedroom?"

"And can you imagine the anorak I'd need, with a hood big enough for four?"

Agoak's face fell.

"Do you plan to carry the baby in your hood?"

"Certainly."

"The traditional way . . ."

"Yes!"

Agoak was seized with an overwhelming urge to tell Judith everything. To let her know that he would be handling the computer, that he had just moved up considerably in the ranks, that nothing would be the same for them again. He wanted to blurt out to her that as the wife of the most important employee of the bank after the manager, she had no need to wear traditional clothing and could indulge herself in the smartest fashions. He was well aware, however, that his argument would carry little weight. Most of the White women in Frobisher wore an anorak and there were as many White babies swaying about in hoods as there were Eskimo babies. So too for mukluks: the only people without them were Whites from the South, who went around in their conventional city boots. It did not take long, however, before the average visitor went to the store to buy himself a pair of these very practical and comfortable snow-boots. In the final analysis, just about everybody wore mukluks and anoraks . . . and had an infant nestled in their hood!

How, then was he to present his case in a convincing way?

His momentary panic over, Agoak began to recover his composure. He felt childish for having had such silly, even fatuous thoughts. Why should his professional accomplishments exercise any influence over the way Judith dressed in a remote town, where everybody had to conduct themselves and even think in much the same manner, since it was the climate that counted, rather than social rank or any citizen's alleged importance. In Montreal or Toronto it would be important — and certainly much easier — to act and dress according to certain social standards, because everything would be different — climate, attitudes, responsibilities, personal relations. But here?

Judith chattered away and buzzed around the house like a woman possessed. Agoak had never heard her talk so long and loud and make so little sense. It was striking to see such a concentration of happiness, an all-embracing force that took hold of the whole being. What struck Agoak most was the luminous quality of Judith's smile. There was a feeling of joy he had never known her to experience before. This served to restore his peace of mind, and for the time being at least, he stopped worrying about the possible impact any rumors about his promotion at the bank might have on Judith in the days to come.

Settled in his armchair with the perpetual cup of hot tea in his hand, Agoak contemplated Judith's noisy and restless mood of elation. It was a sight to behold, something Agoak could never have imagined. Judith was a new woman, with new and unsuspected facets of herself to reveal. She was behaving so differently that once or twice the thought briefly crossed Agoak's mind that the woman standing before him was not Judith at all but someone who was a complete stranger to him.

However the couple's real discoveries that evening took place in bed. Judith had been so beside herself with joy when making dinner that she had burned it and so they had ended up eating sandwiches. Agoak opened a bottle of wine which they sipped slowly while they talked about the child who was on the way . . . except that poor Agoak, who was still being the gracious listener, could hardly get a word in edge-wise, since Judith had become so talkative.

When at last they were drunk with both wine and happiness and decided to go to bed, Agoak did not have to exercise any initiative. That evening it was Judith who had her clothes off first, hurrying Agoak along, helping him undress faster, pulling him impatiently into bed, pouncing on him immediately, taking him as he would take her, drawing out his desires, nibbling him, sniffing at him, swallowing his penis and then his sperm, beginning the arousal all over again, despite Agoak's pleadings, masturbating as she sucked his joy, trembling with a series of intense orgasms, until the moment came when she straddled her male, forced him into her and brought them to one last, powerful simultaneous orgasm. And throughout this display of unbridled passion Judith whispered, murmured, sighed and moaned the same refrain, "Thank you! Thank you! Thank you!"

Morning came and had the courtesy not to be dull and overcast. During the night high winds had dispersed the clouds and the result, despite the polar cold, was a clear day with a captivating quality of unreality which left a ridge of gold along the horizon.

Agoak felt a great sense of relief as he stood at the window waiting to go to work. He was, as usual, all alone in the house, since Judith was already on duty at the coffee shop. This reddish-gold line at the horizon, this horizon towards which he was headed on a pretty well clear path, felt almost symbolic and he could hardly avert his glance from it.

It was a peaceful moment. Agoak thought to himself that Judith now had a source of happiness all her own, like a bright, bubbly spring at which to slake her thirst.

At work Agoak discovered that his wife's pregnancy was the news of the day among the Eskimo women on the staff. Even the manager seemed to be in on it, because he gestured to Agoak through the glass partition in his office by putting his hands together and shaking them back and forth, in the signal for victory. Later he came over to whisper congratulations in his ear, and it then occurred to Agoak that if this piece of news had already travelled so far so fast, the one about the computer, and his role in its operation, would not take long to make the rounds either.

Any doubts disappeared with the arrival of his first English customers. All of them wore a proud expression as they congratulated Agoak — not, this time, over Judith's pregnancy, but over the business of the computer terminal.

Yes, news certainly did travel fast in Frobisher. But then that was the fate of remote cities, cut off from civilization, like Schefferville, Labrador City, Fermont and so many others: it was almost impossible to keep a secret in any of them. People of all different sorts are thrown together on a daily basis, while sensational events are few and far between, so that the merest rumor can take on headline proportions. As with Judith's pregnancy and Agoak's sudden promotion.

When he walked into the coffee shop on his break, Agoak knew that even at this early juncture, Judith already knew everything. She strode right over to him the moment he sat down in one of the booths. Agoak detected a strange mixture of contentment and anxiety on her face. Before she could open her mouth, Agoak asked her, "How do you feel this morning?"

The note of concern in his voice appeared to disarm Judith. She laughed softly and shook her head in a coquettish way.

"Look at me," she said smiling, "how do you think I feel?"

"Happy," said Agoak.

"You're right, that's exactly how I feel — happy. I feel as if I'm wearing a protective shield of happiness around me, like a suit of armor."

Though the waitresses were not supposed to do so, Judith sat down in the booth beside her husband.

"I hear you're something of a computer expert."

"Only on the terminal, at the tail end of the process."

"The what?"

"I'll explain all that later. So you've heard the news, have you?"

"Yes. And I felt like an idiot. I didn't know what people were talking about. Why didn't you let me know sooner?"

Agoak looked away and wondered how best to answer her question, without going into details. He was conscious of the time and of the responsibilities that awaited them both. His reply came in a calm, measured voice, though one which gave hints of a new-found and largely untested strength of will.

"What I tried to accomplish," he said, "I wanted to accomplish in secret, to make it a big surprise. I wanted to prove something and I had to do it alone, without any outside help."

"And what was it you wanted to prove?"

"What an Inuk can do if given the chance."

Judith sat for a while staring at the floor and thinking. Then she looked Agoak right in the eyes and said in a somewhat brusque tone, "You mean how easily an Inuk can become a White if he wants to?"

She got up and left. She came back with her husband's coffee, put it on the table and left again before Agoak, who had one finger in the air, could get out what he was on the verge of saying.

For Agoak, the rest of the day brought a mixture of varied emotions, a kind of bizarre and cacophonous rhapsody which ran from euphoria to remorse. The man had been through the whole emotional gamut in the last two days. Unfortunately, the positive experiences were not quite enough to outweigh the negative ones. Agoak felt an abyss opening up between him and Judith, in spite of the fact he was confident of having acted with the best of motives. As far as he was concerned, he had nothing to reproach himself for. Say what she might, Judith would never convince him he was some sort of traitor for having wanted to improve his lot in life, escape from the dire conditions of his childhood, move up the ladder of success. What had all that got to do with being a traitor? Father Ricard himself had endorsed Agoak's plans and testified as to their soundness. Could a man whose family still lived in conditions of unimaginable physical misery, without any realistic hope for the future, be blamed for wanting to improve his lot and rise above conditions no human being should be compelled to tolerate?

If he had been successful, it was certainly not at his family's expense. They had not been asked to make any sacrifices for his sake. It was by working in the summer and saving his money that Agoak paid for the privilege of going away to school. Though the government covered certain educational costs for Eskimos at all levels of schooling, this still left other expenses for the student to pay. Agoak had made certain his father was never obliged to pay these expenses for him. He had earned every necessary dollar himself and didn't owe anything to anybody, least of all his family.

And now he was being treated like a leper, a pariah, for having ambitions he saw as absolutely justifiable.

How he would have liked to be in Povungnituk just at that moment, sitting and discussing the problem with Father Ricard — and perhaps entrusting him with the task of persuading Judith to take a different stand on things! But here in Frobisher, whom could he approach? Whom would Judith be prepared to listen to? Who might manage to make her see the light? Not one of the people who came to mind fulfilled the basic condition: not being White, at least not the sort of White who was typical of the majority in Frobisher. There weren't, after all, twenty Father Ricards in all the world. Agoak might have gone so far as to say that there was only one. Judith just might accept advice from him; she certainly wouldn't from anyone else. There seemed to be no solution . . . unless of course they were to go to Povungnituk.

Agoak worked through his day as best he could. There had been some problems at the counter for a while which had kept him absorbed. Later on he had received some telexes from Montreal concerning the computer link and he had had to study these and begin drafting his reply.

When he got home he was too tired to take offence at Judith's less than enthusiastic welcome. He ate in silence, then went to his armchair and turned on the TV. Later, much later, when the news was over and it was time for bed, he said to Judith in a non-committal tone, "How would you like to go to Povungnituk one of these days?"

"Did you want to see your family?"

"For one thing."

"I've got no desire to see mine."

Agoak was about to say: 'Why not? — they're Eskimos who live the traditional life, drinking, brawling, stealing . . .', but he restrained himself and just nodded his head. Judith cleared away their cups, locked the doors and was about to turn out the lights, when she suddenly turned to Agoak and said, "You want me to have a talk with Father Ricard, don't you . . .?"

Astonished by Judith's perspicacity, Agoak stared at her coldly, "And what if I do?"

"What would be the point?"

Agoak waved his hand vaguely in the air and replied, "To try to make you understand some things I think he can explain better than I can."

"I understand perfectly well," said Judith. "In fact, I understand too well. I don't need his explanations. I haven't made any declarations of war, so don't go looking for targets to shoot at."

They left it at that, since even though Agoak had wanted to have the whole thing out, Judith hadn't left him the chance to do so. When he walked into the bedroom, she was already in bed with her back turned to him. He stood there for a moment wondering if he should say anything more, but as she wasn't budging, he went to bed as well. A little while later he leaned over and whispered to the back of her neck, "Judith . . ."

She jerked impatiently and said, "I've got a hard day's work waiting for me tomorrow, and so do you. Let's be sensible and get some sleep."

Agoak debated for a moment as to whether he should re-open the discussion, but decided that Judith was right, she had to get up early to be at work by seven, and he had plenty to do himself, especially with the new arrangements at the bank. He fell into a troubled sleep, his mind assailed by nightmares.

The next morning, with Judith already gone, Agoak slowly sipped his coffee as he sat at the kitchen table. Everything seemed to be getting more complicated by the hour; every happy piece of news brought something unpleasant in its wake. A certain thought came welling up in Agoak's mind as he recalled the conversation they had had one evening with their White friends and Nochasak.

Judith seemed to have been saying that she would leave her children free to make their own decisions about the future. Did this mean she would let them return to the ancient Inuit way of life if they wished to do so? And wouldn't this, more than anything, more than ever, create an unbridgeable gap between him and his wife?

Agoak, sitting alone with his coffee, had never felt less happy. He thought back to when he was first seeing Judith and to their attempts at reaching a mutual understanding. It had taken months before they were really talking. As he mulled this over, Agoak suddenly realized that he had often talked at length about his future plans, but had hardly ever heard an opinion on the subject from Judith, no words of encouragement, certainly nothing like positive enthusiastic support. Something more like polite and neutral silence.

As he set off for work, his mind was a whirl of confusion over how to deal with Judith. He felt helpless and sick at heart. His idea of taking her to see Father Ricard and trying to fire up her enthusiasm had already met with a miserable defeat. She had seen through his ploy and from now on she would be suspicious. If there was another way to look at the issue, or someone else who could help, Agoak was unable to see what, or who, this might be. The worst thing of all was that Judith had never really explained how she felt about all this. She had said some pretty harsh things, she had accused Agoak of treachery, she had made some murky claims about his doing nothing to help the most underprivileged Inuit — but she had never made it clear what form this help might take. The truth was, as Agoak had to admit, that up till then their arguments had been based more on emotion than anything else. Judith had expressed her fears, but had not attempted to understand them. She put a lot of stock in gut reactions, but refused to discuss the facts. It was inconceivable to Agoak that she would refuse to acknowledge that they were well-off now and had a rosy future in store. It seemed equally inconceivable that she could have more or less admitted to a longing for the nomadic life in igloo and tent, for the precarious sort of existence led by

Inuit who could not, or would not, take advantage of the progress achieved in the Arctic. True, the progress in question was the work of the White man, but since for the moment this was more than the Inuit were capable of, was it not best to take advantage of what was being offered? And at the same time build up an Eskimo society which would eventually assume a new role in partnership with White society, and create opportunities for the Inuk to enjoy well-being, respect and access to the whole world, if his needs and tastes so dictated? . . .

Agoak had never yet managed to put this vision of things into words. He was pretty sure, moreover, that Judith would never hear him out if he attempted to do so. Agoak was still completely baffled as to why. His whole being, with its stake in mathematical precision, rebelled at the idea that a formula for life as clear as his could be so thoroughly misunderstood and in fact rejected out of hand by Judith.

As he walked into the bank, Agoak had an idea. He had suddenly thought of someone who might know how to handle a discussion with Judith. Agoak was resigned to the fact that he was never going to make Judith listen. Someone who might manage it, however, was Nochasak. It was worth a try, at least.

He worked away and felt a little better. Like a drowning man who tries to save himself by clutching at flotsam, Agoak clung to the idea that Nochasak would succeed where he had failed.

He skipped his coffee-break and decided against sending an explanation to Judith with a teller who was on her way to the coffee shop. He telephoned the airport, where Nochasak worked, and announced he was coming out to eat with him at the canteen. He asked the bank manager to give him some extra time off at lunch, and when twelve o'clock sounded he headed off for his appointment with Nochasak in the Nanook taxi.

His fellow Inuk was surprised.

"I thought you ate in the place Judith works at," he said.

"Things are different today," replied Agoak. "I can safely say that things are different today."

They ordered their meals, and when the young waitress was gone, Agoak looked Nochasak right in the eye.

"I need your help," he said.

"I'll do what I can, count on it. Oh, I almost forgot to congratulate you. Judith called my wife. You're expecting a child. That's fantastic! I hope for you it's a boy."

"I'll take what comes," said Agoak. "Anyway, thank you . . ."

Nochasak watched him fidget for a moment, then finally, to help him get started, said, "You've got problems, I gather."

"Yes, I must confess, I do."

"It can't be money."

"No."

"In fact I also learned you gave your boss quite a shock at the bank."

"Yes."

"Something to do with computers."

"That's right."

"It's always nice," said Nochasak, "when an Inuk can make a White sit up and take notice like that. . . . So what about these problems?"

"Something's been going on, and I've got two ideas I'd like to try out."

"First things first: what's been going on?"

"It's Judith."

"Oh?"

"Nochasak, have you noticed anything lately?"

"No, nothing in particular."

Then he added discreetly, "It all depends what you want to know."

"Judith doesn't approve of my having a career."

"What?"

"What I mean is, a career in the White world. Sometimes I wonder if she wouldn't like to see me become a nomad."

"The two of you together?"

"That's the idea."

"And the children you may have?" pursued Nochasak. "Like the ancient Eskimos?"

"Exactly."

Nochasak weighed his words carefully, "My wife and I hadn't guessed it in exactly those terms, but we had noticed that Judith stays pretty quiet whenever you talk about your future plans. There was one occasion when she seemed to be in a rage because you were speaking well of your boss. It was no big deal, it happened one minute and was gone the next. But we did begin to wonder."

"I've begun to wonder too and all the answers I come up with have me scared."

"She wants both of you to go back to the traditional life?"

"Nochasak, I just don't know. I can't manage to get her into a real discussion, the kind of thing where we could speak our minds and get it over with once and for all."

"It's crazy," said Nochasak. "A couple having a falling out like that so soon after getting married."

"And it's no little falling out," said Agoak. "Believe me, it's serious."

"I thought she was happy about being pregnant."

"She is, and it's beautiful to see. But at the same time I know she's terribly unhappy."

"Because of your promotion at the bank?"

"Yes, among other things."

"She must be pleased, with the salary. . . ."

"From what I can tell, she's afraid we might go and live in the South, in a big city."

"Might you?"

Agoak thought before answering.

"I've worked hard since the age of sixteen to get where I am," he said. "I don't like the idea of having to put limits on my ambition and depriving myself of the chance to finish what I started."

"I understand."

"If finishing what I started means ending up in Toronto, why should I stay stuck in Frobisher or any place like it?"

"Personally," said Nochasak, "I've never wanted to leave here."

"Why not?"

"Because of my wife, perhaps. She has the same fears about the South. She's always said this was the perfect town for us. It's got stores, people, electricity, running water, well-paid jobs. Going elsewhere, we'd lose what we have here."

"That sounds like Judith's line of reasoning, if I understood it correctly."

"Well?"

"I can't stay stuck here. I've got my sights aimed higher, much higher."

"Have you explained all this to Judith?"

Agoak didn't answer. Instead he asked Nochasak, "Has your wife ever called you a traitor?"

"No."

"Mine has."

"That's strange. Did she elaborate?"

"That's the trouble, I don't know what she thinks or what she wants. Sometimes I get the feeling she'd really like to live the ancient life, running behind a dog-sled, eating raw meat in the igloo. . . . But at other times, I don't know, I just don't know."

"She wouldn't like to go and live in Toronto, for example?"

"I don't think so."

"Neither would my wife," said Nochasak.

Agoak was no longer sure whether he had done the right thing in asking for Nochasak's help.

"Have you ever thought of going to live in Toronto or somewhere?" he asked his friend.

"Yes, I have."

"Would you have gone out of necessity, to improve your lot, really make something of your life?"

"When I was younger, yes. I would have liked to work in the control tower at the airport here, and end up working at Dorval or Malton or even in the States."

"Would you have gone against your wife's wishes?"

"I wouldn't have gone alone."

"What if she hadn't wanted to go with you?"

"I would've stayed."

"Does that mean that's what I should do? Is that what you'd advise?"

"No. First of all, everyone has his own life, his own story, his own motives, his way of seeing things. Another thing: I was just a laborer. I'm a foreman today, but I had no special training. I was strong, I liked working, I was always punctual, and I had no desire to lead a nomadic life. I wasn't a man with special skills, like you, able to speak two languages."

"Almost three," interjected Agoak. "I won't have any trouble perfecting my French."

"Fine. Which means you could do great things if you left. That's different. On the other hand, if you stay here, with the pile of skills you have, and Frobisher pushes ahead just a little, you could carve out a nice future for yourself."

"I know," said Agoak, "but I want to feel free to choose exactly what's right for me. Exactly what's right."

"Which means getting Judith to agree to following you to the ends of the earth, right?"

"Yes. Or else she stays behind."

Nochasak looked at him with an expression of shock and dismay.

"You mean . . .?"

Agoak sighed and bit his lower lip. He looked gloomy as he stared at the floor.

"Yes, I know what you're thinking, Nochasak, and you're right. I love that woman. What I just said was cruel. If I didn't love her so much, do you think I'd feel so bad? I want her to understand, to share my dreams, to encourage my career. Everything you've mentioned, everything I'm capable of, my prospects here or elsewhere, I know none of that has anything to do with real Eskimo life. And it shouldn't. There comes a point where you have to leave the past behind, cut the cord. Or else become part savage again, like in the old days. Tell me, am I a traitor?"

"No. But Judith thinks so, does she?"

"Yes, that's what I was saying."

"How did she put it? In what connection?"

"I think it had something to do with my not giving help to the nomads, how it was all very well for me to have my skills and be well thought of at the bank, but what was I doing for the nomads? As it happened, there was one who went by the house that day with his wife and three children, riding a couple of sleds."

For Agoak, the really unpleasant part of the whole episode had been the moment when Judith prevented him from speaking to the Eskimo family in question, after they had all congregated in the coffee shop. He couldn't explain why, but he had taken this gesture of Judith's very badly. It had him completely baffled. He described the episode to Nochasak.

"From all you've said, it's hard to know what she's driving at. She must have something in mind, but I can't see where that leaves you."

"From time to time, I have to recommend a nomad for a loan at the bank. There are some who are responsible, who've proved they're good risks, despite the uncertainties they have to live with. Seal hunters, Inuit who take caribou for their hides, who work trap-lines on a regular basis for the Hudson's Bay Company or fish for char on a commercial basis. As long as we know we can trust them, we never turn them away. And since I can converse with the Inuit in Inuktitut, I've managed to get a number of new customers accepted at the bank. I've also helped some of the old-timers get organized and plan their work a bit better. I think that's helping out my own kind in a way my personal abilities and development will allow. Nochasak, I'm fully aware that I'm far from. . . ."

"Have you explained what you've just told me to Judith?"

"No, not really."

"Why not?"

"I figured she wouldn't be interested."

"Are you sure?"

"At first, she was spending all her time daydreaming around the house. When I got home at night . . . you know, we were newlyweds. . . ."

"Yes, I understand."

"At dinner I'd talk a bit about what I did at the bank, but I was pretty sure she didn't have the faintest idea what my work actually involved. When she opened an account, it turned out to be the first one she'd ever had and it was a mystery to her. How could she have understood what I had to tell her about the bank?"

"You could have kept it simple. If you've been able to help out some of the nomadic Inuit, you certainly could have found the words to make her understand."

What Agoak wanted was to get Judith's undivided attention long enough to be able to describe his working day to her in his own words. For Judith had never appreciated that her husband was busy doing everything in his power to see that as many worthy, self-respecting Inuit as possible shared the fruits of his years of personal service.

Agoak didn't bother to explain all this to his friend. He felt Nochasak had understood not only the emotional aspects of their falling out, but also its more strictly ideological side, for lack of a better term. There was no need to say more.

"So what you'd like," said Nochasak, "is for me to try and explain things to Judith."

"Yes."

"On your behalf, you mean."

"Yes, since I don't feel I get through to her when I talk."

"The only problem is getting her alone. I'm at work all day and so is she."

"Can I suggest something? Let's arrange to go bowling this evening. At the last minute I'll have some piece of work to finish up at the bank and I won't join you till later, late enough so you'll have had a chance to talk to her. It's a little sneaky, but it's the only choice we have."

They agreed on the plan and Agoak got up to leave.

"I never suspected we'd reach an understanding so easily."

Agoak felt a sense of relief. He had never been quite sure that Nochasak would be willing to get involved or even that he would understand. But things were working out. The scheme for getting them together was plausible enough and Judith was unlikely to see anything suspicious in it. Which meant there might be some resolution to the problem that very evening. Was this hoping for too much?

Whatever happened in the next several hours, Agoak made up his mind to be optimistic rather than pessimistic. He breezed through his work at the bank. He didn't let his worries get in the way and in fact accomplished more than his fair share, in spite of everything. Agoak was proud of what he had done that day and as the afternoon came to a close, he realized that the excuse about having to come back in the evening was no lie. He had done so much at the counter and with the manager, who had to give final approval to some of the transactions, that he had been forced to neglect his regular duties, ones which could not be put off until the next day. He really did have to make up for lost time that evening.

CHAPTER VII

Encountering Judith back at the house at five o'clock wasn't easy for Agoak. If they had only lived in a big city, where excuses came easily and were hard to verify. . . . But Frobisher was worse than a village. Everybody knew everything. Judith would most certainly have learned already that her husband had eaten at the airport with Nochasak. It was therefore important that she have no doubts about the motives for their meeting

"Where were you all day?" she asked her husband.

"At the airport."

"I know."

"Then why do you ask?"

"You didn't come for your break, you didn't come for lunch."

"I ate with Nochasak at the airport."

"I know that too."

"Well?"

"You might have let me know."

Agoak risked a testy remark.

"With the mood you've been in these days . . ."

Judith stood by the stove with her arms folded across her chest, looking at him.

"We've been waiting for some office furniture which is late. I went to see Nochasak so he'd telex Montreal and find out what was going on."

There was a grain of truth in what Agoak had said. It was a happy coincidence, because the girls at the bank, who were a prime source of news for Judith, would back him up. And before parting company with Nochasak, Agoak had tipped him to the story. For the moment his cover was secure.

"Since I was already out at the airport by lunchtime, I ate with Nochasak."

"Without telling me?"

"That's right."

Agoak finished his dinner. There was virtually nothing to break the silence. He sensed that Judith had her doubts and was waiting until the next day when she could check up. For the rest, she was perfectly aware she had not been in a mood designed to elicit a man's affection and concern. Was this perhaps the moment for Judith to make a clean breast of her troubles?

Though she said little and gave no promise of unburdening herself, Judith did manage a smile or two and spoke in a mild-mannered way, with the result that there was no real tension over the table. Slowly Agoak relaxed. It was perhaps to be hoped that the evening would go well and that before retiring, he and Judith would have finally found the key to a common vocabulary which had hitherto eluded them.

Suddenly Agoak was reminded of computer languages, which are so baffling to the uninitiated and yet so straightforward for those who have mastered them. It was just a matter of knowing the right passwords. He grinned at the idea. Judith noticed and looked quizzically at her husband. But Agoak was afraid to begin explaining himself, for fear of letting the cat out of the bag, so he returned to his dinner, while Judith, who had paused a moment to see if the little mystery was about to be cleared up, shrugged her shoulders and resumed eating as well.

They were watching the news afterwards, when the telephone rang. From what Judith was saying, Agoak guessed it was Nochasak's wife at the other end. After a moment Judith said, "Wait, I'll go ask him."

She turned towards Agoak and said in an unassuming tone, "Nochasak and his wife would like to go bowling with us tonight."

Agoak struck a thoughtful pose, then looked up just as Judith said, "Do you feel like it?"

Agoak nodded.

"Sure, why not?"

"That'll be fine," said Judith into the phone, "What time? Eight? We'll meet you there. Bye bye!"

They refrained from speaking while they got ready. Judith had mentioned she had to iron a blouse and she set about the task briskly. At one point Agoak heard her humming while she ironed. He felt good inside. Things were definitely taking a turn for the better. There was a light at the end of the tunnel.

"Judith," he said all of a sudden.

She put down the iron and looked at her husband.

"After the day I had at the bank, I'm afraid I'm behind in my work."

"I'm not going there all alone!" she exclaimed.

"I'm not suggesting you should. You go and meet Nochasak and his wife. I'll do a few minutes' work at the bank, then join you a bit later."

"What, at ten o'clock?"

"No, I've got an hour's worth, less if anything, I promise."

"Okay."

She finished her ironing and went to the bedroom to change, while Agoak quietly rinsed and stacked the dinner dishes in preparation for the next day's washing-up, a chore he had long since taken over because of the discrepancy in their working hours.

When Judith came out of the bedroom, she was ready to leave. She nodded to indicate the dishes in the sink, looked at Agoak and muttered, "Thanks, I'd forgotten about them."

They parted company in front of the bank, Judith going on towards the bowling alley while her husband unlocked the door of his place of work. Agoak felt confident Nochasak and his wife would know how to talk to Judith. A lot could get said in an hour's time.

Agoak worked away, feeling serene and at peace with himself. By and by he was relieved to see he had finished up what he came to do. He left, locking the door behind him, as the clock struck nine.

Just as he stepped outside, Judith arrived, walking at a brisk pace.

"Come on," she said to him.

She grabbed him firmly by the arm and started pulling him in the direction of the house.

"What's going on . . .?" Agoak protested weakly.

"We'll talk about it at home," she said, keeping up her relentless pace. Agoak tried to blurt something out again further on, but Judith stopped him with a peremptory wave of the hand.

"Home I said!"

The door closed and Judith whipped off her anorak in a single motion.

"You want to talk?" she asked.

"Yes . . . This is no way to live."

"You were the one who put Nochasak up to this trick tonight!" she said harshly.

Her hands opened and closed in a convulsive movement, her features were drawn, tears welled up in her eyes.

"Hold on," said Agoak. "You're starting things off on the wrong foot already. I don't even know why you're upset."

"You don't?"

"All I can do is guess," he said quietly. "How do you expect us to reach some kind of understanding? This has been going on for weeks. We're no further ahead, our marriage is going to the dogs and we're hurting each other without even knowing why."

Judith looked down at the floor, humbled. Her voice began to break.

"Nochasak had some pretty unpleasant observations to make tonight. Maybe he's right."

"Judith, are you afraid of what might happen if we go and live in the South, in a big city?"

"Yes."

"Is there some specific reason you're afraid?"

"I'm not sure."

"You've never been to the South, Judith, and you've never known anyone to come back the worse for it."

"Yes I have."

"Who?"

"Lukasi Maniapik."

"Oh, him!"

"He lived in Montreal for three years. What was he like when he came back?"

"He was already drinking too much before he left to go there. He got into trouble down there and went to prison."

"They say he killed somebody."

"No, it was attempted murder, he didn't actually kill anybody, and apparently the judge was lenient because Lukasi was an Eskimo who wasn't used to big cities and easy access to liquor."

"There, you see?"

"Judith, think for a minute. Can you, in all honesty, compare Lukasi to a man like me?"

"I'm not saying that!"

"You're not? The way you tell it, the proof that big cities are dangerous is that Lukasi, who was a drunken bum to begin with, went to Montreal and became even more of a drunken bum. Is that apt to happen to me?"

She shook her head.

"I guess not."

"You *guess* not?"

Suddenly she burst out laughing.

"You're right, you're not like Lukasi at all."

"Let's face it: if your family, as you know them, decided to plop themselves down in Montreal or Toronto or Winnipeg, it'd be a total disaster."

"I know."

"Now be honest, do you really think that you or I would be running the same risk?"

Judith took a long breath.

"I know, I know. But there'd be other things to worry about."

"What things?" asked Agoak insistently. "What things?"

"We have everything we need here," Judith said slowly. "I used to know people who had visited here or come here to live. They all used to say that in Frobisher, an Inuk was well treated if he behaved well, that he could get work and didn't have to go without anything. People would also tell me about schools for the children, all the things there were to do, the friends there were to be made. I wasn't worried about coming here."

"But you would be about going to Montreal?"

"Yes."

"But why? Even an Eskimo, if he knows what I know, can always find work there."

"How many Eskimos are there in Montreal or any of your other cities? How many?"

"I don't know, very few. There are barely a couple of hundred Inuit in the South, in all the cities put together, if you don't count those who are just there for school or training programs."

"You see?"

"I see that as Inuit we'd be all alone, but even here we've got White friends. Down there, we'd simply have more, that's all. We speak the same language. You and I can both function in English . . ."

"With them we can."

"Yes, obviously, with them."

"But here we speak Inuktitut, our own language. In Montreal I'd have nobody to speak it with but you."

"And the children."

"You don't think for a minute that in a big city immigrants like us would ever convince their children to speak Inuktitut, do you? You know perfectly well they'd want to speak French or English."

"In Montreal, and in Toronto, I've heard lots of Italian children speaking their own language!"

"And how many Italians are there? Or Jews, or Germans? They've all got one another for support. I hear they've even got newspapers and radio and television programs in their own languages. And schools too!"

"We've got all that here," said Agoak.

"Exactly!" exclaimed Judith. "We've got it here, but we'll never have it in the South. We'd need a hundred thousand, two hundred thousand Inuit living there, whereas here we're in a position of strength. We're treated well, we have what we need. The Whites respect Inuit who work hard and live right. That's what you don't seem to understand, Agoak. We're getting somewhere in this town and I like that, it feels good. I could spend the rest of my life in Frobisher and be perfectly happy. Even if things got very expensive and I had to keep working for years, I wouldn't mind. But if we were in a big city, with all those Whites, with weather that was too hot and humid, wet snow, air pollution . . . and having to speak English day after day, without ever being able to speak Inuktitut. . . . Tell me honestly, don't you find yourself speaking English at work all day long?"

"No."

"Oh?"

"I've never really noticed. Half the customers are Inuit. The tellers are too. . . ."

"Just like the people at the movie-house, the bowling lanes, the airport. . . . The list goes on and on. It's the same for me at work: at least half the customers are Inuit or speak the language, the girls I work with are Inuit. Even the cook is an Inuk. Things would never be like that in the South, for either of us."

"So what you're saying is that you'd rather stay here. But not because you want to interfere with my career plans."

"Absolutely not, provided you limit them to what you can achieve in Frobisher, where your own kind are in the majority."

"And what if I don't limit myself?"

"What do you mean?"

"What if I was still determined to go all the way, despite everything?"

"And end up in some big city?"

"For example."

"What is it you want to know?"

"Would you come with me?"

"I know what you're thinking, Agoak. You know something about computers and you feel they've only got a limited use here."

"You're on the right track."

"Agoak, I read and watch television and keep up with what's going on in the world. I'll bet you that even if Nordair isn't making full use of computers yet. . . ."

"As far as I know," interrupted Agoak, "they already use them in the South, around Hamilton and the other places they serve."

"But not here?"

"No."

"Do you think things will be like that for long? I'm positive Nordair and other companies will soon be using computers. The government too, for that matter."

"They do say it's just a question of time," admitted Agoak.

"Well then, you could work full-time on computers, if you had a mind to. You'd be practically the only computer expert here, so there'd be almost no competition. You've got a vacation coming up next summer. There's nothing to prevent you from taking more correspondence courses, then going to Toronto during your vacation to get more practical training. No, Agoak your future is right here, among your own kind, in your own climate, where you can speak your language every evening — and even for most of the day if you want. Some day soon, you'll be able to pass along your skills to other Inuit, who may want to follow in your footsteps. You have a career to pursue here, if you want. . . ."

"You've given this a lot of thought."

"I have, yes. I might have talked about it sooner . . . I'm sure I would have in Povungnituk, if you'd trusted me, if you'd talked to me about what you were doing, what you wanted to do. But you did everything in secret, as though I couldn't appreciate what was going on. I don't talk much, Agoak, I'm aware of that. I don't say everything that's on my mind, but I keep my eyes open and I listen carefully. I retain things and I'm aware of the awful complexities of White society. While I wouldn't want to live in that society, I know we can benefit from the sort of progress the White man has brought to the Arctic. If we really want to enjoy it and get the most out of it, we should stay where we are, working hard with the skills we have."

Agoak stared at Judith in astonishment.

"I think I underestimated you," he said.

"You just didn't trust me, that's all. You thought I was an idiot because I went around without saying much and was happy just to give you love and affection."

"I must confess I really didn't know you."

"That's true, you didn't. It's just not like me to have long talks like the one we've just had. And I was getting frustrated because it looked like you were never going to understand my feelings — unless I drew you a picture, as our friends the Smiths say. I was reacting as a woman, emotionally, from the heart. I finally had to get around to telling you what I thought. And I have."

"Stay in Frobisher," mused Agoak. "Be *the* computer expert, train other Inuit. Make a career within our own little society. . . ."

"Yes!"

"Maybe that's not such a bad idea."

"It's not a bad idea at all!"

"I had the impression you wanted us to return to the nomadic life, like the ancient Inuit. . . ."

"You had that impression because I never really explained how I was thinking. Let's just say I didn't express myself very well," said Judith. "I understood what I was saying and I thought I was making myself clear. I was talking about not forgetting our origins, of being proud of them, and also about understanding the nomads."

"And helping them too!"

"Yes, especially by becoming an Inuk who's achieved something. Not just at the bank, either. It's important to serve as an example and the way to do that is to stay here, not go running off to the big city. You want to be a computer expert, fine! The only thing is, make sure those computers of yours can help *them* too, especially some of our young people, the ones who have something to offer, like you, and who could benefit by being introduced to this new world. That, to my way of thinking, is the really essential thing: you make the most of whatever advantages you've enjoyed and then pass the benefit of your experience along to other Inuit. That, as philosopher Bernard Desloges would have said, is happiness, or the next best thing anyway. It's all up to you."

Agoak, who had been listening attentively to Judith all this time, was well nestled down into his armchair, with his elbows propped up and his fingers intertwined in front of his chest. He looked pensive.

"Do you want some tea?" she asked.

Agoak nodded affirmatively and Judith went about preparing some. Agoak stared into space, lost in some reverie from which he emerged only when he began sipping the bitter, scalding beverage. He made a face, pursed his lips and sat back in his chair, with the cup balanced on the arm.

"I'm giving all this serious consideration," he said to Judith. "More than you can imagine. I'm trying to come around to your way of thinking."

Judith who had poured some tea for herself as well, was seated at an angle along one side of the table. She took a sip and savored it as she watched her husband.

"You might as well think about it at your leisure. It's not something that needs an answer. I'll see over the next few days whether you're still obsessed with the idea of leaving no matter what."

Agoak got up and marched around the living room with his hands in his pockets.

"I don't think it needs as much thinking about as all that," he said. "You were right. I created this big dream for myself, when there was no real reason to. It didn't have to take me to the four corners of North America, because it can be realized right here, after all. And we'll never be as well off anywhere else as we can be here. I have to admit it, Judith, you were right. I'm only sorry I wasn't able to see that for myself and that you had to live through some unpleasant moments."

"You had to live through some too. As far as I'm concerned, I feel sorry about not being able to make you understand my reasoning any better."

A great sense of peace — and a comforting silence — filled the house. Judith was cuddled up on Agoak's lap and he held her tenderly in his arms. Agoak felt blissfully relaxed. He smiled and Judith caressed his lips with the tip of her finger.

"What are you thinking about?" she said.

"I was thinking that in her own peculiar way, and without even knowing it, old Kuksuk was right when she yelled at me about being a traitor and having an evil spirit, an *agiortok*, in the head."

His tone became serious again, almost sombre.

"Judith, that event is something I just can't get out of my mind."

"What event?"

"When I dragged her by the arm back to her house and she was yelling insults at me. I really was betraying my own kind by wanting to emigrate to Toronto."

"Was that where you wanted to go?"

"I figured I had more of a future there than anywhere else. She was right, the poor old thing. Tomorrow I'll tell her I'm going to stay."

"You're going to stay?"

"And I'll take her a bottle of wine too."

"You're really going to stay?"

"Yes, Judith."

CHAPTER VIII

One of the things that had been aired the evening of their mutual discovery continued to haunt Agoak over the course of several days. It had come up long after their exchange of explanations, after Judith had finally spoken her mind.

For a while they just sat and exchanged caresses. As they became aroused, they set about exploring each other's bodies with their hands, unleashing a slow swell of desire which stirred their muscles. They found themselves on a straight-backed kitchen chair. They were both naked, their clothes strewn on the floor, the lights extinguished. Judith was astride Agoak's member, devouring it in long, rhythmic thrusts while he fondled her breasts, sucked her nipples and covered her neck with kisses. When Judith's hoarse moans signalled the oncoming orgasm, Agoak took hold of her hips and used his added strength to help drive his instrument of pleasure even deeper into her. They reached their climax together and Judith drenched Agoak's muscular thighs with her juices, while Agoak inundated Judith's vagina with his sperm.

They returned to the armchair, still naked but now blissfully tired, and snuggled up in the dark, where they spoke in a whisper to each other, as if they were afraid of waking up someone in the next room. This prompted Agoak to remark, "We're whispering. Nobody's asleep."

Judith giggled.

"Yes there is," she said, "and we have to be careful not to wake them."

"Who?" asked Agoak, intrigued.

"Someone," replied Judith.

Agoak pulled himself up in the chair a little and tried to catch the expression on Judith's face.

"Sweetheart, you're crazy in the head."

"No. I'm talking about the old Agoak and the old Judith, the ones from yesterday. They've gone to sleep, they've gone bye-bye. If we don't wake them up, they'll never come back. Let's try not to wake them."

Agoak threw his head back and laughed. He played with a wisp of Judith's hair.

"How would you like it if I was even more Eskimo?" he said after a while.

"You're not going to wake up the old couple are you?"

"No, I'm perfectly serious. Do you think we've lost touch with the real Inuit?"

"Perhaps a little, yes. But I want you to understand something: it's more in our attitude that we've lost touch with them. I think it's fine to be the way we are. The only thing is, there are some Inuit who haven't got as far as us and we tend to forget about them from day to day."

Agoak pushed Judith gently off his lap and made her sit on one arm of the chair.

"Am I getting that heavy already?" said Judith with a laugh. "I thought I still had a way to go."

"You know it's got nothing to do with that," said Agoak. "I've just had an idea and I'd like to discuss it."

"What's that?"

"Talking about not losing touch with the nomadic Eskimos makes me realize that I haven't done any of the things they do for a long time."

"Like what?" asked Judith a little anxiously.

"Like hunting for seal."

She laughed softly and kissed Agoak.

"Oh, is that all? I was afraid you were thinking of going on a long excursion by dog-sled!"

"Not at all," protested Agoak. "We want to get back to nature, but we don't want to overdo it. Going on a seal hunt would be enough."

"In the middle of winter?"

"Sure. It's quite easy in open water, but once the ice has set in, it's a real challenge. As long as we're going to do it at all, I'd rather give it a try in this kind of weather. I'll ask Nochasak to come along. Maybe we could go next Sunday."

"Can I come along too?" asked Judith.

"Of course!"

Agoak now had to get the expedition organized and that gave him cause for concern. Nothing seemed to work out quite as Agoak imagined it would. The first thing he realized was that Inuk or not, he wasn't actually equipped to go and hunt anything at all. The situation was much the same for Nochasak, who had given his only remaining rifle to his elder son two years previously. Between them they had no guns, no ammunition, not even a hunting knife. A visit to the store was in order and this Nochasak and Agoak did one day on their lunch-hour. When they came out, they were well equipped and ready for anything. Agoak bought both a rifle and a shotgun for himself, then another rifle and shotgun, as well as three 100-round boxes of ammunition for each weapon and three hunting knives of different sizes, with leather sheathes.

Nochasak was flabbergasted.

"You've got a whole arsenal there," he commented.

"Judith expressed interest in coming along with us. How about your wife?"

"I doubt it. She leads a sedentary life here in Frobisher and hasn't been on a hunting expedition since the children were small, a good twenty years ago. Even the times I've gone she hasn't wanted to come along. She used to go out a lot as a girl with her father and her brothers, but as she says herself, that's all behind her now."

"Judith used to hunt when she was younger too. But that was with the men in her family, who are all drunkards. It couldn't have been very pleasant."

Judith was happy. The arms Agoak had purchased were among the best, and she handled them with obvious relish. She apparently knew quality when she saw it.

"I used to be afraid of guns and afraid of hunting when I lived at home," she said. "I never knew when one of my drunken relatives might start firing a gun at random. Whenever they were cleaning their guns in the house, I'd start to shake all over and I'd hide somewhere as far away as possible. I'd often go hide in the mission, for example, just to be far away. And whenever they forced me to go on a hunt with them, I'd be terrified from start to finish."

She stroked the long, smooth barrels and smiled.

"It'll be completely different with you, Agoak. I'll go as often as you like."

"Do you know how to handle a gun?"

Judith worked the bolt of her rifle in a convincing manner.

"Certainly," she replied. "I just might be the one who gets the seal on Sunday!"

That evening Agoak pondered what Judith had said. Maybe she

was right; maybe she was more likely to make a kill than he was. Apart from anything else, he had stopped hunting while still very young. As his father had not hunted and he didn't have any brothers or sisters his own age, his hunting had been confined almost exclusively to childhood expeditions with young friends. He had done so little hunting, so long ago, that he barely remembered the essentials. He probably still remembered how to shoot, because that's a skill you don't lose. But could he actually hunt?

At one point he asked Nochasak, "Do you remember what's involved in hunting seal?"

"Oh yes. I go on seal hunts every year, both winter and spring."

Hearing Judith say she was likely to be the one to make the first kill didn't really surprise Agoak, even if it left him feeling a little unsettled. He kept coming back to the idea that Judith wanted more than anything for him to be an Inuk. Unfortunately, he had long ago forgotten the most basic rituals of the traditional way of life. He had become estranged from both the primitive outlook and the daily activities with which it was associated. Coming as he did from a family who had chosen to earn their living from something as sendentary as stone carving, living his life divorced from the ancient Eskimo traditions, which he knew only second-hand, by word of mouth, Agoak now realized that while he had come a long way in a short time, retracing his steps would be a good deal more difficult. And what would Judith think if the expedition turned out to be something of a failure? That would certainly make Agoak look bad. How would that make Judith feel?

Of course, they had had a searching discussion about the future of their relationship, about their future together. Judith's own attachment to the traditional Eskimo costume was unequivocal. What did she have in mind for Agoak. That he had come to look like a White or like an Inuk? Perhaps the hunt would bring them face to face with some stark realities. Agoak had his pride to think of, first as a man, then as an Inuk, and the prospect of being humiliated filled him with anxiety. . . . The hunt had been his idea and it would be difficult to back out now. As he went to bed that evening, he wondered if it had been such a good idea after all. He had a fitful sleep.

Sunday arrived and the morning seemed favorable.

"I've probably heard hundreds of seal-hunt stories being recounted," Agoak said to his friend as they stood outside packing their gear. "I guess I never paid attention. In any case, I never absorbed much. So once the three of us get out there, don't be surprised if I'm a little hesitant. I don't really know anything about it."

Nochasak explained a few things.

"In the spring, you can hunt seal in the open water or, anywhere there are islands, on beaches or rock outcroppings by the shore. In winter it's different. The seal is under the ice, where he's hollowed out an *agloo* for himself, a kind of chamber with an air-hole. That's where he comes to breathe. If the weather's very cold, you can see the mist of his breath and even his black snout as it pokes up through the ice. Or you can go looking for the hole, but that takes much longer. Once you've found it, you enlarge it enough to give you easy access to the chamber underneath. You wait a little while somewhere close by, keeping absolutely still, and sometimes the seal will haul out and stay on the ice for a few moments. If you're a good shot, you stay where you are, wait for the mist and fire at his snout. If you think you've hit him, you enlarge the hole and with a little luck he'll be there, dead, floating in the chamber. But it's not always that simple. Sometimes he doesn't die so quickly. I can remember times when I've had to poke around under the ice to find him. It's definitely much easier in the spring."

Agoak nodded in agreement.

"The best thing to do is follow you and Judith and just see how it goes."

"Of course."

"The important thing for me, if I'm going to take a shot, is that I don't miss."

"What does Judith have to say about it all?"

"She says she's going to make the first kill!"

"Fine, let her have her opinion, see she gets her chance."

But Agoak was not sure things would be so simple. They left the house by snowmobile and headed for the wide-open expanse of the bay, which still had only a sprinkling of snow on it. Agoak had a queasy feeling in the pit of his stomach.

He realized that proposing this hunting expedition had been more or less an act of bravado on his part and that he was about to reap the rather chancy consequences. It perhaps would have been better to prove himself by undertaking feats about which he felt more confident, which the Eskimo that refused to die in Judith might still find convincing . . . but it was too late for second thoughts.

"It can't be helped," Agoak mused as he rode along with his wife in the sled behind Nochasak's snowmobile. "I played the wrong hand, but I've played it. If I lose out, I'll have nobody to blame but myself."

It took them a good hour to reach the spot Nochasak thought would serve them best in their endeavor. They had left at dawn, or what passes for dawn in the Arctic, where night and day are difficult to distinguish, and they were scarcely aware of the passing of time. All around them was a bluish half-light, while the long reddish-gold line of the midnight sun stretched along the flat, endless horizon.

Nochasak stopped the machine, slowly climbed out, looked carefully in every direction, took a few steps and crouched down to scan the surface of the ice as far as the eye could see.

Judith then stirred, got out of the sled and went and crouched at an angle to Nochasak. She too kept as still as possible and looked carefully out over the vast whiteness.

Not wanting to be left behind, Agoak followed suit. He recalled the technique of looking for the breath which Nochasak had mentioned and he was anxious to find out if he could spot a seal for himself that way.

The three dark masses in their furry anoraks remained as motionless as statues for a long time. Agoak reminded himself that keeping still was essential. Any animal living on such flat, deserted wastes was sensitive to, and shy of, the slightest movement. Before the seal came too far out of its air-hole, it would scrutinize the landscape and dive to the depths at the slightest suspicion of anything unusual. It would then be some time until it reappeared. Agoak, like his two companions, was therefore most careful not to budge while he examined every inch of the icy plain.

Although in his heart of hearts he felt cut off from what he termed the "real" Inuit, Agoak was in fact the first to whistle a quiet signal to the others that he had spotted something. Some distance away, in the blue air just above the ice, two puffs of mist had appeared, lit from behind by the morning sun, which hung low over the horizon. Agoak did not move right away, but waited till they appeared again. Several minutes passed before the seal came back to the surface. This time, perhaps because he was paying more attention, the puff of vapor seemed higher, clearer and sharper. Using instincts he never imagined he still possessed, he trained his eyes carefully on certain barely discernable features of the terrain and committed them to memory. First he noticed there was a slight depression in the ice and a little beyond that, a rounded, but clearly defined hump lying directly to the right of the spot where the first two puffs had appeared.

With the third puff, which he had no trouble getting a fix on in the surrounding landscape, Agoak alerted his companions. Nochasak immediately crawled over to the spot where Agoak was crouched down.

"Did you see something?" he whispered.

He too was following instincts he thought he had long since lost. He spoke as quietly as possible, knowing how acute the seal's hearing was and how easily sound travelled through ice which had little snow cover. But he had enough to go on now that the mist had been spotted. It remained to get close to the animal's agloo, so that they could put the rest of their strategy into action.

Nochasak then said to Agoak and Judith, who had also joined them, "We're going to walk very carefully, almost on tip-toes, over to the agloo."

"Should we be ready to fire?" asked Judith.

"The ice isn't too thick," replied Nochasak, "so I think we'd be better off enlarging the hole. I think the seal will haul out on to the ice."

"How do you know?" asked Agoak in a curious tone.

"It's not a matter of knowing," said Nochasak. "Apparently, it's quite unpredictable. The Inuit I've hunted with, including some of the real old-timers, have told me it's not something you can really predict."

"I guess we'll just have to wait and see," said Agoak. "I've had hunters tell me the same thing."

"I remember from when I was young and used to go out hunting," commented Judith in turn, "that both methods were used. However, a hole in the ice meant we should wait. It was safer. But you still have to be very careful not to miss the seal, otherwise he'll be back in the water in two seconds and you won't see him again for a long time."

"We can do it either way," said Nochasak. "Get closer or shoot at the mist from here."

"It takes a good shot to make a kill that way," said Agoak.

"An expert," said Judith. "There was someone like that in Povungnituk who never missed, apparently."

"It certainly wasn't me," said Agoak.

"No, it wasn't, Agoak," said Judith giggling.

"And I'm way out of practice," added Nochasak. "How about you, Judith?"

She threw up her hands.

"You expect me to take a chance on spoiling everything?"

"Okay," said Nochasak, "we'll go and dig out the hole. Follow me — and don't make any noise."

They moved back to the sled, guided by Nochasak, and pulled out their axes. Then Agoak took the lead and, with their eyes riveted to the irregularities in the ice which acted as their reference points, they walked along as quietly as possible. Agoak raised his arm once, in midstride, to point to the puffs of mist, which seemed to drift higher and higher as they got closer and closer.

They all stopped for a moment when they realized how near they were to their goal. From that location it was possible to make out the hole itself: it was darker than the surrounding ice and stood out quite distinctly in the faint light. The seal had dived back into the water, so they began moving forward again, more cautiously than ever. Nochasak whispered, "It's getting tricky now. We can't be too close to the agloo when he comes up to breathe, otherwise he'll notice us here and might disappear for good."

Timing themselves on the basis of the seal's breathing cycle, they stopped in their tracks a little farther on, and just then the mist reappeared. It took them several minutes, inching carefully forward, before they reached the vicinity of the agloo. There they stopped again, crouched down and waited. They despaired of ever seeing the seal again. Then, all of a sudden, they spotted the creature's snout poking up through the ice, heard him draw a long, hoarse breath and watched the warm mist rise into the air. The next moment he was gone. Nochasak was on his feet in a flash, ax in hand, chopping furiously. Responding with similar alacrity, Judith and Agoak rushed to Nochasak's side, where they too began working feverishly at their millenial task, as though it were second nature to them.

As they chopped away, Nochasak said, "He's gone down a long way, to feed. When he comes back, we'll have to be in position."

Then, more by intuition than experience, Nochasak grunted a warning to the other two.

"Watch it, he's on his way!"

They moved back a few feet and waited in a crouch. The hole was bigger now and the seal hesitated momentarily. He swam back and forth, looking around as he did, but saw and heard nothing. Feeling emboldened, he thrust his muzzle a little farther out of the water, exhaled noisily and then, with a long whistling sound, inhaled the brisk fresh air.

As soon as he had dived to the depths again, the three Inuit returned to their task. This time when Nochasak sounded the alert, there was an opening in the ice measuring at least one square metre. The weather was not yet cold enough for the green, sluggish waters of Frobisher Bay to freeze over very quickly. They waited again for the seal to return and familiarize himself with the sudden changes in his environment. He disappeared once more, and the three hunters all loaded their rifles and moved back rapidly about twenty metres, where they crouched down motionless, their weapons at the ready.

There was nothing more they could do. Either the seal would keep coming up simply to breathe and then dive again, or else he would haul out onto the ice to give his exhausted muscles a rest from continuous swimming. It all depended on what the beast had been up to during the preceding hours. And that, of course, was something nobody knew but the seal himself. All the three hunters could do, therefore, was wait.

Trusting entirely to their instincts now, the three Inuit sat on the ground with their weapons in place, aiming at the newly enlarged hole in the vastness of the ice. The stamina which they were able to call upon was strictly atavistic; no White could ever tolerate the strain on the constitution which built up over such long periods of time. Even Agoak, the least seasoned of them all and the one most sheltered from such trials, held his position without moving a muscle. He was curious himself to see how long he could last and was surprised to discover that he did not feel weakened by the ordeal.

The time wore on. The seal kept coming up for air at regular intervals and showed no real signs of concern, nor much curiosity either. The silence and the stillness reassured him. He kept breathing his fill, then disappearing again. At one point Nochasak sighed in an uncharacteristic way, but neither Judith nor Agoak paid any attention. They maintained their vigil, hardly venturing to blink their eyes.

Suddenly, Agoak was overcome by a strange sense of foreboding and the next moment, to his great surprise, the seal appeared and began to roll up onto the ice. Half-way out of the water he paused and clung to the edge of the ice, while he took a long, careful look at his surroundings. Nothing stirred; there were no signs of life. Feeling reassured, the seal pulled himself out of the water and onto the ice in a series of slow, flowing movements, then, breathing a long sigh of relief, stretched out on the ice, where he made himself a kind of nest in the thin layer of snow.

The shots rang out, a split-second apart: the seal was thrown into the air, then fell back dead. It was quite apparent that the first shot had been fired by Judith and that, from the motion of the seal's body, she had hit it right in the head. The glory was incontestably hers.

Judith stood up, smiling timidly and gesturing in a manner that indicated disbelief. And in an equally disbelieving tone of voice, she repeated over and over again, "I killed him! I killed him!"

Then, turning to her husband and to Nochasak, she said, "Excuse me."

Agoak just laughed.

"You should see yourself right now," he said. "You look like a little girl who's just been caught in the act."

Judith couldn't help laughing either.

"What a surprise!" she said. "I was sure one of you would get him first."

They went over to have a look at their prey. Judith's bullet had indeed struck the head, right in the middle. They noticed two other wounds, one in the neck and the other right down near the tail.

Pointing to this last wound, Agoak made a face and said, "That must be mine." He then added, to the great amusement of the others, "It's a good thing for me I'm an accountant and not a nomad who has to hunt to stay alive. Mind you," he said, pointing to his wife, "if I was, I'd have Judith with me and I could manage."

Agoak could not have put it better.

Nochasak went off to get the snowmobile and drove it back to the spot where the seal's remains lay. He got out his knife and pointed to the carcass.

"I can flense it right here," he said. "We'll take what we want and throw the rest back in the water so the wolves won't come for it."

But Judith seemed to have another idea in mind.

"There's something I'd like to do," she said, smiling at Agoak. "It would be just like the old days."

"What were you thinking of?" asked Agoak.

"I'd like to take the seal back to the house and cut it up there."

"You want to do it yourself?" asked Agoak.

"Yes. I used to do it all the time in Povungnituk."

"And you want to do it in the house?"

"Yes."

"Where?"

"On the kitchen floor."

"Right on the kitchen floor?"

"I can clean it up afterwards. Will you let me, Agoak?"

The two Inuit looked at each other. They both shrugged their shoulders.

"If you'd really like to, Judith."

"I would," said Judith. "That way we'll be sure to get the best pieces, and we can share the booty with Nochasak. Do you enjoy having seal at home?" she asked the Inuk.

"We don't eat it very often, but when we do we really enjoy it."

"You'll have more than your fill this time!"

They set about getting the animal moved. It was a good-sized male, weighing about 100 kilos. After the two men had heaved it onto the sled, the little group headed in the direction of town, the lights from which gave a reddish tinge to the sky.

Back at the house, Agoak, who had been mulling things over during the return journey, seemed less enthusiastic. Judith was dismayed to see him pulling a long face as they carted the seal into the kitchen.

"Something's come over you," said Judith. "Look at yourself. . . ."

Agoak was pouting.

"What's the matter?" asked Judith.

"Do you realize what butchering it in the house will involve?"

"Yes."

"Do we have to be true to our roots by splattering blood and guts all over the place?"

Nochasak seemed to be amused by Agoak's question. Judith burst out laughing.

"For God's sake, Agoak, let's just do it. You're like a dog who's afraid of his own shadow."

"No, really, do you have any idea what kind of a mess a butchered seal is going to make in here?"

The White man's outlook had apparently so affected Agoak's thinking that Judith and Nochasak felt cause for concern over his reaction. Powerless to overcome his aversion, Agoak was also aware that he was upsetting Judith. She had made her request. Did this mean she was really anxious for a wholesale return to the traditional life? Or had he misunderstood?

It was the moment of truth. Agoak stared in grim silence at the carcass lying on the ground and felt incapable of either going on or turning back. Coming to terms with his aversion, on the one hand, and exercising his authority in order to stop Judith, on the other, were equally untenable alternatives. The ink was hardly dry on the peace treaty they had signed only a few days before, and it would not do to run roughshod over it already. But Agoak couldn't remain ambivalent forever. A decision had to be made and Agoak's decision was to wash his hands of the problem, in effect, to break his word. He said brusquely, "You can do whatever suits you. I'm going out." As he reached the door he turned around and added, "You can interpret this any way you like."

Thanks to Agoak's gesture, they were right back to square one again. Even after he was long gone, Judith was still standing by the seal with an expression of astonishment on her face. She seemed saddened, but not angered, by what had happened. She lifted her head and looked at Nochasak.

"I think I went too far," she said.

He shook his head pensively.

"Too far, too fast," he said. "You weren't brought up in the same way as him. As he points out, his family led a sit-down life and earned their living like Whites. He left home quite young to go to school. He probably never saw a seal being butchered, whereas it's nothing unusual for you. . . . Yes, I think you did go too far."

"I guess I shouldn't have," she muttered.

"On the other hand," continued Nochasak, "did you see how Agoak behaved today? He was like a real, honest-to-goodness Inuk out there. It was Agoak who saw the seal's breath first."

Judith wrung her hands and between clenched teeth said, "I actually saw it before him — but I didn't want to say anything."

There was a pause, then Nochasak said, "So did I."

Judith sighed, walked around the carcass of the seal and stopped at Nochasak's side, touching his arm.

"I think the best thing would be for you to take the seal with you. If you've still got any meat a little while from now, you can give me some to put in the freezer. For the time being, however, I'd better just forget about it."

Then, in a tone of humility, she added, "We did the wrong thing just now."

"So we did," Nochasak added in agreement.

Thus, while originally designed to placate Judith, the seal hunt had managed to ruin what might otherwise have been a most enjoyable Sunday.

In a contrary frame of mind and with his pace accelerated by pent-up anger, Agoak had quickly covered the distance to the hotel and now sat in the bar slowly sipping a beer. He drew up a mental balance-sheet for the day and found positive feelings on the credit side. On the debit side, however, was this notion of Judith's about butchering the seal at home, which she seemed to think would be barely more complicated than slicing up a loaf of bread for dinner. It was obviously not quite as simple as that; what was not so obvious, on the other hand, was the strange compulsion that lay behind her actions. Was it inherited? Agoak could not rule out the possibility. But was it also necessary for him, for Agoak, to be influenced in his every word and deed by the past? He was in a position to help his fellow Inuit, to lend them support, to promote their success. He could be a hero to them in today's terms; a man revered and respected. He didn't mind the idea of being a social catalyst; but he saw no necessity for any return to the past. Agoak had ancestors who had eaten human flesh. Did this mean Judith was liable to suggest they devour someone on a future Sunday outing, in deference to tradition?

The idea was ridiculous and Agoak knew full well that nothing of the sort was about to happen. Still, such a far-fetched notion seemed to him the logical extension of Judith's line of reasoning.

The bar was exasperatingly noisy, smokey and jammed with people. Agoak stayed put because he knew how to withdraw and become deaf and blind to what was around him. Besides, it would be no better elsewhere. The coffee shop was also packed. It was just as well to stay here, absorbed in his own thoughts, so he could sort things out.

What he could not get over was being asked to embrace two mutually incompatible ways of life. For him it was enough to live in harmony with those around him. Such harmony engendered mutual respect, and made race unimportant. Accomplishing the goals one had set for oneself seemed to him to be enough. On the other hand, he had no quarrel with the way his ancestors had lived. There had been good reason for it. They did not wander the length and breadth of the Arctic out of some misplaced desire for freedom, but rather in the interests of sheer survival. Agoak had nothing to reproach them for. Yet certain behavioral patterns, even if common to an entire people, could always change. It was no longer necessary for any Inuk to pursue his survival over vast distances. Nowadays it was possible for him to stay put and survive, once he realized what opportunities lay close at hand.

So it was for Agoak, who certainly had no objections to blazing a trail for as many Inuit as needed his help. But in order to accomplish this on their behalf, was it absolutely necessary for him to adopt their way of life down to the last detail? They had all lived — and as it happened some of them still lived — off the wildlife that roamed that part of the world. They had done this for so long that they were perhaps no longer capable of changing course and could only barge blindly ahead, indifferent to the opportunities being offered them for a new and comparatively comfortable existence.

Agoak thought back to the evening in Toronto which he had spent at an English folk festival. Everything about it, the costumes, the food, the songs, the dancing, drew on Anglo-Saxon tradition. But the next day, as Agoak was quick to notice, the past was put aside for the sake of the present, something he found quite understandable. Furthermore, the sense of nostalgia evoked had a restrained quality about it and stopped short of any excessively romanticized view of the past. He was finally able to put his finger on what bothered him about Judith's attitude: she had a yearning for the past, but was incapable of distinguishing beneficial traditions from those that were simply irrelevant or unpalatable.

There was nothing Agoak could do about the fact that gutting, skinning and butchering a seal made him sick, and always had. He had agreed to Judith's request in a moment of weakness, while they were still outdoors, stimulated by the bracing fresh air and wide open spaces. But once back in the warmth of the house, he recalled the foul smell and gelatinous consistency of seal guts laid bare by the knife. He had only ever had to witness such a scene twice as a boy and both times he had thrown up violently. Everything in him rebelled at the very thought.

How could he explain to his wife that, as an Inuk born and bred, he had so little enthusiasm for the ancient customs? What did being a man signify for Judith? Agoak was still mystified about her feelings and had no desire to be enlightened on the subject just at the moment.

Ensconced in the bar of the hotel, Agoak continued to mull over the events of the previous several hours, and even took stock of his life as a whole. Yet one thought began pressing in on him with greater and greater urgency: he had to return home. He waved his hand, asked for the bill, paid and left.

His watch read six o'clock. Had there been enough time? Agoak might walk in the door and find that the butchering was still not finished. However, a vague childhood memory told him less time was needed than had elapsed that afternoon. As he walked out of the building, he could see his house in Ikaluit, although from this distance he could not make out anything through the windows.

He was back in the twinkling of an eye. As he got closer he noticed that Nochasak's snowmobile was gone. That was a good sign. He quickened his pace and strode through the door. Judith, who had been watching television, got up to greet her husband. The kitchen, including the double sink, was clean, and everything seemed to be in place. Agoak gave Judith a puzzled look.

"I didn't flense the seal after all," she said slowly. "I gave it to Nochasak. He'll be bringing a little meat for us to put in the freezer."

Agoak was astonished, but despite a burning curiosity, he said nothing.

"Agoak," said Judith, "I'm sorry."

"Sorry for what?"

"For what I did. I was cruel and insensitive. It's not a thing somebody who loves you should have done."

"You're crazy!"

"Yes, I know. I was and I still am. It's all my fault. I said all the wrong things. Can you forgive me?"

"I thought it was really important for you to flense the seal yourself."

"No! I said that . . . I don't know why I said it. Maybe because I thought it would be fun. It brought back nice memories."

"You see?"

"Not necessarily nice memories, I wouldn't want to relive any of that. I think when I first flensed a seal, I had a kind of need to tear flesh. It was subconscious revenge against my family for the life I had to lead."

"Judith, try to forget."

"Yes, I know I should try to. But when I saw the carcass on the ice, it brought so many things flooding back that I couldn't think straight anymore. I didn't even bother to ask you how you felt about the whole thing. It never occurred to me that you might look at it differently. When Nochasak reminded me after you left that you grew up with a family who worked indoors and never went hunting, I realized what I'd done, but by then it was too late. So I gave the carcass to Nochasak. All of a sudden, I didn't want it anymore."

"What have you been doing all this time?" asked Agoak.

"I just sat down. I thought you'd be at the hotel, but since you hardly drink at all, I wasn't worried."

"You could've come to get me."

"I didn't want to be with other people. I had to do some thinking, because I realized once again I hadn't said everything I should have said, or maybe I just didn't say it the right way. Agoak, I'm an Eskimo woman and I'm proud of the fact that we come from an ancient culture and that our people managed to survive very well under extremely bad conditions. And I know they'll meet other challenges if they have to. But in spite of what I'm saying, I'm also very proud of having received an education from the Whites. I'm determined to remain an Inuk, but not to the point where it spoils our life. I'm going to behave in a perfectly rational way, Agoak, just like you, because that's the only way we can live right now."

She smiled and wrapped her arms around him.

"And that's the last time I'll ever suggest we gut and butcher a seal on the kitchen floor, I promise."

Despite their reconciliation, and the sense of physical release attained before they switched off the lights, Agoak and Judith slept badly, though this had nothing to do with the nervous tension built up over the day. They had had nothing more to say to each other for the moment and were well disposed to enjoying a good night's sleep. The problem was the ruckus created by Tomasic Papik's dogs.

In the middle of winter, Frobisher is not a particularly peaceful place, day or evening, least of all on a Sunday. During the week, the splutter of snowmobile engines, along with the occasional Bombardier carrying freight or passengers, forms an ever-present backdrop of sound. By evening the heavy-duty vehicles are back in the garage, but the snowmobiles can still be heard, since both Whites and Inuit use them for transport, or simply for recreational purposes. For some years now dogs have been getting rarer and rarer, and only the real nomads are still likely to arrive in town with a pack of Huskies. Ikaluit had not seen a single dog until that Sunday, when Tomasic Papik, Agoak's neighbor three doors away, turned up around noon, for no apparent reasons, with two magnificent teams of Huskies, who were as pure in their breeding as they were boisterous, irascible, noisy and quarrelsome.

Though most of Frobisher was finally asleep, the air was filled with the cacophonous, age-old sound of dogs yelping and howling, a sound utterly characteristic of the Arctic, even if it is one now largely replaced by the high-pitched drone of the snowmobile.

CHAPTER IX

The days went by and life returned to normal. If the engine had been misfiring for a while, it was now back in tune and running as it should. Agoak and Judith took up where they had left off, without regret or remorse.

And then, one fateful afternoon, while Agoak chatted with a customer at the bank and Judith busied herself serving a group of Inuit at a table in the coffee shop, an aircraft loomed over Resolution Island and the Strait of Gabriel and made contact with the control tower in Frobisher.

"Request pattern, request pattern."

The plane identified itself. It was a Lear jet of Canadian registry. From where the Lear was just at that moment, it would have taken a Beaver, Otter or DC-3 some time to reach its destination, but this was a jet-propelled aircraft and it flew at speed. No sooner had it asked for flight path information than it was radioing:

"Request permission to land. Give instrument reading and strip number."

Again the pilot gave his call letters.

A few minutes later, the sleek, elegant craft touched down on the runway. Two men climbed out and immediately began inquiring, "Is there anywhere to eat? Come on, come on!"

They were hungry and wanted some action out of the ground crew. They also needed directions and it was in fact Nochasak, who happened to be crossing the tarmac at that particular moment, who explained to them where to find the Bombardier which would take them to the coffee shop. At that time of day, with the hotel dining room not yet open, it was the most presentable spot to have a bite to eat.

And so it was that on this particular day two men walked into the nearly deserted coffee shop, where it became Judith's responsibility to serve them. Fate works in strange ways, for while Emilie Outsanuk was working the same shift as Judith, she was not the one who happened to take these particular orders. How easily it could have been otherwise.

The men were White, but of a sort Judith had rarely seen before. What struck her about them right away was the quality of their clothes. They were brand new, and Judith had never seen fabric so fine or so beautifully cut. Their watches, their rings, the cigarette case and the lighter which lay on the table, all attested to the fact they were rich and very sure of themselves, even arrogant. They stared incessantly at Judith, examining her up and down, taking in every detail. She felt them undressing her with their eyes. She had pretty breasts and, under normal circumstances, she was proud of the fact. But standing by their table she felt as though she were stark naked and the piercing stares were actually fondling her breasts. She shuddered and went stiff with resentment. A strange sense of revulsion swept through her. The two men in question were young and handsome as gods as well. But there was something written on their faces, something Judith couldn't quite understand and didn't want to understand. She was pleasant all the same. She had to be. The manager was nearby and keeping a close watch on the two strangers and no doubt on Judith as well.

What really unsettled her was being confronted once again by an attitude she had known as a child, when Whites of this kind would come through Povungnituk and act in an insulting manner, addressing the Inuit in a tone at once condescending and threatening. This kind of arrogance, though rare in the Arctic today, was something Judith could never tolerate, especially now that she was part of Frobisher society and expected to be treated accordingly.

Somehow the two men were almost polite with her, even if they seemed rather too fascinated by her body, her hair, her smile . . . and even said so! At the same time, they insisted on talking to her as though she were a child.

"How old are you?"

She suppressed her resentment and smiled, as she felt obliged to do, going so far in fact as to look a little flirtatious, since the customer is, after all, always right.

"Old enough to be married," she replied. "What can I get you?"

The one who looked to be the older of the two made a face, closed his eyes and asked, "Do you know what a club sandwich is?"

He asked the question in a contemptuous tone, as though expecting an answer in the negative.

"Of course I do," said Judith dryly.

This seemed to disappoint them and the younger one gave a facetious smile.

"So bring two club sandwiches."

"We have three kinds," said Judith. She handed them the menus she'd been holding. "Would you like to choose one?" She turned on her heel and said as she left, "I'll be right back."

She walked over towards the cash, where Emilie Outsanuk was standing idle for the moment. The manager came over and looked at Judith.

"Everything okay?" he asked, more by way of a warning than anything else.

"I don't know who those two are," said Judith in a rage, "but I could just kill them!"

"Shhh . . .," said the manager.

Emilie put her fingertips on Judith's arm.

"Do you want me to take over?"

"No," said Judith brusquely, "I can manage."

She returned to the table and stood tapping her heel.

"Are you ready to order?"

"What time does the hotel dining room open?" asked one of the men.

"Six o'clock," said Judith.

"We'll wait. Bring us some coffee."

Judith went to get the two coffees, brought them to the table and returned to the cash desk, turning her back to the two strangers. Other customers drifted in and were served by Emilie, while Judith sat alone with her elbows on the counter, fully aware that the two men were still staring at her.

Emilie stopped in midstream to say to Judith, "They just won't give up, and now they're whispering to each other while they look you over."

Judith shrugged her shoulders.

"I'm off in ten minutes, then they're all yours."

She tried to get the men out of her mind and instead planned what she would do after she finished her shift and returned home. That Saturday they had done a huge shopping at the meat and grocery department of the Bay. After checking the cupboards, the refrigerator and the freezer, Judith had decided their supplies were altogether too low and so with Agoak's approval, they had purchased roast upon roast — beef, pork, even lamb — an enormous turkey, several good-sized capons and a large quantity of canned goods, which included several more meat items among them. As Judith had said with a giggle to Agoak, "I got up feeling like some meat this morning and look what it's done for us. We're going to go broke at these prices!"

"Still," said Agoak, "we had hardly anything left in reserve."

As she got ready to go home, it occurred to Judith that a hefty steak would make a delicious dinner. Unfortunately, what she had purchased was already in the freezer and couldn't be used that quickly. For just such a contingency — leaving aside the canned goods — there was some bacon in the refrigerator, though that would hardly make a real feast. She made a mental note to be better organized next day and take out something to thaw in time for dinner, then resigned herself to fixing bacon and eggs for Agoak that evening. If prepared with the appropriate amount of love, that would do for this once.

After her moment of frustration had passed and she had recovered her good humor, she set off for Ikaluit, striding along vigorously, humming and whistling, feeling enormously content and somehow rejuvenated.

She strode into the house at the same brisk pace, in the same mood of elation, closed the door behind her and set about tidying up a bit and doing a few of the usual daily chores. At five o'clock she started the dinner, so that by the time Agoak got back home, the bacon would be cooked and the eggs would be ready for the frying pan. With some toast, slices of cheddar and a few pickles, it would be a simple but restorative meal. Judith performed her tasks with a sense of joy.

After Judith had gone and their coffees were paid for, the two visitors left the coffee shop in an unhurried manner. They stepped outside and glanced around at their environment in the sombre light of the midnight sun. But what they were concentrating their attention on was Judith as she walked down the hill towards Ikaluit. One of them, the younger of the two, laughed sarcastically.

"Shall we?" he said.

The other man looked undecided. He hesitated.

"What's the matter, Bob?" asked the younger man.

His companion shook his head doubtfully as he examined their surroundings, the big building behind them, the layout of the rest of the town. The other man was straining at the leash.

"She's only a native!" he exclaimed, in the sort of tone characteristic of an American talking about Blacks. They finally made up their minds and started walking slowly in the direction of the house which they had just seen Judith enter. They made their way cautiously through the snow, something they were obviously unaccustomed to doing. Nor were their expensive boots of much help either.

"What do you want from her?" asked the older man.

"Oh you know, talk to her, kiss her a little, see if she's as built as she looks. I've never had a chance to see an Eskimo's tits before and I don't want to miss the opportunity.

"And what if she makes a fuss?" he asked, pointing to the town all around. "It's no village."

"What're you worried about? Do you think anybody here listens to the natives?" he said, again stressing the word "natives" in a tone of profound contempt. He gave a cavalier wave of the hand.

"I'll throw a few American tens on the floor and you just watch how fast she gets down on her hands and knees to pick them up. After that I guarantee you she'll head for the bedroom with us and show us a real good time for our trouble. Did you see those eyes? Wave a few bucks in front of them and watch them light up."

"What if there's somebody else in the house?"

"We'll check that out. We can always make up some story. . . ."

They had arrived in front of the house and through the window they could see Judith moving around. They could also see the table was set.

"She's alone," said the younger man.

The one called Bob whispered, "You're right, she really is good-looking."

"You see? You're horny for her too."

"I wouldn't kick her out of bed, that's for sure. Anyway, we're practically at the North Pole, thousands of miles from home, so we deserve a little fun."

"I think we're going to have a ball tonight."

Judith had just begun removing the first few strips of bacon from the package when the door suddenly burst open. Someone had barged in without even knocking.

Judith was astonished to see the two customers from the coffee shop standing there. They looked tall and imposing in the low-ceilinged house. Their voices were loud and harsh and they snickered sarcastically. Thunderstruck and momentarily at a loss for words, Judith stared at the intruders, then managed to blurt out, "What are you doing here? What do you want?"

The men just kept laughing and moving towards her, drowning out the poor girl's protests with their brutal comments.

"What do you want?!" she said again, almost screaming.

"I think maybe we want to use the phone," replied one of the men in a tone of mock deference.

"There isn't any telephone here! Get out of here!"

By this time, however, the younger man had already grabbed her. He held her by the waist with one arm as he tried to take hold of a breast with the other hand. Judith struggled as best she could, but before long both men were wrestling with her and tearing off her clothes. Judith managed to grab the pan in which the bacon had started to fry and threw the boiling fat in the younger man's face. He howled with rage and punched Judith right in the face as hard as he could. With her lip split open, her nose bleeding and her cheek bruised, Judith fell back, stunned by the blow. In a sudden burst of fury, the two men tore off the rest of her clothes, then the older man threw her on the floor and held her down while his companion pulled out his penis and drove it into the girl. He pounded away at her with his lower body, determined to achieve immediate gratification. Judith screamed and writhed as she attempted to dislodge the huge glistening organ, but her assailants were too strong and kept her pinned to the floor.

Just then, Agoak came in, unnoticed. Still wearing his parka and mukluks, he ran straight into the bedroom, in a blind, terrible rage. He grabbed a rifle and a hunting knife and bounded into the kitchen. He fired a shot and wounded the younger man, who had been raping Judith. The two men leapt to their feet, but a second shot struck the older man. Then with his knife held high over his head, Agoak sprang on the two wounded men like a crazed panther. He stabbed and slashed in broad strokes, hacking off strips of clothing and skin and flesh. Nothing could stop him, neither the assailants' pleas for mercy nor their feeble attempts at defending themselves. Agoak continued at his butchery until the two men finally collapsed, half-naked, with blood pouring from a dozen wounds, their costly outfits cut to ribbons. As they moaned in agony, they tried their best to push away this madman who was bent on killing them.

"Stop, stop," pleaded one of them. "We'll give you money, a whole lot of money. . . ."

He was unable to complete his sentence because just then Agoak drove his knife through the man's skull, killing him instantly. His companion, who was still naked below the waist, lay panting and writhing pathetically on the kitchen floor. Agoak sliced off his penis with one stroke of his blade. The man let out a terrible, inhuman scream, a sound filled with the most atrocious fear and pain. Then Agoak finished him off.

Without a moment's hesitation he cut off the other man's penis and hurled it to the ground. Then he fell to his knees and began to cry. Judith, who was slumped against the wall, was crying as well. Her face was contorted and her whole body trembled. A low, whimpering sound such as a wounded animal might make issued from the back of her throat. Her hands opened and closed in a series of spasmodic movements.

They remained in this position for some time. When the initial shock had passed, it was Judith who rose from the floor first. She had calmed somewhat, but her lips were pinched and her eyes hollow. She picked her way over to Agoak, who was rocking back and forth with his arms swaying at his side, his hands covered in blood. He looked dazed.

The two bodies lay in a heap on the floor, butchered beyond recognition. Scattered about everywhere were bits of clothing and human flesh which had been hacked from the victims during Agoak's savage attack with the knife, while not far from the window lay the two bloodied penises.

Judith took Agoak by the arm, helped him up and led him to the kitchen table. She pulled out a chair and sat him down before saying, "I'll make some fresh tea."

Nothing stirred in Frobisher; the house was absolutely still as well. Agoak slowly took in what was around him. He twitched a few times and put his head in his hands. He sat there for a while as Judith just stood staring at the white wall behind him.

By and by the water began to sing in the electric kettle, until the sound changed into a quiet burbling. That seemed to be enough to break the tension. Agoak raised his head and Judith put some tea in the pot. As she was pouring the boiling water, Agoak said in a very grave voice, "It's done."

Judith turned around sharply. Agoak repeated what he had said in the same tone and motioned half-heartedly with his hands.

"It's done, everything's ruined. We're finished. . . ."

Judith had moistened a cloth and was busy sponging the blood from her cut lip and injured nose, as well as from the long gash she had over her cheekbone.

Agoak pushed back his chair and got up. He stood beside the two bodies with his hands in his pockets and contemplated his deed.

"What are we going to do?" asked Judith.

"Head north," replied Agoak.

"What?"

"Make a getaway. Go north to the top of Baffin Island, as far as Ellesmere if we have to."

"How will we live?"

"The way the others do, the way our ancestors did before us."

"Agoak!"

"Do you think we have any choice? I've killed two Whites, two rich Whites at that."

"Do you know who they were?"

"Now I do, yes. I saw them and got curious. It wasn't hard to get the information. The control tower talked to Dorval to find out who the two of them might be. They're rich Americans. They cause trouble everywhere they go. Even here, as you can see."

"What now, Agoak?"

He stretched out his hands and announced in his mournful tone, "I killed them. All I can do is flee."

Then he threw back his shoulders, assumed a resolute and determined expression and said to Judith, "You'll have to give me a hand getting everything ready."

THE INUIT

Theories and Things

10/9/81

→ *Theories and Things*

(Willard Van Orman)

W. V. Quine

191

The Belknap Press of
Harvard University Press
Cambridge, Massachusetts
and London, England
1981

Library of Congress Cataloging in Publication Data

Quine, W. V. (Willard Van Orman)
    Theories and things.

    Bibliography: p.
    Includes index.
    1. Philosophy—Miscellanea. I. Title.
B68.Q56   191   81–4517
ISBN 0–674–87925–2   AACR2

To

Bob and Rosalie

Preface

The first and longest essay in this collection, very nearly a title essay, is a decoction of several of my recent papers and lectures on what the assuming of objects means and how it helps. Four subsequent essays are new to the literature; two of these may still reappear in colloquium proceedings. The remaining twenty-one items in the collection are garnered from scattered publications and revised none or in varying degrees. Seven of them date from the sixties; the rest are recent, two being still in press as I write.

Themes of ontology, epistemology, and semantics are pursued in the first five essays. Then comes an unaccustomed venture into ethics, followed by three pieces on philosophy in retrospect and two reviews of contemporary philosophers of science. Essays 12 to 14, next, reflect my dim view of intensional objects and modal logic. The ensuing six are occupied with logic proper, or what I deem proper, and the nature of mathematics. The next item, number 21, is less essay than medley, and it is followed by a short piece on metaphor and two on public relations. The drift away from philosophy becomes complete in two essays with which the book concludes. They are two examples from among six reviews in geography and lexicography that I wrote in a somewhat playful spirit in the sixties, and I include them in that same spirit. They do not add to the philosophical content which it is the purpose of this volume to convey.

In many of these essays, as in previous writings, I have been helped by suggestions from Burton Dreben. To him and to David Kaplan and Donald Davidson I am indebted also for good advice regarding the volume as a whole.

Harvard University
February 1981

Contents

Theories and Things

◆ Things and Their Place in Theories

Our talk of external things, our very notion of things, is just a conceptual apparatus that helps us to foresee and control the triggering of our sensory receptors in the light of previous triggering of our sensory receptors. The triggering, first and last, is all we have to go on.

In saying this I too am talking of external things, namely,

This is a revised and amplified version of "What is it all about?" an essay first published by the United Chapters of Phi Beta Kappa in *The American Scholar*, Winter 1980–1981. That essay was the Gail Caldwell Stine Memorial Lecture that I gave at Mount Holyoke College in April 1980 and soon afterward at Oakland University in Michigan, Uppsala University in Sweden, and the University of Iceland. The content derived largely from two of my four Immanuel Kant Lectures (Stanford University, February 1980) and developed out of lectures that I gave ten to twelve months earlier at Tallahassee, Ann Arbor, Berkeley, Los Angeles, Madison, Louvain-la-Neuve, Aix-en-Provence, and the Collège de France under such titles as "How and why to reify" and "Les étapes de la réification."

The present version incorporates substantial passages also from three other publications: "Whither physical objects?" (*Boston Studies in the Philosophy of Science*, vol. 39, pp. 497–504, copyright © 1976, D. Reidel Publishing Co., Dordrecht, Holland), "Facts of the matter" (R. Shahan, ed., *American Philosophy from Edwards to Quine*, Norman: University of Oklahoma Press, 1977), and "The variable and its place in reference" (Z. van Straaten, ed., *Philosophical Subjects: Essays Presented to P. F. Strawson*, Oxford: Oxford University Press, 1980). Bits are drawn also from my replies to critics in three periodicals now in press: *Sintaxis* (Montevideo), the *Southwestern Journal of Philosophy*, and *Midwest Studies in Philosophy*.

people and their nerve endings. Thus what I am saying applies in particular to what I am saying, and is not meant as skeptical. There is nothing we can be more confident of than external things—some of them, anyway—other people, sticks, stones. But there remains the fact—a fact of science itself—that science is a conceptual bridge of our own making, linking sensory stimulation to sensory stimulation; there is no extrasensory perception.

I should like now to consider how this bridging operation works. What does it mean to assume external objects? And what about objects of an abstract sort, such as numbers? How do objects of both sorts help us in developing systematic connections between our sensory stimulations?

The assuming of objects is a mental act, and mental acts are notoriously difficult to pin down—this one more than most. Little can be done in the way of tracking thought processes except when we can put words to them. For something objective that we can get our teeth into we must go after the words. Words accompany thought for the most part anyway, and it is only as thoughts are expressed in words that we can specify them.

If we turn our attention to the words, then what had been a question of assuming objects becomes a question of verbal *reference* to objects. To ask what the *assuming* of an object consists in is to ask what *referring* to the object consists in.

We refer by using words, and these we learn through more or less devious association with stimulations of our sensory receptors. The association is direct in cases where the word is learned by ostension. It is thus that the child learns to volunteer the word 'milk', or to assent if the word is queried, in the conspicuous presence of milk; also to volunteer the word so as to induce the presence of milk.

The mechanism in such a case is relatively clear and simple, as psychological mechanisms go. It is the conditioning of a response. To call it objective reference, however, is premature. Learning the expression 'milk' in this way, by direct association with appropriate stimulations, is the same in principle as learning the sentence 'It's windy' or 'It's cold' or 'It's raining' by direct association with appropriate stimulations. It is we in our adult ontological sophistication that recognize the word 'milk' as referring to an object, a substance, while we are less ready to single out an object of reference for 'It's windy' or 'It's cold' or 'It's raining'. This is the contrast that we need eventually to analyze if we are to achieve a satisfactory analysis of what to count as objective reference; and it is not a contrast that obtrudes in the primitive phase of learning by ostension. The word 'milk', when uttered in recognition or when queried and assented to, is best regarded at first as a sentence on a par with 'It's windy', 'It's cold', and the rest; it is as if to say 'It's milk'. It is a one-word sentence. All of these examples are *occasion* sentences, true on some occasions of utterance and false on others. We are conditioned to assent to them under appropriate stimulation. There is no call to read into them, as yet, any reference to objects.

The view of sentences as primary in semantics, and of names or other words as dependent on sentences for their meaning, is a fruitful idea that began perhaps with Jeremy Bentham's theory of fictions.[1] What Bentham observed was that you have explained any term quite adequately if you have shown how all contexts in which you propose to use it can be paraphrased into antecedently intelligible language. When this is recognized, the philosophical analysis of concepts or explication of terms comes into its own. Sentences come to be seen as the primary repository of meaning, and words are seen as imbibing their meaning through their use in sentences.

Recognition of sentences as primary has not only expedited philosophical analysis; it has also given us a better picture of how language is actually learned. First we learn short sentences, next we get a line on various words through their use in those sentences, and then on that basis we manage to grasp longer sentences in which those same words recur. Accordingly the development leading from sensory stimulation to objective reference is to be seen as beginning with the flat conditioning of simple occasion sentences to stimulatory events, and advancing through stages more forthrightly identifiable with objective reference. We have

1. See Essay 7 below.

still to consider what the distinguishing traits of these further stages might be.

As long as the word 'milk' can be accounted for simply as an occasion sentence on a par with 'It's raining', surely nothing is added by saying that it is a name of something. Nothing really is said. Similarly for 'sugar', 'water', 'wood'. Similarly even for 'Fido' and 'Mama'. We would be idly declaring there to be designata of the words, counterparts, shadows, one apiece: danglers, serving only as honorary designata of expressions whose use as occasion sentences would continue as before.

The outlook changes when individuative words emerge: words like 'chair' and 'dog'. These differ from the previous examples in the complexity of what has to be mastered in learning them. By way of mastery of any of those previous words, all that was called for was the ability to pass a true-false test regarding points or neighborhoods taken one at a time. It is merely a question, in the case of Fido or milk, of what visible points are on Fido or on milk and what ones are not. To master 'dog' or 'chair', on the other hand, it is not enough to be able to judge of each visible point whether it is on a dog or chair; we have also to learn where one dog or chair leaves off and another sets in.

In the case of such words, individuative ones, the idea of objective reference seems less trivial and more substantial. The word 'dog' is taken to denote each of many things, each dog, and the word 'chair', each chair. It is no longer an idle one-to-one duplication, a mirroring of each word in an object dreamed up for that exclusive purpose. The chairs and dogs are indefinite in number and individually, for the most part, nameless. The 'Fido'-Fido principle, as Ryle called it, has been transcended.

However, this contrast between the individuatives and the previous words does not become detectable until a further device has become available: predication. The contrast emerges only when we are in a position to compare the predication 'Fido is a dog' with the predication 'Milk is white'. Milk's being white comes down to the simple fact that whenever you point at milk you point at white. Fido's being a dog does not come down to the simple fact that whenever you point at Fido you point at a dog: it involves that and more. For whenever you point at Fido's head you point at a dog, and yet Fido's head does not qualify as a dog.

It is in this rather subtle way that predication creates a difference between individuative terms and others. Prior to predication, such words as 'dog' and 'chair' differ in no pertinent way from 'milk' and 'Fido'; they are simple occasion sentences that herald, indifferently, the presence of milk, Fido, dog, chair.

Thus reference may be felt to have emerged when we take to predicating individuative terms, as in 'Fido is a dog'. 'Dog' then comes to qualify as a general term denoting each dog, and thereupon, thanks again to the predication 'Fido is a dog', the word 'Fido' comes at last to qualify as a singular term naming one dog. In view then of the analogy of 'Milk is white' to 'Fido is a dog', it becomes natural to view the word 'milk' likewise as a singular term naming something, this time not a body but a substance.

In *Word and Object* and *The Roots of Reference* I have speculated on how we learn individuative terms, predication, and various further essentials of our language. I will not go further into that, but will merely remind you of what some of these further essentials are. Along with singular predication, as in 'Milk is white' and 'Fido is a dog', we want plural predication: 'Dogs are animals'. Along with monadic general terms, moreover, such as 'dog' and 'animal', we want dyadic ones, such as 'part of', 'darker than', 'bigger than', and 'beside'; also perhaps triadic and higher. Also we want predication of these polyadic terms, at least in the singular: thus 'Mama is bigger than Fido', 'Fido is darker than milk'. Also we want the truth functions—'not', 'and', 'or'—by means of which to build compound sentences.

Now a further leap forward, as momentous as predication, is the *relative clause*. It is a way of segregating what a sentence says about an object, and packaging it as a complex general term. What the sentence

Mont Blanc is higher than the Matterhorn but the Matterhorn is steeper

says about the Matterhorn is packaged in the relative clause:

object that is not as high as Mont Blanc but is steeper.

Predicating this of the Matterhorn carries us back in effect to the original sentence.

The grammar of relative clauses can be simplified by rewriting them in the 'such that' idiom:

> object x such that Mont Blanc is higher than x but x is steeper.

This keeps the word order of the original sentence. The 'x' is just a relative pronoun written in mathematical style. We can change the letter to avoid ambiguity in case one relative clause is embedded in another.

The relative clause serves no purpose in singular predication, since such predication just carries us back to a sentence of the original form. Where it pays off is in plural predication. Without relative clauses, the use of plural predication is cramped by shortage of general terms. We could still say 'Dogs are animals' and perhaps 'Small dogs are amusing animals', but it is only with the advent of relative clauses that we can aspire to such heights as 'Whatever is salvaged from the wreck belongs to the state'. It becomes:

> Objects x such that x is salvaged from the wreck are objects x such that x belongs to the state.

In general, where 'Fx' and 'Gx' stand for any sentences that we are in a position to formulate about x, relative clauses open the way to the plural predication:

> Objects x such that Fx are objects x such that Gx.

Once we have this equipment, we have the full benefit of universal and existential quantification. This is evident if we reflect that '$(x)Fx$' is equivalent to '(x) (if not Fx then Fx)' and hence to:

> Objects x such that not Fx are objects x such that Fx.

I said that reference may be felt to emerge with the predicating of individuatives. However, it is better seen as emerging by degrees. Already at the start the sentences 'Fido' and 'Milk', unlike 'It's raining', are learned by association with distinctively salient portions of the scene. Typically the salience is induced by pointing. Here already, in the selectivity of salience, is perhaps a first step toward the eventual namehood of 'Fido' and 'Milk'. Predications such as 'Milk is white' further enhance this air of objective reference, hinging as they do on a coinciding of saliences. Thus contrast the predication 'Milk is white' with 'When night falls the lamps are lit'. 'When' here is a connective comparable to the truth functions; it just happens to deliver standing sentences rather than occasion sentences when applied to occasion sentences. 'Milk is white' likewise can be viewed as a standing sentence compounded of the occasion sentences 'Milk' and 'White', but it says more than 'When there is milk there is white'; it says '*Where* there is milk there is white'. The concentration on a special part of the scene is thus doubly emphasized, and in this I sense further rumblings of objective reference.

Predications such as 'Milk is white' still afford, even so, little reason for imputing objective reference. As already remarked, we might as well continue to use the purported names as occasion sentences and let the objects go. A finite and listed ontology is no ontology.

Predication of individuatives, next, as in 'Fido is a dog', heightens reference in two ways. The concentration on a special part of the scene is emphasized here more strongly still in 'Milk is white', since Fido is required not merely to be contained in the scattered part of the world that is made up of dog; he is required to fill one of its discrete blobs. And the more telling point, already noted, is that 'dog' transcends the 'Fido'-Fido principle; dogs are largely nameless.

Even at this stage, however, the referential apparatus and its ontology are vague. Individuation goes dim over any appreciable time interval. Thus consider the term 'dog'. We would recognize any particular dog in his recurrences if we noticed some distinctive trait in him; a dumb animal would do the same. We recognize Fido in his recurrences in learning the occasion sentence 'Fido', just as we recognize further milk and sugar in learning 'Milk' and 'Sugar'. Even in the absence of distinctive traits we will correctly concatenate momentary canine manifestations as stages of the same dog as long as we keep watching. After any considerable lapse of observation, however, the question of identity of unspecified dogs simply does not arise—not at the rudimentary stage of language learning. It scarcely makes sense until we are in a position to say such things as that in general if *any* dog undergoes such and such then in due course that *same* dog will behave thus and so. This sort of general talk about long-term causation becomes possible only with the advent of quantification or its equivalent, the relative clause in plural predication. Such is the dependence of individuation, in the time dimension, upon relative clauses; and it is only with full individuation that reference comes fully into its own.

With the relative clause at hand, objective reference is indeed full blown. In the relative clause the channel of reference is the relative pronoun 'that' or 'which', together with its recurrences in the guise of 'it', 'he', 'her', and so on. Regimented in symbolic logic, these pronouns give way to bound variables of quantification. The variables range, as we say, over all objects; they admit all objects as values. To assume objects of some sort is to reckon objects of that sort among the values of our variables.

II

What objects, then, do we find ourselves assuming? Certainly bodies. The emergence of reference endowed the occasion sentences 'Dog' and 'Animal' with the status of general terms denoting bodies, and the occasion sentences 'Fido' and 'Mama' with the status of singular terms designating bodies.

We can see how natural it is that some of the occasion sentences ostensively learned should have been such as to foreshadow bodies, if we reflect on the social character of ostension. The child learns the occasion sentence from the mother while they view the scene from their respective vantage points, receiving somewhat unlike presentations. The mother in her childhood learned the sentence in similarly divergent circumstances. The sentence is thus bound to be versatile, applying regardless of angle. Thus it is that the aspects of a body in all their visual diversity are naturally gathered under a single occasion sentence, ultimately a single designation.

We saw how the reification of milk, wood, and other substances would follow naturally and closely on that of bodies. Bodies are our paradigmatic objects, but analogy proceeds apace; nor does it stop with substances. Grammatical analogy between general terms and singular terms encourages us to treat a general term as if it designated a single object, and thus we are apt to posit a realm of objects for the general terms to designate: a realm of properties, or sets. What with the nominalizing also of verbs and clauses, a vaguely varied and very untidy ontology grows up.

The common man's ontology is vague and untidy in two ways. It takes in many purported objects that are vaguely or inadequately defined. But also, what is more significant, it is vague in its scope; we cannot even tell in general which of these vague things to ascribe to a man's ontology at all, which things to count him as assuming. Should we regard grammar as decisive? Does every noun demand some array of denotata? Surely not; the nominalizing of verbs is often a mere stylistic variation. But where can we draw the line?

It is a wrong question; there is no line to draw. Bodies are assumed, yes; they are the things, first and foremost. Beyond them there is a succession of dwindling analogies. Various expressions come to be used in ways more or less parallel to the use of the terms for bodies, and it is felt that corresponding objects are more or less posited, *pari passu;* but there is no purpose in trying to mark an ontological limit to the dwindling parallelism.

My point is not that ordinary language is slipshod, slipshod though it be. We must recognize this grading off for what it is, and recognize that a fenced ontology is just not implicit in ordinary language. The idea of a boundary between being and nonbeing is a philosophical idea, an idea of technical science in a broad sense. Scientists and philosophers seek a comprehensive system of the world, and one that is oriented to reference even more squarely and utterly than ordinary language. Ontological concern is not a correction of a lay thought and practice; it is foreign to the lay culture, though an outgrowth of it.

We can draw explicit ontological lines when desired. We can regiment our notation, admitting only general and singular terms, singular and plural predication, truth functions, and the machinery of relative clauses; or, equivalently and more artificially, instead of plural predication and relative clauses we can admit quantification. Then it is that we can say that the objects assumed are the values of the variables, or of the pronouns. Various turns of phrase in ordinary language that seemed to invoke novel sorts of objects may disappear under such regimentation. At other points new ontic commitments may emerge. There is room for choice, and one chooses with a view to simplicity in one's overall system of the world.

More objects are wanted, certainly, than just bodies and substances. We need all sorts of parts or portions of substances. For lack of a definable stopping place, the natural course at this point is to admit as an object the material content of any portion of space-time, however irregular and discontinuous and heterogeneous. This is the generalization of the primitive and ill-defined category of bodies to what I call physical objects.

Substances themselves fall into place now as physical objects. Milk, or wood, or sugar, is the discontinuous four-dimensional physical object comprising all the world's milk, or wood, or sugar, ever.

The reasons for taking the physical objects thus spatio-temporally, and treating time on a par with space, are overwhelming and have been adequately noted in various places.[2] Let us pass over them and ponder rather the opposition to the four-dimensional view; for it is a curiosity worth looking into. Part of the opposition is obvious misinterpretation: the notion that time is stopped, change is denied, and all is frozen eternally in a fourth dimension. These are the misgivings of unduly nervous folk who overestimate the power of words. Time as a fourth dimension is still time, and differences along the fourth dimension are still changes; they are merely treated more simply and efficiently than they otherwise might be.

Opposition has proceeded also from the venerable doctrine that not all the statements about the future have truth

2. E.g., in my *Word and Object*, pp. 170ff.

values now, because some of them remain, as of now, causally undetermined. Properly viewed, however, determinism is beside the point. The question of future truths is a matter of verbal convenience and is as innocuous as Doris Day's tautological fatalism "Que será será."

Another question that has been similarly linked to determinism, wrongly and notoriously, is that of freedom of the will. Like Spinoza, Hume, and so many others, I count an act as free insofar as the agent's motives or drives are a link in its causal chain. Those motives or drives may themselves be as rigidly determined as you please.

It is for me an ideal of pure reason to subscribe to determinism as fully as the quantum physicists will let me. But there are well-known difficulties in the way of rigorously formulating it. When we say of some event that it is determined by present ones, shall we mean that there is a general conditional, true but perhaps unknown to us, whose antecedent is instantiated by present events and whose consequent is instantiated by the future event in question? Without some drastic limitations on complexity and vocabulary, determinism so defined is pretty sure to boil down to "Que será será" and to afford at best a great idea for a song. Yet the idea in all its vagueness retains validity as an ideal of reason. It is valid as a general injunction: look for mechanisms.

This has been quite a spray, or spree, of philosophical miscellany. Let us now return to our cabbages, which is to say, our newly generalized physical objects. One of the benefits that the generalization confers is the accommodation of events as objects. An action or transaction can be identified with the physical objects consisting of the temporal segment or segments of the agent or agents for the duration. Misgivings about this approach to events have been expressed, on the grounds that it does not distinguish two acts that are performed simultaneously, such as walking and chewing gum. But I think that all the distinctions that need to be drawn can be drawn, still, at the level of general terms. Not all walks are gum chewings, nor vice versa, even though an occasional one may be. Some things may be said of an act on the score of its being a walk, and distinctive things may be said of it on the score of its being a chewing of gum, even though it be accounted one and the same event. There are its crural features on the one hand and its maxillary features on the other.

A reason for being particularly glad to have accommodated events is Davidson's logic of adverbs,[3] for Davidson has shown to my satisfaction that quantification over events is far and away the best way of construing adverbial constructions.

Our liberal notion of physical objects brings out an important point about identity. Some philosophers propound puzzles as to what to say about personal identity in cases of split personality or in fantasies about metempsychosis or brain transplants. These are not questions about the nature of identity. They are questions about how we might best construe the term 'person'. Again there is the stock example of the ship of Theseus, rebuilt bit by bit until no original bit remained. Whether we choose to reckon it still as the same ship is a question not of 'same' but of 'ship'; a question of how we choose to individuate that term over time.

Any coherent general term has its own principle of individuation, its own criterion of identity among its denotata. Often the principle is vague, as the principle of individuation of persons is shown to be by the science-fiction examples; and a term is as vague as its principle of individuation.

Most of our general terms individuate by continuity considerations, because continuity favors causal connections. But even useful terms, grounded in continuity, often diverge in their individuation, as witness the evolving ship of Theseus, on the one hand, and its original substance, gradually dispersed, on the other. Continuity follows both branches.

All this should have been clear without help of our liberal notion of physical object, but this notion drives the point home. It shows how empty it would be to ask, out of context, whether a certain glimpse yesterday and a certain glimpse today were glimpses of the same thing. They may or may not have been glimpses of the same body, but they certainly were glimpses of *a* same thing, a same physical object; for the con-

---

3. "The logical form of action sentences."

tent of any portion of space-time, however miscellaneously scattered in space and time that portion be, counts as a physical object.

The president or presidency of the United States is one such physical object, though not a body. It is a spatially discontinuous object made up of temporal segments, each of which is a temporal stage also of a body, a human one. The whole thing has its temporal beginning in 1789, when George Washington took office, and its end only at the final takeover, quite possibly more than two centuries later. Another somewhat similar physical object is the Dalai Lama, an example that has been invigorated by a myth of successive reincarnation. But the myth is unnecessary.

A body is a special kind of physical object, one that is roughly continuous spatially and rather chunky and that contrasts abruptly with most of its surroundings and is individuated over time by continuity of displacement, distortion, and discoloration. These are vague criteria, especially so in view of molecular theory, which teaches that the boundary of a solid is ill defind and that the continuity of a solid is only apparent and properly a matter of degree.

The step of generalization from body to physical object follows naturally, we saw, on the reification of portions of stuff. It follows equally naturally on molecular theory: if even a solid is diffuse, why stop there?

We can be happy not to have to rest existence itself on the vague notions of body and substance, as we would have to do if bodies and substances were our whole ontology. Specific individuatives such as 'dog' or 'desk' continue, like 'body', to suffer from vagueness on the score of the microphysical boundaries of their denotata, as well as vagueness on the score of marginal denotata themselves, such as makeshift desks and remote ancestors of dogs; but all this is vagueness only of classification and not of existence. All the variants qualify as physical objects.

Physical objects in this generous sense constitute a fairly lavish universe, but more is wanted—notably numbers. Measurement is useful in cookery and commerce, and in the fullness of time it rises to a nobler purpose: the formulation of quantitative laws. These are the mainstay of scientific theory,[4] and they call upon the full resources of the real numbers. Diagonals call for irrationals, circumferences call for transcendentals. Nor can we rest with constants; we must quantify over numbers. Admitting numbers as values of variables means reifying them and recognizing numerals as names of them; and this is required for the sake of generality in our quantitative laws.

Measures have sometimes been viewed as impure numbers: nine miles, nine gallons. We do better to follow Carnap[5] in construing each scale of measurement as a polyadic general term relating physical objects to pure numbers. Thus 'gallon xy' means that the presumably fluid and perhaps scatterd physical object x amounts to y gallons, and 'mile xyz' means that the physical objects x and y are z miles apart. Pure numbers, then, apparently belong in our ontology.

Classes do too, for whenever we count things we measure a class. If a statistical generality about populations quantifies over numbers of people, it has to quantify also over the classes whose numbers those are. Quantification over classes figures also in other equally inconspicuous ways, as witness Frege's familiar definition of ancestor in terms of parent: one's ancestors are the members shared by every class that contains oneself and the parents of its members.

Sometimes in natural science we are concerned explicitly with classes, or seem to be—notably in taxonomy. We read that there are over a quarter-million species of beetles. Here evidently we are concerned with a quarter-million classes and, over and above these, a class of all these clasess. However, we can economize here. Instead of talking of species in this context, we can make do with a dyadic general term applicable to beetles: 'conspecific'. To say that there are over a quarter-million species is equivalent to saying that there is a class of over a quarter-million *beetles* none of which are conspecific. This still conveys impressive information, and it still requires reification of a big class, but a class only of beetles and not of classes.

4. See Essay 18, below.
5. *Physikalische Begriffsbildung.*

This way of dodging a class of classes is not always available. It worked here because species are mutually exclusive.

Note the purely auxiliary role of classes in all three examples. In counting things we are more interested in the things counted than in their class. In the genealogical example the concern is with people, their parentage and ancestry; classes entered only in deriving the one from the other. In the example of the beetles, classes were indeed out in the open—even inordinately so, I argued. But even so, it is because of an interest still strictly in beetles, not classes, that one says there are so many species. The statement tells us that beetles are highly discriminate in their mating. It conveys this sort of information, but more precisely, and it makes auxiliary reference to classes as a means of doing so. Limited to physical objects though our interests be, an appeal to classes can thus be instrumental in pursuing those interests. I look upon mathematics in general in the same way, in its relation to natural science. But to view classes, numbers, and the rest in this instrumental way is not to deny having reified them; it is only to explain why.

III

So we assume abstract objects over and above the physical objects. For a better grasp of what this means, let us consider a simple case: the natural numbers. The conditions we need to impose on them are simple and few: we need to assume an object as first number and an operator that yields a unique new number whenever applied to a number. In short, we need a progression. Any progression will do, for the following reasons. The fundamental use of natural numbers is in measuring classes: in saying that a class has n members. Other serious uses prove to be reducible to this use. But any progression will serve *this* purpose; for we can say that a class has n members by saying that its members are in correlation with the members of the progression up to n—not caring which progression it may be.

There are ways of defining specific progressions of classes, no end of ways. When we feel the need of natural numbers we can simply reach for members of one of these progressions instead—whichever one comes handy. On the basis of natural numbers, in turn, it is possible with the help of classes to define the ratios and the irrational numbers in well-known ways. On one such construction they turn out to be simply certain classes of natural numbers. So, when we feel the need of ratios and irrationals, we can simply reach for appropriate subclasses of one of the progressions of classes. We need never talk of numbers, though in practice it is convenient to carry over the numerical jargon.

Numbers, then, except as a manner of speaking, are by the board. We have physical objects and we have classes. Not just classes of physical objects, but classes of classes and so on up. Some of these higher levels are needed to do the work of numbers and other gear of applied mathematics, and one then assumes the whole hierarchy if only for want of a natural stopping place.

But now what are classes? Consider the bottom layer, the classes of physical objects. Every relative clause or other general term determines a class, the class of those physical objects of which the term can be truly predicated. Two terms determine the same class of physical objects just in case the terms are true of just the same physical objects. Still, compatibly with all this we could reconstrue every class systematically as its complement and then compensate for the switch by reinterpreting the dyadic general term 'member of' to mean what had been meant by 'not a member of'. The effects would cancel and one would never know.

We thus seem to see a profound difference between abstract objects and concrete ones. A physical object, one feels, can be pinned down by pointing—in many cases, anyway, and to a fair degree. But I am persuaded that this contrast is illusory.

By way of example, consider again my liberalized notion of a physical object as the material content of any place-time, any portion of space-time. This was an intuitive explanation, intending no reification of space-time itself. But we could just as well reify those portions of space-time and treat of them instead of the physical objects. Or, indeed, call them physical objects. Whatever can be said from the old point of view can be paraphrased to suit the new point of view, with no effect on the structure of scientific theory or on its links with observational evidence. Wherever we had a predication '*x* is a *P*', said of a physical object *x*, we would in effect read '*x* is the place-time of a *P*'; actually we would just reinterpret the old '*P*' as 'place-time of a *P*', and rewrite nothing.

Space separately, or place anyway, is an untenable notion. If there were really places, there would be absolute rest and absolute motion; for change of place would be absolute motion. However, there is no such objection to place-times or space-time.

If we accept a redundant ontology containing both physical objects and place-times, then we can indeed declare them distinct; but even then, if we switch the physical objects with their place-times and then compensate by reinterpreting the dyadic general term 'is the material content of' to mean 'is the place-time of' and vice versa, no one can tell the difference. We could choose either interpretation indifferently if we were translating from an unrelated language.

These last examples are unnatural, for they work only if the empty place-times are repudiated and just the full ones are admitted as values of the variables. If we were seriously to reconstrue physical objects as place-times, we would surely enlarge our universe to include the empty ones and thus gain the simplicity of a continuous system of coordinates.

This change in ontology, the abandonment of physical objects in favor of pure space-time, proves to be more than a contrived example. The elementary particles have been wavering alarmingly as physics progresses. Situations arise that curiously challenge the individuality of a particle, not only over time, but even at a single time. A field theory in which states are ascribed directly to place-times may well present a better picture, and some physicists think it does.

At this point a further transfer of ontology suggests itself: we can drop the space-time regions in favor of the corresponding classes of quadruples of numbers according to an arbitrarily adopted system of coordinates. We are left with just the ontology of pure set theory, since the numbers and their quadruples can be modeled within it. There are no longer any physical objects to serve as individuals at the base of the hierarchy of classes, but there is no harm in that. It is common practice in set theory nowadays to start merely with the null class, form its unit class, and so on, thus generating an infinite lot of classes, from which all the usual luxuriance of further infinites can be generated.

One may object to thus identifying the world with the output of so arbitrarily chosen a system of coordinates. On the other hand, one may condone this on the ground that no numerically specific coordinates will appear in the laws of truly theoretical physics, thanks to the very arbitrariness of the coordinates. The specificity of the coordinates would make itself known only when one descends to coarser matters of astronomy, geography, geology, and history, and here it is perhaps appropriate.

We have now looked at three cases in which we interpret or reinterpret one domain of objects by identifying it with part of another domain. In the first example, numbers were identified with some of the classes in one way or another. In the second example, physical objects were identified with some of the place-times, namely, the full ones. In the third example, place-times were identified with some of the classes, namely, classes of quadruples of numbers. In each such case simplicity is gained, if to begin with we had been saddled with the two domains.

There is a fourth example of the same thing that is worth noting, for it concerns the long-debated dualism of mind and body. I hardly need say that the dualism is unattractive. If mind and body are to interact, we are at a loss for a plausible mechanism to the purpose. Also we are faced with the melancholy office of talking physicists out of their cherished conservation laws. On the other hand, an aseptic dualistic parallelism is monumentally redundant, a monument to everything multiplicacious that William of Ockham so rightly deplored. But now it is easily seen that dualism with or without interaction is reducible to physical monism, unless disembodied spirits are assumed. For the dualist who rejects disembodied spirits is bound to agree that for every state of mind there is an exactly concurrent and readily specifiable state of the accompanying body. Readily specifiable certainly; the bodily state is specifiable simply as the state of accompanying a mind that is in that mental state. But then we can settle for the bodily states outright, bypassing the mental states in terms of which I specified them. We can just reinterpret the mentalistic terms as denoting these correlated bodily states, and who is to know the difference?

This reinterpretation of mentalistic terms is reminiscent of the treatment of events that I suggested earlier, and it raises the same question of discrimination of concurrent events. But I would just propose again the answer that I gave then.

I take it as evident that there is no inverse option here, no hope of sustaining mental monism by assigning mental states to all states of physical objects.

These four cases of reductive reinterpretation are gratifying, enabling us as they do to dispense with one of two domains and make do with the other alone. But I find the other sort of reinterpretation equally instructive, the sort where we save nothing but merely change or seem to change our objects without disturbing either the structure or the empirical support of a scientific theory in the slightest. All that is needed in either case, clearly, is a rule whereby a unique object of the supposedly new sort is assigned to each of the old objects. I call such a rule a proxy function. Then, instead of predicating a general term 'P' of an old object x, saying that x is a P, we reinterpret x as a new object and say that it is the f of a P, where 'f' expresses the proxy function. Instead of saying that x is a dog, we say that x is the lifelong filament of space-time taken up by a dog. Or, really, we just adhere to the old term 'P', 'dog', and reinterpret it as 'f of a P', 'place-time of a dog'. This is the strategy that we have seen in various examples.

The apparent change is twofold and sweeping. The original objects have been supplanted and the general terms reinterpreted. There has been a revision of ontology on the one hand and of ideology, so to say, on the other; they go together. Yet verbal behavior proceeds undisturbed, warranted by the same observations as before and elicited by the same observations. Nothing really has changed.

The conclusion I draw is the inscrutability of reference.

To say what objects someone is talking about is to say no more than how we propose to translate his terms into ours; we are free to vary the decision with a proxy function. The translation adopted arrests the free-floating reference of the alien terms only relatively to the free-floating reference of our own terms, by linking the two.

The point is not that we ourselves are casting about in vain for a mooring. Staying aboard our own language and not rocking the boat, we are borne smoothly along on it and all is well; 'rabbit' denotes rabbits, and there is no sense in asking 'Rabbits in what sense of "rabbit"?' Reference goes inscrutable if, rocking the boat, we contemplate a permutational mapping of our language on itself, or if we undertake translation.

Structure is what matters to a theory, and not the choice of its objects. F. P. Ramsey urged this point fifty years ago, arguing along other lines, and in a vague way it had been a persistent theme also in Russell's *Analysis of Matter*. But Ramsey and Russell were talking only of what they called theoretical objects, as opposed to observable objects.

I extend the doctrine to objects generally, for I see all objects as theoretical. This is a consequence of taking seriously the insight that I traced from Bentham—namely, the semantic primacy of sentences. It is occasion sentences, not terms, that are to be seen as conditioned to stimulations. Even our primordial objects, bodies, are already theoretical —most conspicuously so when we look to their individuation over time. Whether we encounter the same apple the next time around, or only another one like it, is settled if at all by inference from a network of hypotheses that we have internalized little by little in the course of acquiring the non-observational superstructure of our language.

It is occasion sentences that report the observations on which science rests. The scientific output is likewise sentential: true sentences, we hope, truths about nature. The objects, or values of variables, serve merely as indices along the way, and we may permute or supplant them as we please as long as the sentence-to-sentence structure is preserved. The scientific system, ontology and all, is a conceptual bridge of our own making, linking sensory stimulation to sensory stimulation. I am repeating what I said at the beginning.

But I also expressed, at the beginning, my unswerving belief in external things—people, nerve endings, sticks, stones. This I reaffirm. I believe also, if less firmly, in atoms and electrons and in classes. Now how is all this robust realism to be reconciled with the barren scene that I have just been depicting? The answer is naturalism: the recognition that it is within science itself, and not in some prior philosophy, that reality is to be identified and described.

The semantical considerations that seemed to undermine all this were concerned not with assessing reality but with analyzing method and evidence. They belong not to ontology but to the methodology of ontology, and thus to epistemology. Those considerations showed that I could indeed turn my back on my external things and classes and ride the proxy functions to something strange and different without doing violence to any evidence. But all ascription of reality must come rather from within one's theory of the world; it is incoherent otherwise.

My methodological talk of proxy functions and inscrutability of reference must be seen as naturalistic too; it likewise is no part of a first philosophy prior to science. The setting is still the physical world, seen in terms of the global science to which, with minor variations, we all subscribe. Amid all this there are our sensory receptors and the bodies near and far whose emanations impinge on our receptors. Epistemology, for me, or what comes nearest to it, is the study of how we animals can have contrived that very science, given just that sketchy neural input. It is this study that reveals that displacements of our ontology through proxy functions would have measured up to that neural input no less faithfully. To recognize this is not to repudiate the ontology in terms of which the recognition took place.

We *can* repudiate it. We are free to switch, without doing violence to any evidence. If we switch, then this epistemological remark itself undergoes appropriate reinterpretation too; nerve endings and other things give way to appropriate proxies, again without straining any evidence. But it is a confusion to suppose that we can stand aloof and recognize all the alternative ontologies as true in their several ways, all the envisaged worlds as real. It is a confusion of truth with evidential support. Truth is immanent, and there is no higher. We must speak from within a theory, albeit any of various.

Transcendental argument, or what purports to be first philosophy, tends generally to take on rather this status of immanent epistemology insofar as I succeed in making sense of it. What evaporates is the transcendental question of the reality of the external world—the question whether or in how far our science measures up to the *Ding an sich*.

Our scientific theory can indeed go wrong, and precisely in the familiar way: through failure of predicted observation. But what if, happily and unbeknownst, we have achieved a theory that is conformable to every possible observation, past and future? In what sense could the world then be said to deviate from what the theory claims? Clearly in none, even if we can somehow make sense of the phrase 'every possible observation'. Our overall scientific theory demands of the world only that it be so structured as to assure the sequences of stimulation that our theory gives us to expect. More concrete demands are empty, what with the freedom of proxy functions.

Radical skepticism stems from the sort of confusion I have alluded to, but is not of itself incoherent. Science is vulnerable to illusion on its own showing, what with seemingly bent sticks in water and the like, and the skeptic may be seen merely as overreacting when he repudiates science across the board. Experience might still take a turn that would justify his doubts about external objects. Our success in predicting observations might fall off sharply, and concomitantly with this we might begin to be somewhat successful in basing predictions upon dreams or reveries. At that point we might reasonably doubt our theory of nature in even fairly broad outlines. But our doubts would still be immanent, and of a piece with the scientific endeavor.

My attitude toward the project of a rational reconstruction of the world from sense data is similarly naturalistic. I do not regard the project as incoherent, though its motivation in some cases is confused. I see it as a project of positing a realm of entities intimately related to the stimulation of the sensory surfaces, and then, with the help perhaps of an auxiliary realm of entities in set theory, proceeding by contextual definition to construct a language adequate to natural science. It is an attractive idea, for it would bring scientific discourse into a much more explicit and systematic relation to its observational checkpoints. My only reservation is that I am convinced, regretfully, that it cannot be done.

Another notion that I would take pains to rescue from the abyss of the transcendental is the notion of a matter of fact. A place where the notion proves relevant is in connection with my doctrine of the indeterminacy of translation. I have argued that two conflicting manuals of translation can both do justice to all dispositions to behavior, and that, in such a case, there is no fact of the matter of which manual is right. The intended notion of matter of fact is not transcendental or yet epistemological, not even a question of evidence; it is ontological, a question of reality, and to be taken naturalistically within our scientific theory of the world. Thus suppose, to make things vivid, that we are settling still for a physics of elementary particles and recognizing a dozen or so basic states and relations in which they may stand. Then when I say there is no fact of the matter, as regards, say, the two rival manuals of translation, what I mean is that both manuals are compatible with all the same distributions of states and relations over elementary particles. In a word, they are physically equivalent. Needless to say, there is no presumption of our being able to sort out the pertinent distributions of microphysical states and relations. I speak of a physical condition and not an empirical criterion.

It is in the same sense that I say there is no fact of the matter of our interpreting any man's ontology in one way or, via proxy functions, in another. Any man's, that is to say, except ourselves. We can switch our own ontology too without doing violence to any evidence, but in so doing we switch from our elementary particles to some manner of proxies and thus reinterpret our standard of what counts as a fact of the matter. Factuality, like gravitation and electric charge, is internal to our theory of nature.

2

✦ *Empirical Content*

The preceding essay was concerned with the empirical significance of the assuming of objects. This one is concerned, yet more abstractly, with empirical significance as such: with the relation of scientific theory to its sensory evidence. As before, my stance is naturalistic. By sensory evidence I mean stimulation of sensory receptors. I accept our prevailing physical theory and therewith the physiology of my receptors, and then proceed to speculate on how this sensory input supports the very physical theory that I am accepting. I do not claim thereby to be proving the physical theory, so there is no vicious circle.

What sort of thing is a scientific theory? It is an idea, one might naturally say, or a complex of ideas. But the most practical way of coming to grips with ideas, and usually the only way, is by way of the words that express them. What to look for in the way of theories, then, are the sentences that express them. There will be no need to decide what a theory is or when to regard two sets of sentences as formulations of the same theory; we can just talk of the theory formulations as such.

The relation to be analyzed, then, is the relation between our sensory stimulations and our scientific theory formulations: the relation between the physicist's sentences on the

---

This piece is adapted from a paper, "Gegenstand und Beobachtung," that I am to present at Stuttgart in June 1981. There are echoes in it of "On empirically equivalent systems of the world."

one hand, treating of gravitation and electrons and the like, and on the other hand the triggering of his sensory receptors. Let us begin by looking at the sentences most directly connected with sensory stimulation. These are the occasion sentences noted in the preceding essay. They are occasion sentences of a special sort, which I call *observation* sentences. By this I do not mean to suggest that they are about observation, or sense data, or stimulation. Examples are 'It's raining', 'It's milk', as before. An observation sentence is an occasion sentence that the speaker will consistently assent to when his sensory receptors are stimulated in certain ways, and consistently dissent from when they are stimulated in certain other ways. If querying the sentence elicits assent from the given speaker on one occasion, it will elicit assent likewise on any other occasion when the same total set of receptors is triggered; and similarly for dissent. This and this only is what qualifies sentences as observation sentences for the speaker in question, and this is the sense in which they are the sentences most directly associated with sensory stimulation.

Naturally the exact same total set of sensory receptors is unlikely to be triggered twice. The more nearly it is approximated, however, the likelier the assent or dissent should be. Naturally, moreover, many of the receptors will be irrelevant to any particular sentence; but this excess is harmless, canceling out. Only the relevant receptors will be triggered on *all* the occasions appropriate to the sentence in question.

The notion of observation sentence can be further refined by allowing for degrees of observationality. Hesitation can then be taken into account. But it is already evident from what I have said that a pretty substantial notion of observation sentence is before us here, despite latter-day skepticism on the subject.

The problem of relating theory to sensory stimulation may now be put less forbiddingly as that of relating theory formulations to observation sentences. In this we have a head start in that we recognize the observation sentences to be theory-laden. What this means is that terms embedded in observation sentences recur in the theory formulations.

What qualifies a sentence as observational is not a lack of
such terms, but just that the sentence taken as an undivided
whole commands assent consistently or dissent consistently
when the same global sensory stimulation is repeated. What
relates the observation sentence to theory, on the other hand,
is the sharing of embedded terms.

When we proceed to look for inferential connections between observation sentences and theory formulations, however, we are caught up in a succession of problems. Problem
1: observation sentences are occasion sentences, whereas
theory is formulated in *eternal* sentences, true or false once
for all. What logical connection can there be between the
two? Evidently we need first to eternalize the observation
sentence. Thus a given utterance of 'It's raining' might be
eternalized to read 'Raining at 42°N and 71°W on March
9, 1981, at 0500'. We thus run headlong into Problem 2, the
problem of determining places and times on an observational
basis. Even if we were to postpone the sophistication of
latitude and longitude by starting rather with place names,
we would still need to explain how to determine by name
where we are at the time and, indeed, how to determine the
date and time of day.

However, suppose for the moment that Problem 2 were
solved. Suppose the eternalized reports of observation were
available. Still we cannot expect scientific theory to imply
such sentences outright. Science normally predicts observations only on the assumption of initial conditions. We arrange an observable situation and then, if our scientific
theory is right, a predicted further observation ensues. What
a scientific theory implies is thus not an eternalized observation sentence outright, but rather a conditional sentence,
what I have called an *observation conditional.*[1] It is a sentence
⌜ If ϕ then ψ ⌝ where ψ is an eternalized observation sentence
and ϕ states the initial conditions. Since the initial conditions are to be observable too, ϕ will also be an eternalized
observation sentence; or perhaps it will be a conjunction of
several, since they may differ from one another in respect
of the places and times.

1. "On empirically equivalent systems of the world."

This brings us to Problem 3. The initial conditions expressed in ϕ refer to times and places at some remove from those referred to in ψ; perhaps at various removes. In allowing this we are stopping short of fundamentals. We are allowing a certain amount of unchecked theory to slip through the net. At the place-time where the predicted observation is due, how does the experimenter know that the supposed initial conditions were fulfilled a while back and some way off? He can have only indirect evidence of this: his memory, his notes, the testimony of others. These are after-effects, from which those past arrangements are inferred. The inference is already a part of scientific theory, however tacit and unconscious. Strictly, all the experimenter has to go on are his present observations. They are paired. One is the immediate initial condition, which may be the present evidence of various past initial conditions ordinarily so called. The other is the predicted observation.

Clearly, then, our observation conditions were too liberal. We should limit our attention to conditional sentences ⌜If ϕ then ψ⌝ where ϕ and ψ stand for eternalized observation sentences referring to one and the same place-time.

Having thus disposed of Problem 3, let us recall Problem 2: the problem of specifying and determining places and times on an observational basis. There is an easy step that bypasses this problem, now that we have required the observation conditional to refer to the same place-time in both its clauses. Namely, we can now dispense with the specification of a place-time and claim, instead, generality. We can withdraw to what I may call *observation categoricals*—sentences like 'Where there is smoke there is fire' or 'When it rains it pours' or 'When night falls the lamps are lit'. These enjoy generality over places and times, but they do not need to be read as assuming a prior ontology of places and times or any implicit universal quantification over them. The construction can be seen rather as a simple one, learned early. The child may learn the component observation sentences 'Here is smoke' and 'Here is fire' by ostension, and then the compound is an eternal sentence that expresses his having become conditioned to associate the one with the other.

The problem of places and times, Problem 2, is thus circumvented. Specifications of place-times are still indispensable to science, but we have kicked them upstairs: we have consigned them to the network of theoretical concepts where they belong, at a comfortable remove from observation.

Here, then, is further progress in relating scientific theory to its sensory evidence. The relation consists in the implying of true observation categoricals by the theory formulation. And how do we know when an observation categorical is true? We never do, conclusively, by observation, because each is general. But observation can falsify an observation categorical. We may observe night falling and the lamps not being lit. We may observe smoke and find no fire.

This characterization fits Popper's dictum that scientific theories can only be refuted, never established. But we do see scope still for intuitive support of theories. An observation categorical gains our confidence as our observations continue to conform to it without exception; this is simple habit formation, or conditioning. A theory formulation, in turn, gains our confidence as the observation categoricals implied by it retain our confidence.

The observation categoricals implied by a theory formulation constitute, we may say, its empirical content; for it is only the observation categoricals that link theory to observation. If two theory formulations imply all the same observation categoricals, they are empirically equivalent.

A theory formulation merely implies its observation categoricals, and is not implied by them, unless it is trivial. Two theory formulations may thus imply all the same observation conditionals without implying each other. They can be empirically equivalent without being logically equivalent.

In fact, they can be empirically equivalent and yet logically inconsistent, incompatible. We can get a trivial example of this situation by simply switching two words that do not appear in any observation sentences—perhaps the words 'molecule' and 'electron'. Thus imagine an exhaustive encyclopedic formulation of our total scientific theory of the world. Imagine also another just like it except that the words 'molecule' and 'electron' are switched. The formulations are empirically equivalent: all the implicative connections between the observation categoricals and the sentences containing the word 'molecule' or 'electron' in the one theory formulation are matched by the same implicative connections in the other theory with the two words rewritten. The observation categoricals remain identical, for they lack those words. Yet the two theory formulations are logically incompatible, for the one attributes properties to molecules that the other formulation *denies* of molecules and attributes to electrons. (I am indebted here to Humphries.)

The natural response to this trivial example is that the two formulations are really formulations of the same theory in slightly different words, and that the one can be translated into the other by switching the two words back. More generally, whenever we find terms, extraneous to the observation categoricals themselves, that can be so reinterpreted throughout one of the theory formulations as to reconcile it with the other theory formulation, and not disturb the empirical content, we see the conflict to be superficial and uninteresting.

Suppose, however, two empirically equivalent theory formulations that we see no way of reconciling by such a reinterpretation of terms. We probably would not know that they are empirically equivalent, for the usual way of finding them so would be by hitting upon such a reinterpretation. Still, let us suppose that the two formulations are in fact empirically equivalent even though not known to be; and let us suppose further that all of the implied observation categoricals are in fact true, although, again, not known to be. Nothing more, surely, can be required for the truth of either theory formulation. Are they both true? I say yes.

But, again, they may be logically incompatible, despite their empirical equivalence. This raises the specter of cultural relativism: each is evidently true only from its own point of view.

However, the specter is easily laid, by a move just as trivial as our recent switch of 'molecule' and 'electron'. Being incompatible, the two theory formulations that we are imagining must evaluate some sentence oppositely. Since they are nevertheless empirically equivalent, that sentence must contain terms that are short on observational criteria. But then we can just as well pick out one of those terms and treat it as if it were two independent words, one in the one theory formulation and another in the other. We can mark this by changing the spelling of the word in one of the two theory formulations.

Pressing this trivial expedient, we can resolve all conflict between the two theory formulations. Both can be admitted thenceforward as true descriptions of one and the same world in different terms. The threat of relativism of truth is averted.

I suggested that the empirical content of a theory formulation consists of its observation categoricals. This definition is appealing in its catholicity. Observation sentences enter it holophrastically, with no regard to internal structure beyond what may go into the logical links of implication between theory formulations and observation categoricals. The language need not be bivalent, it need not be realistic, it need not even have anything clearly recognizable as terms or as reference, or any recognizable ontology. The one grammatical construction that we need specifically to recognize is the one that combines observation sentences two by two into observation categoricals. Since this construction has the very primitive effect of expressing conditioned expectations, something to the purpose doubtless exists in any language, however exotic.

❧ *What Price Bivalence?*

A good scientific theory is under tension from two oppos-
ing forces: the drive for evidence and the drive for system.
Theoretical terms should be subject to observable criteria,
the more the better, and the more directly the better, other
things being equal; and they should lend themselves to systematic laws, the simpler the better, other things being
equal. If either of these drives were unchecked by the other,
it would issue in something unworthy of the name of scientific theory: in the one case a mere record of observations,
and in the other a myth without foundation.

What we settle for, if I may switch my metaphor from
dynamics to economics, is a trade-off. We gain simplicity of
theory, within reason, by recourse to terms that relate only
indirectly, intermittently, and rather tenuously to observation. The values that we thus trade off one against the other
—evidential value and systematic value—are incommensur-
able. Scientists of different philosophical temper will differ
in how much dilution of evidence they are prepared to accept
for a given systematic benefit, and vice versa. Such was the
difference between Ernst Mach and the atomists. Such is the
difference between the intuitionists and the communicants
of classical logic. Such is the difference between the Copen-
hagen school of quantum physicists and the proponents of
hidden variables. Those who prize the evidential side more
are the readier to gerrymander their language in such ways

Reprinted from the *Journal of Philosophy* 78 (1981), with additions.

as to excise one or another sheaf of undecidable sentences, even though without hope of excising all. Those who prize the systematic side more are the readier to round language out, gaining smoothness and tolerating, to that end, some increment of adipose tissue.

We stalwarts of two-valued logic buy its sweet simplicity at no small price in respect of the harboring of undecidables. We declare that it is either true or false that there was an odd number of blades of grass in Harvard Yard at the dawn of Commencement Day, 1903. The matter is undecidable, but we maintain that there is a fact of the matter. Similarly for countless similar trivialities. Similarly for more extravagant undecidables, such as whether there was a hydrogen atom within a meter of some remote point that we may specify by space-time coordinates. And similarly, on the mathematical side, for the continuum hypothesis or the question of the existence of inaccessible cardinals. Bivalence is, as Dummett argues (pp. 145–165), the hallmark of realism.

I propose in the present pages neither to defend bivalence nor to repudiate it. My inclination is to adhere to it for the simplicity of theory that it affords, but my purpose now is to acknowledge the costs.

Besides the realists's undecidable matters of fact, with respect to physical objects or infinite cardinal numbers, there is also the vagueness of terms to reckon with; and bivalence raises issues also in this domain. The culmination of these latter troubles is the sorites paradox, the ancient paradox of the heap. If removal of a single grain from a heap always leaves a heap, then, by mathematical induction, removal of all the grains leaves a heap. Russell's latter-day version is no less familiar: if the loss of a hair renders no man bald, then neither does the loss of any number of them. Bivalence seals the paradox, requiring as it does at each stage that the statement that a heap remains, or that the man is bald, be univocally true or false.

The paradox is engendered by vague terms generally. Moreover, as Crispin Wrights points out, a term is apt to be vague if it is to be learned by ostension, since its applicability must admit of being judged on the spot and so cannot hinge on fine distinctions laboriously drawn. Exceptions to this can be contrived, as by Dummett (p. 265), but still the evident moral is that we are deep in contradiction before we finish acquiring the bare ostensive beginnings of cognitive language.

What saves us is that at that stage we are too naive to appreciate our predicament; mathematical induction is a theoretical adjunct, not yet acquired. When we do reach the point of positing numbers and plying their laws, then is the time to heed the contradictions and to take steps. One expedient that often serves is abandonment of a vague absolute term in favor of a relative term of comparison. The expedient is familiar in the case of such terms as 'big', 'tall', and 'heavy', and it works equally for 'bald': we may abandon 'bald' in favor of 'balder than'. The case of 'heap' is somewhat more awkward, however, and 'mountain' yet more so. Here the clearer course is to keep the absolute term but to resolve its vagueness by arbitrary stipulations.

'Mountain' affords a rich example, for there is the vagueness of acceptable altitude, the vagueness of boundary at the base, and the consequent indecision as to when to count two summits as two mountains and when as one. Possible stipulations are as follows. Leaving foreign planets conveniently aside, we may define a mountain as any region of the earth's surface such that (a) the boundary is of uniform altitude, (b) the highest point, or one of them, is at an inclination of at least ten degrees above every boundary point and twenty degrees above some, and is at least a thousand feet above them, and (c) the region is part of no other region fulfilling (a) and (b). (Theorem: the boundary of a mountain is the outermost contour line that lies wholly within ten degrees of steepness from the summit and partly within twenty.)

It is in this spirit that what had been learned as observation terms may be redefined, on pain of paradox, as theoretical terms whose application may depend in marginal cases on protracted tests and indirect inferences. The sorites paradox is one imperative reason for precision in science, along with more familiar reasons.

Not that it is customary in general to devise such precise criteria. Partial steps are taken as needed, and the tacit fic-

tion is adopted that other terms are subject to precise limits
that we are not bothering to settle. Some terms are adopted
from observation language and incorporated into scientific
language with their edges refined, others are incorporated
as if refined; and sufficient unto the day is the evil thereof.
We are thus enabled to make do with our bivalent logic and
our smooth and simple arithemetic, including mathematical
induction.

To take this attitude is merely to recognize and acquiesce
in what Waismann called the open texture of empirical
terms. To reason *as if* our terms were precise seems pretty
straightforward as long as we see that they could be made
precise by arbitrary stipulations whenever occasion might
arise. However, Unger has lately argued that the problem
runs deeper. Diminish a table, conceptually, molecule by
molecule: when is a table not a table? No stipulations will
avail us here, however arbitrary.

Each removal of a molecule leaves a physical object, yes, in
my liberal sense of the term—namely, the material content
of a portion of space-time. A table contains a graded multitude of nested or overlapping physical objects each of which
embodies enough of the substance to have qualified as a table
in its own right, but only in abstraction from the rest of the
molecules. Each of these physical objects would qualify as a
table, that is, if cleared of the overlying and surrounding
molecules, but should not be counted as a table when still
embedded in a further physical object that so qualifies in
turn; for tables are meant to be mutually exclusive. Only
the outermost, the sum of this nest of physical objects, counts
as a table.

Yet something remains of Unger's point. There remains
the question how much to include in the table in the way of
superficial or hovering molecules. We cannot simply rule that
the table passes muster both with and without various of the
marginal molecules, for, again, tables are mutually exclusive; only one is present. Now this case differs from the
ancient example of the heap, or the example of baldness, in
that we cannot settle the demarcation of the table even by an
arbitrary ruling. We were able to stipulate an arbitrary
minimum to the number of grains in a heap, and a maximum

to the numbers of hairs on a bald head, but we are at a loss
to frame a convention for the molecular demarcation of the
surface of a table. Words fail us.

The question about the grass of 1903 hinged, one felt,
on a robust matter of fact. Still, being clearly undecidable,
the question makes empirical sense to us only by analogy
and extrapolation. It makes sense because we often do count
things, and are prepared even to count present blades of
grass. We project these vivid notions into the inaccessible
past as a matter of course, such is the organization of our
system of the world. The physicist has done more of the
same, and only more extravagantly, in giving us the makings
of our idle question about the hydrogen atom. This undecidable question, like the one about the grass, makes empirical
sense to us only by virtue of the devious connections between
our systematic theory of the world and the various observations to which the system as a whole is answerable. The connections are more complex and more tenuous in this case
of the hydrogen atom than in the case of the grass of 1903,
but the question is still, for the bivalent-minded, a question
of objective fact.

One has a different feeling about the question of the heap,
or of baldness: that it is a mere question of words, to be
settled by a stipulation. Yet these and the others are all
equally questions within a manmade verbal fabric, connected
only more or less remotely with observation—too remotely,
in all four cases, to be decidable. In what way, then, are the
questions of heaps and baldness matters of convention, and
the others matters of fact? One way to bring out the contrast is in terms of our physical theory itself, in full acceptance of bivalence. Namely, the number of the blades of
grass and the presence of a hydrogen atom are physically
determined by the spatio-temporal distribution of microphysical states, unknown though it be. Where to draw the
line between heaps and nonheaps, on the other hand, or between the bald and the thatched, is not determined by the
distribution of microphysical states, known or unknown; it
remains an open option.

On this score the demarcation of the table surface is on a
par with the cases of heaps and baldness. But it differs from

those cases in not lending itself to any stipulation, however
arbitrary, that we can formulate; so it can scarcely be called
conventional. It is neither a matter of convention nor a matter of inscrutable but objective fact. Yet we are committed,
nevertheless, to treating the table as one and not another
of this multitude of imperceptibly divergent physical objects. Such is bivalence.

At this point one might defend bivalence by arguing that
no actual sentence can hinge for its truth or falsity on
demarcations of a table surface that are too subtle for us to
formulate. But I find this defense unsatisfying. It is in the
spirit of bivalence not just to treat each closed sentence as
true or false; as Frege stressed, each general term must be
definitely true or false of each object, specifiable or not. If
the term 'table' is to be reconciled with bivalence, we must
posit an exact demarcation, exact to the last molecule, even
though we cannot specify it. We must hold that there are
physical objects, coincident except for one molecule, such
that one is a table and the other is not.

One might then despair of bivalence and proceed discon-
solately to survey its fuzzy and plurivalent alternatives in
hopes of finding something viable, however unlovely. Or one
might dig in one's heels—recalcitrate, in a word—and accept this démarche as a lesson rather in the scope and limits
of the notion of linguistic convention.

Bivalence is a basic trait of our classical theories of nature. It has us positing a true-false dichotomy across all the
statements that we can express in our theoretical vocabulary,
irrespective of our knowing how to decide them. In keeping
with our theories of nature we have viewed all such sentences as having factual content, however remote from observation. In this way simplicity of theory has been served.
What we now observe is that bivalence requires us further
to view each general term, for example 'table', as true or
false of objects even in the absence of what we in our bivalent way are prepared to recognize as objective fact. At
this point, if not before, the creative element in theory-
building may be felt to be getting out of hand, and second
thoughts on bivalence may arise.

It may still be noted in mitigation that the notion of physical object in the liberal sense involves no such quandary, covering as it does indiscriminately all the competing candidates for the title of table. It and other notions of austere physical theory remain in the clear. It is only the commonsense classifications of physical objects that come into question.

4

✒ On the Very Idea of a Third Dogma

Truth, meaning, and belief are sticky concepts. They stick together. That meaning and truth were somehow closely related was evident before Russell's eponymous *Inquiry* and after, but it was left to Davidson to recognize Tarski's theory of truth as the very structure of a theory of meaning. This insight was a major advance in semantics. Tarski had indeed called his theory of truth a study in semantics, but one felt constrained to add that it was semantics only in a broad sense, belonging more specifically to the theory of reference and not to the theory of meaning. That constraint now lapses.

The pairing of meaning and belief is another point stressed by Davidson. They can be separated, like Siamese twins, only by artificial means. If we try to construe an unknown language, we may assume at best that the observed utterance describes the given situation as the speaker, not we, believes it to be. What we take the utterance to mean will then hinge on what we take the speaker to believe and vice versa. The utterance and the situation are the end points of a diagonal whose resolution into rectangular components, meaning and belief, depends on how we tilt the grid.

But it is the remaining pair, truth and belief, that seems to me to have got unobservedly stuck. I shall argue that it is because of conflating these at a crucial point that Davidson abandons what he calls the third dogma, thereby parting the last mooring of empiricism. He writes that "this . . .

dualism of scheme and content, of organizing system and something waiting to be organized, cannot be made intelligible and defensible. It is itself a dogma of empiricism, a third dogma. The third, and perhaps the last, for if we give it up it is not clear that there is anything distinctive left to call empiricism."[1] Against this purported dogma he argues that, "the notion of fitting the totality of experience, like the notion of fitting the facts, or being true to the facts, adds nothing intelligible to the simple concept of being true . . . Nothing, . . . no *thing*, makes sentences and theories true: not experience, not surface irritations, not the world."[2]

He rightly protests in these pages and elsewhere that it is idle to say that true sentences are sentences that fit the facts, or match the world; also pernicious, in creating an illusion of explanation. There is nothing to add to Tarski's analysis, Davidson rightly urges, so far as the concept of truth is concerned. Where I sense a conflation of truth and belief, however, is in his referring to "the totality of experience" and "surface irritations" on a par with "the facts" and "the world." The proper role of experience or surface irritation is as a basis not for truth but for warranted belief.

If empiricism is construed as a theory of truth, then what Davidson imputes to it as a third dogma is rightly imputed and rightly renounced. Empiricism as a theory of truth thereupon goes by the board, and good riddance. As a theory of evidence, however, empiricism remains with us, minus indeed the two old dogmas. The third purported dogma, understood now in relation not to truth but to warranted belief, remains intact. It has both a descriptive and a normative aspect, and in neither aspect do I think of it as a dogma. It is what makes scientific method partly empirical rather than solely a quest for internal coherence. It has indeed wanted some tidying up, and has had it.

The last section of my "Two Dogmas of Empiricism"[3] is cited by many writers in varied moods, and Davidson has not spared it. It is where I represented total science as "a

---

1. "On the very idea of a conceptual scheme," p. 11.
2. *Ibid.*, p. 16.
3. Reprinted in *From a Logical Point of View*.

man-made fabric which impinges on experience only along the edges. Or, to change the figure, . . . a field of force whose boundary conditions are experience." It was an interim indication of an attitude, and an attitude that I still hold. My noncommittal term 'experience' awaited a theory.

Within four years I was referring more committally to surface irritations. I took this line so as to discourage a phenomenalistic interpretation. Our typical sentences are about bodies and substances, assumed or known in varying degrees, out in the world. Typically they are not about sense data or experiences or, certainly, surface irritations. But some of them are elicited by surface irritations, and others are related to surface irritations in less direct and more tenuous ways.

If there was still an unintended overtone of sensory quality in my reference to surface irritation, it was effectively banished by the time I wrote *Word and Object;* for there I wrote explicitly of the triggering of sensory receptors. Nobody could suppose that I supposed that people are on the whole thinking or talking about the triggering of their nerve endings; few people, statistically speaking, know about their nerve endings.

Putting matters thus physiologically was of a piece with my naturalism, my rejection of a first philosophy underlying science. Empiricist discipline, however, is not lost thereby. The fabric celebrated in my old metaphor is with us still. As before it is a fabric of sentences accepted in science as true, however provisionally. The ones at the edges are occasion sentences. Moreover, they are occasion sentences of a special sort, namely, ones whose acceptance as true on any given occasion is apt to be prompted by the firing of associated sets or patterns of receptors on that occasion. The tribunal, to worry another of my old metaphors, is just the firing of the receptors.

I assume no awareness of the firing or any interim contemplation of sense data. I treat of stimulus and response. The response is assertion of the occasion sentence or assent to it. Typically the sentence is one that treats of external objects and is not devoid of theoretical terms. The link between the stimulus and the response is forged in some cases by simple conditioning or ostension and in other cases by analogy or verbal explanation, but it becomes a direct and immediate connection once it is formed.

Where empiricist discipline persists is partly in the relative firmness of this link between a goodly store of occasion sentences and concurrent stimulation, and partly in a high degree of dependence upon these occasion sentences on the part of sentences in the interior of the fabric. It is a matter of degree of responsivness, a matter of more and less responsible science, of better and worse.

It seems that in Davidson's mind the purported third dogma is somehow bound up with a puzzling use on my part of the phrase "conceptual scheme." The "dualism of scheme and content" deplored in my first quotation from Davidson bears a trace of this, as does the title of his essay. In conclusion, then, let me clarify the status of the phrase. I inherited it some forty-five years ago through L. J. Henderson from Pareto, and I have meant it as ordinary language, serving no technical function. It is not, as architects say, a supporting member. A triad—conceptual scheme, language, and world—is not what I envisage. I think rather, like Davidson, in terms of language and the world. I scout the *tertium quid* as a myth of a museum of labeled ideas. Where I have spoken of a conceptual scheme I could have spoken of a language. Where I have spoken of a very alien conceptual scheme I would have been content, Davidson will be glad to know, to speak of a language awkward or baffling to translate.

Somewhere I suggested a measure of what might be called the remoteness of a conceptual scheme but what might better be called the conceptual distance between languages. The definition hinges on changes in the lengths of sentences under translation. Given a pair of sentences from the two languages, sentences that are acceptable translations of each other, select a shortest equivalent of each of the sentences within its language. Compare these two shortest equivalents in respect of length, and compute the ratio. When this has been done for every pair of sentences that are acceptable translations of each other, strike the average of all those ratios. This measures the conceptual distance between the two languages.

Sentences are infinitely numerous, for want of a limit on length, and so therefore are pairs of sentences. The striking of that average ratio is consequently no simple matter of division; we must consider limits of infinite series. There is also the indeterminacy of translation to contend with, but we can accommodate that by so choosing our manual of translation, from among the multitude of empirically correct ones, as to minimize that average ratio of lengths of sentences that we are angling for.

What I have offered is not, I hardly need say, an effective procedure. But it does afford a definition of a sort, and one that is not much vaguer than the notion of acceptable translation on which it depends.

The vagueness of the notion of acceptable translation is not, indeed, a vagueness to belittle. If there is a question in my mind whether a language might be so remote as to be largely untranslatable, and hence beyond the reach even of the definition of remoteness that I have simulated above, that question arises from the vagueness of the very notion of translation. We are already accustomed, after all, to cutting corners and tolerating rough approximations even in neighborly translation. Translatability is a flimsy notion, unfit to bear the weight of the theories of cultural incommensurability that Davidson effectively and justly criticizes.

5

Use and Its Place
in Meaning

Words and phrases refer to things in either of two ways. A
name or singular description *designates* its object, if any.
A predicate *denotes* each of the objects of which it is true.
Such are the two sorts of reference: designation and denotation. We are often told, and rightly, that neither sort is to
be confused with *meaning*. The descriptions 'the author of
Waverley' and 'the author of *Ivanhoe*' designate the same
man, after all, but differ in meaning; and a predicate may
denote each of many things while having only one meaning.

There are no restraints on what can be referred to. All
sorts of things are designated and denoted. On the other
hand, a meaning is apparently some special sort of thing.
But just what?

You would think we would know. The word 'meaning' is a
common noun, a very common noun, on the tip of everyone's
tongue. It occurs in a few frequent phrases. We ask the

The opening pages of this essay were those of "Cognitive meaning"
The Monist, vol. 62:2, April 1979, and are reprinted with the permission of the editor and the publisher. The rest was presented under the
present title in a symposium on meaning and use that was held in
Jerusalem in April 1976 in memory of Bar-Hillel. It appeared in the
symposium volume *Meaning and Use* (Avishai Margalit, ed., copyright © 1979, D. Reidel Publishing Co., Dordrecht, Holland), pp. 1–8,
and meanwhile in *Erkenntnis* 13 (copyright © 1978, D. Reidel), likewise pp. 1–8.

meaning of a word; we give the meaning of a word; we speak of knowing the meaning of an expression; we speak of an expression as having or lacking meaning; and we speak of expressions as alike in meaning. But one context in which we do not normally encounter the word 'meaning' is the context 'a meaning is'; 'a meaning *is* such and such'. The question. 'What is a meaning?' thus qualifies as a peculiarly philosophical question.

Meanings are meanings of expressions, so I had better begin by explaining my use of the expression 'expression'. An expression, for me, is a string of phonemes—or, if we prefer to think in terms of writing, a string of letters and spaces. Some expressions are sentences. Some are words. Thus when I speak of a sentence, or of a word, I am again referring to the sheer string of phonemes and nothing more. I must stress this because there is a widespread usage to the contrary. The word or sentence is often thought of rather as a combination, somehow, of a string of phonemes and a meaning. Homonyms are thus treated as distinct words. This usage is often convenient in the study of language, and in its proper place I have no quarrel with it. But it cannot be allowed here, because our purpose is to isolate and clarify the notion of meaning.

A meaning, still, is something that an expression, a string of phonemes, may *have,* as something external to it in the way in which a man may have an uncle or a bank account. It has it by virtue of how the string of phonemes is used by people. The same expression, the same string, may by coincidence turn up in two languages and mean differently in them. It may mean in two ways even in a single language; and then it is called ambiguous. But it remains, in any sense, one and the same expression. On this approach ambiguity and homonymy are on a par: what is concerned in either case is a single string of phonemes.

The point is that the notion of an expression must not be allowed to presuppose the notion of meaning. One may suspect, however, that my identifying expressions with strings of phonemes is then self-defeating, because the notion of a phoneme is itself commonly so defined as to presuppose the notion of sameness and difference of meaning. Two acoustically distinguishable sounds are counted as occurrences of the same phoneme if substitution of the one sound for the other leaves meanings unaffected. Now this appeal to meaning is happily not needed. We can simply say that two sounds count as occurrences of the same phoneme if the substitution has no effect on a speaker's readiness to assent to any sentence.

Expressions, then, are strings of phonemes in this innocent sense, and it is expressions that are to have meanings. What sort of things these meanings are is the question before us. But actually we are rather rushing matters in supposing there to be such things as meanings; for one can perhaps talk of meaning without talking of meanings.

Thus let us start rather with the verb 'mean' as an intransitive verb. An expression means; meaning is what it does, or what some expressions do. To say that two expressions are alike in meaning, then, is to say that they mean alike. Some expressions sound alike, some mean alike. It is significant that when we ask for the meaning of an expression we are content to be given another expression on a par with the first—like it in meaning. We do not ask for something that the two of them mean. The French idiom is more to the point: *cela veut dire*.

We could wish for further light on just what an expression is doing when it means, and how it does it, but we need not seek anything that the expression is doing it to—anythings that gets meant. We are not tempted to if we take 'mean' as intransitive.

In a longer view, however, this bid for ontological economy is idle. For, once we understand what it is for expressions to mean alike, it is easy and convenient to invoke some special objects arbitrarily and *let* them be meant—thus reconstituting our verb as transitive. In choosing a domain of objects for this purpose and assigning them to expressions as their so-called meanings, all that matters is that the same one be assigned always and only to expressions that mean alike. If we can manage this, then we can blithely say thereafter that expressions that mean alike *have* the *same meaning*. We should merely bear in mind that 'mean alike' comes first, and the so-called meanings are then concocted.

How do we concoct them? I said it was easy. Just take each meaning as a set of expressions that mean alike. The meaning of an expression is the set of all expressions that mean like it. Clearly this definition, which is by no means new, meets the stated requirement: it assigns the same meaning to two expressions if and only if they mean alike. The air of artificiality is no drawback, since there was no preconception as to what sort of thing a meaning ought to be.

So we see that if we know what it is for expressions to mean alike, the rest is easy. And we would seem to know, if facile lip service were indicative; but it is not. Fluency and clarity are poorly correlated.

Wittgenstein has stressed that the meaning of a word is to be sought in its use. This is where the empirical semanticist looks: to verbal behavior. John Dewey was urging this point in 1925. "Meaning," he wrote (p. 179), "... is primarily a property of behavior." And just what property of behavior might meaning then be? Well, we can take the behavior, the use, and let the meaning go.

How, then, may we set about studying the use of words? Take a decidedly commonplace and unambiguous word: 'desk'. What are the circumstances of my use of this word? They include, perhaps, all the sentences in which I ever have used or shall use the word, and all the stimulatory situations in which I uttered or shall utter those sentences. Perhaps they include all the sentences and stimulatory situations in which I *would* use the word. The sentences and stimulatory situations in which I *would now* use the word might even be said to constitute the *meaning* of the word for me now, if we care to rehabilitate the dubious term 'meaning'. However, the range of sentences and stimulatory situations concerned is forbiddingly vast and ill organized. Where is one to begin?

For a provisional solution, consider what we often actually do when asked the meaning of a word: we define the word by equating it to some more familiar word or phrase. Now this is itself a quick way of specifying the range of sentences and situations in which the word is used. We are specifying that range by identifying it with the range of sentences and stimulations in which the other and more familiar word or phrase is used. Happily we can spare ourselves the trouble of cataloguing all those sentences and situations, because our pupil has already mastered the use of the more familiar word or phrase.

We may persist, then, in the old routine of giving meanings by citing synonyms. The behavioral doctrine of meaning does not oppose that. What the behavioral doctrine of meaning contributes is theoretical: it purports to explain this synonymy relation itself, the relation between the word whose meaning is asked and the more familiar word or phrase that we cite in reply. The behavioral doctrine tells us that this relation of synonymy, or sameness of meaning, is sameness of use.

The method of giving the meaning of a word by citing a synonym is convenient but very limited. It accounts for only a small minority of the entries in a dictionary. Often the lexicographer will resort to what he calls a distinction of senses: he will cite several partial synonyms, some suitable in some kinds of context and others in others. When he does this, he has to distinguish the kinds of context by providing a general characterization of each, usually by reference to subject matter. And in many cases there is no such appeal even to partial synonyms; the use of a word can be taught in other ways. In general, given any sentence all of whose words are familiar except the word in question, what needs to be taught is how to paraphrase that sentence into an equivalent whose words are all familiar.

General instructions for paraphrasing the sentential contexts of a word into unproblematic sentences: such is the lexicographer's job. The citing of a direct synonym is just one form that such instructions may take, and it is feasible less often than not. What is more to the point than the relation of synonymy of words to words and phrases, then, as a central concept for semantics, is the relation of semantical equivalence of whole sentences. Given this concept, we readily define the other: a word is synonymous to a word or phrase if the substitution of the one for the other in a sentence always yields an equivalent sentence.

And when do sentences count as semantically equivalent? A provisional answer from the behavior point of view is evi-

dent: they are equivalent if their use is the same. Or, trying
to put the matter less vaguely, we might say that they are
equivalent if their utterance would be prompted by the same
stimulatory situations.

But clearly this will not do. They cannot both be uttered
at once; one must be uttered to the exclusion of the other.
On any occasion where one of the sentences is uttered, moreover, there must have been a cause, however trivial, for uttering it rather than the other. It may hinge merely on a phonetic accident: the choice of a word in the one sentence may
have been triggered by a chance phonetic resemblance to a
word just previously heard. Clearly we ask too much if we
ask of two equivalent sentences that they be prompted by
all the same stimulations. And anyway, if a criterion required actually comparing the stimulatory conditions for
the volunteering of sentences, it would surely be hopeless in
practice; for utterances are on the whole virtually unpredictable. The motives for volunteering a given sentence can
vary widely, and often inscrutably: the speaker may want to
instruct, or console, or surprise, or amuse, or impress, or
relieve a painful silence, or influence someone's behavior by
deception.

We can cut through all this if we limit our attention to
the *cognitive* equivalence of sentences; that is, to the sameness of truth conditions. We are then spared having to
speculate on the motives or circumstances for volunteering
a sentence. Instead we can arrange the circumstances ourselves and volunteer the sentence ourselves, in the form of
a query, asking only for a verdict of true or false. Cognitively equivalent sentences will get matching verdicts, at
least if we keep to the same speaker. He can be mistaken
in his verdicts, but no matter; he will then make the same
mistake on both sentences.

I remarked that it would be too much to require of two
equivalent sentences that their utterance be prompted by
all the same stimulations. Now, however, we are evidently
in an opposite difficulty: we are requiring too little. We are
requiring only that the speaker believe both or disbelieve
both or suspend judgment on both. This way lies little more
than material equivalence, not cognitive equivalence.

The solution to this difficulty is to be found in what John Stuart Mill called concomitant variation. To get this effect we must limit our attention for a while in yet another way: we must concentrate on occasion sentences. These, as opposed to standing sentences, are sentences whose truth values change from occasion to occasion, so that a fresh verdict has to be prompted each time. Typically they are sentences that contain indexical words, and that depend essentially on tenses of verbs. Examples are 'This is red' and 'There goes a rabbit'; these might be designated more particularly as observation sentences. Further examples are 'He is a bachelor' and 'There goes John's old tutor'; these do not qualify as observation sentences, but still they are occasion sentences. The truth value of 'He is a bachelor' varies with the reference of the pronoun from occasion to occasion; similarly the truth value of 'There goes John's old tutor' depends both on the varying reference of the name 'John' and on who happens to be passing down the street at the time. Now if our interrogated informant is disposed to give matching verdicts on two such occasion sentences on every occasion on which we query the two sentences, no matter what the attendant circumstances, then certainly the two sentences must be said to be cognitively equivalent for him. One such pair is 'He is a bachelor' and 'He is an unmarried man'. Another such pair, for a particular speaker, may be 'There goes John's old tutor' and 'There goes Dr. Park'.

These two pairs of examples differ significantly from each other, in that the second pair qualifies as cognitively equivalent only for a particular speaker, or a few speakers, while the first pair would qualify as cognitively equivalent for each speaker of the language. It is the difference between cognitive equivalence for an individual, or for an idiolect, and cognitive equivalence for a language. It is the latter that we are interested in when we expound the semantics of a language. Cognitive equivalence for the individual, however, is the prior notion conceptually, that is, in respect of criterion. Two occasion sentences are equivalent for him if he is disposed, on every occasion of query, to give them matching verdicts or, on doubtful occasions, no verdict.

The summation over society comes afterward: the sentences are equivalent for the language if equivalent for each speaker taken separately.

This unanimity requirement works all right for our core language, Basic English so to say, which all English speakers command. However, when recondite words are admitted, a pair of occasion sentences may fail of cognitive equivalence for an ignorant speaker merely because of misunderstanding. If we still want to count those two sentences cognitively equivalent for the language, we may do so by relativizing the unanimity requirement to an elite subset of the population.

Cognitive equivalence of two occasion sentences for a speaker consists in his being disposed to give matching verdicts when queried in matching stimulatory circumstances. We can easily make this notion of stimulatory circumstances more explicit. It is a question of the external forces that impinge on the interrogated subject at the time, and these only insofar as they affect his nervous system by triggering his sensory receptors. Thanks to the all-or-none law, there are no degrees or respects of triggering to distinguish. So, without any loss of relevant information, we may simply identify the subject's external stimulation at each moment with the set of his triggered receptors. Even this identification is very redundant, since the triggering of some receptors will have no effect on behavior, and the triggering of some receptors will have no different effect from what the triggering of other neighboring receptors would have had. However, the redundancy is harmless. Its effect is merely that two occasion sentences that are cognitively equivalent, in the sense of commanding like verdicts under identical stimulations, will also command like verdicts under somewhat unlike stimulations.

Each overall momentary stimulation of our interrogated subject is to be identified, I have suggested, with a subset of his receptors. The stimulation that he undergoes at any moment is the set of receptors triggered at that moment. This makes good sense of sameness and difference of stimulation of that person from moment to moment. It does not make sense of sameness of stimulation of two persons, since two persons do not share the same receptors. They do not even have exactly homologous receptors, if we get down to minutiae. But this is all very well, for I am not having to equate stimulations between persons. The notion of cognitive equivalence of occasion sentences for a single person rests on sameness and difference of stimulations of that person alone, and the subsequent summation over society appeals then to cognitive equivalence for each separate person, with no equating of stimulations between persons.

I feel that the relation of cognitive equivalence is in good shape, so far as occasion sentences are concerned. The relation is defined for the individual and for society, and the definition can be applied by a routine of query and verdict. There remain, of course, the other sentences—the standing sentences.

There remain also the single words, and their relation of synonymy to other words and phrases. We saw earlier that this relation presents no difficulty, once we have fixed the relation of equivalence of sentences. One word is synonymous to another word or phrase if substitution of the one for the other always yields equivalent sentences. Or, now that our equivalence relation for sentences is cognitive equivalence, we should say that a word is *cognitively* synonymous to a word or phrase if substitution of the one for the other always yield cognitively equivalent sentences. Granted, the relation even of cognitive equivalence of sentences is now under control only for occasion sentences. However, I think this is already enough to settle cognitive synonymy of words to words and phrases across the board. If a given word is interchangeable with a given word or phrase in all occasion sentences, invariably yielding a cognitively equivalent sentence, then I think the interchangeability can be depended on to hold good in all standing sentences as well.

If this be granted, then a conceptual foundation for cognitive synonymy is pretty firmly laid. The courses, as stonemasons call them, are as follows. First there is the relation of sameness of overall stimulation of an individual at different times. This is defined, theoretically, by sameness of triggered receptors. Next there is the relation of cognitive equivalence of occasion sentences for the individual. This is defined by his disposition to give matching verdicts when the two sentences are queried under identical overall stimulations. Next there is the relation of cognitive equivalence of occasion sentences for the whole linguistic community. This is defined as cognitive equivalence for each individual. Finally there is the relation of cognitive synonymy of a word to a word or phrase. This is defined as interchangeability in occasion sentences *salva aequalitate*. We could take the nominal further step, if we liked, and define the cognitive meaning of a word as the set of its cognitive synonyms.

Strictly speaking, this interchangeability criterion of synonymy requires some awkward reservations regarding the positions in which the substitutions are allowable. For instance, it would never do to require interchangeability within direct quotations; and this reservation extends, in diminishing degrees, to indirect quotation and other idioms of propositional attitude. I shall pass over this difficulty, for it is a familiar and perennial one, and I have nothing new to say about it.

Anyway we must remember that the synonymy of words and phrases, however well defined, is not the mainstay of lexicography. What are wanted in general, as I said earlier, are instructions for paraphrasing the sentential contexts of a word into unproblematic sentences by whatever means; the citing of a direct synonym is just one form that such instructions can sometimes take. The relation of equivalence of occasion sentences offers a foundation equally, however, for all this. If the use of a word can be pinned down by instructions for paraphrasing its sentential contexts at all, I expect it can be pinned down by instructions for paraphrasing just those contexts that are occasion sentences.

If we may measure the familiarity of words by their frequency, we may perhaps schematize the task of the monoglot lexicographer as follows. Let us define a *gloss* of a sentence *s*, with respect to one of its words *w*, as any cognitively equivalent sentence lacking *w* and containing only other words of *s* and words of higher frequency than *w*. A word may be called *reducible* if all occasion sentences that contain it admit of such glosses with respect to it. The lexicographer's task, then, is a systematic specification of glosses of occasion sentences with respect to all reducible words. This leaves him doing nothing about the irreducible words, which constitute the core language. I welcome this outcome on the whole, for the monoglot lexicographer's compulsive explanations of irreducible words have been a waste. But he should still add a few supplementary cognitive equivalences for the benefit of speakers whose frequencies diverge somewhat from the national average. For instance he should continue to define 'gorse' as 'furze' *and* 'furze' as 'gorse'.

I am of course stopping short still of the needs of practical lexicography in one conspicuous respect: I am attending only to the cognitive side, ignoring emotional and poetic aspects. Regarding those further aspects I have nothing to suggest.

My consideration of cognitive equivalence has been limited to occasion sentences thus far, and I have urged that occasion sentences already provide a broad enough base for lexicography. However, there is no need to limit cognitive equivalence to occasion sentences. We can extend the relation into standing sentences in several fragmentary but substantial ways. Standing sentences grade off into occasion sentences, after all. Verdicts on occasion sentences have to be prompted anew on each occasion, while verdicts on standing sentences may stand for various periods. The shorter the periods, the more the sentence resembles an occasion sentence. The more it resembles an occasion sentence, the more applicable our criterion of cognitive equivalence: the criterion of like verdicts under like stimulation. We might even extend this criterion to all standing sentences, provided that we take it only as a necessary condition of cognitive equivalence and not a sufficient one. For occasion sentences it is necessary and sufficient.

From another angle a sufficient but not necessary condition of cognitive equivalence can be brought to bear on standing sentences. Namely, we can exploit the relation of cognitive synonymy, which I already defined on the basis of cognitive equivalence of occasion sentences. One standing sentence is cognitively equivalent to another if it can be transformed into the other by a sequence of replacements of words or phrases by cognitive synonyms. This sufficient condition can be broadened by submitting the standing sentences not just to substitution of synonyms but also to other sort of paraphrase: sorts that have already been found to preserve cognitive equivalence among occasion sentences. These conditions do not quite add up to a definition of cognitive equivalence for standing sentences. If a pair of standing sentences meets the necessary condition and not the proposed sufficient one, the question of their cognitive equivalence has no answer. But in their incomplete way the conditions do make the notion widely applicable to standing sentences. Meanwhile it is defined for occasion sentences, and this, I have urged, is basis enough for cognitive lexicography.

I have been concerned in all these remarks with monoglot semantics, not polyglot; not translation. Criteria are harder to come by in the polyglot domain, particularly in the case of radical translation, where there are no bilinguals to exploit. The most serious difference is this: cognitive equivalence for a single individual is definable for occasion sentences generally, by sameness of verdict under sameness of stimulation; but between two individuals this definition carries us little beyond the observation sentences.[1]

If a bilingual is available, we can treat the two languages as his single tandem language; and then we can indeed define cognitive equivalence of occasion sentences generally, for him, even between the languages. But this is still cognitive equivalence only for him and not for a linguistic community, or pair of communities. Only if we have a whole subcommunity of bilinguals can we summate over the individuals, as we did in the monoglot case, and derive a bilingual relation of cognitive equivalence of occasion sentences at the social level. The polyglot case thrives, it would seem, just to the extent that it can be treated as monoglot. Thus the theory I have been developing here has no bearing, that I can see, on the indeterminacy of translation.

1. See my *Word and Object*, pp. 41–49.

6

On the Nature of Moral Values

Imagine a dog idling in the foreground, a tree in the middle distance, and a turnip lying on the ground behind the tree. Either of two hypotheses, or a combination of them, may be advanced to explain the dog's inaction with respect to the turnip: perhaps he is not aware that it is there, and perhaps he does not want a turnip. Such is the bipartite nature of motivation: belief and valuation intertwined. It is the deep old duality of thought and feeling, of the head and the heart, the cortex and the thalamus, the words and the music.

The duality can be traced back to the simplest conditioning of responses. A response was rewarded when it followed stimulus a, and penalized when it followed b; and thereafter it tended to be elicited by just those stimulations that were more similar to a than to b according to the subject's inarticulate standards of similarity. Observe then the duality of belief and valuation: the similarity standards are the epistemic component of habit formation, in its primordial form, and the reward-penalty axis is the valuative component.

The term 'belief' of course ill fits this primitive level. Even the term 'similarity standard' requires a word of caution:

This essay was written for A. I. Goldman and J. Kim, eds., *Values and Morals* (copyright © 1978, D. Reidel Publishing Co., Dordrecht, Holland, pp. 37–46), a volume in honor of Brandt, Frankena, and Stevenson. It was reprinted in *Critical Inquiry* 5 (1979).

such implicit standards of similarity are ascribed to the subject only on the behavioral basis of the experiments themselves, experiments in the reinforcement and extinction of his responses. The experiments afford at the same time a criterion for comparing the subject's implicit values, along the reward-penalty axis. His values are easier to plot, however, than his similarities. They are largely recognizable from innate reflexes, such as wincing, even without recourse to experiments in reinforcement and extinction. Moreover, they stand in the simple dyadic relation of better and worse, whereas similarity is at least triadic: a is more similar to b than to c. The evaluations thus line up in a single dimension, while the similarities may be expected to require more dimensions.

Clearly all learning, all acquisition of dispositions to discriminatory behavior, requires in the subject this bipartite equipment: it requires a similarity space and it requires some ordering of episodes along the valuation axis, however crude. Some such equipment, then, must precede all learning; that is, it must be innate. There need be no question here of awareness, or of ideas, innate or otherwise. It is a matter rather of physiological details of our complex and incontestably innate nervous system, which determine our susceptibilities to the reinforcement and extinction of responses. Those details are perhaps not yet fully understood, but we need know little to be assured that what is required for all learning must not have been learned.

Our innate similarity space is our modest head start on the epistemic side, for it is the starting point for induction. Induction consists, primitively, in the expectation that similar episodes will have similar sequels; and the similarity concerned is similarity by our subjective lights. In our innate likes and dislikes we have our modest head start on the valuative side, and then induction is our guide to worthwhile acts. I find it instructive to dignify the lowly neural phenomenon of reinforcement and extinction in these subjectivist terms, for its represents that neural phenomenon as technology in the small: the use of inductive science for realizing values.

Our similarity space is progressively changed and elaborated as our learning proceeds. Similarity standards that led to bad predictions get readjusted by trial and error. Our inductions become increasingly explicit and deliberate, and in the fullness of time we even rise above induction, to the hypothetico-deductive method.

Likewise our ordering of sensory episodes along the valuation axis is progressively changed and elaborated. In some cases an epistemic factor contributes to the change. We learn by induction that one sort of event tends to lead to another that we prize, and then by a process of transfer we may come to prize the former not only as a means but for itself. We come to relish the sport of fishing as much as we relish the fresh trout to which it was a means. Values get shifted also in other ways—perhaps something to do with chemistry, in the case of the acquired taste for strong peppers or anchovies. Or in more baffling ways, if one moves on to Schönberg or Jackson Pollock.

The transmutation of means into ends, just now illustrated by fishing, is what underlies moral training. Many sorts of good behavior have a low initial rating on the valuation scale, and are indulged in at first only for their inductive links to higher ends: to pleasant consequences or the avoidance of unpleasant ones at the preceptor's hands. Good behavior, insofar, is technology. But by association of means with ends we come gradually to accord this behavior a higher intrinsic rating. We find satisfaction in engaging in it and we come to encourage it in others. Our moral training has succeeded. There are exceptions to this pattern of development, I regret to say, but happily not among my readers.

The penalties and rewards by which the good behavior was inculcated may have included slaps and sugar plums. However, mere show of approval and disapproval on the parent's part will go a long way. It seems that such bland manifestations can directly induce pleasure and discomfort already in the very young. Perhaps some original source of sensual satisfaction, such as a caress, comes to be associated very early with the other more subtle signs of parental approval, which then come to be prized in themselves.

The distinction between moral values and others is not an easy one. There are easy extremes: the value that one places on his neighbor's welfare is moral, and the value of peanut brittle is not. The value of decency in speech and dress is moral or ethical in the etymological sense, resting as it does on social custom; and similarly for observance of the Jewish dietary laws. On the other hand, the eschewing of unrefrigerated oysters in the summer, though it is likewise a renunciation of immediate fleshly pleasure, is a case rather of prudence than of morality. But presumably the Jewish taboos themselves began prudentially. Again a Christian fundamentalist who observes the proprieties and helps his neighbors only from fear of hell-fire is manifesting prudence rather than moral values.[1] Similarly for the man with felony in his heart who behaves himself for fear of the law. Similarly for the child who behaves himself in the course of moral training; his behavior counts as moral only after these means get transmuted into ends. On the other hand, the value that the child attaches to the parent's approval is a moral value. It had been a mere harbinger of a sensually gratifying caress, if my recent suggestion is right, but has been transmuted into an end in itself.

It is hard to pick out a single distinguishing feature of moral values, beyond the vague matter of being somehow irreducibly social. We do better to recognize two largely overlapping classes of moral values. *Altruistic* values are values that one attaches to satisfactions of other persons, or to means to such satisfactions, without regard to ulterior satisfactions accruing to oneself. *Ceremonial* values, as we might say, are values that one attaches to practices of one's society or social group, again without regard to ulterior satisfactions accruing to oneself. Definitions appealing explicitly to behavioral dispositions rather than thus to hidden motivations would be desirable, but meanwhile a vague sketch such as this can be of some help if we do not overestimate it.

It is clear from the foregoing examples of prudential taboos, hell-fire, repressed felony, and child training, that two members of a society may value an act equally and yet the

---

1. Bernard Williams, pp. 75f, questions the disjointness of these alternatives. I am construing them disjointly.

value may be moral for the one and prudential for the other. But we like to speak also of the moral values or moral code or morality of a society as a whole. In so doing we may perhaps be taken to mean those values that are implemented by social sanctions, plus any further values that are moral values for most of the members individually.

I follow Schlick in placing the moral values in among the sensual and aesthetic values on an equal footing. Some non-moral values, for instance that of fishing, are subject to transmutation of means into ends, and some are innate, and some accrue in other ways. But so it is in particular with moral values: some accrue by transmutation of means into ends, through training, and some perhaps require no training.

Schlick, like Hume, set great store by sympathy: by the pleasure and sorrow that are induced by witnessing others' pleasure and sorrow. We have these susceptibilities, he believed, without training. If they are somehow gene-linked, it would be interesting to understand the mechanism. This would then account also for the previous point, the infant's early responsiveness to signs of parental approval and disapproval, as a special case.

Tinbergen in his study of herring gulls determined what simple configurations on paper served to rouse the chick to an expectant attitude, as if toward its mother, and what configurations would arouse a complementary attitude in the hen. He noted a human analogue in the simple formula for 'cuteness': fat cheek, big eye, negligible nose. Disney knew how to induce audible female cooing in the movie theater with a few strokes of the pen. The herring gull's response is instinctive; must ours, in this case, be otherwise? Again the rabbit that squeals from between the wolf's jaws is making an instinctive response that is altruistic in a functional sense; for the squeal does not deter the wolf, but it warns other rabbits. Hereditary altruism at its heroic extreme raises a genetic question, if the young martyr is not to live to transmit his altruistic genes; but biologists have proposed an answer. Altruism is mainly directed to close kin, and they transmit largely the same genes.

I represented our moral values as falling into two over-

lapping classes, the altruistic and the ceremonial. The classes
overlap in two ways. Altruistic values are in part institu-
tionalized and so may take on an added ceremonial appeal.
Conversely, there is altruistic value in so behaving as not to
offend against a neighbor's ceremonial values.

There are also cross-classifications, imposed by considerations of origin. Some values, in the altruistic category, perhaps issue freely from an innate faculty of sympathy, unless this class is empty and sympathy is an acquired taste.
Some, in the ceremonial category, are embraced out of senti-
ments of solidarity; thus the dietary observances in some
cases, and the old school tie. The basis here is perhaps sympathy still, in an attenuated way. Further, in any event, there
are both altruistic and ceremonial values that are inculcated
by precept, unsupported still by palpable reward or punishment. This is already a case of training in its mild way, a
case of transmutation of means into ends; the good behavior
is indulged in at first as a means to the ethereal end of parental or social approval, and only afterward comes to be
valued as an end in itself. Finally, there is moral training by
recourse to palpable reward or punishment over and above
parental or social attitude. Few of us are of such saintly
docility as to need no training of this earthier kind. But in
due course, here again, means get transmuted into ends, and
conscience is further fortified.

I remarked that this account places the moral values in
among the sensual and aesthetic ones. By the same token it
represents each of us as pursuing exclusively his own private
satisfactions. Thanks to the moral values that have been
trained into us, however, plus any innate moral beginnings
that there may have been, there is no clash of interests as we
pursue our separate ways. Our scales of values blend in
social harmony.

I am using the first-person plural rather narrowly here,
to include my readers and myself but not as many further
persons as I could wish. There are those—I mention no
names—whose moral training has been neglected or has not
proved feasible. Their ordering of values has remained in
such a state that these persons stand to maximize their
satisfactions by battening on our good behavior while cheat-

ing on their own. Society accommodates such misfits by introducing penalties to offset the imbalance in their values.

The moral values tend by virtue of their social character to be more uniform from person to person, within a culture, than many sensual and aesthetic values. Hence the tendency with regard to the latter to allow that *de gustibus non disputandum est,* while ascribing absoluteness and even divine origin to the moral law.

Hypotheses less extravagant than that of divine origin account well enough for such uniformity as obtains among moral values, even apart from possible innate components. It is merely that these values are passed down the generations, imposed by word of mouth, by birch rod and sugar plum, by acclaim and ostracism, fine, imprisonment. They are imposed by society because they matter to society, whereas aesthetic preferences may be left to go their way.

Language, like the moral law, was once thought to be God-given. The two have much in common. Both are institutions for the common good. Taken together they reflect, somewhat, the primitive duality of belief and valuation on which I remarked at the beginning. Language promotes the individual's inductions by giving him access to his neighbor's observations and even to his neighbor's finished inductions. It also helps him influence his neighbor's actions, but it does this mainly, still, by conveying factual information. On the other hand, the moral law of a society, if successful, coordinates the actual scales of values of the individuals in such a way as to resolve incompatibilities and thus promote their overall satisfaction.

In language there is a premium on uniformity of usage, to facilitate communication. In morality there is a premium on uniformity of moral values, so that we may count on one another's actions and rise in a body against a transgressor. In language as in morality the uniformity is achieved by instruction, each generation teaching the next. In the case of language there is less recourse to birch rod and sugar plum, because the rewards of conformity are built in. In morals, private deviations such as theft can augment one's satisfactions unless one's values have been rearranged by moral training or offset by external sanctions; but in language, private deviation directly defeats one's own immediate purpose by obscuring one's message. There is, however, an exception: lying is a deviation in verbal behavior that can work to one's private advantage. The utility of language for each of us hinges on a predominance of truthfulness on the part of others, but any of us can enjoy that advantage and lie a little too, to his private profit. Thus it is that the liar invites the reproaches not of the orthoepist but of the moralist. Moral values need to be instilled into him that will offset the values served by lying. Failing that, we may incapacitate his future lies by spreading warnings.

For the usefulness of a language it is required that most speakers associate the same expression with the same sort of object, but it does not matter how the expression sounds as long as all members of the society make it sound about alike. An expression to the same purpose in another language can therefore differ utterly and it will not matter, if the two societies do not seek to communicate. Language thus tends to extreme uniformity within isolated societies and chaotic diversity between them. We see linguistic gradation in the world, but only because of gradations in the intimacy of communication.

Moral values may be expected to vary less radically than language from one society to another, even when the societies are isolated. True, there are societies whose bans and licenses boggle our sheltered imaginations. But we can expect a common core, since the most basic problems of societies are bound to run to type. Morality touches the common lot of mankind as the particularities of sound and syntax do not. Where language touches the common lot is rather in the intelligence and influence that the sounds and syntax serve to convey. Thus any variation of morality from culture to culture invites comparison perhaps with the variation of world view or scientific outlook from culture to culture, but certainly not with the extravagant variation of language.

When we set about comparing moralities from culture to culture, assessing variations and seeking the common core, we may begin by considering how to separate the native's moral values from his other values. How much of what he does or refrains from doing is attributable to mistaken notions of causal efficacy on his part, and accountable therefore to misguided prudence rather than to moral scruples? He may believe in so full a complement of supernatural sanctions as to leave no scope for moral values as distinct from prudential ones. In this event we can do no better than recur to our derivative concept of the morality of a society, as distinct from that of an individual. The question then becomes that of determining what behavior is implemented by socially established rewards and penalties. This standard will fail us too, however, if the society is so successfully indoctrinated regarding supernatural sanctions that no social enforcement is called for. At this point the most we can do is compare the native's acts with ours in situations where our qualify as moral acts by our own lights. We will observe whether he respects property, and, if he does not, whether he seems worried and furtive in taking it. We will observe whether he kills harmless creatures without meaning to eat them. We will try to observe whether he is promiscuous in his love life, and, if so, whether he is furtive about that. We can observe his behavior, when he lets us, and we can applaud or reprehend it in our way.

Moral contrasts are not, of course, so far to seek. Disagreements on moral matters can arise at home, and even within oneself. When they do, one regrets the methodological infirmity of ethics as compared with science. The empirical foothold of scientific theory is in the predicted observable event; that of a moral code is in the observable moral act. But whereas we can test a prediction against the independent course of observable nature, we can judge the morality of an act only by our moral standards themselves. Science, thanks to its links with observation, retains some title to a correspondence theory of truth; but a coherence theory is evidently the lot of ethics.

Scientific theories on all sorts of useful and useless topics are sustained by empirical controls, partial and devious though they be. It is a bitter irony that so vital a matter as the difference between good and evil should have no comparable claim to objectivity. No wonder there have been efforts since earliest times to work a justification of moral values into the fabric of what might pass for factual science.

For such, surely, were the myths of divine origins of moral law.

There is a legitimate mixture of ethics with science that somewhat mitigates the methodological predicament of ethics. Anyone who is involved in moral issues relies on causal connections. Ethical axioms can be minimized by reducing some values causally to others; that is, by showing that some of the valued acts would already count as valuable anyway as means to ulterior ends. Utilitarianism is a notable example of such systematization.

Causal reduction can serve not only in thus condensing the assumptions but also in sorting out conflicts. Thus take the question of white lies. If we once agree to regard truthfulness as good only as a means to higher moral ends, rather than as an ultimate end in itself, then the question becomes a question essentially of science, or engineering. On the one hand, the utility of language requires a preponderance of truthfulness; on the other hand, the truth can cause pain. So one may try to puzzle out a strategy.

Causal reduction is often effective in resolving moral conflicts not only within the individual but between individuals. One individual disputes another's position on some point of morals. The other individual tries to justify his position instrumentally, hence by causal reduction to some ulterior end which they both value. The first individual is then either persuaded or proceeds to contest the causal reduction, in which case the issue has been gratefully transformed into a cognitive question of science. This way of resolving moral issues is successful to the extent that we can reduce moral values causally to other moral values that command agreement. There must remain some ultimate ends, unreduced and so unjustified. Happily these, once identified, would tend to be widely accepted. For we may expect a tendency to uniformity in the hereditary component of morality, whatever it may be, and also, since the basic problems of societies are much alike, we may expect considerable agreement in the socially imposed component when it is reduced to fundamentals.

Even in the extreme case where disagreement extends irreducibly to ultimate moral ends, the proper counsel is not one of pluralistic tolerance. One's disapproval of gratuitous torture, for example, easily withstands one's failure to make a causal reduction, and so be it. We can still call the good good and the bad bad, and hope with Stevenson that these epithets may work their emotive weal. In an extremity we can fight, if the threat to the ultimate value in question outweighs the disvalue of the fighting.

There remains the awkward matter of a conflict of ultimate values within the individual. It could have to do with the choice of a career, or mate, or vacation spot. The predicament in such a nonmoral case will concern only the individual and a few associates. When the ultimate values concerned are moral ones, on the other hand, and more particularly altruistic ones, the case is different; for the individual in such a dilemma has all society on his conscience.

The basic difficulty is that the altruistic values that we acquire by social conditioning and perhaps by heredity are vague and open-ended. Primitively the premium is on kin, and primitively therefore the very boundary of the tribe itself in its isolation constitutes a bold boundary between the beneficiaries of one's altruism and the alien world. Nowadays the boundary has given way to gradations. Moreover, we are prone to extrapolate; extrapolation was always intrinsic to induction, that primitive propensity that is at the root of all science. Extrapolation in science, however, is under the welcome restraint of stubborn fact: failures of prediction. Extrapolation in morals has only our unsettled moral values themselves to answer to, and it is these that the extrapolation was meant to settle.

Today we unhesitatingly extrapolate our altruism beyond our close community. Most of us extend it to all mankind. But to what degree? One cannot reasonably be called upon to love even one's neighbor quite as oneself. Is love to diminish inversely as the square of the distance? Is it to extend, in some degree, to the interests of individuals belonging to other species than our own? As regards capricious killing, one hopes so; but what of vivisection, and of the eating of red meat?

One thinks also of unborn generations. Insofar as our moral standards were shaped by evolution for fostering the survival of the race, a concern for the unborn was assured. One then proceeds, however, as one will, to systematize and minimize one's ethical axioms by reducing some causally to others. This effort at system-building leads to the formulation and scrutiny of principles, and one is then taken aback by the seeming absurdity of respecting the interests of non-existent people: of unactualized possibilities. This counter-revolutionary bit of moral rationalization is welcome as it touches population control, since the blind drive to mass procreation is now so counter-productive. But the gratification is short-lived, for the same rationalization would seem to condone a despoiling of the environment for the exclusive convenience of people now living.

It need not. A formulation is ready to hand which sustains the moral values that favor limiting the population while still safeguarding the environment. Namely, it is a matter of respecting the future interests of people now unborn, but only of future actual people. We recognize no present unactualized possibilities.

Thus we do what we can with our ultimate values, but we have to deplore the irreparable lack of the empirical checkpoints that are the solace of the scientist. Loose ends are untidy at best, and disturbingly so when the ultimate good is at stake.

7

Five Milestones
of Empiricism

In the past two centuries there have been five points where empiricism has taken a turn for the better. The first is the shift from ideas to words. The second is the shift of semantic focus from terms to sentences. The third is the shift of semantic focus from sentences to systems of sentences. The fourth is, in Morton White's phrase, methodological monism: abandonment of the analytic-synthetic dualism. The fifth is naturalism: abandonment of the goal of a first philosophy prior to natural science. I shall proceed to elaborate on each of the five.

The first was the shift of attention from ideas to words. This was the adoption of the policy, in epistemology, of talking about linguistic expressions where possible instead of ideas. This policy was of course pursued by the medieval nominalists, but I think of it as entering modern empiricism only in 1786, when the philologist John Horne Tooke wrote as follows: "The greatest part of Mr. Locke's essay, that is, all which relates to what he calls the abstraction, complexity, generalization, relation, etc., of ideas, does indeed merely concern language" (p. 32).

7

7
This essay is part of a paper that I presented under the title "The pragmatists' place in empiricism" at a symposium at the University of South Carolina in 1975. The paper will be published by the University of South Carolina Press in the symposium volume *Pragmatism, Its Sources and Prospects.*

British empiricism was dedicated to the proposition that only sense makes sense. Ideas were acceptable only if based on sense impressions. But Tooke appreciated that the *idea* idea itself measures up poorly to empiricist standards. Translated into Tooke's terms, then, the basic proposition of British empiricism would seem to say that words make sense only insofar as they are definable in sensory terms.

At this point, trouble arises over grammatical particles: what of our prepositions, our conjunctions, our copula? These are indispensable to coherent discourse, yet how are they definable in sensory terms? John Horne Tooke adopted a heroic line here, arguing that the particles were really ordinary concrete terms in degenerate form. He advanced ingenious etymologies: 'if' was 'give', 'but' was 'be out'. However, this line was needless and hopeless. If we could make concrete terms do all the work of the grammatical particles, we could make them do so without awaiting justification from etymologists. But surely we cannot, and there is no valid reason to want to; for there is another approach to the problem of defining the grammatical particles in sensory terms. We have only to recognize that they are *syncategorematic*. They are definable not in isolation but in context.

This brings us to the second of the five turning points, the shift from terms to sentences. The medievals had the notion of syncategorematic words, but it was a contemporary of John Horne Tooke who developed it into an explicit theory of contextual definition; namely, Jeremy Bentham. He applied contextual definition not just to grammatical particles and the like, but even to some genuine terms, categorematic ones. If he found some term convenient but ontologically embarrassing, contextual definition enabled him in some cases to continue to enjoy the services of the term while disclaiming its denotation. He could declare the term syncategorematic, despite grammatical appearances, and then could justify his continued use of it if he could show systematically how to paraphrase as wholes all sentences in which he chose to imbed it. Such was his theory of fictions:[1] what he called paraphrasis, and what we now call contextual definition. The

1. See Ogden.

term, like the grammatical particles, is meaningful as a part of meaningful wholes. If every sentence in which we use a term can be paraphrased into a sentence that makes good sense, no more can be asked.

Comfort could be derived from Bentham's doctrine of paraphrasis by all who may have inherited Locke's and Hume's misgivings over abstract ideas. Reconsidered in the spirit of John Horne Tooke, these misgivings become misgivings over abstract terms; and then Bentham's approach offers hope of accommodating such terms, in some contexts anyway, without conceding an ontology of abstract objects. I am persuaded that one cannot thus make a clean sweep of all abstract objects without sacrificing much of science, including classical mathematics. But certainly one can pursue those nominalistic aims much further than could have been clearly conceived in the days before Bentham and Tooke.

Contextual definition precipitated a revolution in semantics: less sudden perhaps than the Copernican revolution in astronomy, but like it in being a shift of center. The primary vehicle of meaning is seen no longer as the word, but as the sentence. Terms, like grammatical particles, mean by contributing to the meaning of the sentences that contain them. The heliocentrism propounded by Copernicus was not obvious, and neither is this. It is not obvious because, for the most part, we understand sentences only by construction from understood words. This is necessarily so, since sentences are potentially infinite in variety. We learn some words in isolation, in effect as one-word sentences; we learn further words in context, by learning various short sentences that contain them; and we understand further sentences by construction from the words thus learned. If the language that we thus learn is afterward compiled, the manual will necessarily consist for the most part of a word-by-word dictionary, thus obscuring the fact that the meanings of words are abstractions from the truth conditions of sentences that contain them.

It was the recognition of this semantic primacy of sentences that gave us contextual definition, and vice versa. I attributed this to Bentham. Generations later we find Frege celebrating the semantic primacy of sentences, and Russell giving contextual definition its fullest exploitation in technical logic. But Bentham's contribution had not been lying ineffective all that while. In the course of the nineteenth century a practice emerged in the differential calculus of using differential operators as simulated coefficients while recognizing that the operators were really intelligible only as fragments of larger terms. It was this usage, indeed, rather than Bentham's writings, that directly inspired Russell's contextual definitions.[2]

In consequence of the shift of attention from term to sentence, epistemology came in the twentieth century to be a critique not primarily of concepts but of truths and beliefs. The verification theory of meaning, which dominated the Vienna Circle, was concerned with the meaning and meaningfulness of sentences rather than of words. The English philosophers of ordinary language have likewise directed their analyses to sentences rather than to words, in keeping with the example that was set by both the earlier and the later work of their mentor Wittgenstein. Bentham's lesson penetrated and permeated epistemology in the fullness of time.

The next move, number three in my five, shifts the focus from sentences to systems of sentences. We come to recognize that in a scientific theory even a whole sentence is ordinarily too short a text to serve as an independent vehicle of empirical meaning. It will not have its separable bundle of observable or testable consequences. A reasonably inclusive body of scientific theory, taken as a whole, will indeed have such consequences. The theory will imply a lot of observation conditionals, as I call them,[3] each of which says that if certain observable conditions are met then a certain observable event will occur. But, as Duhem has emphasized, these observation conditionals are implied only by the theory as a whole. If any of them proves false, then the theory is false, but on the face of it there is no saying which of the component sentences of the theory to blame. The observation conditionals cannot be distributed as consequences of the

2. See Whitehead and Russell, 2d ed., p. 24.
3. See Essay 2 above.

several sentences of the theory. A single sentence of the theory is apt not to imply any of the observation conditionals. The scientist does indeed test a single sentence of his theory by observation conditionals, but only through having chosen to treat that sentence as vulnerable and the rest, for the time being, as firm. This is the situation when he is testing a new hypothesis with a view to adding it, if he may, to his growing system of beliefs.

When we look thus to a whole theory or system of sentences as the vehicle of empirical meaning, how inclusive should we take this system to be? Should it be the whole of science? or the whole of *a* science, a branch of science? This should be seen as a matter of degree, and of diminishing returns. All sciences interlock to some extent; they share a common logic and generally some common part of mathematics, even when nothing else. It is an uninteresting legalism, however, to think of our scientific system of the world as involved *en bloc* in every prediction. More modest chunks suffice, and so may be ascribed their independent empirical meaning, nearly enough, since some vagueness in meaning must be allowed for in any event.

It would also be wrong to suppose that *no* single sentence of a theory has its separable empirical meaning. Theoretical sentences grade off to observation sentences; observationality is a matter of degree, namely, the degree of spontaneous agreement that the sentence would command from present witnesses. And while it may be argued that even an observation sentence may be recanted in the light of the rest of one's theory, this is an extreme case and happily not characteristic. And in any event there will be single sentences at the other extreme—long theoretical ones—that surely have their separable empirical meaning, for we can make a conjunctive sentence of a whole theory.

Thus the holism that the third move brings should be seen only as a moderate or relative holism. What is important is that we cease to demand or expect of a scientific sentence that it have its own separable empirical meaning.

The fourth move, to methodological monism, follows closely on this holism. Holism blurs the supposed contrast between the synthetic sentence, with its empirical content, and the analytic sentence, with its null content. The organizing role that was supposedly the role of analytic sentences is now seen as shared by sentences generally, and the empirical content that was supposedly peculiar to synthetic sentences is now seen as diffused through the system.

The fifth move, finally, brings naturalism: abandonment of the goal of a first philosophy. It sees natural science as an inquiry into reality, fallible and corrigible but not answerable to any supra-scientific tribunal, and not in need of any justification beyond observation and the hypothetico-deductive method. Naturalism has two sources, both negative. One of them is despair of being able to define theoretical terms generally in terms of phenomena, even by contextual definition. A holistic or system-centered attitude should suffice to induce this despair. The other negative source of naturalism is unregenerate realism, the robust state of mind of the natural scientist who has never felt any qualms beyond the negotiable uncertainties internal to science. Naturalism had a representative already in 1830 in the antimetaphysician Auguste Comte, who declared that "positive philosophy" does not differ in method from the special sciences.

Naturalism does not repudiate epistemology, but assimilates it to empirical psychology. Science itself tells us that our information about the world is limited to irritations of our surfaces, and then the epistemological question is in turn a question within science: the question how we human animals can have managed to arrive at science from such limited information. Our scientific epistemologist pursues this inquiry and comes out with an account that has a good deal to do with the learning of language and with the neurology of perception. He talks of how men posit bodies and hypothetical particles, but he does not mean to suggest that the things thus posited do not exist. Evolution and natural selection will doubtless figure in this account, and he will feef free to apply physics if he sees a way.

The naturalistic philosopher begins his reasoning within the inherited world theory as a going concern. He tentatively believes all of it, but believes also that some unidentified portions are wrong. He tries to improve, clarify, and understand the system from within. He is the busy sailor adrift on Neurath's boat.

8

Russell's Ontological
Development

The twentieth century began, as many of you know, in 1901.
Russell was twenty-eight and had published three books: one
on politics, one on mathematics, and one on philosophy. Late
next summer the century will be two-thirds over. Russell's
books have run to forty, and his philosophical influence, direct and indirect, over this long period has been unequaled.

Russell's name is inseparable from mathematical logic,
which owes him much, and it was above all Russell who made
that subject an inspiration to philosophers. The new logic
played a part in the philosophical doctrines that Russell propounded during the second decade of this century—doctrines
of unsensed sensa and perspectives, logical constructions and
atomic facts. These doctrines affect our thinking today both
directly and through supervening schools of thought. The
impact of logical empiricism upon present-day philosophy is
to an important degree Russell's impact at one remove, as
the references in Carnap and elsewhere generously attest.
Moreover, Wittgenstein's philosophy was an evolution from
views that Russell and the young Wittgenstein had shared.
The Oxford philosophy of ordinary language must admit,
however bleakly, to a strong strain of Russell in its origins.

A symposium paper, reprinted from the *Journal of Philosophy* 63
(1966). A few lines have been dropped and others permuted because
of coverage by Essay 7 above.

I think many of us were drawn to our profession by Russell's books. He wrote a spectrum of books for a graduated public, layman to specialist. We were beguiled by the wit and a sense of newfound clarity with respect to central traits of reality. We got memorable first lessons in relativity, elementary particles, infinite numbers, and the foundations of arithmetic. At the same time we were inducted into traditional philosophical problems such as that of the reality of matter and that of the reality of minds other than our own. For all this emergence of problems the overriding sense of newfound clarity was more than a match. In sophisticated retrospect we have had at points to reassess that clarity, but this was a sophistication that we acquired only after we were hooked.

Russell spoke not only to a broad public, but to a broad subject matter. The scatter of his first three books set a precedent to which his books of the next six decades conformed. Some treat of education, marriage, morals, and, as in the beginning, politics. I shall not venture to guess whether the world is better for having heeded Russell in these farther matters to the degree that it has, or whether it is better for not having heeded him more. Or both.

Instead I shall talk of Russell's ontological development. For I must narrow my scope somehow, and ontology has the virtue of being central and not unduly narrow. Moreover, Russell's ontology was conditioned conspicuously by both his theory of knowledge and his logic.

In *Principles of Mathematics*, 1903, Russell's ontology was unrestrained. Every word referred to something. If the word was a proper name, in Russell's somewhat deviant sense of that phrase, its object was a *thing;* otherwise a *concept.* He limited the term 'existence' to things, but reckoned things liberally, even including instants and points of empty space. And then, beyond existence, there were the rest of the entities: "numbers, the Homeric gods, relations, chimeras, and four-dimensional spaces" (p. 449). The word 'concept', which Russell applied to these nonexistents, connotes mereness; but let us not be put off. The point to notice, epithets aside, is that gods and chimeras are as real for Russell as numbers. Now this is an intolerably indiscriminate ontology.

Take impossible numbers: prime numbers divisible by 6. It must in some sense be false that there are such; and this must be false in some sense in which it is true that there are prime numbers. In this sense are there chimeras? Are chimeras then as firm as the good prime numbers and firmer than the primes divisible by 6?

Russell may have meant to admit certain chimeras (the possible ones) to the realm of being, and still exclude the primes divisible by 6 as impossibles. Or he may, like Meinong, have intended a place even for impossible objects. I do not see that in *Principles of Mathematics* Russell faced that question.

Russell's long article on Meinong came out in *Mind* in installments the following year. In it he criticized details of Meinong's system, but still protested none against the exuberance of Meinong's realm of being. In the same quarterly three issues later, however, a reformed Russell emerges: the Russell of "On Denoting" (1905), fed up with Meinong's impossible objects. The reform was no simple change of heart; it hinged on Russell's discovery of a means of dispensing with the unwelcome objects. The device was Russell's theory of singular descriptions, that paradigm, as Ramsey has said, of philosophical analysis. It involved defining a term not by presenting a direct equivalent of it, but by what Bentham called *paraphrasis:* by providing equivalents of all desired sentences containing the term.[1] In this way, reference to fictitious objects can be simulated in meaningful sentences without our being committed to the objects. Frege and Peano had allowed singular description the status of a primitive notation; only with Russell did it become an "incomplete symbol defined in use."

The new freedom that paraphrasis confers is our reward for recognizing that the unit of communication is the sentence and not the word. This point of semantical theory was long obscured by the undeniable primacy, in one respect, of words. Sentences being limitless in number and words limited, we necessarily understand most sentences by construction from antecedently familiar words. Actually there

1. See Essay 7 above.

is no conflict here. We can allow the sentences a monopoly of full "meaning," in some sense, without denying that the meaning must be worked out. Then we can say that knowing words is knowing how to work out the meanings of sentences containing them. Dictionary definitions of words are mere clauses in a recursive definition of the meanings of sentences.

Russell's preoccupation with incomplete symbols began with his theory of singular descriptions in 1905. But it continued and spread, notably to classes. For background on classes we must slip back a few years. Classes were an evident source of discomfort to Russell when he was writing *Principles of Mathematics*. There was, for one thing, his epoch-making paradox. Burali-Forti had found a paradox of classes as early as 1897, but it concerned infinite ordinal numbers, and could be accommodated, one hoped, by some local adjustment of theory. On the other hand, Russell's simple paradox of the class of all classes not belonging to themselves struck at the roots. It dates from 1901, when, as Frege expressed it to Russell, arithmetic tottered.

Russell's accommodation of the paradoxes, his theory of types, came only in 1908. In *Principles*, 1903, we find no more than tentative gropings in that direction. But *Principles* evinces much discomfort over classes also apart from the paradoxes. The further source of discomfort is the ancient problem of the one and the many. It seems strange now that Russell saw a problem in the fact that a single class might have many members, since he evidently saw no problem in the corresponding fact that a single attribute, or what he then called a class-concept, might apply to many things. What made the difference was that, in the bipartite ontology of *Principles of Mathematics*, classes counted as things rather than as concepts; classes existed. Russell observed against Peano that "we must not identify the class with the class-concept," because of extensionality: classes with the same members are the same (p. 68). Since the class was not the class-concept, Russell took it not to be a concept at all; hence it had to be a thing. But then, he felt, it ought to be no more than the sum of the things in it; and here was his problem of the one and the many.

We saw that in 1905 Russell freed himself of Meinong's

impossibles and the like by a doctrine of incomplete symbols. Classes were next. In his 1908 paper, "Mathematical Logic as Based on the Theory of Types," there emerges not only the theory of types but also a doctrine of incomplete symbols for explaining classes away. This latter doctrine is designed precisely to take care of the point Russell had made against Peano in connection with extensionality. Russell's contextual definition of class notation gave the benefit of classes, namely, extensionality, without assuming more than class-concepts after all.

Seeing Russell's perplexities over classes, we can understand his gratification at accommodating classes under a theory of incomplete symbols. But the paradoxes, which were the most significant of these perplexities, were not solved by his theory of incomplete symbols; they were solved, or parried, by his theory of types. One is therefore startled when Russell declares in "My Mental Development" that his expedient of incomplete symbols "made it possible to see, in a general way, how a solution of the contradictions might be possible."[2] If the paradoxes had invested only classes and not class-concepts, then Russell's elimination of classes would indeed have eliminated the paradoxes and there would have been no call for the theory of types. But the paradoxes apply likewise, as Russell knew, to class-concepts, or propositional functions. And thus it was that the theory of types, in this its first full version of 1908, was developed expressly and primarily for propositional functions and then transmitted to classes only through the contextual definitions.

The startling statement that I quoted can be accounted for. It is linked to the preference that Russell was evincing, by 1908, for the phrase 'propositional function' over 'class-concept'. Both phrases were current in *Principles of Mathematics;* mostly the phrase 'propositional function' was visibly meant to refer to notational forms, namely, open sentences, while concepts were emphatically not notational. But after laying waste Meinong's realm of being in 1905, Russell trusted concepts less and favored the more nominalistic tone of the phrase 'propositional function', which bore the double

2. Schilpp, *Philosophy of Bertrand Russell*, p. 14.

burden. If we try to be as casual about the difference between use and mention as Russell was fifty and sixty years ago, we can see how he might feel that, whereas a theory of types of real classes would be ontological, his theory of types of propositional functions had a notational cast. Insofar, his withdrawal of classes would be felt as part of his solution of the paradoxes. This feeling could linger to 1943, when he wrote "My Mental Development," even if its basis had lapsed.

We, careful about use and mention, can tell when Russell's so-called propositional functions must be taken as concepts, more specifically as attributes and relations, and when they may be taken as mere open sentences or predicates. It is when he quantifies over them that he reifies them, however unwittingly, as concepts. This is why no more can be claimed for his elimination of classes than I claimed for it above: a derivation of classes from attributes, or concepts, by a contextual definition framed to supply the missing extensionality. On later occasions Russell writes as if he thought that his 1908 theory, which reappeared in *Principia Mathematica*, disposed of classes in some more sweeping sense than reduction to attributes.

Just how much more sweeping a reduction he was prepared to claim may have varied over the years. Hahn and other readers have credited him with explaining classes away in favor of nothing more than a nominalistic world of particulars and notations. But Russell early and late has expressly doubted the dispensability of universals. Even if we were ingeniously to paraphrase all talk of qualities, for instance, into an idiom in which we talk rather of similarity to chosen particulars instancing those qualities, still, Russell more than once remarked, we should be left with one universal, the relation of similarity. Now here, in contrast to the class matter, I think Russell even concedes the Platonists too much; retention of the two-place predicate 'is similar to' is no evidence of assuming a corresponding abstract entity, the similarity relation, as long as that relation is not invoked as a value of a bound variable. A moral of all this is that inattention to referential semantics works two ways, obscuring some ontological assumptions and creating an illusion of others.

What I have ascribed to confusion can be ascribed to indifference; for we are apt to take pains over a distinction only to the degree that we think it matters. Questions as to what there is were for Russell of two sorts: questions of existence in his restricted sense of the term, and residual questions of being—questions of what he came to call 'subsistence'. The questions as to what subsists evidently struck him as less substantial, more idly verbal perhaps, than questions as to what exists. This bias toward the existential would explain his indiscriminate bestowal of subsistence in *Principles of Mathematics*. True, he called a halt in 1905 with his theory of descriptions; but on that occasion he was provoked by the impossibility of Meinong's impossibles. And he had even put up with those for a time. Moreover, Russell continued to be very prodigal with subsistence even after propounding his theory of descriptions. We find him saying still in 1912 that "nearly all the words to be found in the dictionary stand for universals."[3]

I am suggesting that through his fourth decade Russell took a critical interest in existential questions but was relatively offhand about subsistential ones. This bias explains his glee over eliminating classes and his indifference over the status of the surviving propositional functions; for we saw that in *Principles* the classes occupied, however uneasily, the existential zone of being. To hold that classes, it there be any, must exist, while attributes at best subsist, does strike me as arbitrary; but such was Russell's attitude.

Russell's relative indifference to subsistence shows again in his treatment of meaning. Frege's three-way distinction between the expression, what it means, and what if anything it refers to, did not come naturally to Russell. In "On Denoting," 1905, he even argued against it. His argument is hard to follow; at points it seems to turn on a confusion of expressions with their meanings, and at points it seems to turn on a confusion of the expression with the mention of it, while elsewhere in the same pages Russell seems clear on both distinctions. The upshot is that "the relation of '*C*' to *C* remains wholly mysterious; and where are we to find the

3. *Problems of Philosophy*, p. 146.

denoting complex '*C*' which is supposed to denote *C*? . . . This
is an inextricable tangle, and seems to prove that the whole
distinction between meaning and denotation has been
wrongly conceived."

In other writings Russell commonly uses the word 'meaning' in the sense of 'reference'; thus " 'Napoleon' means a
certain individual" and " 'Man' means a whole class of such
particulars as have proper names."[4] What matters more
than terminology is that Russell seldom seems heedful,
under any head, of a subsistent entity such as *we* might call
the meaning, over and above the existent object of reference.
He tends, as in the 1905 paper "On Denoting," to blur that
entity with the expression itself. Such was his general tendency with subsistents.

For my own part, I am chary of the idea of meaning, and,
furthermore, I think Russell too prodigal with subsistent
entities. So it would be odd of me to criticize Russell for not
recognizing meanings as subsistent entities. However, the
outcome that wants criticizing is just that, for want of distinctions, Russell tended to blur meaninglessness with failure
of reference. This was why he could not banish the king of
France without first inventing the theory of descriptions. To
make sense is to have a meaning, and the meaning is the
reference; so 'the king of France' is meaningless and 'The
king of France is bald' is meaningful only by being short for
a sentence not containing 'the king of France'. Well, even if
the theory of descriptions was not needed in quite this way,
it brought major clarifications and we are thankful for it.

Russell's tendency to blur subsistent entities with expressions was noticed in his talk of propositional functions. It is
equally noticeable in what he says of propositions. In *Principles of Mathematics* he describes propositions as expressions, but then he speaks also of the unity of propositions
(p. 50), and of the possibility of infinite propositions (p.
145), in ways ill suited to such a version. In "Meinong's Theory," 1904, he speaks of propositions as judgments (p. 523).
There is similar oscillation in *Principia Mathematica*.

But by the time of "The Philosophy of Logical Atomism,"

4. *Analysis of Mind*, pp. 191, 194.

1918, the oscillation has changed direction. At one point in this essay we read, "a proposition is just a symbol" (p. 185) ; at a later point we read rather, "Obviously propositions are nothing . . . To suppose that in the actual world of nature there is a whole set of false propositions going about is to my mind monstrous" (p. 223). This repudiation is startling. We had come to expect a blur between expressions and subsistent entities, concepts ; what we get instead of subsistence is nothingness. The fact is that Russell has stopped talking of subsistence. He stopped by 1914. What would once have counted as subsisting has been disposed of in any of three ways : identified with its expression, or repudiated utterly, or elevated to the estate of out-and-out existence. Qualities and relations come to enjoy this elevation ; Russell speaks in "The Philosophy of Logical Atomism" of "those ultimate simples, out of which the world is built, . . . that . . . have a kind of reality not belonging to anything else. Simples . . . are of an infinite number of sorts. There are particulars and qualities and relations of various orders, a whole hierarchy" (p. 270).

Russell's abandonment of the term 'subsistence' was an improvement. It is a quibbling term ; its function is to limit existence verbally to space-time and so divert attention from ontological commitments of other than spatio-temporal kind. Better to acknowledge all posits under an inclusive and familiar heading. Posits too dubious for such recognition will then be dropped, as were propositions in some sense.

As for propositions, in particular, we saw Russell in this essay taking them as expressions part of the time and part of the time simply repudiating them. Dropping then the ambiguous epithet, we might take this to be Russell's net thought: there are no nonlinguistic things that are somehow akin to sentences and asserted by them.

But this is not Russell's thought. In the same essay he insists that the world does contain nonlinguistic things that are akin to sentences and asserted by them ; he merely does not call them propositions. He calls them facts. It turns out that the existence of nonlinguistic analogues of sentences offends Russell only where the sentences are false. His facts are what many of us would have been content to call true propositions. Russell himself called them that in 1904,[5] propositions then being judgments; and in the 1918 essay now under discussion he allows them full-fledged existence. "Facts belong to the objective world" (p. 183). True, he says a page earlier that "when I speak of a fact I do not mean a particular existing thing"; but he is here distinguishing between fact and thing only as between sorts of existents, paralleling the distinction between sentences and names. Facts you can assert and deny; things you can name (p. 270). Both exist; 'thing' has ceased to be coextensive with 'existent'.

Russell in this 1918 essay acknowledges Wittgenstein's influence. Russell's ontology of facts here is a reminder of Wittgenstein, but a regrettable one. Wittgenstein thought in his *Tractatus* days that true sentences mirrored nature, and this notion led him to posit things in nature for true sentences to mirror; namely, facts.

Not that Wittgenstein started Russell on facts. Russell was urging a correspondence between facts and propositions in 1912,[6] when he first knew Wittgenstein; and he equates facts with true judgments as early, we saw, as 1904. Russell had his own reason for wanting facts as entities, and Wittgenstein abetted him.

Russell was receptive to facts as entities because of his tendency to conflate meaning with reference. Sentences, being meaningful, had to stand to some sort of appropriate entities in something fairly like the relation of naming. Propositions in a nonsentential sense were unavailable, having been repudiated; so facts seemed all the more needed. They do not exactly serve as references of false sentences, but they help. For each true or false sentence there *is* a fact, which the sentence asserts or denies according as the sentence is true or false. This two-to-one variety of reference became for Russell even a central trait distinguishing sentences from names, and so facts from things.[7]

Russell continued to champion facts, right through his *In-*

5. "Meinong's theory," p. 523.
6. *Problems of Philosophy*, pp. 198ff.
7. "Philosophy of logical atomism," pp. 187, 270.

quiry into Meaning and Truth and into *Human Knowledge,* 1948. In *Human Knowledge* the term applies not only to what true statements assert, but to more: "Everything that there is in the world I call a 'fact' " (p. 143).

Russell's predilection for a fact ontology depended, I suggested, on confusion of meaning with reference. Otherwise I think Russell would have made short shrift of facts. He would have been put off by what strikes a reader of "The Philosophy of Logical Atomism": how the analysis of facts rests on analysis of language. Anyway Russell does not admit facts as fundamental; atomic facts are atomic as facts go, but they are compound objects.[8] The atoms of Russell's logical atomism are not atomic facts but sense data.

In *Problems of Philosophy,* 1912, Russell had viewed both sense data and external objects as irreducible existents. We are acquainted with sense data beyond peradventure, he held, whereas our belief in external objects is fallible; still, speaking fallibly, both are real. Our belief in external objects is rooted in instinct, but it is rational of us, he held, to accept such dictates of instinct in the absence of counterevidence (p. 39). This cheerful resignation echoes Hume and harmonizes also with the current Oxford way of justifying scientific method: scientific method is part of what 'rational' means.

Two years later, in *Our Knowledge of the External World,* Russell was more sanguine. Here it was that sense data became logical atoms for the construction of the rest of the world. Already in *Problems* he had talked of private worlds of sense data and the public space of physics, and of their correlations. Now we find him using these correlations as a means of identifying external objects with classes of sense data. He identifies the external object with the class of all the views of it in private worlds, actual and ideal. In so doing he also pinpoints each of the private worlds as a point in public space.

It was a great idea. If executed with all conceivable success, it would afford translation of all discourse about the

---

8. "Philosophy of logical atomism," pp. 195f, 270; *Our Knowledge of the External World,* p. 54.

external world into terms of sense data, set theory, and logic. It would not settle induction, for we should still be in the position of predicting sense data from sense data. But it would settle the existence of external things. It would show that assumption superfluous, or prove it true; we could read the result either way.

It would neatly settle the ontology of the external world, by reducing it to that of the set theory of sense data. In *Our Knowledge of the External World*, moreover, Russell wrote as though he had eliminated classes, and not just reduced them to attributes (see pp. 224f); so he would have looked upon the project, if successful, as resting on an ontology of sense data alone (see p. 153). But by 1918 he thought better of this point, as witness the recognition of "qualities and relations . . . a whole hierarchy" lately quoted.

In *Our Knowledge of the External World* Russell expressed no confidence that the plan he sketched could be fully realized. In his sketch, as he remarked, he took other minds for granted; moreover, he broached none of the vast detail that would be needed for the further constructions, except for a few illustrative steps. But the illustrations gave a vivid sense that the concepts of *Principia Mathematica* could be helpful here and the many ingenious turns and strategies of construction that went into *Principia* could be imitated to advantage. A strategy much in evidence is definition by abstraction—what Whitehead came to call *extensive abstraction*, and Carnap *quasi-analysis*.

It was left to Carnap, in 1928, to be inspired to press the plan. Russell's intervening works, "The Philosophy of Logical Atomism," *Analysis of Matter*, and *Analysis of Mind* might in view of their titles have been expected to further it, but they did not. The dazzling sequel to *Our Knowledge of the External World* was rather Carnap's *Der logische Aufbau der Welt*. Carnap achieved remarkable feats of construction, starting with sense data and building explicitly, with full *Principia* techniques and *Principia* ingenuity, toward the external world. One must in the end despair of the full definitional reduction dreamed of in recent paragraphs, and it is one of the merits of the *Aufbau* that we can see from it where the obstacles lie. The worst obstacle seems to be that the assigning of sense qualities to public place-times has to be kept open to revision in the light of later experience, and so cannot be reduced to definition. The empiricist's regard for experience thus impedes the very program of reducing the world to experience.[9]

Russell meanwhile was warping his logical atomism over from its frankly phenomenalistic form to what, influenced by Perry and Holt, he called "neutral monism."[10] Neutrality here has a bias, as it often has in politics; Russell's neutral particulars are on the side of sense data. Still, a drift has begun, and it continues. It does not reach the physicalistic pole, even in *Human Knowledge;* but there is an increasing naturalism, an increasing readiness to see philosophy as natural science trained upon itself and permitted froo uoe of scientific findings. Russell had stated the basis for such an attitude already in 1914: "There is not any superfine brand of knowledge, obtainable by the philosopher, which can give us a standpoint from which to criticize the whole of the knowledge of daily life. The most that can be done is to examine and purify our common knowledge by an internal scrutiny, assuming the canons by which it has been obtained."[11]

9. This ironic way of putting the matter is due to Burton Drohen
10. Cf. *Analysis of Mind*, p. 25, *Analysis of Matter*, ch. 37.
11. *Our Knowledge of the External World*, p. 71.

On Austin's Method

Once there were but a handful of therapeutic positivists and a multitude of chronic metaphysicians. Now there are therapists in every college. The epidemic has been stemmed and the therapy is routine. How are the veteran therapists hereafter to occupy their minds? One way is by directing their efforts against a continuing but less virulent form of the infection, namely, against philosophical perplexity in the lay mind. Ryle in his *Dilemmas* had a successful go at this. Another way is by continuing the kind of language study that went into the therapy, but continuing it now as a line of pure research. Characteristic writings of Austin's seem to fit in here.

Austin's technique, as Urmson has described it in this symposium, is a mode of introspective inquiry into semantics, conducted by native speakers in groups. It is an inquiry that is continuous with portions of linguistics, and probably capable both of benefiting from professional work in that field and of supplementing it. Despite its philosophical antecedents, it is an inquiry whose affinities in linguistics are not in theoretical linguistics; they are in lexicography. It is an inquiry into subtle differences in the semantics, or circumstances of use, of selected English phrases.

Semantic theory is plagued by the lack of an acceptable

A résumé of this symposium paper appeared in the *Journal of Philosophy* 62 (1965), and the whole in K. T. Fann, ed., *Symposium on J. L. Austin* (London: Routledge, 1969).

general definition of meaning. A definition of meaning simply as circumstances of use is inadequate because of vagueness as to how much may relevantly be included under 'circumstances'. However, that general problem of demarcating the circumstances is a problem that plagues semantic theory and not lexicographic practice, or, in particular, Austin's kind of inquiry. As long as one limits oneself to volunteering specific circumstances of use of expressions, the problem of meaning does not arise. There is a certain immunity in the concrete case.

The nature of this immunity may be clarified by an analogy from proof theory. Consider the notion of a mechanical method. In order to prove or even clearly state Gödel's theorem of the incompletability of number theory, or Church's theorem of the undecidability of quantification theory, we have to define the notion of a mechanical method; and recursiveness was the answer. But in showing the decidability of a theory we need no definition of mechanical method; we just present a method which everyone would call mechanical. Similarly Austin was able to present specific circumstances of use without broaching the problem of meaning.

For that matter, the same can be said of what Carnap calls explication—the sort of conceptual reduction that figures prominently in the philosophy of mathematics and elsewhere. Each explication stands on its own merits, without broaching the general problem of synonymy or meaning. But I digress.

Austin's manner of semantic inquiry contrasts with main trends in linguistics in being avowedly introspective. Any linguist certainly introspects his language much of the time, but Austin was unusual in adhering to introspective data exclusively. Such data are said to be untrustworthy because of their subjectivity, but, as Urmson explained, Austin had an ingenious remedy for that: he gained objectivity by group introspection.

This remedy is an instance of a perhaps more widely useful strategy. In its general form the strategy consists in exploiting the subjective and then objectifying it afterward by a social summation over individual subjects. The strategy has uses also apart from the introspective situation. Thus suppose some exotic field linguist from overseas were here testing us to see what things we apply various terms to. He would find, by induction from sample tests, that each of us will apply the term 'pup' on sight to just the things to which each of us will apply 'young dog'. In this way he will discover that our terms 'pup' and 'young dog' are coextensive. But he could not, by that method, equate 'bachelor' with 'unmarried man'; for no two of us will even apply 'bachelor' on sight to all and only the same persons, let alone 'unmarried man', given our differences in acquaintance and information. However, our visiting linguist can still equate 'bachelor' with 'unmarried man' after all if he resorts to the strategy of first studying each subject in isolation and only afterward objectifying by a social summation. He will find that each of us will apply 'bachelor' just when *he* will apply 'unmarried man'.

Let me broach next the utterly boring question, as Urmson called it, of how to classify Austin's introspective semantics. Is it to be called philosophy? To call it that does not, from Austin's point of view as described by Urmson, say much about it; philosophy is "a heterogeneous set of enquiries." I applaud this casual attitude toward the demarcation of disciplines. Names of disciplines should be seen only as technical aids in the organization of curricula and libraries; a scholar is better known by the individuality of his problems than by the name of his discipline. If deans and librarians class some of his problems as philosophical, that is no reason for him to be concerned with other problems that they class as philosophical: his further concerns might just as well be problems that are classed as linguistic or mathematical. For that matter, naming disciplines even fosters philosophical error. To take the most glaring case, why do people insist on viewing all parts of physics, however theoretical, as in some degree empirical, and all parts of mathematics, however practical, as purely formal? No such contrast would emerge sentence by sentence, or problem by problem, without reference to the nominal demarcation of disciplines. But again I digress.

Does calling Austin's distinctive activity philosophical say *anything* about it? The one salient trait of philosophical inquiries, according to Austin as represented by Urmson, is that for want of standard methods they have not yet hived off under some special name. This criterion is not helpful. The want of standard methods in Austin's work is surely not so dire as to prevent its hiving off under the special name of linguistics.

Actually Austin's work has a genuine tie to philosophy, in a more substantial sense than just what hasn't hived off. It cames in his choice of idioms for analysis. He was no Baconian inductivist, amassing random samples of the world or of the dictionary and scanning them with untendentious eye for unpreconceived uniformities. The *arrière pensée* of *How to Do Things with Words* emerges toward the end of that book: it is "an inclination to play Old Harry with . . . (1) the true/false fetish, (2) the value/fact fetish" (p. 150).

That book would have been different, in respect of one of its avowed motives at any rate, if Austin had appreciated Tarski's work on truth. Ironically, I think it was overattention to a demarcation of disciplines that deprived him of Tarski's insights. It was overattention to the demarcation of the study of English usage. But this in turn was due, I think, to a basic impatience with philosophical perplexity.

There are two ways of rising to problems. Thus take the perturbations of Mercury. I suppose that before Einstein some astronomers pondered these with an eager curiosity, hoping that they might be a key to important traits of nature hitherto undetected, while other astronomers saw in them a vexatious anomaly and longed to see how to explain them away in terms of instrumental error. Attitudes toward philosophical problems vary similarly, and Austin's was of the negative kind. Hence his tendency to limit a philosophical venture to the study of word usage; for language criticism was the method of therapeutic positivism, the method of the *Ueberwindung der Metaphysik*.

What counts as true even for Tarski's theory of truth is language, granted. But the value of Tarski's theory stands forth only if at the second level, talking *of* truth, we look beyond language to logic.

In his scintillating essay "Truth," Austin himself went

part way down Tarski's path. In a footnote he even cited Tarski's paradigm, " 'It is raining' is true if and only if it is raining," and commented: "So far so good." Then he looked into usage to add to the story. Tarski, in contrast, concentrated on the mathematical significance of his paradigm. For all its surface triviality, the paradigm is quickly shown to have extraordinary powers. For one thing, it suffices, of itself, to determine truth uniquely. If there are two truth predicates 'True$_1$' and 'True$_2$', both fulfilling the paradigm, then the two are coextensive. More remarkable still, as Tarski showed, not even one truth predicate can quite fulfill the paradigm, on pain of contradiction. Yet, as he went on to show in the more laborious stretches of his "Wahrheitsbegriff," a predicate fulfilling the paradigm can after all be constructed suitable to any preassigned language that is fixed in vocabulary and formal in its logical structure, provided that we bring to the construction certain set-theoretic aids from beyond the bounds of the preassigned language itself. A conclusion that follows from all this is the openness of set theory: for each consistent set theory there is a stronger. This follows also from Gödel's work; and Tarski's work strikingly illuminates Gödel's.

The problem of the perturbations of Mercury turned out to be one of the keys to the relativity of space and time, and the problem of truth turned out to be one of the keys to the relativity of set theories.

I quoted Austin as saying that *How to Do Things with Words* was prompted in part by an animus against the true/false fetish. Yet the relevance of the book to the fetish is not clear, if we think of truth in terms of Tarski's paradigm. The paradigm works for evaluations, after all, as Smart has noticed (1965), as well as for statements of fact. And it works equally for performatives. 'Slander is evil' is true if and only if slander is evil, and 'I bid you good morning' is true of us on a given occasion if and only if, on that occasion, I bid you good morning. A performative is a notable sort of utterance, I grant; it makes itself true; but then it is true. There are good reasons for contrasting and comparing performatives and statements of fact, but an animus against the true/false fetish is not one of them.

Developments in *How to Do Things with Words* that were prompted directly or indirectly by Austin's animus against the true/false fetish are best understood rather as explorations of the gulf between sentence and statement. His work on this will doubtless be continued by others. As for "the value/fact fetish," his work seems rather to depict the intertwining of value and fact than to discredit the distinction—though someone may discredit it. Anyway his inclination to play Old Harry with those two fetishes has issued in perceptive work that should be relevant to the philosophy of law and other domains.

Historians of science tell us that science forges ahead not by an indiscriminate Baconian inductivism but by pursuing preconceptions, even mistaken ones. I see in Austin's work this kind of progress.

10

Smart's Philosophy and Scientific Realism

The Oxford-style philosopher, so influential nowadays, turns his good ear to the dictates of unspoiled common sense and his other to science. Historians of science itself, not to be outdone, take to belittling the force of evidence and saying how fashion spins the plot. Even leading quantum physicists have been known to impute reality primarily to ordinary things, their experimental equipment, as against the diminutive objects of their theory.

In refreshing contrast, South Australia's professor of philosophy J. J. C. Smart propounds in *Philosophy and Scientific Realism* "an unashamedly realistic view of the fundamental particles of physics . . . Indeed," he pursues, "I would wish to go further than merely to defend the physicist's picture of the world as an ontologically respectable one. I would wish to urge that the physicist's language gives us a *truer* picture of the world than does the language of ordinary common sense" (pp. 18, 47). With science dominating our lives and progressing ever faster on ever more frontiers, it is strange that such a view needs urging. Strange but true.

In fact, Smart declares not just for science but for physics. There have been materialists who held that living things,

Reprinted with permission from *The New York Review of Books*, July 9, 1964. Copyright © 1964 Nyrev, Inc.

though material, were subject to biological and psychological laws that were irreducible in principle to laws of physics. Such was the materialism of emergence. Smart's materialism is more robust.

Seeing how right-minded the book is, how congenial to one's own way of thinking, one expects its value to lie rather in persuading others than in instructing oneself. But on this score there are pleasant surprises. One of them comes on the heels of Smart's denial of emergence in biology and psychology. "Not only do I deny the existence of emergent laws and properties," he writes (p. 52), "but I even deny that in biology and psychology there are laws in the strict sense at all." The propositions of biology and psychology are local generalizations about some terrestrial growths of our acquaintance. In principle they are on a par with natural history and geography, or with consumers' reports. This is true, he urges, even of propositions about cell division. If they "are made universal in scope, then such laws are very likely not universally true. If they are not falsified by some queer species or phenomenon on earth they are very likely falsified elsewhere in the universe. The laws of physics, by contrast, seem to be truly universal" (pp. 54f).

Biology runs deeper, he grants, than cell division. There are the chromosome, the virus, the gene, nucleic acid, and the genetic code. Propositions on these matters are presumably broader in scope, admittedly more theoretical, and potentially more explanatory than other propositions in biology. Just so; and they are more nearly physico-chemical.

Physics investigates the essential nature of the world, and bioliogy describes a local bump. Psychology, human psychology, describes a bump on the bump. Remarkable it is, and a matter of philosophical bemusement down the ages, that some parochial sensory responses and thought processes up in that bump of a bump should be equal to the physicist's business of encompassing the essential nature of the world. It takes an ingenious bit of triangulating from way off center.

This reflection goes well with a point that Smart makes about color. Color dominates our sensory experience; things that contrast in color are emphatically in contrast. Yet, and here is Smart's point, color differences seldom bear interestingly upon physical laws. The reason is that a mixed color can look to us like a pure one, and yet its looking like that pure one hinges on special mechanisms in us which could be otherwise and perhaps are otherwise in other creatures. "Extraterrestrial beings could be expected to have a similar concept of length or electric charge to ours, but we would not expect their colour concepts, supposing they had any, to correspond to ours in any simple manner . . . To see the world *sub specie aeternitatis* . . . we must eschew the concepts of colour and other secondary qualities" (p. 84).

It is along this line that Smart makes sense of the traditional philosophical distinction between primary and secondary qualities, and simultaneously accounts for its importance. The primary qualities—length, shape, weight, hardness, and the like—are the ones that enter most simply into physical laws.

Largely the book is given over to standard topics of controversy: physicalism versus phenomenalism, the mind-body problem, man the machine, freedom and responsibility, the reality of the future. I have hinted how the first one comes out: physicalism wins. For arguments the reader is referred to the book, and Godspeed. In each of these further confrontations likewise, as the reader will have begun to guess, right wins out: the body, the machine, responsibility, the future.

In the mind-body affair it is restful to see mental states identified unapologetically with bodily ones, and no semantic hedging. There are answers, simply, to stock objections.

On man as machine, latter-day antimechanists have invoked Gödel's theorem, which says that no formal proof procedure can encompass number theory. Smart, defending a mechanistic view, takes issue with this rather wistful application of Gödel's great theorem. Where man rises above the limitations of formal proof procedure, Smart suggests, is in the informal and largely inconclusive maneuvers of scientific method; and a computing machine could in principle be programmed to do the same.

Smart agrees with Hobbes that freedom and determinism are not antithetical; determined acts count as free when mediated through the agent in certain ways. The division of acts into some for which a man is regarded as responsible, and others for which he is not, is part of the social apparatus of reward and punishment: responsibility is allocated where rewards and punishments have tended to work as incentives and deterrents.

Such, in important part, is the use of "he could." There is also another use, as Smart observes: one which is on a par with "it could," as in "it could have broken." He links this use to incompleteness of information regarding the causal circumstances. I applaud this as a general attitude toward the modalities of possibility and necessity; they turn upon our own abstraction from particulars, for instance through our ignorance of them, rather than upon the nature of the world.

There is a conception, which Smart scouts, of the present moment as advancing through time at an inexorable pace of sixty seconds per minute. There is a notion also that sentences about the future are as yet neither true nor false, and that otherwise fatalism would reign and striving would be useless. These confusions are popular and in part Aristotelian. In the writings of Donald Williams (pp. 262–307) and others they have been set to rights with all clarity. Still, Smart adds distinctive touches in setting them to rights again. There incidentally emerges in the course of this exposition an arresting contrast between probability and truth. "Probable," he brings out, is an *indicator* word like 'I,' 'you,' 'now,' 'then,' 'here,' 'there': a word whose reference depends on the occasion of its use. For a statement of specific fact is true once and for all, if at all, whether we know it or not, but even so it may be more or less probable from occasion to occasion. The modality of probability ends up thus in a limbo of subjectivity, where the modalities of possibility and necessity just preceded it.

The book is couched in words unminced though uncontentious. A tendency to mince, in such right-minded writings, may be due in part to writers' awareness that people think these ideas are morally pernicious. But Smart handles this moral dilemma rather by taking it by the horns, in five final pages on materialism and values. I am happy to report that the materialist gains his moral victory hands down.

11

Goodman's Ways of Worldmaking

Ways of Worldmaking is a congeries. Not indeed an incongruous congeries, as of congers and costermongers, but withal a congeries to conjure with. For all its slenderness it offers us a philosophy of style, a philosophy of quotation, a philosophy of art, a philosophy of optical illusion, and a philosophy of nature. It is this last that packages the lot and gives it a name. The looseness of the package is in keeping with the philosophy that assembles it; for the doctrine is that there are many worlds, none all-embracing.

There is currently a Leibniz revival that has philosophers luxuriating in a continuum of possible worlds. One sterling virtue of Nelson Goodman's philosophy is that it is no part of that. Goodman means all his worlds to be actual. Proceeding then to try to penetrate what one hopes is a figure of speech, one finds that where the purported multiplicity really lies is not so much in worlds as in versions: world versions. I cannot quite say versions of the world, for Goodman holds that there is no one world for them to be versions of. He would sooner settle for the versions and let the world or worlds go by.

His doctrine rests partly on an appreciation of the creative component in natural science. Even the most rudimen-

Reprinted with permission from *The New York Review of Books*, November 23, 1978. Copyright © 1978 Nyrev, Inc.

tary of scientific laws is a generalization beyond the instances observed. There are divergent ways of generalizing from the same observations; some ways relatively simple, others arbitrarily gerrymandered.

We settle tentatively on the simplest one, but we may be forced off it by later observations. Even in observation itself there is a creative component: we overlook features irrelevant to our concerns, we perceive broad forms and gloss over discontinuities, we round out and round off. And at the other extreme, in the high flights of theoretical physics, man's creativity is overwhelming. Physical theory is indeed uncannily successful in the corroborations that it predicts and in the power over nature that it confers, but even so it is ninety-nine parts conceptualization to one part observation. May there not be some radically alternative conceptual structure, undreamt of, that would fit all the past observations and all the predicted ones equally well, and yet be untranslatable into our scheme? Our own physical theory and that one would be two world versions, equally sound. Two versions of *the* world? But what world is that? To describe it we must retreat into one or the other version; they share no neutral description. Recognize the two versions, Goodman says, and leave it at that.

This much will already estrange many of Goodman's readers. Not me. But then he presses on where I falter. Another world version that he treats with respect is the commonsense one which depicts a world not of atoms and electrons and nuclear particles but of sticks, stones, people, and other coarse objects. He sees further world versions, more fragmentary, in the styles of various painters. Thus he contrasts the world of Rembrandt with the world of Rouault and the world of Picasso. Shunning even the restraints of representational art, he forges on to abstract painting and to music: here again are world versions in their lesser ways. How, when they depict nothing? Well, they refer in another way: they stand as *samples* of interesting strains or qualities. There is a significant continuity, Goodman argues, between exemplification and depiction as well as between depiction and description.

One feels that this sequence of worlds or versions founders

in absurdity. I take Goodman's defense of it to be that there is no reasonable intermediate point at which to end it. I would end it after the first step: physical theory. I grant the possibility of alternative physical theories, insusceptible to adjudication; but I see the rest of his sequence of worlds or world versions only as a rather tenuous metaphor.

Why, Goodman asks, this special deference to physical theory? This is a good question, and part of its merit is that it admits of a good answer. The answer is not that everything worth saying can be translated into the technical vocabulary of physics; not even that all good science can be translated into that vocabulary. The answer is rather this: nothing happens in the world, not the flutter of an eyelid, not the flicker of a thought, without some redistribution of microphysical states. It is usually hopeless and pointless to determine just what microphysical states lapsed and what ones supervened in the event, but some reshuffling at that level there had to be; physics can settle for no less. If the physicist suspected there was any event that did not consist in a redistribution of the elementary states allowed for by his physical theory, he would seek a way of supplementing his theory. Full coverage in this sense is the very business of physics, and only of physics.

Anyone who will say, "Physics is all very well in its place" —and who will not?—is then already committed to a physicalism of at least the nonreductive, nontranslational sort stated above. Hence my special deference to physical theory as a world version, and to the physical world as the world.

Component essays in Goodman's congeries are rewarding quite apart from the polycosmic motif that strings them together. There is a bright one on samples, which dramatizes in deft parables the relation of sample to purpose. A swatch represents its bolt in point of texture, pattern, and color, but, unlike a sample cupcake, it deviates in size and shape. But a swatch can also be used to exemplify swatches; and then, he observes, its size and shape count for much and its particular texture, pattern, and color for little.

The chapter on quotation explores the possibility of analogues of quotation, direct and indirect, in painting and music. Goodman finds that depictions of picture frames will

not quite do as analogues of quotations marks, and that indirect quotation has better affinities in painting than direct.
Both sorts of quotation come off badly in music. The reasons
he gives for these similarities and contrasts afford some
worthwhile semantical insights.

The chapter on perception begins with the familiar illusion induced by closely paired flashes, which the eye per-
ceives as a single moving light. Remarkable variations of
this phenomenon are then reported, stemming from experiments by Paul Kolers. Illusions can be created of elaborate
permutations of position along quite unexpected lines, ac-
companied by changes of shape. Analogous affects are not
obtainable in the case of changes of color, and Goodman
offers an ingenious and convincing reason why they should
not be.

In his chapter on art he dismisses the traditional problem
of defining a work of art. He shows that the notion is hopelessly entangled with the fancied distinction in metaphysics
between internal and external relations, between intrinsic
and extrinsic, between essence and accident, which he laud-
ably rejects. He finds more significance in describing the
circumstances in which a thing functions as art; and it is as
a means to this venture that his discussion of swatches and
other samples fits in.

There are engaging passages. The scientist

seeks systems, simplicity, scope; and when satisfied on these scores
he tailors the truth to fit . . . He as much decrees as discovers the
laws he sets forth, as much designs as discerns the patterns he
delineates.

. . . we must distinguish falsehood and fiction from truth and
fact; but we cannot, I am sure, do it on the ground that fiction is
fabricated and fact found.

. . . the philosopher like the philanderer is always finding himself stuck with none or too many.

How can anyone this sensitive to words have coined
'acquacentric'? Why the Italian, or indeed anything to do
with Latin, when he could have played 'hydrocentric'
straight?

12

On the Individuation
of Attributes

For a while I propose to treat tolerantly of attributes, or
properties. Usually I have taken a harsher line. Classes,
down the years, I have grudgingly admitted; attributes not.
I have felt that if I must come to terms with Platonism, the
least I can do is keep it extensional. For this brief space,
however, it will be convenient to keep the question of the
existence of attributes in abeyance, or even to talk as if
they existed.

Attributes are classes with a difference. That is, corresponding to one and the same class there may be several
different attributes. The point is that no two classes have
exactly the same members, but two different attributes may
be attributes of exactly the same things. Classes are identical
when their members are identical; such is the principle of individuation of classes. On the other hand, attributes, I have
often complained, have no clear principle of individuation.

Faulty individuation has nothing to do with vagueness of
boundaries. We are accustomed to tolerating vagueness of
boundaries. We have little choice in the matter. The boundaries of a desk are vague when we get down to the fine structure, because the clustering of the molecules grades off; the

Reprinted from A. R. Anderson, R. B. Marcus, and R. M. Martin, eds.,
The Logical Enterprise: Essays for Frederick B. Fitch (New Haven:
Yale University Press, 1975).

allegiance of any particular peripheral molecule is indeterminate, as between the desk and the atmosphere. However, this vagueness of boundaries detracts none from the sharpness of our *individuation* of desks and other physical objects. What the vagueness of boundaries amounts to is this: there are many almost identical physical objects, almost coextensive with one another, and differing only in the inclusion or exclusion of various peripheral molecules. Any one of these almost coextensive objects could serve as the desk, and no one the wiser; such is the vagueness of the desk. Nevertheless they *all* have their impeccable principle of individuation; physical objects are identical if and only if coextensive. Where coextensiveness is not quite fully *verifiable*, neither is identity, but the identity is still well *defined*, though the desk is not. Specification is one thing, individuation another. Physical objects are well individuated, whatever else they are not. We know what it takes to distinguish them, even where we cannot detect it.

It then follows that the classes of physical objects are well individuated too, since their identity consists simply in the identity of the members. But what, on the other hand, is the principle of individuation of attributes? Thus grant me that any creature with a heart has kidneys and vice versa. The class of hearted creatures and the class of kidneyed creatures are identical. Still, we are not prepared to identify the attribute of heartedness with that of kidneyedness. Coextensiveness of attributes is not enough. What more, then, is wanted?

I forget who it was—let me call him Zedsky—that offered an interestingly exasperating answer to this question. The necessary and sufficient condition for identity of attributes is quite as clear, he contended, as the notions of class and member—notions with which I evidently have no quarrel. For we have only to look to Russell's general definition of identity, which explains identity for attributes and anything else. In general, objects x and y are identical if and only if they are members of just the same classes. So attributes, in particular, are identical if and only if they are members of exactly the same classes of attributes. This of course is an exasperating defense; but it is interesting to consider why.

We might object to Zedsky's answer in the following way. He says that attributes are identical when the classes that they belong to are identical. But when are such classes identical? They are classes of attributes. They are identical when their members are identical; that was the principle of individuation of classes. It was a good principle of individuation of classes of physical objects, since we had a good prior standard of identity of physical objects. But it is useless for classes of attributes; we cannot appeal to identity of the members, failing a prior standard of individuation of attributes, these being the members. Zedsky is evidently caught in a circle, individuating attributes in terms of identity of classes whose individuation depends on that of attributes.

Zedsky might answer in turn by protesting that the Russellian definition which he is applying to attributes does not really mention identity of classes. When expressed in words it seems to do so: attributes are identical when the classes that they belong to are identical. But it is simpler in symbols, and says nothing of identity of classes. What is required in order that attributes A and B be identical is simply that (z) $(A \epsilon z . \equiv . B \epsilon z)$. This formula contains only the single variable 'z' for classes of attributes, and no mention of identity.

What this shows is that we must look a little deeper. The real reason why the formula does not clarify the individuation of attributes is not that it mentions identity of classes of attributes, but that it mentions classes of attributes at all. We have an acceptable notion of class, or physical object, or attribute, or any other sort of object, only insofar as we have an acceptable principle of individuation for that sort of object. There is no entity without identity. But the individuation of classes of attributes depends, we saw, on the individuation of attributes. This, then, is why we are not satisfied with an account of the individuation of attributes which, like Zedsky's, depends on the notion of classes of attributes at all.

These thoughts on attributes remind us that classes themselves are satisfactorily individuated only in a relative sense. They are as satisfactorily individuated as their members.

Classes of physical objects are well individuated; so also, therefore, are classes of classes of physical objects; and so on up. Classes of attributes, on the other hand, are as badly off as attributes. The notion of a class of things makes no better sense than the notion of those things.

We may do well, with this relativism in mind, to cast an eye on the credentials of set theory. It turns out that the usual systems of set theory still stand up to the demands of individuation very well, if we assume that the ground elements or individuals of the system are physical objects or other well-individuated things rather than ill-individuated things such as attributes. For, we saw how classes of well-individuated things are well individuated; therefore so are classes of such classes; and so on up.

This takes care of the usual systems of set theory, which exclude *ungrounded* classes. A class is ungrounded if it has some member which has some member which . . . and so on downward *ad infinitum*, never reaching bottom. The system of my "New Foundations"[1] does have ungrounded classes, and so does the system of my *Mathematical Logic;* and it could be argued that for such classes there is no satisfactory individuation. They are identical if their members are identical, and these are identical if *their* members are identical, and there is no stopping. This, then, is a point in favor of the systems that bar ungrounded classes.

Our reflections on individuation have brought out a curious comparison of three grades of stringency. We can never quite specify the desk, from among various nearly coincident physical objects, because of vagueness at the edges. Yet its individuation, we saw, was quite in order. And we saw further that though with Zedsky we can define identity for attributes by applying Russell's general definition, still the individuation of attributes is not in order. These examples suggest that specification makes the most stringent demands, individuation is less stringent, and mere definition of identity is less stringent still.

I think I have adequately explained why Zedsky's account of the identity of attributes does not solve the problem of

their individuation. But it may be worthwhile still, for the
sake of a shift of perspective, to answer Zedsky again along
a somewhat different line. For this we must consider sentences. How do we ever actually specify any particular attribute *or* any particular class? Or, for that matter, any
particular proposition? Ordinarily, basically, we do so by
citing an appropriate sentence. For specifying an attribute
or a class it will be an open sentence, like '*x* has a heart,' giving the attribute of heartedness and the class of the hearted.
For specifying a proposition it will be a closed sentence. Attributes, classes, and propositions are what we may call, in
a word, *epiphrastic*. I am not saying that these entities are
somehow ontologically dependent on sentences, or even that
sentences can be formulated to fit all attributes or classes or
propositions. I am saying how one ordinarily proceeds when
one does succeed, if at all, in specifying any one attribute or
class or proposition.

   This being the case, the question of individuation of attributes becomes in practice a question of how to tell whether
two open sentences express the same attribute. How should
the two sentences be related? We may object to Zedsky that
while his citation of Russell defines identity of attributes,
it does not say how two sentences should be related in order
to express an identical attribute. However, this objection
needs tightening; he can rise to the new demand. By an easy
adaptation of Russell's definition he can tell us how two sentences should be related. Thus let us represent the two sentences as '*Fx*' and '*Gx*', open sentences as they are. For '*Fx*'
and '*Gx*' to express the same attribute, then, Zedsky can tell
us, all that is required is that the attribute of being an *x*
such that *Fx*, and the attribute of being an *x* such that *Gx*,
belong to the same classes of attributes. In this rejoinder,
Zedsky would simply be repeating the frustrating old Russell definition, but stretching it so as to squeeze the sentences
'*Fx*' and '*Gx*' in, and thus meet our demand for a relation between sentences. Sentences '*Fx*' and '*Gx*' express the same
attribute, so Zedsky would be telling us, just in case those
sentences are so related that $(z) (x[Fx] \; \epsilon \; z \; . \equiv . \; x[Gx] \; \epsilon \; z)$.

   What can we say to this? We have a pat answer, which we
can carry over from the earlier argument. This is unsatis-

factory in individuating attributes because, again, it assumes prior intelligibility of the notion of a class z of attributes. Indeed this is doubly unsatisfactory, for it assumes the notion of attribute also in the abstraction notation '$x[\quad]$', 'the attribute of being an x such that'.

So we now see that when we ask for a relation of sentences that will individuate attributes, we must require that the relation be expressed without mention of attributes. The notion of attribute is intelligible only insofar as we already know its principle of individuation.

Observe, in contrast, how well the corresponding requirement is met in the individuation of classes. I began by saying that classes are identical when their members are identical; but what we now want is a satisfactory formulation of a relation between two open sentences 'Fx' and 'Gx' which holds if and only if 'Fx' and 'Gx' determine the same class. The desired formulation is of course immediate: it is simply '$(x)(Fx \equiv Gx)$'. It does not talk of classes; it does not use class abstraction or epsilon, and it does not presuppose classes as values of variables. It is as pure as the driven snow. Classes, whatever their foibles, are the very model of individuation on this approach.

Can we do anything similar for attributes? Some say we can. Open sentences 'Fx' and 'Gx' express the same attribute, they say, if and only if they entail each other; if and only if the biconditional formed from them is analytic. Or, to put the matter into modal logic, the requirement is that $(x)\square(Fx \equiv Gx)$. Thus formulated, the requirement for identity of attributes is the same as the requirement for the identity of classes, but with the necessity operator inserted. For my part, however, I find this sort of account unsatisfactory because of my doubts over the notion of analyticity—to say nothing of modal logic.

Propositions are of course on a par with attributes. Two closed sentences are said to express the same proposition when they entail each other; when their biconditional is analytic, or holds necessarily. And I find the account similarly unsatisfactory.

I have contrasted classes with attributes in point of individuation. But I must stress that this is their only contrast. I must stress this fact because I have lately come to appreciate, to my surprise, that an old tendency still persists among philosophers to regard classes and attributes as radically unlike. It persists as an unarticulated feeling. I have been unable to elicit clear theses on the point, but I think I have sensed the association of ideas.

There seems to be an unarticulated feeling that a class is best given by enumeration. For large classes this is impossible, granted; but still it is felt that you know a class only insofar as you know its members. But may we not say equally that you know an attribute only insofar as you know what things have it? Well, the two cases are felt to differ. One cause of this feeling is perhaps an unconscious misreading of the principle that a class is "determined" by its members: as if to say that to find the class you must find its members. All it really means for classes to be determined by their members is that classes are the same that have the same members.

There seems, moreover, to be an unarticulated feeling that a class of widely dispersed objects is itself widely extended in the world, unwieldy, and hard to envisage. One cause of this feeling is perhaps an unconscious misreading of 'extension' or 'extensional'. The feeling is encouraged, and also evinced, by the use of such words as 'aggregate' to explain the notion of class, as if classes were concrete heaps or swarms. Indeed, the word 'class' itself, as if to say a fleet of ships, originated in this attitude. Likewise the word 'set'.

In contrast to all this, there is no reluctance to recognize that an attribute is normally specified by presenting an open sentence or predicate. The readiness to recognize this for attributes, despite not recognizing it for classes, is due perhaps to an unconscious tendency to confuse attributes with locutions, predicates. Indeed 'predicate' has notoriously been used in both senses, as was 'propositional function'. Attributes are thus associated with sentential conditions, while classes are associated with rosters or with heaps and swarms.

I am driven thus to psychological speculation as my only means of combatting the false contrast of class and attribute, because this misconception does not stand forth as an explicit thesis to refute. It is a serious misconception still, for it leads some philosophers to prefer attributes to classes, as somehow clear or more natural, even when they do not propose to distinguish between coextensive attributes. Let us recognize rather that if we are always to count coextensive attributes as identical, attributes *are* classes. Let us recognize that classes, like attributes, are abstract and immaterial, and that classes, like attributes, are epiphrastic. You specify a class not by its members but by its membership condition, its open sentence. Any proper reason to prefer attributes to classes must hinge only on distinctions between coextensive attributes.

Such distinctions are indeed present and called for in modal logic. Also, as we saw, the acceptance of modal logic carries with it the acceptance of a way of individuating attributes. Anyone who rejects this way of individuating attributes also rejects modal logic, as I do. Now it may be supposed that the only use of attributes is in model logic. If this supposition is true, there is no individuation problem for attributes; either we accept the individuation given by modal logic or we reject modal logic and so have no need of attributes. However, this supposition is uncertain; there may be a call for attributes independent of modal logic. Perhaps they are wanted in a theory of causality. In this event the problem of the individuation of attributes remains with us.

In an essay of 1958 called "Speaking of Objects,"[2] I raised the question whether we might just acquiesce in the faulty individuation of attributes and propositions by treating them as twilight entities, only real enough to be talked of in a few limited contexts, excluding the identity context. The plan is rather reminiscent of Frege on propositional functions. For his propositional functions may well be seen as attributes, and he accorded them only a shadowy existence: they were *ungesättigt*. It is a question of moderating the maxim "No entity without identity" to allow half-entity without identity. I raised the question in passing and remarked only that such a course would require some refashioning of logic. I propose now to explore the matter a bit further.

If we continue to speak of attributes as members of classes,

2. Reprinted in *Ontological Relativity*, pp. 1–25.

then we cannot dodge the question of identity of attributes. For given this much, we can coherently ask whether attributes A and B belong to all the same classes, and to ask this is to ask whether they are identical, even failing any *satisfactory* principle of individuation. If, therefore, we are to waive individuation for attributes, we must disallow class membership on the part of attributes.

In set theory, then, we find a possible candidate for the office of attribute, namely, *ultimate classes*. The phrase is mine, but the notion goes back to von Neumann, 1925. Some historians claim to find it already in Julius König, 1905, and even in Cantor, 1899; but this hinges on a question of interpretation.[3] Anyway, an ultimate class is a class that does not belong to any classes. In *Mathematical Logic* I called them nonelements. Often in the literature they are called proper classes. This perverse terminology has its etiology: they are classes *proper* as opposed to sets. But it *is* perverse; 'ultimate' is more suggestive.

The admitting of ultimate classes is one of the various ways of avoiding the antinomies of set theory, such as Russell's paradox. In the face of ultimate classes we can no longer ask, with Russell, about the class of all those classes that are not members of themselves. Since ultimate classes are members of none, the nearest we can come to Russell's paradoxical class is the class of all those *sets*, or nonultimate classes, that are not members of themselves. This is an ultimate class, and not a member of itself, and there is no contradiction.

Such was the purpose of ultimate classes. Russell avoided the antinomies by means rather of his theory of types, of course, and did not have the notion of an ultimate class. Still this notion induces, retroactively, some nostalgic reverberations also in Russell's writings. Away back in *Principles of Mathematics* Russell was exercised over the class as many and the class as one. The ultimate class, had he seen it, he might have seen as a class that existed only as many and not as one. Or, again, recall Russell's introduction to the second edition of Whitehead and Russell's *Principia Mathematica*.

---

3. See my *Set Theory and Its Logic*, p. 302.

There, influenced by Wittgenstein's *Tractatus*, Russell entertained the maxim that "a propositional function occurs only through its values." This echoes Frege on the *ungesättigt*. It is not clear how to make a coherent general doctrine of this maxim, without giving up general set theory. But the maxim does nicely fit the notion of an ultimate class. Being capable only of having members and not of being members, ultimate classes may be likened to propositional functions that occur only through their values.

Ultimate classes had as their purpose the avoidance of the antinomies, but perhaps we can now put them to another purpose: to serve as attributes. Ultimate classes are incapable of being members, and so are not captured by identity as Russell defines it; and identity conditions were all that stood between class and attribute. Reviving Russell's phrases, we can say that an attribute is a class as many, while a set is a class as one. An attribute is a propositional function that occurs only through its values.

Russell's definition of identity, however, now needs reconsideration. Membership on the part of ultimate classes has not been degrammaticized; it is merely denied. Hence Russell's definition of identity *can* be applied to ultimate classes, and it gives an absurd result: ultimate classes are all members of exactly the same classes, namely none, and are hence all identical—despite differing in their members. But here we are merely faced with the known and obvious fact that that definition of identity does not work for theories that admit objects belonging to no classes.

There *is* a way of constructing a suitable definition of identity within *any* theory, even a theory in which there is no talk of class and member at all. It is the method of exhaustion of the lexicon of predicates. A trivial example will remind you of how it runs. Suppose we have just two primitive one-place predicates '*F*' and '*G*', and one two-place predicate '*H*', and no constant singular terms or functors; just quantifiers and truth functions. Then we can define '$x = y$' as

$$Fx \equiv Fy \, . \, Gx \equiv Gy \, . \, (z)(Hxz \equiv Hyz \, . \, Hzx \equiv Hzy),$$

thus providing substitutivity in atomic contexts. The full logic of identity can be derived. The method obviously extends to any finite lexicon of primitive predicates, and it defines, every time, genuine identity or an indistinguishable facsimile: indistinguishable within the terms of the theory concerned.

We have just now run a curious course. In order to shield attributes from the identity question, we tried to shield them from membership in classes, such being Russell's definition of identity. But in so doing, and thus likening attributes to ultimate classes, we have disqualified Russell's definition of identity and thus nullified our motivation.

In conclusion let us briefly consider, then, how attributes must fare under our generalized approach to identity by exhaustion of predicates. Let us vaguely assume a rich, all-purpose lexicon of predicates, no mere trio of predicates as in the last example. Certain of these predicates will be desirable in application to attributes. One such is the two-place predicate 'has'; we want to be able to speak of an object as having an attribute. Many other predicates will be useless in application to attributes; thus it would be false, at best, to affirm, and useless, at best, to deny, that an attribute is pink or divisible by four. Ryle branded such predications category mistakes; he declared them meaningless and so did Russell in his theory of types. So did Carnap.

Over the years I have represented a minority of philosophers who preferred the opposite line: we can simplify grammar and logic by minimizing the number of our grammatical categories and maximizing their size. Instead of agreeing with Carnap that it is meaningless to say 'This stone is thinking about Vienna', and with Russell that it is meaningless to say 'Quadruplicity drinks procrastination', we can accommodate these sentences as meaningful and trivially false. Stones simply never think, as it happens, and quadruplicity never drinks.

For our present inquiry into attributes, however, we are bound to take rather the line of Ryle, Russell, and Carnap. We must separate the serious predications from the silly ones. We must think in terms of a many-sorted logic with many sorts of variables, some of which are grammatically attachable to some predicates and some to others. Then we can look to that partial lexicon of just those predicates that are attachable to attribute variables and to attribute names; and we can proceed to define identity of attributes by exhaustion of just those predicates. If we keep those predicates to just the ones that may seriously and usefully be affirmed of attributes, and denied of attributes, then the identity relation defined by exhaustion of those predicates should be just right for attributes.

Stated less cumbersomely, what we are seeking as an identity relation of attributes is a relation which assures interchangeability, *salva veritate*, in all contexts that are worthwhile for attribute variables. Let us try, then, to name a few such contexts. One conspicuous one we have named is the context 'has'. On the other hand, a context that is still unwelcome, presumably, is the membership context: we do not want to recognize the question of membership of attributes in classes. For if membership of attributes in classes were accepted, we could again apply Russell's shortcut definition of identity, and so again we would have identity of attributes without any instructive principle of individuation. For that matter, even the 'has' context is presumably welcome only when the mention of attributes is restricted to the right-hand side; for we do not want to recognize attributes of attributes. If we recognized them, we could say that attributes are identical when they have all the same attributes, and so again we would have identity of attributes without any instructive principle of individuation. For the same reason, of course, a primitive predicate of identity would be an unwelcome context for attribute variables; and so would contexts where attributes are counted. Thus we should be prepared, at least until solving our identity problem, to abstain from saying that Napoleon had all the attributes of a great general save one—though remaining free to say that Napoleon had all the attributes of a great general.

This last example, of course, mentions attributes only in the same old 'has' context. *Are* there other desirable contexts, or are all desirable contexts of attribute variables parasitic on 'has' and reducible to it by paraphrase?

In the latter event, our definition of identity of attributes by exhaustion of lexicon is the work of a moment. The relevant lexicon is meager indeed, having 'has' as its only member; and thus attributes come out identical if exactly the same things *have* them. In this event, attributes are extensional; we might as well read 'has' as membership, and call attributes classes; but they are classes as many, not as one, for we are declaring it ungrammatical to represent them as members of further classes. They occur only through their values. They are ultimate classes, except that now we do not deny their membership in other classes; we degrammaticize it. Some set-theorists, Bernays among them,[4] have already taken this line with ultimate classes too.

If on the other hand there are desirable contexts of attribute variables that do not reduce to 'has', then let us have a list of them in the form of a list of appropriate primitive predicates of attributes. Given the list, we know how to define identity of attributes in terms of it. It should be possible to produce the list, and thus to individuate attributes, if attributes really serve any good purpose not served by classes.

4. See my *Set Theory and Its Logic*, p. 313. On identifying attributes with ultimate classes see Geach, *Logic Matters*, p. 233.

13

Intensions Revisited

For the necessity predicate, as distinct from the necessity functor 'Ц', I shall write 'Nec'. I affirm it of a sentence, to mean that the sentences is a necessary truth, or, if one like, analytic. Whatever its shortcomings in respect of clear criteria, the predicate is more comfortable than the sentence functor, for it occasions no departure from extensional logic. Hence there would be comfort in being able to regard '□' as mere shorthand for 'Nec' and a pair of quotation marks— thus '□(9 is odd)' for 'Nec '9 is odd' '. But it will not do. In modal logic one wants to quantify into necessity contexts, and we cannot quantify into quotations.

We can adjust matters by giving 'Nec' *multigrade* status :[1] letting it figure as an *n*-place predicate for each *n*. As a two-place predicate it amounts to the words 'is necessarily true of' ; thus Nec('odd', 9). As a three-place predicate it amounts to those same words said of a two-place predicate and two objects; thus Nec('<', 5, 9). And so on up. In terms now of multigrade 'Nec' we can explain the use of '□' on open sentences. We can explain '□(x is odd)', '□(x < y)', etc., as short for 'Nec('odd', x)', 'Nec ('<', x, y)', etc.[2] There is no longer an obstacle to quantifying into '□(x is odd)', '□(x < y)', etc. since the definientia do not quote the variables.

Reprinted from *Midwest Studies in Philosophy* 2 (1977).

1. The word was first used by Goodman, at my suggestion.
2. Kaplan anticipated this procedure in his third footnote.

This multigrade use of 'Nec' is much like my multigrade treatment in 1956 of the verbs of propositional attitude.[3] Critics of that paper reveal that I have to explain—what I thought went without saying—that the adoption of a multigrade predicate involves no logical anomaly or any infinite lexicon. It can be viewed as a one-place predicate whose arguments are sequences. As for the use of quotation, it of course is reducible by inductive definition to the concatenation functor and names of signs.

Perhaps also a caution is in order regarding two ways of taking 'necessarily true'. The sentence '9 is odd' is a necessary truth; still, that the form of words '9 is odd' means what it does, and is thus true at all, is only a contingent fact of social usage. Of course I intend 'Nec' in the former way. Similarly for its polyadic use, applied to predicates.

Commonly the predicate wanted as argument of 'Nec' will not be available in the language as a separate word or consecutive phrase. At that point the 'such that' functor serves. For example, the definiens of '$\Box((x + y)(x - y) = x^2 - y^2)$' is:

$$\text{Nec}('zw \; {}_3 \; ((z + w)(z - w) = z^2 - w^2)', x, y).$$

The 'such that' functor, '$zw \; {}_3$' in this example, connotes no abstraction of classes or relations or attributes. It is only a device for forming complex predicates, tantamount to relative clauses.[4]

When predication in the mode of necessity is directed upon a variable, the necessity is *de re*: the predicate is meant to be true of the value of the variable by whatever name, there being indeed no name at hand. 'Nec('odd',x)' says of the unspecified object x that oddity is of its essence. Thus it is true not only that Nec('odd', 9), but equally that Nec('odd', number of planets), since this very object 9, essence and all, happens to *be* the number of the planets. The 'Nec' notation accommodates *de dicto* necessity too, but differently: the term concerned *de dicto* is within the quoted sentence or predicate. Thus 'Nec '9 is odd' ', unlike 'Nec('odd', 9)', is *de*

3. "Quantifiers and propositional attitudes," reprinted in *Ways of Paradox*.

4. See Essay 1 above, §I.

dicto, and 'Nec 'number of planets is odd' ', unlike 'Nec ('odd', number of planets)', is false.

De re and *de dicto* can be distinguished also in terms of '□', but along other lines. When the term concerned is a variable, there is nothing to distinguish; *de re* is *de rigueur*. When it is not a variable, we keep it in the scope of '□' for *de dicto*:

□ (number of planets is odd)   (false)

and bring it out thus for *de re*:

(1) ($\exists x$) (x = number of planets. □(x is odd)).   (true)

In the system of definitions of '□' in terms of 'Nec' we observe a radical twist: '□(x is odd)' and '⊓(number of planets is odd)' look alike in form, as do 'Nec ('odd', x)' and 'Nec('odd', number of planets)', but the translations do not run true to form. '⊓(x is odd)' and '□(number of planets is odd)' stand rather for the dissimilar formulas 'Nec('odd', x)' and 'Nec 'number of planets is odd' ', whereas what stands for 'Nec('odd', number of planets)' is (1).

Definitional expansion of '□' thus goes awry under substitution of constants for variables. This is legitimate; unique eliminability is the only formal demand on definition. What the irregularity does portend is a drastic difference in form between the modal logic of '□' and such laws as govern its defining predicate 'Nec'. Drastic difference there is indeed. In particular the distinction between *de re* and *de dicto* is drawn with a simpler uniformity in terms of 'Nec' than in terms of '□'.

Some simplification of theory can be gained by dispensing with singular terms other than variables in familiar fashion: primitive names can be dropped in favor of uniquely fulfilled predicates and then restored as singular descriptions, which finally can be defined away in essentially Russell's way. That done, we can explain '□' fully in terms of 'Nec' and vice versa by this schematic biconditional :

(2) $\Box F x_1 x_2 \ldots x_n \equiv \text{Nec} ('F', x_1, x_2, \ldots, x_n)$.

Here n may be 0. A certain liberty has been taken in quoting a schematic letter.

It may be noted in passing that '□' on the left of (2) could alternatively be viewed not as a sentence functor but as a predicate functor, governing just the '*F*' and forming a modal predicate '□*F*'.[5]

The reconstruction of '□' in terms of 'Nec' has lent some clarity to the foundations of modal logic by embedding it in extensional logic, quotation, and a special predicate. Incidentally the contrast between *de re* and *de dicto* has thereby been heightened. But the special predicate takes some swallowing. In its monadic use it is at best the controversial semantic predicate of analyticity, and in its polyadic use it imposes an essentialist metaphysics. Let me be read, then, as expounding rather than propounding. I am in the position of a Jewish chef preparing ham for a gentile clientele. Analyticity, essence, and modality are not my meat.

If these somber reflections make one wonder whether 'Nec' may be more than we need for '□', a negative answer is visible in (2) : they are interdefinable.

A project that I shall not undertake is that of codifying laws of 'Nec' from which those of modal logic can be derived through the definitions. The laws of 'Nec' would involve continual interplay between quotations and their contents. Obviously we would want:

$$\text{Nec '...' } \supset \text{ ...,}$$

where the dots stand for any closed sentence. Also, where '——' and '...' stand for any closed sentences, we would want 'Nec '—— ≡ ...'' to assure the interchangeability of '——' with '...' inside any quotation preceded by 'Nec'. This is needed for the substitutivity of '□ (—— ≡ ...)' in the modal logic. Also we would need corresponding laws governing the polyadic use of 'Nec' in application to predicates; and here complexities mount. No doubt modal logic is better codified in its own terms; such is the very utility of defining '□' instead of staying with 'Nec'. The latter is merely of conceptual interest in distilling the net import of modal logic over and above extensional logic.

Necessity *de dicto* is notoriously resistant to the substitu-

---

5. For a study of the truth theory of a predicate functor to just this effect see Peacocke.

tivity of identity. When only variables are concerned, the question does not arise; for they figure only *de re*, or, as I have often put it, only in referential position. Moreover, we have decided that only variables *are* concerned, definitions aside. Still, let us consider how singular terms fare when restored definitionally as descriptions. Expanded by those definitions, an identity joining two descriptions or a description and a variable obviously implies the corresponding universally quantified biconditional. We may be sure therefore that even in *de dicto* positions, where substitutivity of simple identity fails, we can depend on substitutivity of necessary identity, $\Box(\zeta = \eta)$; this is assured by the substitutivity of '$\Box(\text{------} \equiv \ldots)$' noted above.

The substitutivity of $\ulcorner\Box(\zeta - \eta)\urcorner$ is gospel in modal logic. Still, some readers are perhaps brought up short by my appeal to $\ulcorner\Box(\zeta = \eta)\urcorner$, as if I did not know that

(3) $(x)(y)(x = y . \supset \Box(x = \text{y}))$.

The point is that I am not free to put ζ and η for 'x' and 'y' in (3). Instantiation of quantifications by singular terms is under the same wraps as the substitutivity of identity.

Let instantiation then be our next topic. From the true universal quantification:

$(x)(x \text{ is a number} . \supset . \Box(5 < x) \vee \Box(5 \geqq x))$

we cannot, one hopes, infer the falsehood:

$\Box(5 < \text{number of planets}) \vee \Box(5 \geqq \text{number of planets})$.

From the truth:

$5 < \text{number of planets} . - \Box(5 < \text{number of planets})$,

again, we cannot, one hopes, infer the falsehood:

$(\exists x)(5 < x . - \Box(5 < x))$.

When *can* we trust the instantial laws of quantification? The answer is implicit in the substitutivity of $\ulcorner\Box(\zeta = \eta)\urcorner$. For, instantiation is unquestioned when the instantial term is a mere variable 'x'; and we can supplant 'x' here by any desired term η, thanks to the substitutivity of $\ulcorner\Box(x = \eta)\urcorner$, if we can establish $\ulcorner(\exists x)\Box(x = \eta)\urcorner$. This last, then, is the condition that qualifies a term η for the instantial role in

steps of universal instantiation and existential generalization in modal contexts. A term thus qualified is what Føllesdal
called a genuine name and Kripke has called a rigid designator.[6] It is a term such that $(\exists x)\,\Box\,(x = a)$, that is, something is necessarily a, where 'a' stands for the term.

Such a term enjoys *de re* privileges even in a *de dicto*
setting. Besides acquitting themselves in instantiation, such
terms lend themselves in pairs to the substitutivity of simple
identity. For, where ζ and η are rigid designators, we are
free to put them for 'x' and 'y' in (3) and thus derive necessary identity.

A rigid designator differs from others in that it picks out
its object by essential traits. It designates the object in all
possible worlds in which it exists. Talk of possible worlds is
a graphic way of waging the essentialist philosophy, but it
is only that; it is not an explication. Essence is needed to
identify an object from one possible world to another.

Let us turn now to the propositional attitudes. As remarked above, my treatment of them in 1956 resembled my
present use of 'Nec'. At that time I provisionally invoked attributes and propositions, however reluctantly, for the roles
here played by mere predicates and sentences. Switching now
to the latter style, I would write:

(4) Tom believes 'Cicero denounced Catiline',

(5) Tom believes 'x ϶ (x denounced Catiline)' of Cicero,

(6) Tom believes 'x ϶ (Cicero denounced x)' of Catiline,

(7) Tom believes 'xy ϶ (x denounced y)' of Cicero,
       Catiline,

depending on which terms I want in referential position—
that is, with respect to which terms I want the belief to be
de re. The multigrade predicate 'believes' in these examples
is dyadic, triadic, triadic, and tetradic.

Whatever the obscurities of the notion of belief, the underlying logic thus far is extensional—as in the case of
'Nec'. But we can immediately convert the whole to an intensional logic of belief, analogous to that of '$\Box$'. Where 'B_i'

6. Kripke, see below, p. 173.

is a sentence functor ascribing belief to Tom, the analogue of the sketchy translation schema (2) is this:

$B_t F x_1 x_2 \ldots x_n \equiv.$ Tom believes 'F' of $x_1, x_2, \ldots, x_n$.

Parallel to (1) we get:

$(\exists x) (x = \text{Cicero} . B_t (x \text{ denounced Catiline}))$,

$(\exists x) (x = \text{Catiline} . B_t (\text{Cicero denounced } x))$,

$(\exists x) (\exists y) (x = \text{Cicero} . y = \text{Catiline} . B_t (x \text{ denounced } y))$

as our transcriptions of the *de re* constructions (5)–(7).

In the 1956 paper I dwelt on the practical difference between the *de dicto* statement:

(8)   Ralph believes '$(\exists x) (x \text{ is a spy})$'

and the *de re* statement 'There is someone whom Ralph believes to be a spy', that is:

(9) $(\exists y)$ (Ralph believes 'spy' of y).

I noted also the more narrowly logical difference between the *de dicto* statement:

(10)   Ralph believes 'Ortcutt is a spy'

and the *de re* statement:

(11)   Ralph believes 'spy' of Ortcutt,

and conjectured that the step of 'exportation' leading from (10) to (11) is generally valid. However, if we transcribe (10) and (11) into terms of 'B_r' according to the foregoing patterns, we get:

(12) $B_r (\text{Ortcutt is a spy})$,

(13) $(\exists x) (x = \text{Ortcutt} . B_r (x \text{ is a spy}))$,

and here the existential force of (13) would seem to belie the validity of the exportation. Sleigh, moreover, has challenged this step on other grounds. Surely, he observes (nearly enough), Ralph believes there are spies. If he believes further, as he reasonably may, that

(14)   No two spies are of exactly the same height,

then he will believe that the shortest spy is a spy. If exportation were valid, it would follow that

Ralph believes 'spy' of the shortest spy,

and this, having the term 'the shortest spy' out in referential position, implies (9). Thus the portentous belief (9) would follow from trivial ones, (8) and belief of (14).

Let us consult incidentally the analogues of (10) and (11) in modal logic. Looking to the transcriptions (12) and (13), we see that the analogous modal structures are '$\Box Fa$' and '$(\exists x)(x = a \,.\, \Box Fx)$'. Does the one imply the other? Again the existential force of the latter would suggest not. And again we can dispute the implication also apart from that existential consideration, as follows [abbreviating (14) and 'there are spies' in conjunction as '14'] :

(15) $\Box (14 \supset .$ the shortest spy is a spy),

(16) $(\exists x)(x =$ the shortest spy $.\, \Box (14 \supset . x$ is a spy)).

Surely (15) is true. On the other hand, granted (14), presumably (16) is false; for it would require someone to be a spy *de re*, or in essence.

Evidently we must find against exportation. Kaplan's judgment, which he credits to Montgomery Furth, is that the step is sound only in the case of what he calls a *vivid* designator, which is the analogue, in the logic of belief, of a rigid designator. And what might this analogue be? We saw that in modal logic a term is a rigid designator if $(\exists x)\Box (x = a)$, where 'a' stands for the term; so the parallel condition for the logic of belief is that $(\exists x)B_t (x = a)$, if Tom is our man. Thus a term is a vivid designator, for Tom, when there is a specific thing that he believes it designates. Vivid designators, analogues of the rigid designators in modal logic, are the terms that can be freely used to instantiate quantifications in belief contexts, and that are subject to the substitutivity of identity—and, now, to exportation.

Hintikka's criterion for this superior type of term was that Tom *know* who or what the person or thing is; whom or what the term designates.[7] The difference is accountable to

7. Hintikka, *Knowledge and Belief.*

the fact that Hintikka's was a logic of both belief and knowledge.

The notion of knowing or believing who or what someone or something is, is utterly dependent on context. Sometimes, when we ask who someone is, we see the face and want the name; sometimes the reverse. Sometimes we want to know his role in the community.[8] Of itself the notion is empty.

It and the notion of essence are on a par. Both make sense in context. Relative to a particular inquiry, some predicates may play a more basic role than others, or may apply more fixedly; and these may be treated as essential. The respective derivative notions, then, of vivid designator and rigid designator, are similarly dependent on context and empty otherwise. The same is true of the whole quantified modal logic of necessity; for it collapses if essence is withdrawn. For that matter, the very notion of necessity makes sense to me only relative to context. Typically it is applied to what is assumed in an inquiry, as against what has yet to transpire.

In thus writing off modal logic I find little to regret. Regarding the propositional attitudes, however, I cannot be so cavalier. Where does the passing of the vivid designator leave us with respect to belief? It leaves us with no distinction between admissible and inadmissible cases of the ex portation that leads from (10) to (11), except that those cases remain inadmissible in which the exported term fails to name anything. It leaves us defenseless against Sleigh's deduction of the strong (9) from (8) and belief of (14). Thus it virtually annuls the seemingly vital contrast between (8) and (9): between merely believing there are spies and suspecting a specific person. At first this seems intolerable, but it grows on one. I now think the distinction is every bit as empty, apart from context, as that of vivid designator: that of knowing or believing who someone is. In context it can still be important. In one case we can be of service by pointing out the suspect; in another, by naming him; in others, by giving his address or specifying his ostensible employment.

Renunciation does not stop here. The condition for being

---

8. Such variation is recognized by Hintikka, *Knowledge and Belief*, p. 149n. For a study of it in depth see Boër and Lycan.

a vivid designator is that $(\exists x)\,\mathrm{B}_t(x = a)$, or, in the other notation, that

$$(\exists x)\,(\text{Tom believes } `y \; 3 \; (y = a)\text{'} \text{ of } x).$$

Surely this makes every bit as good sense as the idiom 'believes of'; there can be no trouble over '$y \; 3 \; (y = a)$'. So our renunciation must extend to all *de re* belief, and similarly, no doubt, for the other propositional attitudes. We end up rejecting *de re* or quantified propositional attitudes generally, on a par with *de re* or quantified modal logic. Rejecting them, that is, except as idioms relativized to the context or situation at hand. We remain less cavalier toward propositional attitudes than toward modal logic only in the unquantified or *de dicto* case, where the attitudes are taken as dyadic relations between people or other animals and closed sentences.

Even these relations present difficulties in respect of criterion. Belief is not to be recognized simply by assent, for this leaves no place for insincerity or sanctimonious self-deception. Belief can be nicely tested and even measured by the betting odds that the subject will accept, allowance being made for the positive or negative value for him of risk as such. This allowance can be measured by testing him on even chances. However, bets work only for sentences for which there is a verification or falsification procedure acceptable to both parties as settling the bet. I see the verb 'believe' even in its *de dicto* use as varying in meaningfulness from sentence to sentence.

Ascribed to the dumb and illiterate animal, belief *de dicto* seems a *contradictio in adjecto*. The betting test is never available. I have suggested elsewhere that some propositional attitudes—desire, fear—might be construed as a relation of the animal to a set of sets of his sensory receptors; but this works only for what I called egocentric desire and fear.[9] I see no way of extending this to belief. Certainly the ascription of a specific simple belief to a dumb animal often can be supported by citing its observable behavior; but a general definition to the purpose is not evident.

9. "Propositional objects," reprinted in *Ontological Relativity*.

Raymond Nelson has ascribed beliefs to machines. He has done so in support of a mechanist philosophy, and I share his attitude. The objects of belief with which he deals are discrete, observable alternatives, and the machine's belief or expectation with respect to them lends itself to a straightforward definition. But this is of no evident help in the kind of problem that is exercising me here. For my problem is not one of reconciling mind and matter, but only a quest for general criteria suitable for unprefabricated cases.

14

Worlds Away

Identifying an object from world to possible world is analogous, it has been suggested,[1] to identifying an object from
moment to moment in our world. I agree, and I want now
to develop the analogy.

Consider my broad conception of a physical object: the
material content of any portion of space-time, however scattered and discontinuous. Equivalently: any sum or aggregate
of point-events. The world's water is for me a physical object, comprising all the molecules of H_2O anywhere ever.
There is a physical object part of which is a momentary
stage of a silver dollar now in my pocket and the rest of
which is a temporal segment of the Eiffel Tower through its
third decade. I am using 'there is' tenselessly (Sellars: 'there
be').

Any two momentary objects, then, taken at different moments, are time slices of some one time-extended physical
object; time slices, indeed, of each of many such. Thus consider the present momentary stage of that sliver dollar in my
otherwise empty pocket; and consider a momentary stage of
that same coin next Tuesday, again in my otherwise empty
pocket. One object of which these two momentary objects
are time slices is the coin. Another object of which they are

---

Reprinted from the *Journal of Philosophy* 73 (1976). Two of the paragraphs near the end have been dropped because of coverage in the
preceding essay.

1. E.g., by Hintikka, *Intentions of Intentionality*, ch. 6.

time slices is the monetary content of my pocket—a discontinuous object that has had some nickel and copper content along the way. A third and more inclusive object of which they are time slices is the total content of my pocket, there being intrusive stages of a key or pillbox. Identification of an object from moment to moment is indeed on a par with identifying an object from world to world: both identifications are vacuous, pending further directives.

Identification of an object from moment to moment takes on content only when we indicate what sort of object we want.[2] The two momentary objects last studied are indeed time slices of *the* same *coin.* If for my convenience my friendly neighborhood banker changes the coin to quarters, then the earlier time slice of my coin and a later scattered time slice of my four coins may be said to be time slices of *the* same *dollar,* in one sense of the word.

Among the myriad ways, mostly uninteresting, of stacking up momentary objects to make time-extended objects, there is one popular favorite: the corporeal. Momentary objects are declared to be stages of the same body by considerations of continuity of displacement, continuity of deformation, continuity of chemical change. These are not conditions on the notion of identity; they are conditions on the notion of body. Most of our common predicates, like 'coin', denote only bodies, and so derive their individuation from the individuation of the predicate 'body'; and individuation is nine parts cross-moment identification. 'Dollar' was a rather labored exception to the bodily mode of integration, and of course countless still more artificial examples can be devised.

Despite men's stubborn body-mindedness, there are good reason for the more liberal ontology of physical objects.[3] All these objects, when I quantify over individuals, are the

2. My point is strangely reminiscent of Geach's contention that "it makes no sense to judge whether x and y are 'the same' . . . unless we add or understand some genral term—'the same F'" (§31). I say "strangely" because I disagree with Geach; I insist that x and y are the same F if and only if x and y are the same, outright, and Fx. Cross-moment identification is another thing; the momentary objects x and y are unwaveringly distinct, but are time slices of perhaps the same F and different G's. See Geach, *Reference and Generality.*

3. See Essay 1 above, §II.

values of my variables. And what, then, would be the analogous values of variables if one were to quantify over individuals in all possible worlds? Simply the sums of physical objects of the various worlds, combining denizens of different worlds indiscriminately. One of these values would consist of Napoleon together with his counterparts in other worlds, if 'counterpart' made sense; another would consist of Napoleon together with sundry utterly dissimilar denizens of other worlds.

Thus quantification over objects across possible worlds does not require us to make any sense of 'counterpart'. Just as any two momentary objects in different moments are shared as time slices not by just one time-extended object but by countless ones, so any two physical objects in different worlds are shared as realizations not by just one intermundane object but by countless ones. Quantification is as straightforward over the one domain as over the other, unless there is some independent trouble with possible worlds.

And indeed there is. It lies elsewhere: not in the quantification, but in the predicates. We saw that in our own world the identification of a physical object from moment to moment makes sense only relative to the principle of individuation of one or another particular predicate—usually, though not necessarily, the predicate 'body' or one of its subordinates. Such cross-moment groupings are indifferent to the actual quantification over physical objects, since the quantification respects all cross-moment groups, however random. But they matter to the predicates. If a sentence begins '(x) (x is a coin .⊃', the physical objects that are going to matter as values of its variable are just the coins; and thus the way of identifying a coin from moment to moment can be relevant to the truth value of the sentence. Since all sentences contain predicates, cross-moment identification of one sort or another is a crucial matter in its proper place.

Similarly, if one quantifies over objects across possible worlds, one needs cross-world identification relative to whatever predicates one uses in such sentences. Typically these predicates, again, will be subordinates of 'body'. Insofar, then, we could accommodate them if we could somehow extend our principle of individuation or integration of bodies so as to identify bodies not just from moment to moment, as we do so well, but from world to world. However, our cross-moment identification of bodies turned on continuity of displacement, distortion, and chemical change. These considerations cannot be extended across the worlds, because you can change anything to anything by easy stages through some connecting series of possible worlds. The devastating difference is that the series of momentary cross sections of our real world is uniquely imposed on us, for better or for worse, whereas all manner of paths of continuous gradation from one possible world to another are free for the thinking up.

To see how quantification into modal contexts depends on cross-world identifications, or counterparts, consider '$(\exists x)\Box Fx$'. The problem is not in the quantification as such, as we saw; 'x' ranges over all manner of ill-assorted cross-world hybrids. 'Fx', however, stands for some sentence built up of 'x' and various predicates and logical constants. Or we may as well think of 'F' itself as a predicate, primitive or defined. The quantification '$(\exists x)\Box Fx$' says that among the objects fulfilling 'F' in our world there is some one (among perhaps many) all of whose counterparts in other possible worlds fulfill 'F'. For this to make sense, we need to make cross-world sense not of 'same object', which is vacuous, but of 'same F'. We need cross-world individuation of the predicate 'F'. Or nearly so. We could manage with a little less. Cross-world individuation of some predicate subordinate to 'F' would suffice if that predicate happened to be fulfilled by one of the objects whose counterparts are all supposed to fulfill 'F'. Here, indeed, is a strategy that can be pressed to advantage: pick the narrowest predicate you can, so long as you can count on it to catch one of the objects whose counterparts are all supposed to fulfill 'F'. For, the narrower it is, the fewer the objects are for which we need to specify counterparts, or cross-world identities. The limit of this strategy, if it can be managed, is a uniquely fulfilled predicate, true of just a single object whose counterparts are all supposed to fulfill 'F'; for then there is just the one object demanding definition of cross-world identity.

Imagine a case where this has been managed. It is asserted that $(\exists x)\Box Fx$, and this is supported by producing a predicate '*G*' that is purportedly fulfilled uniquely by an *x* such that □ *Fx*. All that then needs to be done to make sense of all this, if not to prove it, is to cite conditions of cross-world identity for the object *x* such that *Gx*. But the analogy of identification over time is still of no help.

Instead of bandying a uniquely fulfilled predicate '*G*', one may forge a corresponding singular term '*g*'. Here, then, is the rigid designator.[4]

Hintikka has explained that he is not a champion of alethic modal logic, the logic of necessity. But he is very much a champion, in two senses, of the modal logic of propositional attitudes. He urges that things are different there. Paths of continuous gradation from one belief world to another are not free for the thinking up. The belief worlds coincide with one another in all details in which the believer believes, and at other points they are still pretty well behaved, being compatible with his beliefs. In large part it does make sense to identify a body from one such world to another.

Yes, but not always. Each belief world will include countless bodies that are not separately recognizable objects of the believer's beliefs at all, for the believer does believe still that there are countless such bodies. Questions of identity of these, from world to world, remain as devoid of sense as they were in the possible worlds of alethic modal logic. Yet how are they to be dismissed, if one is to quantify into belief contexts? Perhaps the values of such variables should be limited to objects that the believer has pretty detailed views about. How detailed? I do not see the markings here of a proper annex to austere scientific language.

4. See the preceding essay.

15

Grades of
Discriminability

An object may be said to be *specifiable*, in a given interpreted formal language, if in that language there is an
open sentence, in one free variable, that is uniquely satisfied
by that object. Two objects are *discriminable* if there is an
open sentence, in one free variable, that is satisfied by one
of the objects and not the other. Objects may be discriminable without being specifiable. It is well known that not all
real numbers are specifiable; yet all are discriminable, as is
evident from the fact that any two reals are separated by a
ratio. For any two reals that are numerals μ and ν such that
the open sentence $\ulcorner x < \mu/\nu \urcorner$ is satisfied by one of the reals
and not by the other.

But discriminability does assure specifiability in the infinite, so to speak. If all the objects of a domain are discriminable, obviously each of them uniquely satisfies the infinite
conjunction—better, the set—of all the open sentences in 'x'
that it satisfies. Each real number is uniquely determined by
the set of all the sentences $\ulcorner x < \mu/\nu \urcorner$ that it satisfies.

Discriminability, in the sense defined, will be referred to
more particularly as *strong discriminability* to distinguish it
from weaker grades to which I now turn. I shall call two
objects *moderately discriminable* if there is an open sentence

Reprinted from the *Journal of Philosophy* 73 (1976).

in two free variables that is satisfied by the two objects in one
order and not in the other order. Objects can be discriminable
in this sense without being strongly discriminable. The
ordinal numbers afford an example. All ordinals are moderately discriminable, since any two of them satisfy the open
sentence '$x < y$' in one order and not the other. Yet they are
not all strongly discriminable. If they were, then, as remarked, each ordinal would be uniquely determined by the
set of the open sentences that it satisfies. Sentences, being
finite in length, are denumerable, so the number of sets of
sentences is the power of the continuum. Thus if the ordinals
were strongly discriminable they would be limited in number to the power of the continuum.

In treating of discriminability I am not assuming in general that the languages concerned contain the predicate '='.
In general, however, whether or not a language contains '=',
there is a familiar sense in which we can speak of the utter
indiscriminability of objects x and y in the language. It is
simply that

(1) $(z_1) (z_2) \ldots (z_n) (Fxz_1z_2 \ldots z_n \supset Fyz_1z_2 \ldots z_n)$

for all n and all open sentences of the language in the role of
'$Fxz_1z_2 \ldots z_n$'. Thus the weakest possible condition of discriminability of objects x and y is that there be an open sentence for the role of '$Fxz_1z_2 \ldots z_n$' such that, contrary to (1),

(2) $(\exists z_1) (\exists z_2) \ldots (\exists z_n) (Fxz_1z_2 \ldots z_n . - Fyz_1z_2 \ldots z_n).$

But in fact this formulation is needlessly cumbersome. Its
purpose is already served by its simplest case, where $n = 0$:
the case '$Fx . - Fy$'. If objects x and y can be discriminated
by a sentence of the form (2) at all, they can already be discriminated by a sentence of the short form '$Fx . - Fy$'. For
(2) implies something of this short form. To see this, ab-
breviate (2) as 'G_yx'; then 'G_yy' is inconsistent; so (2) implies '$G_yx . - G_yy$'.

Here, then, is the definition of *weak discriminability*, the
weakest possible: satisfaction of a sentence of the form
'$Fx . - Fy$'. This definition looks equivalent to the definition
of strong discriminability; 'Fx' stands for an open sentence
that is satisfied, it would seem, by the one object and not the

other. Actually the definitions are far from equivalent; we shall find that weak discriminability is even weaker than moderate discriminability. The reason for failure of equivalence is that a sentence of the form 'Fx . $- Fy$' can have 'x' and 'y' as sole free variables and yet not be the conjunction of two sentences that have 'x' and 'y' respectively as sole free variables. This can happen because of an extra occurrence of 'x' or 'y' hidden, so to speak, in the 'F'. It happened at the end of the preceding paragraph, where '$G_y x$. $- G_y y$' was recognized as a correct substitution instance of 'Fx . $- Fy$'.

To show that weak discriminability differs not only from strong but also from moderate discriminability, I need a lemma regarding the logic of identity.

Lemma. If an open sentence is built up of just '$=$' and variables by quantification and truth functions, then in any infinite universe it is equivalent to a mere truth function of equations of its free variables. (Equivalent in the sense of agreeing in truth value for all values of the variables.)

Proof by elimination of quantifiers, as follows. Translate universal quantifications into existential, and then drive quantifiers inward by putting their scopes into alternational normal form, distributing the quantifiers through the alternations, and exporting any unbound components of conjunctions. Banish any self-identities by obvious reductions. Each innermost quantification is now of this sort:

$$(\exists z)\,(z = u_1 . z = u_2 . \ldots . z = u_m . z \neq v_1 . z \neq v_2 . \ldots . z \neq v_n)$$

But we can drop '$(\exists z)$' and '$z = u_1$' here, putting 'u_1' for 'z' in the further clauses (if any). Or if $m = 0$, we can mark the quantification true and resolve it out, since the infinitude of the universe assures that

$$(\exists z)\,(z \neq v_1 . z \neq v_2 . \ldots . z \neq v_n)$$

In this way each innermost quantifier disappears and no new free variables emerge.

To see now that weak discriminability is weaker than moderate, consider an interpreted language with '$=$' as sole predicate and an infinite universe. Any of its sentences whose free variables are 'x' and 'y' is equivalent, by the lemma, to a truth function of '$x = x$', '$y = y$', and '$x = y$', hence to '$x = y$' or '$x \neq y$' or '$\top$' or '$\bot$'. So none of its sentences in two free variables is satisfied by objects in one order and not the other. So none of its objects are moderately discriminable. Yet any two of its objects are weakly discriminable, satisfying as they do the sentence '$x = x \cdot x \neq y$', which has the form '$Fx . - Fy$'.

Ivan Fox has suggested to me another criterion of discriminability: that the objects satisfy some irreflexive sentence in two free variables. Since any sentence of the form '$Fx . - Fy$' is irreflexive [i.e., $(z) - (Fz . - Fz)$], any objects that are weakly discriminable in my sense are discriminable in his. So, since my weak discriminability is minimal, his is equivalent. (Or, to argue this converse anew, let us represent his irreflexive sentence as '$H_y x$'. Because of the irreflexivity, any two objects satisfying '$H_y x$' satisfy '$H_y x . - H_y y$', which has the form '$Fx . - Fy$'.)

We can trim Fox's criterion a little by requiring not that his open sentence be irreflexive, but just that it be reflexively false of one of the objects to be discriminated. Clearly, the equivalence argument above is unimpeded by this emendation. Thus phrased, the criterion of weak discriminability is this: a sentence in two variables is satisfied by the two objects but not by one of them with itself. This version may be preferred to my earlier equivalent—viz., satisfaction of a sentence of the form '$Fx . - Fy$'—on two counts: it calls for no consideration of hidden occurrences of 'x' and 'y', and it fits the style of the definitions of specification and strong and moderate discrimination. Let us see them together. A sentence in one variable *specifies* an object if satisfied by it uniquely. A sentence in one variable *strongly discriminates* two objects if satisfied by one and not the other. A sentence in two variables *moderately discriminates* two objects if satisfied by them in one order only. A sentence in two variables *weakly discriminates* two objects if satisfied by the two but not by one of them with itself.

But the earlier way of stating weak discriminability retains interest for its subtle contrast with strong discriminability: we had '$Fx . - Fy$' on the one hand and 'Fx' and '$- Fy$' on the other. It is remarkable that there is yet another grade of discriminability between the two.

May there even be many intermediate grades? The question is ill defined. By imposing special conditions on the form or content of the open sentence used in discriminating two objects, we could define any number of intermediate grades of discriminability, subject even to no linear order. What I have called moderate discriminability, however, is the only intermediate grade that I see how to define at our present high level of generality.

16

Lewis Carroll's Logic

.

Lewis Carroll has meant much to most of us. Some of us do not outgrow him. There are playful absurdities in his tales that tickle the logical mind. Now and again a passage of his can be aptly quoted in the course of some philosophical analysis, and the quotation sensibly leavens the lump. A posthumous new book of his after lo these eighty years is an event not to be lightly passed over.

Curiosity is twice piqued, in logico-philosophical minds, when the new book turns out to be *Symbolic Logic*. These minds were already cognizant of a Part 1, 1896, of two hundred modest pages. It ran into four editions, as Lewis Carroll called them, in the space of ten months. Despite its austere title it was accessible to children, as it was meant to be. Parts 2 and 3 were already projected at that time, the one Advanced and the other Transcendental. What is now newly before us is Part 2. Modern logic was little beyond its formative stage in Carroll's day, so the more romantic among us might look to his newly revealed Advanced Logic in hopes of finding historically interesting anticipations at least, and perhaps even new light on live topics. The editor of the volume, W. W. Bartley III, evinced and encouraged this romantic attitude in his advance publicity, which appeared in 1972 as an article in the *Scientific American.*

Carroll worked on Part 2 up to his death in 1898. Much

Reprinted from the *Times Literary Supplement*, London, August 26, 1977.

of it was typeset while the work was in progress. Professor Bartley has retrieved the galley proofs, running to 145 pages. He has eked this material out with twenty-eight pages from his own hand, sixteen pages from Carroll's notes and letters, and thirty pages of facsimiles, photographs, and humorous drawings from other sources. Part 2, thus synthesized, is just the second half of the volume that is now before us; for Bartley has also reprinted Part 1 and prefixed forty pages of editorial introduction.

Let us then begin with a retrospective look at Part 1, Elementary. It was not a pioneer work. It was innocent of what may properly be called modern logic, though this had already come abruptly into being seventeen years before, at the hands of Gottlob Frege, in 1879. There was indeed little reason for Carroll to have known of Frege, whose work was long unappreciated; but by Carroll's day Frege's crucial idea had been rediscovered in America by Charles Sanders Peirce (1885) and the science had been progressing apace in three countries. Ernst Schröder was developing it at book length in 1890, 1891, and 1895. Giuseppe Peano had shown glimmerings in 1888 and a firm command in publications of 1893–1895. But Carroll's link with the logical literature bridged all this latter-day turbulence and reached back to John Venn's unregenerate book of the same title, *Symbolic Logic* (1881). Our editor does state that Carroll knew of Peirce, but no influence is evident. Further, he quotes Eric Temple Bell as saying of Carroll that "as a mathematical logician, he was far ahead of his British contemporaries." The word "British" is vital here, but even so the "far" is debatable.

Let me explain the distinctive trait of modern logic. It has often been said that traditional logic treated only of attributes, while modern logic handles also relations. But this contrast is apt to be misunderstood, particularly since Carroll himself emphasizes something he calls relation.

Logic, old or new, traces implications. If one sentence is implied by another, or jointly by several, the connections normally depend on a sharing of terms in varying contexts. Thus, to adapt a syllogism of Carroll's,

> None but the brave deserves the fair,
> Some braggarts are not brave,
> Therefore some braggarts do not deserve the fair.

Now the shared term 'deserves' is relational, certainly. It applies to people in pairs; x deserves y. But our syllogism does not hinge on it, because the term has an unvarying context: 'deserves the fair'. It is rather this latter three-word term as a whole that is relevant to the structure of our syllogism, and it expresses a mere attribute of people taken one at a time: x deserves the fair.

In contrast there is this time-honored example from Jungius:

> Circles are figures,
> Therefore whoever draws a circle draws a figure.

The structure that sustains this implication can be elicited only by attending to the relational term draws. If we bundle this term off as a mere part of two monolithic attributional terms, 'draws a circle' and 'draws a figure', the required structure is lost.

Implications that depend thus essentially on relational terms are what were not covered in any systematic way by the old logic, and are covered smoothly and exhaustively by the new. The trivial example from Jungius gives no hint of the vastness of this coverage. Modern logic is a serious branch of mathematics, and an elegant one.

Syllogisms, for all their slightness, had been the mainstay of formal logic down the centuries. Rules were devised for spotting the valid syllogism—descriptive rules rather than computation. Innovations of an algebraic kind did emerge a few times, by way of expediting the work and widening the coverage. George Boole's work around 1850 was the start of a more continuous development in this vein. At that time Augustus DeMorgan even ventured a little algebra of relations, suited to the Jungius example and the like, but this was rather a foreshadowing of modern logic than the real thing. It was not very systematic, and the coverage was spotty.

W. Stanley Jevons removed some kinks from Boole's methods. Venn continued in this line, and also presented a convenient method of diagrams for testing syllogisms and other simple inferences. All this was again a theory purely of attributes, not relations.

Venn, we saw, was Carroll's point of departure. The departure is inconsiderable. Carroll uses a different style of diagrams, and his algebraic notation adheres less slavishly to arithmetical analogies. His notation has the virtue of distinguishing between connectives of terms and connectives of sentences; this was a departure from the usage of Venn and his predecessors, but already usual in the new logic outside Carroll's orbit. Carroll himself does not strictly observe it in his later work.

Carroll has a compact notation of subscripts. Where 'x' stands for a term, e.g., 'angels', 'x_0' means that there are no x and 'x_1' means that there are some x. Thus 'xy_0' means there are no xy, or in other words that no x are y, and 'xy_1' means that some x are y. To affirm 'x_1' and 'xy_0' jointly he writes 'x_1y_0'. Correspondingly then we would expect 'x_0y_1' to affirm 'x_0' and 'xy_1' jointly, but these are incompatible, so Carroll puts 'x_0y_1' to another use: to mean that x_0 or xy_1. We may guess from this that the algebraic notation is for him less a medium of calculation than a shorthand. The thought is borne out as we read on: he is given to testing implications by descriptive rules rather than by algebraic transformations. In this respect his kinship is even more with the age-old syllogistic tradition than with Boole and his followers.

But he does decidedly improve the old treatments of the syllogism. Alumni of old-fashioned schools will recall that there were twenty-four valid moods of the syllogism, classified into four figures. Carroll reassociates negation with the predicate term, thus reading 'are-not y' as 'are non-y'; further he allows the subject term likewise to be negative; and finally he drops the distinction between subject and predicate. The effect is that twelve of the old moods are absorbed into the other twelve, and twelve new ones emerge that were not traditionally covered. He has doubled the coverage and simplified the rules. Instead of four figures he counts three.

After syllogisms, then what? Carroll's answer: the sorites. A sorites is an implication that has many premises and can be resolved into a chain of syllogisms. Carroll's whimsy has had outlets in his examples of syllogisms, but it is in his soriteses, as he calls them, that he pulls all stops. A typical one has these six premises:

No husband, who is always giving his wife new dresses, can be a cross-grained man.

A methodical husband always comes home for his tea.

No one, who hangs up his hat on a gas jet, can be a man that is kept in proper order by his wife.

A good husband is always giving his wife new dresses.

No husband can fail to be cross-grained, if his wife does not keep him in proper order.

An unmethodical husband always hangs up his hat on the gas jet.

The problem is to find the conclusion, which is that a good husband always comes home for his tea, and to derive it in a chain of valid syllogisms. At this point Carroll does indeed come out with something algorithmic: a routine for symbolizing the premises and successively canceling terms from them. Each such step changes two sentences into an intermediate conclusion, and the process terminates with the conclusion of the lot.

In its opening pages Part 1 is sweepingly ontological. "The Universe contains *Things* . . . Things have *Attributes*." Carroll then adverts to "a Mental Process, in which we imagine that we have put together, in a group, certain Things. Such a group is called a Class." We expect classes to differ from one another only in respect of their members; but no. "Things that weigh a ton and are easily lifted by a baby" constitute one empty class, he holds, while "towns paved with gold" constitute another. Why then talk of classes, over and above attributes?

"A Class, containing only one member, is called an Individual." In thus failing to distinguish unit classes from their members he continues, characteristically, the succession from Boole through Venn. Frege and Peano had by then appreciated how imperative the distinction is, but theirs was another world.

Carroll defends the syllogism against detractors who impute to it the fallacy of "begging the question." This criticism is familiar and feeble, but Carroll's defense is outrageous. He represents the detractors as claiming "that the whole Conclusion is involved in *one* of the Premisses," and then he easily counters the criticism by saying that "the Conclusion is really involved in the *two* Premisses taken together." The children, to whom Part 1 is in part addressed, are the only readers who are apt to believe that anyone really claimed "that the whole Conclusion is involved in *one* of the Premisses." Carroll sets those children a poor example of intellectual morality.

I have been describing Part 1, which is the reprint. Since it was meant to be accessible to children, it may be excused for remaining at essentially the syllogistic level. Let us look at last to Part 2, Advanced. It is the place for historically significant bits, if such there be.

It begins with a little period piece on another traditional issue of roughly the same negligible magnitude as the one about whether the syllogism is question-begging. This is the dispute over whether 'All x are y' implies that there are x. The medieval rules of the syllogism favor this implication. Modern logic gains symmetry and simplicity by according a primary role rather to a reading of 'All x are y' that does not require there to be x. Ordinary usage of these words perhaps varies on the point, and no matter, since anyone can add a phrase for precision when desired. Carroll comes off badly here. He professes actually to prove the implication, arguing from other implications that have no stronger claims and are palpably equivalent. It is a sorry display of question-begging, as the editor recognizes.

Carroll is contentious. He presently shows himself so again, in an impassioned plea for his reinterpretation of 'are-not y' as 'are non-y'. I casually praised this move, above, for the simplified treatment of the syllogism that it affords; but Carroll carps. He lashes out against "The Logicians" for their "perfectly *morbid* dread of negative Attributes, which makes them shut their eyes like frightened children"; an "unreasoning terror." His defensiveness shows itself soon again, when he proceeds to argue the superiority of his diagrams over Venn's. He objects that one of Venn's compartments cannot be shaded, being the whole of outer space; he knew full well that we easily shade enough of it to get on with.

The rudimentary algebraic notation that he used in his treatment of syllogisms and sorites in Part 1 now undergoes a slight augmentation: a sign for 'or' is added. With its help his three so-called figures of the syllogism are now extended to six. The added forms differ increasingly from syllogisms hitherto so called; but they continue to have three terms, all attributional.

Next the editor interposes some logical charts that he found among Carroll's papers and has contrived, with one exception, to interpret. Most of them are variants of a single chart, best visualized in three dimensions as made up of thirteen points on a tetrahedron. The points stand for 'There are x', 'All x are y', 'No x are y', 'Some x are y', and various more complex combinations, and the formula in the middle of any line is implied by those at the ends.

What next? Back to the sorites! He presents an algorithm that takes the form of a genealogical tree. Given any number of premises, the procedure finds the appropriate conclusion, if any, and establishes it. It is required that each premise and the conclusion have either the form 'All $xyz \ldots$ are $uvw \ldots$' or the form 'There are no $xyz \ldots$', with any number of terms negated. (His fifth example exceeds this requirement in two of its twenty-four premises, but he reduces the two to form.)

There follows a series of fanciful examples, some with as many as fifty premises and more terms. Such are the Problem of the School-Boys, the Pork-Chop Problem, Froggy's Problem, and many others. This material is drawn largely from pieces of Carroll's other than the incomplete galley proofs of Part 2. Froggy's Problem had appeared in *Antaeus* with cartoons by Gorey, of *Amphigory;* they are reproduced. Some of the problems Carroll solves by his tree method, with variations. As the editor remarks, an air of sleuthing prevails; "it is almost as if Sherlock Holmes had commissioned Carroll to aid in the education of poor Dr. Watson." Some problems proceed independently of symbolic devices, and these grade off into the ancient paradox "I am lying" and lesser puzzles.

Some of these are presented at length in that leisurely narrative style of Carroll's that we love so well. One of them, "What Achilles said to the Tortoise," appeared first in *Mind* and is familiar to philosophers. Many letters of Carroll's regarding various of the problems are included in the book, mainly letters to John Cook Wilson. The principal controversy arose over Carroll's so-called Barber-Shop Paradox, and spread beyond Carroll and Wilson to Venn, Sidgwick, Russell, and others. It is not the celebrated paradox about shaving. It is a flimsy thing, and can puzzle no one who is clear in his mind about 'if'.

The editor has annotated the volume throughout, often helpfully. In his introduction we find an interesting account of his intermittent quest, over a period of fifteen years, for the unpublished material. He says it all began with uneasiness over the use that Ryle, Stephen Toulmin, and I had made of "What Achilles said to the Tortoise." He wanted to see whether some unpublished papers might illuminate Carroll's intentions. He quotes Ryle and Toulmin as citing Carroll's piece to support their doctrine that universal hypotheses are not truths but mere "inference licenses." He could not quote me to the point, for I have never accepted or written about that doctrine of universal hypotheses. Where I cited Carroll's piece, I was just making Carroll's own point, which is quite clear in his piece, and giving due credit. As for the doctrine regarding universal hypotheses, certainly it was not Carroll's, nor did Ryle and Toulmin suppose it was; they were deliberately pressing forward from Carroll on their own. Still, we can be thankful for Bartley's misunderstanding if it led to this substantial addition to the Carroll corpus.

Considering Bartley's long pursuit of Carroll's papers and his arduous editing, one expects him to be Carroll's champion. He claims somewhat less for Carroll, however, than he did in the 1972 *Scientific American*. He then represented Carroll's tree method as a general method of deciding validity, or implication, throughout the nonrelational part of logic. This, as he remarked, would be an anticipation of something that was achieved after a fashion by Leopold Löwenheim in 1915 and in a practicable way by Heinrich

Behmann in 1922. Actually the scope of Carroll's method is narrower; I indicated it above. Bartley still sees in Carroll's trees "a striking resemblance . . . to a method of 'Semantic Tableaux' " used in recent decades by Evert Beth and Jaakko Hintikka, but in fact this resemblance again is superficial, for the difference in yield is vast. Also Bartley makes too much of Carroll's observations on the liar paradox. But again we can be thankful for some excess of enthusiasm if it was a condition of the service that Bartley has done us.

It is our admiration of Lewis Carroll's other works that lends interest to this one. The volume also offers further gratification on its own account to all who respond to Lewis Carroll's magic touch. Those who are puzzle fanciers, in particular, can revel in the book for many long evenings.

17

Kurt Gödel

Kurt Gödel was born on April 28, 1906, in Brünn, or Brno, Moravia. He was a son of Rudolf Gödel and Marianne, née Handschuh. He entered the University of Vienna in 1924. On February 6, 1930, he received his doctorate in mathematics.

His doctoral dissertation was a proof of the completeness of the first-order predicate calculus. This calculus is the basic department of modern formal logic; there are some who even equate it to logic, in a defensibly narrow sense of the word. Its formulas represent forms of sentences, with variables in place of predicates. Its valid formulas are the ones that go over into true sentences no matter what predicates are put for the variables. What Gödel proved was that every one of the valid formulas admits of formal proof by any of various current proof procedures.

Such completeness was expected. A logician who expected the contrary would have been at pains to strengthen the known proof procedures in hopes of achieving completeness. But an actual proof of completeness was less expected, and a notable accomplishment. It came as a welcome reassurance. Thoralf Skolem in Oslo had already published results in 1929 and earlier which, taken together, may in retrospect be interpreted as anticipating this completeness theorem. Those papers were rather vague on the point, however, and Gödel's work was independent of them.

Reprinted from the *Year Book* for 1978 of the American Philosophical Society.

Gödel had finished this work when 1930 dawned. Before that year was over, his next theorem had been published and its proof had been received for publication; and it was this theorem that sealed his immortality. In contrast to his completeness theorem, this was a theorem of incompletability: the incompletability of elementary number theory. The completeness of the predicate calculus had been, as I said, expected; one merely wanted the proof. On the other hand, the incompletability of elementary number theory came as an upset of firm preconceptions and a crisis in the philosophy of mathematics.

Elementary number theory is the modest part of mathematics that is concerned with the addition and multiplication of whole numbers. Whatever sound and usable rules of proof one may devise, some truths of elementary number theory will remain unprovable; this is the gist of Gödel's theorem. Given any proof procedure, he showed how to construct a sentence purely in the meager notation of elementary number theory that can be proved if and only if it is false. But wait: the sentence cannot be proved and yet be false, if the rules of proof are sound. So it is true but unprovable.

We used to think that mathematical truth consisted in provability. Now we see that this view is untenable for mathematics as a whole, and even for mathematics in any considerable part; for elementary number theory is indeed a modest part, and it already exceeds any acceptable proof procedure.

Specialists will note that in this sketch I resort to vagueness now and again to round off some technical corners.

In the same epoch-making paper Gödel adduced also a further theorem, as corollary to the main one. The gist of it is that a mathematical theory cannot ordinarily be proved to be free of internal contradiction except by resorting to another theory that rests on stronger assumptions, and hence is less reliable, than the theory whose consistency is being proved. Like the incompletability theorem, this corollary has a melancholy ring. Still it has been found to be of positive utility when we are concerned to prove that one theory is stronger than another: we can do so by proving in the one theory that the other is consistent.

The techniques that went into Gödel's proof of incompletability have had utility elsewhere too. They have been instrumental in the rapid development of a vigorous new branch of mathematics, known in part as hierarchy theory and in part as recursive number theory, or recursion theory. The latter has played a major role in the theory of computers.

In the years 1932–1935 Gödel communicated further technical results regarding logical provability in the course of ten short papers. He continued at Vienna as Privatdozent until 1938, but visited America in 1934 to lecture at the Institute of Advanced Study. In 1938 he married Adele Porkert, of Vienna, and moved with her to Princeton as a permanent member of the Institute for Advanced Study. They had no children. Gödel became an American citizen in 1948 and was promoted in 1953 to a professorship at the Institute, where he remained until his death on January 14, 1978.

Gödel's third great discovery was announced in an abstract in 1938 and expounded in full in 1940: the consistency of the continuum hypothesis and of the axiom of choice.

The axiom of choice runs as follows. Suppose a great lot of sets, all mutually exclusive and none of them empty; then there will also be a set containing exactly one member from each. This axiom rings true, and it can be proved as long as the sets in question are finite in number. But for infinite cases no proof is known: none from more obvious beginnings. Yet there are many interesting theorems about infinite sets and infinite numbers that depend for their proofs on the axiom of choice. Accordingly, Gödel's new theorem was welcome; for he proved that the axiom of choice could be added to the usual axioms of set theory without engendering contradiction.

The continuum hypothesis says in effect, of any infinite lot of objects, that either they can be exhausted by assigning each to a distinct whole number or else the real numbers can be exhausted by assigning each real number to a distinct one of those objects. This, unlike the axiom of choice, can scarcely be said to ring true; it rings no bell. There is also a generalized continuum hypothesis, yet farther out. Suffice it to say that these hypotheses resist both proof and disproof from more obvious beginnings, and that they cut a conspicuous figure in the theory of infinite numbers. Gödel's new theorem established that the continuum hypothesis, simple or generalized, can be added to the usual axioms without engendering contradiction.

His way of proving all this, concerning both the axiom of choice and the continuum hypothesis, was every bit as valuable as what he proved. His proof revealed a skeletal structure, economical as can be, that meets all the demands of the usual set theory. This structure, and the assurance of its adequacy, have figured fruitfully in subsequent research also apart from questions of consistency of the axiom of choice and the continuum hypothesis.

What Gödel proved about the axiom of choice and the continuum hypothesis was, we saw, that they can be added to the usual axioms of set theory without engendering contradiction. Now Paul J. Cohen has since proved further that they can be denied without engendering contradiction. They thus hang in midair, undetermined by accepted mathematical principles. We have here a notable postscript to Gödel's already devastating incompleteness theorem. That theorem told us that any given proof procedure, if sound, will leave some mathematical questions (indeed infinitely many) undecidable. And now in the axiom of choice and the continuum hypothesis we have two dramatic examples: two long-studied mathematical questions that are in principle undecidable on the basis of recognized mathematical principles.

Do these results cast doubt on the objectivity of mathematical truth? Or do they reveal unsuspected limits to the power of the mind? Gödel was reluctant to accept either conclusion. His brief subsequent writings reflect a preoccupation with this issue. He believed in the reality of the abstract objects of mathematics and in the capacity of the human mind to apprehend them intuitively. He thought it possible for the mind to transcend formal proof procedures and thus not be bound by his incompleteness theorem. He thought that finer future intuitions about sets might still settle the question of the axiom of choice and the continuum hypothesis.

He propounded no systematic philosophy, but we see him leaning to idealism or even to an old-fashioned rationalism. He particularly admired the rationalist Leibnitz, who had himself anticipated something of mathematical logic. And in a brief contribution to the Einstein volume in Schilpp's Library of Living Philosophers we find Gödel arguing that the general theory of relativity lends support to an idealist position.

Gödel was a slight, frail man. He complained of chronic stomach trouble and was sensitive to cold weather. He could be seen on a warm day trudging along a Princeton street in an overcoat. He said that he and his wife once tried the New Jersey shore for a summer vacation, but found it too cold for comfort.

He had a strong sense of duty. He would pore interminably over the writings of candidates for the Institute for Advanced Study, even though they were only candidates for a year's membership and the writings were remote from his field. He was kind but not outgoing; his interlocutor had to retain the initiative. Such were his achievements, however, that interlocutors with the requisite initiative were by no means wanting.

In 1951 Gödel and John von Neumann shared the Einstein Award and Gödel received an honorary degree at Yale. Harvard followed suit the next year, and Amherst and Rockefeller in later years. Gödel became a member of the American Philosophical Society in 1961. He was a member also of the National Academy of Sciences and the American Academy of Arts and Sciences and a foreign member of the Royal Society, the British Academy, and the Institut de France.

18

Success and Limits
of Mathematization

The two conspicuous traits of mathematics are, first, precision, and, second, the availability of algorithms and rigorous proofs. We regiment a technical language with a view to achieving the most efficient formulation we can of the regularities that hold good of the subject matter; and in some cases this effort produces an algorithm, rendering the laws recognizable by computation. In other cases one settles for a proof procedure, consisting perhaps of a compact codification of so-called axioms and some rules for generating further laws from them.

Mathematical language is the far extreme of this sort of progress. Mathematization is what this progress may be called, if only in its farther reaches.

There has been a perverse tendency to think of mathematics primarily as abstract or uninterpreted and only secondarily as interpreted or applied, and then to philosophize about application. This was the attitude of Russell at the turn of the century, when he wrote that in pure mathematics "we never know what we are talking about, nor whether what we are saying is true."[1] He expressed the same attitude less

This piece, plus two initial pages here omitted, was my contribution to a symposium under this title at the sixteenth International Congress of Philosophy, Düsseldorf, 1978.

1. *Mysticism and Logic*, p. 75. The passage dates from 1901.

wittily thus: "Pure mathematics is the class of all propositions of the form 'p implies q', where p and q are propositions containing one or more variables, the same in the two propositions, and neither 'p' nor 'q' contains any constants except logical constants."[2] On this view all that is left to the mathematician, for him to be right or wrong about, is whether various of his uninterpreted sentence schemata follow logically from his uninterpreted axiom schemata. All that is left to him is elementary logic, the first-order predicate calculus.

This disinterpretation of mathematics was a response to non-Euclidean geometry. Geometrics came to be seen as a family of uninterpreted systems. The first geometry to be studied was indeed abstracted from the technology of architecture and surveying in ancient Egypt, but it is to be reckoned as pure mathematics only after disinterpretation; such was the new view. From geometry the view spread to mathematics generally.

What then of elementary arithmetic? Pure number, pure addition, and the rest would be viewed as uninterpreted; and their application, then, say to apples, would consist perhaps in interpreting the numbers five and twelve as piles of apples, and addition as piling them together.

I find this attitude perverse. The words 'five' and 'twelve' are at no point uninterpreted; they are as integral to our interpreted language as the word 'apple' itself. They name two intangible objects, numbers, which are *sizes of* sets of apples and the like. The 'plus' of addition is likewise interpreted from start to finish, but it has nothing to do with piling things together. Five plus twelve is how many apples there are in two separate piles of five and twelve, without their being piled together.

The expressions 'five', 'twelve', and 'five plus twelve' differ from 'apple' in not denoting bodies, but this is no cause for disinterpretation; the same can be said of such unmathematical terms as 'nation' or 'species'. Ordinary interpreted scientific discourse is as irredeemably committed to abstract objects—to nations, species, numbers, functions, sets—as it

2. *Principles of Mathematics*, p. 3.

is to apples and other bodies. All these things figure as
values of the variables in our overall system of the world.
The numbers and functions contribute just as genuinely to
physical theory as do hypothetical particles.

Arithmetic is a paragon, certainly, of the mathematical
virtues. Its terms are precise and they lend themselves to
an admirable algorithm. But these virtues were achieved
through the progressive sharpening and regimenting of
terms and idioms while they remained embedded in the
regular interpreted language. Arithmetic is related to unregimented language in the same way as is the logic of truth
functions; there is no call for disinterpretation followed by
application. The case of set theory, again, is similar; it comes
of a sharpening and regimenting of ordinary talk of properties or classes. Arithmetic, logic, and set theory are purely
mathematical, but their purity has nothing to do with disinterpretation; all it means is that the arithmetical, logical,
and set-theoretic techniques are formulated without recourse to locutions from outside the arithmetical or logical
or set-theoretic part of our general vocabulary. Purity is not
uninterpretedness.

A progressive sharpening and regimenting of ordinary
idioms: this is what led to arithmetic, symbolic logic, and
set theory, and this is mathematization. Once it has been
achieved by arduous evolution in one domain, it may sometimes be achieved swiftly in another domain by analogy; for
the mathematical notation that was developed in one domain
may, by *r*einterpretation, be put to use in another. A simple
example is the reinterpretation of truth functions as electric
circuits. An even simpler example is the use of graphs in
economics and elsewhere. Geometry, to begin with, is a
sharpening and regimenting of existing idioms regarding
physical space, the space of taut strings and light rays and
trajectories; by reinterpretation, afterward, what had originally designated a curve in physical space might be reinterpreted as expressing a relation between supply and
demand, or between employment and national product, or between the sine of an angle and the size of the angle. These
analogical reinterpretations have fostered the unfortunate
conception of mathematics as basically uninterpreted.

Analogy also takes another line. After some subject matter has been well mathematized and has come to enjoy a smooth algorithm, the mathematician may construct another and this time genuinely uninterpreted system in *partial* analogy. He may do so by denying one of the component laws, or by generalizing on some special feature. Such was the origin of the non-Euclidean geometries and n-dimensional geometry. Systematic variation of this sort, on a wholesale basis, is the business of abstract algebra. Some of the systems thus produced find useful interpretations afterward, but the driving force is not that; it is intellectual curiosity regarding the structures themselves. There is thus no denying the magnitude of the role played in modern mathematics by uninterpreted systems. It is the tail that has come to wag the dog. What I was deploring, however, in deploring the all too popular view represented by the early Russell, was the failure to recognize the existence—let alone the philosophical importance—of the little old dog itself.

In a higher sense, even abstract algebra and the abstract geometrical studies may be said to be fully interpreted studies after all; they are chapters of set theory. A group, for instance, is simply a function of a certain sort. It is any associative two-place function having a unique identity element and for each element an inverse. But a two-place function is a set of triples, and thus group theory is the part of set theory that explores the properties common to functions that meet these conditions. Other abstract algebras can be identified with other set-theoretic structures in a similar spirit.

Mathematics can stand aloof from application to natural science also without being uninterpreted. Higher set theory is a striking case of this. I already urged that set theory, arithmetic, and symbolic logic are all of them products of the straightforward mathematization of ordinary interpreted discourse—mathematization *in situ*. Set-theoretic laws come of regimenting the ways of reasoning about classes or properties, ways of reasoning that already prevailed more or less tacitly in natural science and ordinary discourse. More particularly, as it happens, this regimentation has been a matter of clearing away implicit contradictions. Once the laws are formulated, however, along as simple and general lines as we can manage, we find that they are rich also in implications that outrun any past or contemplated uses, implications regarding infinite sets and transfinite numbers. Bifurcations emerge, moreover, over the axiom of choice or the continuum hypothesis or the existence of inaccessible numbers, where there is a free option between alternative principles without there being any effect on applications in natural science. Mathematicians are driven to pursue these matters by the same disinterested intellectual curiosity that impels them into abstract algebras and odd geometries; yet in this case, unlike those, there has been no departure from interpreted theory.

The branch of mathematics that is most widely and conspicuously used is elementary arithmetic. Next come the parts of mathematics that are built on arithmetic: the algebra of real and complex numbers, the theory of functions, the differential and integral calculus. The ubiquitous use of elementary arithmetic was to be expected, since all sorts of things can be counted and many of them are worth counting. After counting comes measurement. A great invention, measurement; it enables us to compare amounts of valuable stuff that does not lend itself directly to counting. It is measurement that makes for the widespread use of the quantitative branches of mathematics beyond elementary arithmetic.

But if the need to compare amounts of valuable stuff was what fostered the invention of measurement, that use of measurement has subsequently been dwarfed by other uses. Measurement is central to natural science because of the predictive power of concomitant variation. Let us therefore turn our attention briefly to prediction, and induction.

Induction, primitively, was a mere matter of expecting that events that are similar by our lights will have sequels that are similar to one another. The larger the class of mutually similar antecedent events may be, all of which have had mutually similar sequels, the stronger is the presumption of a similar sequel the next time around. But the presumption is increased overwhelmingly if variations among the antecedent events can be correlated with variations in the sequels. For this purpose measurement is brought to bear. Measurement is devised for some varying feature of the otherwise similar antecedent events, and also for some varying feature of the otherwise similar sequels, and a constant ratio or some other simple correlation is established between the two variations. Once this is achieved, a causal connection can no longer be doubted.

Hence the advantage, for science, of quantitative terms; and they are eagerly sought for the various branches of science. These terms and the methods of measuring will differ from branch to branch, but the purely numerical part of the apparatus will be the same for all. Hence the very general scientific utility of analysis, or quantitative mathematics.

Because of the power of these methods, and ultimately the predictive power of concomitant variation, sciences clamor to be quantitative; they clamor for something to measure. This is both good and bad. It is very good indeed if the measurable quantity can be found to play a significant role in the subject matter of the science in question. It is bad if in the quest for something to measure the scientist turns his back on the original concerns of his science and is borne away, however smoothly, on a tangent of trivialities. Ills of mathematization, as well as successes, can be laid to the quest for quantitativity.

It is in the quantitative that mathematization exerts its most overwhelming attraction. More exotic branches of mathematics, however, uninterpreted to begin with, are likewise enlisted for application now and again: topology, perhaps, or Hilbert space. In such cases again there is the duality of good and evil to reckon with. A happy mathematization can work wonders, and the hope of such gains is always the ostensible motive of mathematization. But there are other contributing drives, counter-productive ones, of which the individual himself is apt to be unaware. There is methodolatry, or the love of gadgetry: the tendency to take more satisfaction in methods than in the results. Also there is the repose, the respite from hard thought and hairy decisions, that a smooth algorithm can bring. In these ways one may be lured into problems that lend themselves to favorable techniques, though they not be the problems most central to one's concerns. The rise of the computer aggravates this danger.

We can sense these tensions already in the following humdrum example, which involves no computers and no appreciable mathematics. Amid the vague and amorphous matters confronting the social anthropologist, there are the clean-cut kinship structures. They loom large in primitive societies, and the anthropologist is glad; for they submit nicely to elementary symbolic logic, and do not need even that. Now it is good that there is this firm structure to which to relate other more important but less tangible factors. I suspect nevertheless that kinship cuts a disproportionate figure in anthropology just because of the methodological solace that it brings.

I have touched on the nature of mathematization, arguing that in its primary form it develops within a science rather than being applied from outside. It is continuous with the growth of precision, and it blossoms at last into algorithms and proof procedures. The most significant continuing force for mathematization was measurement, because of the benefits of concomitant variation. Finally I noted the danger of being seduced, by the glitter of algorithm, into mathematizing one's subject off the target. But I should say something, still, about the famous formal limits to mathematization that are intrinsic to the mathematics itself.

Building on Gödel's work, Alonzo Church and Alan Turing showed in 1936 that mathematization in the fullest sense is too much to ask even for so limited a subject as elementary logic. They proved that there can be no complete algorithm, no decision procedure, for the first-order predicate calculus. There is, of course, a complete proof procedure for that calculus. However, it follows from the Church-Turing theorem that there cannot even be a complete proof procedure for nonprovability in that calculus. From this it follows further that there cannot be a complete proof procedure for any branch of mathematics in which proof procedures can be modeled. Elementary number theory is already one such branch; hence Gödel's original incompleteness theorem.

Besides these necessary internal limitations on proof and algorithm, there is commonly also a voluntary one in the case of a natural science. Mathematize as he will, and seek algorithms as he will, the empirical scientist is not going to aspire to an algorithm or proof procedure for the whole of his science; he would not want it if he could have it. He will want rather to keep a large class of his sentences open to the contingencies of future observation. It is only thus that his theory can claim empirical import.

19

On the Limits of Decision

Because these congresses occur at intervals of five years, they make for retrospection. I find myself thinking back over a century of logic. A hundred years ago George Boole's algebra of classes was at hand. Like so many inventions, it had been needlessly clumsy when it first appeared; but meanwhile, in 1864, W. S. Jevons had taken the kinks out of it. It was only in that same year, 1864, that DeMorgan published his crude algebra of relations. Then, around a century ago, C. S. Peirce published three papers refining and extending these two algebras—Boole's of classes and DeMorgan's of relations. These papers of Peirce's appeared in 1867 and 1870. Even our conception of truth-function logic in terms of truth tables, which is so clear and obvious as to seem inevitable today, was not yet explicit in the writings of that time. As for the logic of quantification, it remained unknown until 1879, when Frege published his *Begriffsschrift;* and it was around three years later still that Peirce began to become aware of this idea, through independent efforts. And even down to little more than a half century ago we were weak on decision procedures. It was only in 1915 that Löwenheim published a decision procedure for the Boolean algebra of classes, or, what is equivalent, monadic quantification theory. It was a clumsy procedure, and obscure in the presentation—the way, again, with new inventions. And it was less

---

A shorter version of this paper appeared in the *Akten des XIV. internationalen Kongresses für Philosophie*, vol. 3, 1969.

than a third of a century ago that we were at last forced, by results of Gödel, Turing, and Church, to despair of a decision procedure for the rest of quantification theory.

It is hard now to imagine not seeing truth-function logic as a trivial matter of truth tables, and it is becoming hard even to imagine the decidability of monadic quantification theory as other than obvious. For monadic quantification theory in a modern perspective is essentially just an elaboration of truth-function logic. I want now to spend a few minutes developing this connection.

What makes truth-function logic decidable by truth tables is that the truth value of a truth function can be computed from the truth values of the arguments. But is a formula of quantification theory not a truth function of quantifications? Its truth value can be computed from whatever truth values may be assigned to its component quantifications. Why does this not make quantification theory decidable by truth tables? Why not test a formula of quantification theory for validity by assigning all combinations of truth values to its component quantifications and seeing whether the whole comes out true every time?

The answer obviously is that this criterion of validity is too severe, because the component quantifications are not always independent of one another. A formula of quantification theory might be valid in spite of failing this truth-table test. It might fail the test by turning out false for some assignment of truth values to its component quantifications, but that assignment might be undeserving of notice because incompatible with certain interdependences of the component quantifications.

If, on the other hand, we can put a formula of quantification theory into the form of a truth function of quantifications which are independent of one another, then the truth table will indeed serve as a validity test. And this is just what we can do for monadic formulas of quantification theory. Herbrand showed this in 1930.

The method exploits what Boole called constituent functions; when adapted to quantificational notation they might be called *constituent quantifications*. For a single predicate letter '*F*' the constituent quantifications are two in number:

'$(\exists x) Fx$' and '$(\exists x) - Fx$'. For two letters 'F' and 'G' they are four in number '$(\exists x) (Fx . Gx)$', '$(\exists x) (- Fx . Gx)$', '$(\exists x) (Fx . - Gx)$', and '$(\exists x) (- Fx . - Gx)$'. For n letters, similarly, there are 2^n constitutent quantifications. They correspond to the cells or uncut regions of the Venn diagram. Each constituent quantification says of its cell that it is not empty. Now Herbrand showed that by distributing and confining quantifiers and expanding conjunctions in familiar ways we can transform any monadic formula of quantification theory, in n predicate letters, into an explicit truth function of the constituent quantifications in those n predicate letters. These constituent quantifications are mutually independent; consequently the truth-table test of validity can be brought to bear on any monadic formula of quantification theory once we put the formula into such a normal form. We simply construct the formula's *Herbrand truth table,* as I shall call it, which assigns a truth value to the formula for each assignment of truth values to all constituent quantifications appearing in the formula's normal form. If we care to exempt the empty universe, as is usual and convenient, we have merely to ignore the simultaneous assignment of falsity to all 2^n constituent quantifications.

Example:

$$(\exists x) (Fx . Gx) \supset (x) (Fx . Hx . \supset . Gx).$$

Expressing it as a truth function of constituent quantifications, we have:

$$(\exists x) (Fx . Gx . Hx) \vee (\exists x) (Fx . Gx . - Hx) . \supset$$
$$- (\exists x) (Fx . - Gx . Hx).$$

It comes out true in five of the eight lines of its Herbrand truth table, namely these:

$(\exists x) (Fx . Gx . Hx)$	$(\exists x) (Fx . Gx . - Hx)$	$(\exists x) (Fx . -Gx . Hx)$
$\bot$	$\bot$	$\top$
$\top$	$\top$	$\bot$
$\bot$	$\top$	$\bot$
$\top$	$\bot$	$\bot$
$\bot$	$\bot$	$\bot$

We have now observed this much kinship between monadic formulas of quantification theory and pure truth functions based on sentence letters : the monadic formula has the constituent quantifications as its mutually independent *truth arguments*, that is, arguments that it is a truth function of, just as the pure truth-functional formula has its sentence letters.

It is also possible, by dividing matters differently, to reveal another kinship. Besides seeing a monadic formula in n letters as one truth function of up to 2^n *constituent quantifications*, we can see it also as corresponding to a set of truth functions, or Boolean functions, of just its n predicate letters. These Boolean functions are the *models*, as I shall call them, of the monadic formula. Diagrammatically speaking, a region of the Venn diagram is a model of a given monadic formula if the formula comes out true when all cells of the region are occupied and all else is empty. For example, the formula '$(x) (Fx \equiv -Gx)$' has three models, '$F\overline{G}$', '$\overline{F}G$', and '$\overline{F}G \lor F\overline{G}$'; also the null region, if we choose to recognize the empty universe. The previous example in three predicate letters has 160 models. Clearly any monadic formula is determined uniquely, to within equivalence, by a list of its models. A valid formula is one whose models comprise all 2^{2^n} Boolean functions of its n predicate letters (minus one for the empty universe).

There is a simple mechanical method for eliciting all the models of a monadic formula. It is cumbersome in practice but worth noting in theory. It proceeds from what I shall call the *exhaustive* Herbrand truth table. The ordinary Herbrand truth table assigns truth values to the constituent quantifications that occur in the formula. The exhaustive one, on the other hand, assigns truth values to all 2^n constituent quantifications in the n predicate letters, whether the quantifications occur in the formula or not. Where n is 2, the table runs to four columns and fifteen rows (if we deduct one for the empty universe) ; where n is 3 it runs to eight columns and 255 rows. Now the models of a monadic formula can be formed from the *favorable* rows of the exhaustive Herbrand truth table, that is, the rows in which the formula comes out true. At each favorable row we simply form the alternation of the constituent quantifications that are marked true in that row, and then delete the quantifiers and bound variables; what remains is a model.

Example: '$(x)(Fx \equiv -Gx)$', expressed as a truth function of constituent quantifications, becomes:

$$- (\exists x)(Fx \cdot Gx) \cdot - (\exists x)(-Fx \cdot -Gx).$$

One of the favorable rows of its exhaustive Herbrand truth table is:

$(\exists x)(Fx \cdot Gx)$	$(\exists x)(-Fx \cdot Gx)$	$(\exists x)(Fx \cdot -Gx)$	$(\exists x)(-Fx \cdot -Gx)$
$\perp$	T	T	$\perp$

The corresponding model is '$\overline{F}G \vee F\overline{G}$'.

So the relation of truth functions to monadic formulas can be seen in two ways: the monadic formula is a truth function of up to 2^n constituent quantifications, and also it is determined by a set of up to $2^{2^n} - 1$ Boolean functions of its n predicate letters.

However viewed, the relation invites extrapolation. Truth-functional formulas are to monadic formulas as monadic formulas are to what dyadic ones? Let us try extrapolating. The truth arguments of the n-letter truth-functional formulas are just the n letters. The truth arguments of the n-letter monadic formulas are the 2^n constituent quantifications. Now the new formulas will be certain n-letter dyadic formulas, having 2^{2^n} truth arguments which are built from the 2^n constituent quantifications as constituent quantifications were built from the n predicate letters. Each of these 2^{2^n} new truth arguments will be, in short, an n-letter super-constituent quantification, and will have this form:

$$(\exists x)[\pm (\exists y)(\pm F_1 xy \cdot \pm F_2 xy \ldots \pm F_n xy).$$
$$\pm (\exists y)(\pm F_1 xy \cdot \pm F_2 xy \ldots \pm F_n xy) \ldots$$
$$\pm (\exists y)(\pm F_1 xy \cdot \pm F_2 xy \ldots \pm F_n xy)]$$

where each '$\pm$' may represent affirmation or negation. The new sort of dyadic formulas to which we are extrapolating will be the truth functions of such super-constituent quantifications.

The n-letter monadic formulas, though they were truth functions of the 2^n constituent quantifications in those letters, were of course not ordinarily written explicitly as truth functions of these. To rewrite them thus was to put them in a certain normal form. Now the same is to be true of our new n-letter dyadic formulas; we may take this new lot as broadly as we please, so long as all are convertible into a normal form which represents them explicitly as truth functions of the super-constituent quantifications in those letters. A natural class of dyadic formulas meeting this requirement is the class of what I shall call the *homogeneous dyadic formulas*, defined as follows: a homogeneous dyadic formula is any formula of quantification theory in which each occurrence of each predicate letter is followed by the specific pair of letters 'xy' in that order, and each of the (possibly numerous) quantifiers containing the letter 'y' stands in the scope of one of the quantifiers containing 'x'. By the same moves by which Herbrand was able to transform any monadic schema into an explicit truth function of constituent quantifications, namely, by distributing and confining quantifiers and expanding conjunctions, we are able also to transform any homogeneous dyadic formula in n predicate letters into an explicit truth function of the super-constituent quantifications in those n letters.

Consider now the nature of a super-constituent quantification, as displayed above. If at first we think of the x as fixed, in that formula, then each line of the formula affirms the nonemptiness or emptiness of a constituent function, or cell of the Venn diagram; and all these 2^n lines together then give the whole story regarding all 2^n cells of some one Venn diagram. Each way of settling all the affirmation-negation signs determines one fully marked Venn diagram for the n predicates. For each particular way of settling all the affirmation-negation signs, therefore, what the whole super-constituent quantification tells us is that that particular Venn diagram is fulfilled by the classes obtained by projecting the relations $F_1, F_2, \ldots, F_n$ on some one object x.

The 2^{2^n} super-constituent quantifications are mutually independent, since a different object x can serve each time.

There is, therefore, a decision procedure for a homogeneous dyadic formula: just put it into normal form and build a whacking truth table on these 2^{2^n} truth arguments. Incidentally we can again exempt the empty universe if we please by ignoring appropriate rows.

We saw how an n-letter monadic formula, besides being a truth function of constituent quantifications, corresponds to a set of Boolean functions of the n letters themselves. Now an n-letter homogeneous dyadic formula can be seen to correspond similarly to a set of monadic formulas in those n letters, and hence to a set of sets of Boolean functions of those n letters.

Another step of extrapolation leads from the homogeneous dyadic formulas to homogeneous triadic formulas, which again are decidable. Their truth arguments are super-super-constituent quantifications. And so on up. In general, the homogeneous k-adic formulas are k-adic formulas of quantification theory meeting restrictions like those noted in the dyadic case; namely, the variables must stand in a fixed order after the predicate letters, and the quantifiers must be nested always in that order.

Our natural tendency to associate monadic quantification theory with general quantification theory is in a way misleading. The monadic has stronger affiliations with truth-function logic than with general quantification theory. All these homogeneous polyadic formulas likewise are, is essential respects, of a piece still with truth-function logic.

What makes the difference between all this and the undecidable general quantification theory is not, we see, the presence of polyadic predicates. What evidently gives general quantification theory its escape velocity is the chance to switch or fuse the variable attached to a predicate letter, so as to play 'Fyx' or 'Fxx' against 'Fxy'.

The mercurial quality of general quantification theory can subsist, we know, in seemingly modest fragments of general quantification theory. The general theory of a single symmetrical dyadic predicate is undecidable.[1] So is the general theory of dyadic formulas in which there is no quantifier

1. Church and Quine.

beyond a single initial cluster ' $(\exists x) (y) (\exists z)$ '.[2] Perhaps the time will come when what makes for undecidability in quantification theory will seem as obvious as the decidability of the monadic case. That time is not yet.

2. Kahr, Moore, and Wang.

20

Predicates, Terms, and Classes

Let me begin by distinguishing three kinds of expressions and noting ways in which they have been confused. Later I shall make some moves that tend rather to merge them again, though without confusion.

The three kinds are *predicates, general terms,* and *class names.* The predicate may be pictured as a sentence with gaps left in it where a singular term could be inserted to complete the sentence. This is what C. S. Peirce called a *rheme.* I am thinking at first only of one-place predicates, but the gaps may still be many, corresponding to recurrences of some one singular term. Or, with Frege, we may regard the predicate not as composed of signs at all, but rather as a *way* of forming a sentence around a singular term. This also was Wittgenstein's conception.

The general term, on the other hand, is a sign or a continuous string of signs. It may be a verb or verb phrase, a noun or noun phrase, an adjective or adjective phrase; these

I read this paper in South Africa in October 1980 and at Boston University in December. Early portions hint somewhat of "Clauses and classes," which I presented to the Société Française de Logique in 1978. That paper was subsequently circulated in the bulletin of the society. The last part of the present paper is adapted, by permission of the American Mathematical Society, from "Predicate functors revisited," which is to appear in the *Journal of Symbolic Logic* copyright © by the Association of Symbolic Logic.

distinctions are immaterial to logic. If we think of a predicate as a sentence with gaps, then a general term is that special sort of predicate where the gap comes at one end. I am still limiting my attention to the monadic.

Finally a class name is not a general term, anyway not until further notice, and not a predicate. It is a singular term, simple or complex, *designating* a single abstract object, a class. The corresponding general term *denotes* any number of objects, each member of the class.

The schematic letter '*F*' in the '*Fx*' of symbolic logic is quite properly called a predicate letter, for '*Fx*' stands for any open sentence in '*x*', however numerous and scattered the occurrences of '*x*' in it may be. On the other hand, the letters '*S*', '*M*', and '*P*', as used in schematizing syllogisms in traditional textbooks, are schematic letters for general terms. The place holders for class names, finally, are genuine bindable variables whose values are classes. They may be general variables such as '*x*' and '*y*', or they may be distinctive ones such as '*α*' and '*β*' in *Principia Mathematica*.

A major part of the traditional exercises in syllogisms consisted in preparing each sentence by recasting it in one of the four categorical forms 'All *S* are *P*', 'No *S* are *P*', 'Some *S* are *P*', and 'Some *S* are not *P*', known as A, E, I, and O : 'A' for 'all', we might say, 'E' for 'exclusion', 'I' for 'intersection', and 'O' for 'overflow'. The job of recasting can be visualized in two stages. First the given sentence had to be paraphrased in such a way as to say explicitly that everything or something satisfying such and such a condition, '*Fx*' let us say, satisfies also or fails to satisfy such and such a further condition, say '*Gx*'. The remaining step consisted in effect in maneuvering the '*Fx*' and '*Gx*' into the forms '*x* is an *S*' and '*x* is a *P*', with nicely segregated general terms in place of '*S*' and '*P*'. This step consisted, thus, in devising general terms coextensive with given predicates. It was the easier step of the two, for there is a uniform grammatical construction to the purpose: the relative clause. We can immediately convert any sentence about an object *a* into the form '*a* is something which' followed by a contorted rendering of the original sentence with pronouns where '*a*' had been.

The relative clause is often and conveniently streamlined

in the 'such that' idiom, which is simpler grammatically: '*a* in an *x* such that *Fx*'. The bound variable prevents ambiguity of cross-reference where clauses are nested. The relative clause, whether in the 'such that' form or the 'which' form, is not a class name but merely a complex general term.

Throughout the history of modern logic there has been a tendency to confuse the general term with the abstract singular. The schematic letters for general terms, in syllogistic logic and elsewhere, were thus commonly viewed as class variables, and the 'such that' clauses were viewed as class names. At the same time there was a laudable reluctance to objectify classes at the elementary level of logic; one saw the wisdom of relegating them to where they were really needed, in ulterior parts of mathematics and elsewhere. In the neo-classical logic, consequently, schematic letters for general terms were avoided, and so was the relative clause, the 'such that' construction. Logicians made do with predicate letters, always with variables or singular constants appended as arguments. Such is the standard schematism of quantification theory or the predicate calculus, and it has regularly been adhered to even in the monadic case, where Boolean algebra can cover the same ground more simply and graphically. It was not appreciated that the letters of Boolean algebra can be received innocently as standing schematically for general terms, and that their Boolean compounds can be seen as standing not for class names but for compound general terms.

Scruples against premature reification of classes or properties were probably what led Frege to stress the *ungesättigt* character of predicates, or what he called functions: they need to be filled in with arguments. I applaud the scruples and I agree about the predicates. What I deplore is his failure to see that general terms can be schematized without reifying classes or properties. This failure was due to the dimness, back then, of the distinction between schematic letters and quantifiable variables. Notice that even his predicate letters creep hesitantly into quantifiers on occasion. He was still feeling his way.

Once we appreciate the ontological innocence of the 'such that' idiom, we can admit it with equanimity to the language of elementary logic. Now what about a compact notation for it? One might think we ought to keep conspicuously clear of the set-theoretic notation '$\{x : Fx\}$', in view of the melancholy history of confusion between general terms and class names. However, I shall now propose quite the contrary: that we write '$\{x : Fx\}$' for our innocent relative clause, and 'ϵ' correspondingly for the innocent copula 'is an' that is the inverse of 'such that', and that we then simply deny that we are referring to classes. I find that this course is suited to a philosophically attractive line on classes.

Here is a myth of genesis of the notion of classes. It need not be true, though it seems fairly plausible. In the beginning there were general terms, including relative clauses, for which I am boldly proposing the notation '$\{x : Fx\}$'. Prodded then by certain analogies, on which I have speculated elsewhere,[1] between general terms and singular terms, people began to let the general terms do double duty as singular terms. Thus they posited a single abstract object for each general terms to designate. They called it a property, but we may slim properties down to classes for the well-known benefits of extensionality.

Quantifying over classes began thus in a confusion of general with singular, but it proved to be a happy accident, enriching science in vastly important ways that I shall not pause over.[2] And then, in the fullness of time, people whom we can name found that not every general term could have its class, on pain of paradox. The relative or 'such that' clauses, written as term abstracts '$\{x : Fx\}$', could continue without restriction in the capacity of general terms, but some of them could not be allowed to double as class names, while the rest of them still could. Where to draw the line is the question what set theory to adopt. Wherever drawn, the distinction is easily expressed:

(1) $$(\exists y)(y = \{x : Fx\})$$

tells us that there is such a class. Mathematics transcends logic at just this point.

1. *Roots of Reference*, pp. 84–88, 97–106.
2. See Essay 1 above, §II.

What we have here is the theory of virtual and real classes as of my *Set Theory and Its Logic,* but seen no longer in terms of virtual classes as simulated classes. The abstracts are seen now as unpretentious relative clauses, some of which may also be class names and some not.

Logic, then, in the narrow sense represented by quantification theory, can make free with the abstraction notation '$\{x: Fx\}$', but with no thought of substituting such an abstract for a variable in instantiating a quantification. Such a move would require a premise of the form (1), which would belong to a higher level of mathematics, namely, set theory.

Recoiling from that higher level, let us see how neat an elementary logic can be based on '$\{x: Fx\}$' in the innocent sense of term abstraction. This will be the only variable-binding operator. In addition I shall assume a copula; not 'ϵ', however, not the singular 'is an', but one of the categorical copulas, as our syllogizing forefathers called them. I shall adopt the universal negative copula, the E of the mediaevals, exclusion. 'S excl P' will mean that the S's exclude the P's; no S are P. We must bear in mind that 'excl' is not a singular verb 'excludes', joining two class names, but a copula, 'no are', or 'exclude'. The plural verb 'exclude' is indeed a copula, from a logical point of view, and is equivalent to 'no are', whereas the singular verb 'excludes' is a dyadic general term predicable of pairs of classes. When the further step is made of positing classes as designata of the general terms, the distinction lapses.

Term abstraction and the categorical copula 'excl' suffice for expressing the truth functions and quantification. We can define as follows.

$$'p \mid q' \quad \text{for} \quad '\{x: p\} \text{ excl } \{x: q\}',$$
$$'- p' \quad \text{for} \quad 'p \mid p',$$
$$'\exists\{x: Fx\})' \quad \text{for} \quad '- (\{x: Fx\} \text{ excl } \{x: Fx\}))'.$$

As usual, 'p' and 'q' are schematic letters for sentences lacking any free variables relevant to the context. The first definition thus exploits vacuous abstraction and delivers the truth function 'not both', Sheffer's stroke function. The last definition gives existential quantification, '$(\exists x)Fx$'. Everyone knows how to proceed from these acquisitions to the rest of the truth functions and universal quantification. So we see that the needs of the predicate calculus are met by just the relative clause and the exclusion copula, without use of the singular copula 'ϵ', 'is an'. The embedded predicate letters 'F', 'G', and so on, do remain in the schematism, with variables always attached, just as in the standard schematism of the predicate calculus. On the other hand, the schematic *sentence* letters are a mere convenience, here as in the standard predicate calculus; we could always use 'Fx' or 'Gy' or the like instead of 'p'. Our notation thus comprises just term abstraction and exclusion and the usual schematism of predicate letters adjoined to variables. The exclusion copula occurs only between abstracts.

The reason for distinguishing between general terms and other predicates was that the predicate was not always a segregated and continuous string of signs. This meant keeping predicate letters attached to their arguments. With term abstracts at our disposal, however, this contrast has less point; the predicate can always be gathered up into a general term by abstraction. We could begin to think of our predicate letter 'F' as a term letter after all, if it were only a question of monadic predicates. But it is not; not now. The schematism of predicate letters that is called for in this encapsulation of the predicate calculus is the usual full array, including 'Fxy' and the rest.

However, this line of thought opens up an interesting alternative course of development that is oriented utterly to general terms, monadic and polyadic. Turning to this new course, we reassess all predicate letters as term letters. When 'F' was a predicate letter, the combination 'Fx' was merely a composite symbol standing for any open sentence containing 'x'. Now that 'F' stands for a general term, on the other hand, the juxtaposing of 'F' and 'x' must be understood as a logical operation of predication, a binary operation upon a general term and a variable. I would now write it with a copula as '$x \epsilon F$' were it not that I want to preserve uniformity with polyadic cases. 'Fxy' comes to express a ternary operation of predication, operating on a dyadic general term and two variables. Correspondingly for '$Fxyz$' and beyond.

Numerical indices will now be wanted on the term letters to indicate the degree of each, that is, the number of places. This is because the attached variables are destined to disappear, as we shall see, so that we can no longer count them to determine degree.

Also other supplementary devices will be introduced. The benefit they will confer is the full analysis and elimination of the relative clause, or abstract, and its variables. Predication will disappear as well.

What I am leading up to is what I have called predicate-functor logic. I published on it in 1960 and again in 1971.[3] My reason for reopening it now is that the logic of term abstraction and exclusion which we have just been seeing affords easy new access to a predicate-functor version.

The purpose of the relative clause was to integrate what a sentence says about an object. Its instrument is the bound variable, which marks and collects scattered references to the object. In predicate-functor logic this work is accomplished rather by a few fixed functors that operate on general terms to produce new general terms. These functors have the effect of variously permuting or fusing or supplementing the argument places. Four will suffice. There are *major* and *minor inversion,* explained thus:

$$(\operatorname{Inv} F^n)\, x_2 \ldots x_n x_1 \equiv F^n x_1 \ldots x_n,$$
$$(\operatorname{inv} F^n)\, x_2 x_1 x_3 \ldots x_n \equiv F^n x_1 \ldots x_n.$$

There is a functor that I call *padding*:

$$(\operatorname{Pad} F^n)\, x_0 x_1 \ldots x_n \equiv F^n x_1 \ldots x_n.$$

Finally there is *reflection,* the self or reflexive functor:

$$(\operatorname{Ref} F^n)\, x_2 \ldots x_n \equiv F^n x_2 x_2 \ldots x_n.$$

3. "Variables explained away," reprinted in *Selected Logic Papers;* "Algebraic logic and predicate functors," reprinted with revisions in the 1976 edition of *Ways of Paradox.* In its elimination of variables the plan is reminiscent of the combinatory logic of Schönfinkel and Curry, but unlike theirs it stays within the bounds of predicate logic.

In iteration these four functors suffice to *homogenize* any two predications—that is, to endow them with matching strings of arguments—and to leave the arguments in any desired order, devoid of repetitions. For example, the heterogeneous predications 'F^5wzwxy' and 'G^4vxyz' are verifiably equivalent to these homogeneous ones:

(Pad Ref Inv inv F^5) $vwxyz$,   (inv Pad G^4) $vwxyz$,

These four functors accomplish the recombinatory work of variables. One further functor suffices for the rest of the burden of the predicate calculus. It is a two-place functor that I call the *divergence* functor. Applied to two $n$adic general terms, it produces a term '$F^n \parallel G^n$' of degree $n - 1$. In particular then '$F^1 \parallel G^1$' is a term of degree 0, that is, a sentence. Its interpretation is to be 'F^1 excl G^1'; 'No F are G'. '$F^2 \parallel G^2$' is to be interpreted as the monadic general term:

$$\{y: \{x: F^2xy\} \text{ excl } \{x: G^2xy\}\}.$$

For example, where 'F^2xy' and 'G^2xy' mean 'x reads y' and 'x understands y', '$(F^2 \parallel G^2)y$' means that y is understood by none who read it. The general term '$F^2 \parallel G^2$' amounts to the words 'understood by no readers thereof'. In general,

(2) $(F^n \parallel G^n)x^2 \ldots x_n \equiv . \{x_1: F^nx_1 \ldots x_n\}$ excl $\{x_1: G^nx_1 \ldots x_n\}$
          $= (\omega_1) (F^n\omega_1 \ldots x_n \mid G^nx_1 \ldots x_n).$

It can now be quickly shown that these five functors, applied in iteration to term letters, are adequate to the whole of the predicate calculus. Abstraction, bindable variables, and predication all go by the board. Functors and schematic term letters remain.

For, consider our last version of the predicate calculus, in terms of term abstraction and the exclusion copula. Given any closed sentence schema S in that notation, we can translate it into terms of our five functors as follows. Choose any innermost occurrence in S of the exclusion copula; that is, any occurrence that is flanked by abstracts devoid of the copula. It is flanked thus:

(3) $\{x: F\ldots\}$ excl $\{x: G\ldots\}$

where the rows of dots stand for rows of variables. Bringing

172

our four combinatory functors to bear, we homogenize the 'F...' and 'G...', giving the variable 'x' initial position in each. Thus (3) goes over into something of this sort:

(4) $$\{x : \Gamma x y_1 \ldots y_n\} \text{ excl } \{x : \Delta x y_1 \ldots y_n\}$$

where 'Γ' and 'Δ' stand for complex general terms built from 'F' and 'G' by the combinatory functors. But (4) reduces by (2) to the single predication ' $(\Gamma \parallel \Delta) y_1 \ldots y_n$'. The variable '$x$' and its abstracts have disappeared. Then we proceed similarly with another innermost occurrence of the exclusion copula. As we continue this procedure, exclusion copulas that were not innermost become innermost and give way to single predications; and variables and abstracts continue to disappear. In the end S reduces to a single predication, '$\Theta z_1 \ldots z_k$'. But S had no free variables; all its variables were bound by abstracts, and all are now gone. So $k = 0$; we are left with merely 'Θ', which is some zero-place term schema, some sentence schema, built up of term letters by the four combinatory functors and the divergence functor.

The five functors that have thus proved adequate to the predicate calculus can in fact be reduced to four. George Myro showed me in 1971 that the two inversion functors can be supplanted by a single functor of permutation, explained thus:[4]

$$(\text{Perm } F^n) x_1 x_3 \ldots x_n x_2 \equiv F^n x_1 \ldots x_n.$$

4. This can be seen with the help of *Ways of Paradox*, 1976, p. 298. The 'p' of that page is 'Perm'. The cropping functor there used is definable as the complement of our present '$F \parallel F$', complement being definable thus: '$-G$' for 'Pad $G \parallel$ Pad G'.

21

Responses

Some of my reading elicits responses in rebuttal or further explanation. Some strikes a responsive chord. The ensuing fragments comprise responses of all three sorts.

RESPONDING TO SAUL KRIPKE[1]

A rigid designator is one that "designates the same object in all possible worlds," or, as Kripke presently corrects himself, "in any possible world where the object in question *does* exist." He reassures us regarding his talk of possible worlds: it is not science fiction, but only a vivid way of phrasing our old familiar contrary-to-fact conditionals. Let us recall then that some of us have deemed our contrary-to-fact conditionals themselves wanting in clarity. It is partly in response to this discomfort that the current literature on possible worlds has emerged. It is amusing to imagine that some of us same philosophers may be so bewildered by this further concept that we come to welcome the old familiar contrary-to-fact conditionals as a clarification, and are content at last to acquiesce in them.

The notion of possible world did indeed contribute to the semantics of modal logic, and it behooves us to recognize the nature of its contribution: it led to Kripke's precocious and

---

1. From a review in the *Journal of Philosophy* 69 (1972) of the Munitz volume. Kripke's essay is "Identity and necessity," pp. 135–164 of that volume.

significant theory of models of modal logic. Models afford consistency proofs; also they have heuristic value; but they do not constitute explication. Models, however clear they be in themselves, may leave us still at a loss for the primary, intended interpretation. When modal logic has been paraphrased in terms of such notions as possible world or rigid designator, where the displaced fog settles is on the question when to identify objects between worlds, or when to treat a designator as rigid, or where to attribute metaphysical necessity.

Kripke makes puzzling use of Bishop Butler.

So, as Bishop Butler said, "everything is what it is and not another thing." Therefore [*sic*], "Heat is the motion of molecules" will be necessary, not contingent. (p. 160)

I can construe the bishop to my own purposes: everything is what it is, ask not what it may or must be.

Kripke's positive ruling on heat and molecules is followed by less positive reflections on mind-body identity.

The identity theorist, who holds that pain is the brain state . . . has to hold that we are under some illusion in thinking that we can imagine that there could have been pains without brain states . . . So the materialist is up against a very stiff challenge. He has to show that these things we think we can see to be possible are in fact not possible. (pp. 162–163)

The materialist will sense the stiffness of this challenge only insofar as he believes in metaphysical necessity. I can read Kripke gratefully as abetting my effort to show what a tangled web the modalist weaves.

RESPONDING FURTHER TO KRIPKE[2]

Kripke writes congenially on ontology and referential quantification, stressing that their connection is trivially assured by the very explanation of referential quantification.

2. From a review in the *Journal of Philosophy* 74 (1977) of Evans and McDowell. Kripke's essay is "Is there a problem about substitutional quantification?" pp. 325–419 of that volume.

The solemnity of my terms 'ontological commitment' and 'ontological criterion' has led my readers to suppose that there is more afoot than meets the eye, despite my protests. For all its triviality the connection had desperately needed stressing because of philosophers such as were fictionalized in "On What There Is"[3] and cited from real life by Church.[4] I am grateful for Kripke's deflationary remarks, for they cannot be repeated too often. But then I am let down by the suggestion that he has "considerable doubts and uncertainties" about "Quine's views on ontological commitment" (p. 327) and that we "need a careful examination of the merits and demerits of Quine's and other criteria for 'ontological commitment'" (p. 415). He, like the others, still thinks after all that there is more afoot than meets the eye.

In the course of a homily on morality in philosophy he rightly deplores that "some philosophical writings of an anti-formalist tendency attribute the particular philosophical views of Russell, Quine, or the Vienna Circle—to mention three examples—to 'the formal logicians'" (p. 409). Forty years ago I likewise was deploring the tendency of anti-formalists to attribute the views of the Vienna Circle to "the symbolic logicians." It is sad that the evil persists, but I find wry amusement in becoming included among its objects.

One of Kripke's moral precepts deplores "the tendency to propose technical criteria with the aim of excluding approaches that one dislikes" (p. 410). He notes in illustration that I adopted a criterion of ontological reduction for no other reason than that it "includes well-known cases and excludes undesired cases."[5] I protest that mine was expressly a quest for an objective criterion agreeing with our intuitive sorting of cases. This is a proper and characteristically philosophical sort of quest, so long as one knows and says what one is doing.

3. Reprinted in my *From a Logical Point of View*.
4. "Ontological commitment."
5. He is referring to "Ontological reduction and the world of numbers," reprinted in *Ways of Paradox*.

RESPONDING TO GROVER MAXWELL[6]

One central plank in Maxwell's platform is that our knowledge of the external world consists in a sharing of structure. This is to my mind an important truth, or points toward one. Structure, in the sense of the word that is relevant to this important truth, is what we preserve when we code information.

Send a man into another room and have him come back and report on its contents. He comes back and agitates the air for a while, and in consequence of this agitation we learn about objects in the other room which are very unlike any agitation of the air. Selected traits of objects in that room are coded in traits of this agitation of the air. The manner of the coding, called language, is complicated and far-fetched, but it works; and clearly it is purely structural, at least in the privative sense of depending on no qualitative resemblances between the objects and the agitation. Also the man's internal state, neural or whatever, in which his knowledge of the objects in that room consists, presumably bears none but structural relations to those objects; structural in the privative sense of there being no qualitative resemblances between the objects and the man's internal state, but only some sort of coding, and, of course, causation. And the same applies to our own knowledge of the objects, as gained from the man's testimony.

I do think there is a substantial resemblance between our internal state, whatever it is, which constitutes our hearsay knowledge of the objects in that room, and the man's internal state, which constitutes his eyewitness knowledge of the objects. This I find plausible on broadly naturalistic grounds. Here then I seem even to be in an odd kind of agreement with Maxwell's doctrine of the relative accessibility of other minds. But I must stress a distinction. What I just now conjectured is that between two men's knowledge of the same

6. This response and the next are reprinted from Imre Lakatos and Alan Musgrave, eds., *Problems in the Philosophy of Science* (copyright © 1968, North-Holland Publishing Co., Amsterdam), pp. 161–163, 200f. Maxwell's essay is "Scientific methodology," pp. 148–160 of that volume, and Yourgrau's is "A budget of paradoxes in physics," pp. 178–199.

things there is a more substantial resemblance than between the knowledge and the things. But publicly observable bodies, still, and not other people's knowledge, are what our firmest knowledge is *about*.

Observation terms are the terms upon whose attribution all members of the speech community tend to agree under like stimulation. Observation terms are the consensus-prone terms, and they owe this trait to their having been learned mostly by ostension, or reinforcement in the presence of their objects, rather than by context or definition. What they apply to are publicly observable bodies, mostly, and not subjective entities, because the learning of language is social.

Thus I do not share Maxwell's doctrine that 'the external world . . . is unobservable'. On the contrary, the external world has had, as a theater of observation, few rivals. I disagree, too, when he denies bodies their color because they are collections of submicroscopic particles. Water remains water gallon by gallon, I say, even though its submicroscopic bits are rather oxygen and hydrogen; there is no paradox in this, and there is none in saying that a table top remains smooth and brown, square inch by square inch, even though its submicroscopic bits are discrete, vibrant, and colorless. The qualities of being aqueous and of being smooth and brown are like swarming, or waging war: they are traits only of a congeries. This does not make them unreal or subjective. There is no call for a predicate to hold of each part of the things it holds of. Even a predicate of shape, after all, would fail that test. It is a modern discovery in particular that aqueousness, smoothness, and brownness resemble squareness and swarming on this score; but it is not a contradiction.

Maxwell's trouble, if he has one, is an unquestioning reification of sense data, Humean impressions, free-floating color patches. If you put the color there on a subjective *Vorhang* or curtain, of course you must leave bodies colorless; for, as Maxwell and I agreed, bodies and our knowledge of them are related only structurally and causally and not by a sharing of qualities. Also, if you keep the curtain, you understandably balk at acknowledging observation of bodies. But the curtain itself is a relic of the days when philosophy aspired to a privileged status, nearer and firmer than natural science. This, not behaviorism, is the excessive empiricism that wants exorcising. Neurath pointed the way, representing philosophy and science as in one and the same boat. Problems dissolve, some of them, when we view perception squarely as a causal transaction between external bodies and talking people, with no curtain to screen them.

RESPONDING TO WOLFGANG YOURGRAU

The word 'paradox' is commonly used, in an inclusive sense, for any plausible argument from plausible premises to an implausible conclusion. Paradox in this broad sense can be a casual affair. A little scrutiny may show that a premise was subtly false, or a step subtly fallacious, or that the conclusion was more plausible than we thought; and so the paradox may be resolved without violence to firm beliefs.

Some philosophers have used the word 'paradox' in a narrower sense, reserving it for cases that compel revision of deeply rooted principles. Such is the usage of those who say that Zeno's paradoxes, the barber paradox, the paradox of the condemned man, Skolem's paradox, and Gödel's incompleteness theorem are not genuine paradoxes. But there is already an established word for paradoxes in the narrow sense; viz., 'antinomy'. So the easier line is to accept the common inclusive use of 'paradox' and then distinguish the crisis-engendering species as antinomies.

Russell's paradox is for me a prime example of antinomy. For Yourgrau it is not, I gather; anyway he does not agree that it contravenes principles 'implicit in . . . common sense'. The question on which we differ is whether there being a class for every formulable membership condition is a principle implicit in common sense.

In any event, both the broad quality of paradox and the narrower quality of antinomy are temporal. What premises and what steps of reasoning are persuasive though faulty, and what conclusions are implausible though true, will vary with the sophistication of the individual and the progress of science; and so, therefore, will paradox. Within paradox, again, the special quality of antinomy will in turn depend on whether what is challenged is a firm tenet of the individual at the time. Besides varying with time and person, moreover, the qualities of both paradox and antinomy are matters clearly of degree and not of kind.

Among the antinomies of set theory and semantics there is indeed a family resemblance, namely a certain air of self-application, or circularity. It is shared also by some paradoxes which are not antinomies, notably Gödel's theorem, the barber paradox, and the paradox of the condemned man, and indeed it is present wherever there is a diagonal argument, with or without an air of paradox. It is not easily read into Skolem's paradox, and it bears none at all on Zeno. But it is so characteristic of paradoxes at their most vivid and of antinomies at their most virulent that perhaps self-application, rather than antinomy or paradox as such, is what wants closer scrutiny and deeper understanding.

For we encounter somewhat this same pattern of self-application also at significant points outside the bounds of logic, set theory, and semantics. A case in the philosophy of science is the paradox of Laplace's sage undertaking to falsify his predictions. Much the same problem takes a serious turn in economics, where a predicted state, for example a price in the stock market, is disturbed by the prediction of it. To cope with this predicament was a central motive of the theory of games. In physics we find an analogy in Heisenberg's indeterminacy principle, which turns on the disturbance of the observed object by the observation of it. If we ever find a unified solution of the antinomies of set theory and semantics, along more natural lines than are now known, these analogies will lead us to expect repercussions in other domains.

RESPONDING TO M. J. CRESSWELL[7]

Cresswell puts his metaphysical question thus: What is it that makes one complete physical theory true and another

7. Reprinted from "Replies to the eleven essays," *Southwestern Journal of Philosophy* 11 (1981), where I answer the contributors to Shahan and Swoyer. Cresswell's essay is "Can epistemology be naturalized?" pp. 110–118 of that volume.

false? I can only answer, with unhelpful realism, that it is the nature of the world. Immanent truth, à la Tarski, is the only truth I recognize. But Cresswell adds helpfully that the question has often been posed rather as an epistemological question, viz., how can we know that the one theory is true and the other false? This is really quite another question, and a more nearly serious one.

There is an obstacle still in the verb 'know'. Must it imply certainty, infallibility? Then the answer is that we cannot. But if we ask rather how we are better warranted in believing one theory than another, our question is a substantial one. A full answer would be a full theory of observational evidence and scientific method.

A quick and metaphorical answer, which Cresswell quotes from me, is that the tribunal of experience is the final arbiter. He complains that my "metaphors about the tribunal of experience never get quite the elaboration we feel they need," and I expect he is right. I can only say that I have poured out the full content, such as it is, of that and other brief metaphors of the last pages of "Two Dogmas"[8] into utterest prose. Such was the purpose of large parts of *Word and Object* and *The Roots of Reference;* and note also Essay 2, above. What I called the experiential periphery in "Two Dogmas" takes form in *Word and Object* as the triggering of nerve endings, and what I called statements near the periphery are recognizable in *Word and Object* as the observation sentences. True, there are scarcely the beginnings here of a full theory of evidence and scientific method; much more to that purpose can be gleaned from works by others.

Cresswell compares my view with Russell's logical atomism and rightly finds them incompatible. "He certainly has no sympathy," he writes of me, "with any theory which would make the atomic facts simple facts about our experience, each logically independent of all others." True, but still it is instructive to compare my observation sentences with this doctrine. They are not about experience, but they are fair naturalistic analogues of sentences about experi-

8. Reprinted in *From a Logical Point of View.*

ence, in that their use is acquired or can be acquired by direct conditioning to the stimulation of sensory receptors. Moreover, simple observation sentences are in most cases independent of one another. The profound difference between my view and Russell's atomism is rather that the rest of the truths are not compounded somehow of the observation sentences, in my view, or implied by them. Their connection with the observation sentences is more tenuous and complex.

Likening me to Bradley, Cresswell saddles me with a realm of reified experience or appearance set over against an inscrutable reality. My naturalistic view is unlike that. I have forces from real external objects impinging on our nerve endings, and I have us acquiring sentences about real external objects partly through conditioning to those neural excitations and partly through complex relations of sentences to sentences.

Our speculations about the world remain subject to norms and caveats, but these issue from science itself as we acquire it. Thus one of our scientific findings is the very fact, just now noted, that information about the world reaches us only by forces impinging on our nerve endings; and this finding has normative force, cautioning us as it does against claims of telepathy and clairvoyance. The norms can change somewhat as science progresses. For example, we once were more chary of action at a distance than we have been since Sir Isaac Newton.

These last reflections give naturalism itself somewhat the aspect of a coherence theory after all, and I wonder if I am getting at last some glimmering of Cresswell's discomfort. Might another culture, another species, take a radically different line of scientific development, guided by norms that differ sharply from ours but that are justified by their scientific findings as ours are by ours? And might these people predict as successfully and thrive as well as we? Yes, I think that we must admit this as a possibility in principle; that we must admit it even from the point of view of our own science, which is the only point of view I can offer. I should be surprised to see this possibility realized, but I cannot picture a disproof.

RESPONDING TO DAVID ARMSTRONG[9]

My views regarding the reality of universals have been frequently misunderstood and, I like to think, even more frequently understood—increasingly so down the years. Misunderstanding does indeed linger, and even in high places. Armstrong, I fear, is not alone in it. Here then is my further effort, brief but vigorous, to set the record straight.

Armstrong espouses a realism of universals, and he objects to what he calls my ostrich nominalism. Ostrich nominalism is indeed objectionable, and not unknown. I could name names. What Armstrong does not perceive is that I, like him, espouse rather a realism of universals.

I have explained early and late that I see no way of meeting the needs of scientific theory, let alone those of everyday discourse, without admitting universals irreducibly into our ontology. I have adduced elementary examples such as 'Some zoological species are cross-fertile', which Armstrong even cites, and Frege's definition of ancestor; also David Kaplan's 'Some critics admire nobody but one another', an ingenious example whose covert dependence on universals transpires only on reduction to canonical notation.[10] Mathematics, moreover, and applied mathematics at that, is up to its neck in universals; we have to quantify over numbers of all sorts, functions, and much else. I have argued that there is no blinking these ontological assumptions; they are as integral to the physical theory that uses them as are the atoms, the electrons, the sticks, for that matter, and the stones. I have inveighed early and late against the ostrichlike failure to recognize these assumptions, as well as the opposite error —"mirage realism," in Devitt's phrase—of unwarranted imputations of ontological assumptions. Such was the burden of my "Designation and Existence" (1939) and "On What There Is" (1948).[11] An explicit standard was needed of what constitutes assumption of objects, and it was obvious enough: values of variables.

---

9. Reprinted from *Pacific Philosophical Quarterly* 61 (1981), where it bears the title "Soft impeachment disowned."

10. See my *Methods of Logic*, 3d ed., 3d and later printings, pp. 238f.

11. Reprinted in *From a Logical Point of View*.

How far could one push elementary mathematics without thus reifying universals? Goodman and I explored this at one point. The formalist, we remarked, was already involved in universals in treating of expression types (a point Armstrong thinks I may have overlooked). A formalism of tokens afforded considerable mileage, but stopped short of full proof theory. Nominalism, ostriches apart, is evidently inadequate to a modern scientific system of the world.

Where then does Armstrong differ with me, misinterpretations aside? For one thing, he differs in failing to suggest a standard of what constitutes assumption of objects, and he imputes assumption of objects in cases which, by my standard, would not count as such. His want of a standard in this regard has the startling incidental effect of reviving in his pages Bradley's old worry about a regress of relations. All those relations of Bradley's are real, but there is no regress, for we can define each of them, from the outermost inward, without referring to those farther in. This is because the use of a two-place predicate is not itself a reference to the relation, however real, that is the extension of the predicate. Such reference would be the work rather of a corresponding abstract singular term, or of a bound variable.

Armstrong differs with me also in neglecting the problem of individuation of universals. Under the head of universals we think first and foremost of properties, or attributes. I make no distinction here. I dropped the one term for the other long ago because of a traditional usage, which I feared might be confusing, that limited properties to essential attributes. This is no longer a connotation that obtrudes. Very well; how are attributes to be individuated? When are they to be counted identical? I have argued that no adequately intelligible standard presents itself short of mere coextensiveness of instances. I have stressed further that classes are abstract objects on a par with attributes, that they are equally universals, and that they differ none from attributes unless in their enjoyment of this clean individuation. So I have individuated them thus and called them classes.

At this point, according to Armstrong, I have "moved beyond [my] original position to some form of Predicate and/or Class Nominalism." Original position? My explicit acceptance of classes and predicates as objects dates from my earliest pertinent publications. But Predicate and/or Class *Nominalism?* Such a nominalism would be an ostrich nominalism indeed. It goes with weasel words like 'aggregates' and 'collections' and 'mere', said of classes, and with crossing the fingers. In "Identity, Ostension, and Hypostasis" (1950)[12] I stressed the impossibility of construing classes as concrete sums or aggregates, and the point has been stressed before, surely, and since. I am a Predicate and Class Realist, now as of yore; a deep-dyed realist of abstract universals. Extensionalist yes, and for reasons unrelated to nominalism.

RESPONDING TO RICHARD SCHULDENFREI[13]

"Sentences have replaced thoughts," according to Schulenfrei's account of my views, "and dispositions to assent have replaced belief." Does he mean that for me there is no more than this to thought and belief? Reading on, I suspect that he does. Then he misunderstands me.

My position is that the notions of thought and belief are very worthy objects of philosophical and scientific clarification and analysis, and that they are in equal measure very ill suited for use as instruments of philosophical and scientific clarification and analysis. If some one accepts these notions outright for such use, I am at a loss to imagine what he can have deemed more in need of clarification and analysis than the things he has thus accepted. For instruments of philosophical and scientific clarification and analysis I have looked rather in the foreground, finding sentences, as Schuldenfrei says, and dispositions to assent. Sentences are observable, and dispositions to assent are fairly accessible through observable symptoms. Linking observables to observables, these and others, and conjecturing causal connections, we might then seek a partial understanding, basically neurological, of what is loosely called thought or belief. This I could applaud, but still it is not what I have been

---

12. Reprinted in *From a Logical Point of View.*

13. Schuldenfrei's paper, "Dualistic physicalism in Quine: a radical critique," is to appear together with this reply in an issue of the Uruguayan quarterly *Sintaxis* devoted to my philosophy.

up to. I have been preoccupied rather with meaning, and meaning of a restricted sort at that: cognitive meaning. Meaning, like thought and belief, is a worthy object of philosophical and scientific clarification and analysis, and like them it is ill-suited for use as an instrument of philosophical and scientific clarification and analysis. On meaning, as on thought and belief, Schuldenfrei seems to have misunderstood me. He has me denying that 'Tom is a bachelor' is synonymous with 'Tom is an unmarried man', 'since they do not meet [my] criterion of identity of meaning." In fact I settle on no criterion, but I do treat those two sentences as paradigmatic of what would have to count as cognitively synonymous by any acceptable standard, and in both *Word and Object* and *The Roots of Reference* I speculate on supporting considerations in terms of verbal behavior.

Schuldenfrei's over-estimation of my rejections on the one hand, and of my pretensions on the other, has caused him to picture me as proffering some pretty bare bones in lieu of a philosophy. He has me equating experience in all its richness with an arid little S-R dialectic of occasion sentences on the one hand, or assents to same, and triggered nerve endings on the other. This is a third instance of the same kind of mistake that I have just now noted twice; I do not thus construe experience. Experience really, like meaning and thought and belief, is a worthy object of philosophical and scientific clarification and analysis, and like all those it is ill-suited for use as an instrument of philosophical clarification and analysis. Therefore I cleave to my arid little S-R dialectic where I can, rather than try to make an analytical tool of the heady luxuriance of experience untamed. In making this ascetic option I am by no means equating the one with the other.

He does not appreciate that in my thought experiments I am using the strategy of isolation, or of divide and conquer, that characterizes theoretical science across the board. A latter-day Galileo, replicating his namesake's experiment, rolls a very hard and almost spherical ball down a very hard and smooth slope in an almost complete vacuum. He excludes interferences so as to isolate one significant factor. It is in this spirit that I begin with occasion sentences, indeed with observation sentences in my special sense; I thus filter out the complexities, complex almost to the point of white noise, that come of the subject's concurrent preoccupations and past experience. It is in the same spirit that I cleave to the method of query and assent, rather than wait for the informant to volunteer unpredictable sentences for inscrutable reasons of his own. It is not a way to encompass thought or even language, but it is a way in. It is a plan for isolating a clearly explicable component of a complex phenomenon. This basic strategy of scientific theory is graphically depicted in Fourier analysis, where an irregular curve is analyzed into a hierarchy of regular curves from which it can be recovered in successive approximations by superposition. To complain of bare bones is like criticizing the physicist for failing to capture the richness of the rain forest.

Even granted my use of the scientists's strategy of isolating components, the components thus isolated are thicker than Schuldenfrei thinks. The episodes of stimulation are not staccato; they are legato, continuous. More, they overlap. Thus in *Word and Object* I allowed for a modulus of stimulation by way of parameter. Nor is the subject passive; on the contrary it was the subject's contributions that made for what I called "interference from within," requiring me in *The Roots of Reference* to settle for less than an operational definition of perceptual similarity. Moreover, the learning of language takes place mostly beyond the simple S-R level, by dint of analogical leaps that make appreciable demands upon the learner's creative imagination. I speculated on this process in a sketchy way in *Word and Object* and more in detail in *The Roots of Reference*.

Schuldenfrei states in an appendix that he wrote his paper without benefit of *The Roots of Reference*, and that this book diverges materially from my previous doctrines. It does not. Stimulus and response play the same part there as in *Word and Object*. Perceptual similarity is what was treated briefly in *Word and Object* under the head of quality space. *The Roots of Reference* enlarges upon the third chapter of *Word and Object* much as *Word and Object* enlarged upon "The Scope and Language of Science" or, indeed the last section of "Two Dogmas of Empiricism."

22

Postscript on Metaphor

Pleasure precedes business. The child at play is practicing for life's responsibilities. Young impalas play at fencing with one another, thrusting and parrying. Art for art's sake was the main avenue, Cyril Smith tells me, to ancient technological breakthroughs. Such also is the way of metaphor: it flourishes in playful prose and high poetic art, but it is vital also at the growing edge of science and philosophy.

The molecular theory of gases emerged as an ingenious metaphor: likening a gas to a vast swarm of absurdly small bodies. So pat was the metaphor that it was declared literally true, thus becoming straightway a dead metaphor; the fancied miniatures of bodies were declared real, and the term 'body' was extended to cover them. In later years the molecules have even been observed through electron microscopy; but I speak of origins.

Or consider light waves. There being no ether, there is no substance for them to be waves of. Talk of light waves is thus best understood as metaphorical, so long as 'wave' is read in the time-honored way. Or we may liberalize 'wave' and kill the metaphor.

Along the philosophical fringes of science we may find reasons to question basic conceptual structures and to grope for ways to refashion them. Old idioms are bound to fail us here,

Reprinted by permission of the University of Chicago Press from an issue of *Critical Inquiry* 5 (1978) comprising the proceedings of a conference on metaphor at the University of Chicago. Copyright © 1978 by the University of Chicago.

and only metaphor can begin to limn the new order. If the venture succeeds, the old metaphor may die and be embalmed in a newly literalistic idiom accommodating the changed perspective.

Religion, or much of it, is evidently involved in metaphor for good. The parables, according to David Tracy's paper, are the "founding language" of Christianity. Exegete succeeds exegete, ever construing metaphor in further metaphor. There are deep mysteries here. There is mystery as to the literal content, if any, that this metaphorical material is meant to convey. And there is then a second-order mystery: why the indirection? If the message is as urgent and important as one supposes, why are we not given it straight in the first place? A partial answer to both questions may lie in the nature of mystical experience: it is without content and so resists literal communication, but one may still try to induce the feeling in others by skillful metaphor.

Besides serving us at the growing edge of science and beyond, metaphor figures even in our first learning of language; or, if not quite metaphor, something akin to it. We hear a word or phrase on some occasion, or by chance we babble a fair approximation ourselves on what happens to be a pat occasion and are applauded for it. On a later occasion, then, one that resembles that first occasion by our lights, we repeat the expression. Resemblance of occasions is what matters, here as in metaphor. We generalize our application of the expression by degrees of subjective resemblance of occasions, until we discover from other people's behavior that we have pushed analogy too far, exceeding the established usage. If the crux of metaphor is creative extension through analogy, then we have forged a metaphor at each succeeding application of that early word or phrase. These primitive metaphors differ from the deliberate and sophisticated ones, however, in that they accrete directly to our growing store of standard usage. They are metaphors stillborn.

It is a mistake, then, to think of linguistic usage as literalistic in its main body and metaphorical in its trimming. Metaphor or something like it governs both the growth of language and our acquisition of it. Cognitive discourse at its most drily literal is largely a refinement rather, characteristic of the neatly worked inner stretches of science. It is an open space in the tropical jungle, created by clearing tropes away.

23

Has Philosophy Lost Contact with People?

What is this thing called philosophy? Professor Adler finds that it has changed profoundly in the past half century. It no longer speaks to the ordinary man or confronts problems of broad human interest. What is *it*? Is there some recognizable thing, philosophy, that has undergone these changes? Or has the mere word 'philosophy' been warped over, applying earlier to one thing and now to another? Clearly Adler is exercised by nothing so superficial as the migratory semantics of a four-syllable word, however resounding. He would say that philosophy is indeed somehow the same subject, despite the deplored changes. To show this he might cite the continuity of its changing history. But continuity is characteristic likewise of the migratory semantics of a tetrasyllable. We may do better at assessing the changing scene if we look rather to actual endeavors and activities old and new, exoteric and esoteric, grave and frivolous, and let the word 'philosophy' fall where it may.

Aristotle was among other things a pioneer physicist and biologist. Plato was among other things a physicist in a way,

This piece was written for *Newsday* by request as a response to a piece by Mortimer Adler. The two were to appear together under the above title. Upon publication, November 18, 1979, what appeared under my name proved to have been rewritten to suit the editor's fancy. This is my uncorrupted text.

if cosmology is a theoretical wing of physics. Descartes and Leibniz were in part physicists. Biology and physics were called philosophy in those days. They were called natural philosophy until the nineteenth century. Plato, Descartes, and Leibniz were also mathematicians, and Locke, Berkeley, Hume, and Kant were in large part psychologists. All these luminaries and others whom we revere as great philosophers were scientists in search of an organized conception of reality. Their search did indeed go beyond the special sciences as we now define them; there were also broader and more basic concepts to untangle and clarify. But the struggle with these concepts and the quest for a system on a grand scale were integral still to the overall scientific enterprise. The more general and speculative reaches of theory are what we look back on nowadays as distinctively philosophical. What is pursued under the name of philosophy today, moreover, has much these same concerns when it is at what I deem its technical best.

Until the nineteenth century, all available scientific knowledge of any consequence could be encompassed by a single first-class mind. This cozy situation ended as science expanded and deepened. Subtle distinctions crowded in and technical jargon proliferated, much of which is genuinely needed. Problems in physics, microbiology, and mathematics divided into subordinate problems any one of which, taken out of context, strikes the layman as either idle or unintelligible; only the specialist sees how it figures in the wider picture. Now philosophy, where it was continuous with science, progressed too. There as elsewhere in science, progress exposed relevant distinctions and connections that had been passed over in former times. There as elsewhere, problems and propositions were analyzed into constituents which, viewed in isolation, must seem uninteresting or worse.

Formal logic completed its renaissance and became a serious science just a hundred years ago at the hands of Gottlob Frege. A striking trait of scientific philosophy in subsequent years has been the use, increasingly, of the powerful new logic. This has made for a deepening of insights and a sharpening of problems and solutions. It has made also for the intrusion of technical terms and symbols which, while serving the investigators well, tended to estrange lay readers.

Another striking trait of scientific philosophy in this period has been an increasing concern with the nature of language. In responsible circles this has not been a retreat from
more serious issues. It is an outcome of critical scruples that
are traceable centuries back in the classical British em-
piricists Locke, Berkeley, and Hume, and are clearer in
Bentham. It has been appreciated increasingly in the past
sixty years that our traditional introspective notions—our
notions of meaning, idea, concept, essence, all undisciplined
and undefined—afford a hopelessly flabby and unmanage-
able foundation for a theory of the world. Control is gained
by focusing on words, on how they are learned and used,
and how they are related to things.

The question of a private language, cited as frivolous by
Adler, is a case in point. It becomes philosophically significant when we recognize that a legitimate theory of meaning must be a theory of the use of language, and that language is a social art, socially inculcated The importance of
the matter was stressed by Wittgenstein and earlier by
Dewey, but is lost on anyone who encounters the issue out
of context.

Granted, much literature produced under the head of linguistic philosophy is philosophically inconsequential. Some
pieces are amusing or mildly interesting as language studies,
but have been drawn into philosophical journals only by
superficial association. Some, more philosophical in purport,
are simply incompetent; for quality control is spotty in the
burgeoning philosophical press. Philosophy has long suf-
fered, as hard sciences have not, from a wavering consensus
on questions of professional competence. Students of the
heavens are separable into astronomers and astrologers as
readily as are the minor domestic ruminants into sheep and
goats, but the separation of philosophers into sages and
cranks seems to be more sensitive to frames of reference.
This is perhaps as it should be, in view of the unregimented
and speculative character of the subject.

Much of what had been recondite in modern physics has
been opened up by popularization. I am grateful for this,
for I have a taste for physics but cannot take it raw. A good

philosopher who is a skillful expositor might do the same with the current technical philosophy. It would take artistry, because not all of what is philosophically important need be of lay interest even when clearly expounded and fitted into place. I think of organic chemistry; I recognize its importance, but I am not curious about it, nor do I see why the layman should care about much of what concerns me in philosophy. If instead of having been called upon to perform in the British television series "Men of Ideas" I had been consulted on its feasibility, I should have expressed doubt.

What I have been discussing under the head of philosophy is what I call scientific philosophy, old and new, for it is the discipline whose latter-day trend Adler criticized. By this vague heading I do not exclude philosophical studies of moral and aesthetic values. Some such studies, of an analytical cast, can be scientific in spirit. They are apt, however, to offer little in the way of inspiration or consolation. The student who majors in philosophy primarily for spiritual comfort is misguided and is probably not a very good student anyway, since intellectual curiosity is not what moves him.

Inspirational and edifying writing is admirable, but the place for it is the novel, the poem, the sermon, or the literary essay. Philosophers in the professional sense have no peculiar fitness for it. Neither have they any peculiar fitness for helping to get society on an even keel, though we should all do what we can. What just might fill these perpetually crying needs is wisdom: *sophia* yes, *philosophia* not necessarily.

24

Paradoxes of Plenty

In the depression of the early thirties a Harvard doctorate brought only even chances of appointment to a college faculty. One of my contemporaries won the degree in philosophy with flying colors and turned at once to train for the civil service, rather than court frustration in the field of his choice. If a man did get a teaching job, his struggles continued. He would prepare nine to fifteen hours of lectures a week, besides grading papers and serving on committees. He would do his professional writing in the evenings and on Sundays and during such weeks of vacation as were not taken up with summer teaching. He would type it himself and buy the eventual reprints out of a meager salary.

If more money were diverted into academic channels, one thought, how Academia might bloom! Talent would be attracted and relieved of burdens, and a renassiance would be assured. Fat chance, in our profit-oriented society, but a man could dream.

The chance proved fatter than one's dreams. War came, and the government launched research programs related to defense. Scientific advisers noted the value, in a long view, of basic research for which no present military use could be claimed. Support was gained under this head for work in pure mathematics for which no military relevance, early or late, could be imagined. Soon there ceased to be lip service to

Reprinted from *Daedalus* 103 (1974).

military ends; the National Science Foundation undertook to support good science simply as such. By sharing the overhead expenses of the university, moreover, the defense contracts and the NSF grants indirectly helped also the departments that were not engaged in the programs. Eventually these departments came in for direct support as well, through the National Endowment for the Humanities. Funds were found also for indigent students, who were thus spared the handicap of having to work their way through college and so were enabled to compete on an equal footing with their rich classmates. Intellectual promise came to be the only requirement for entering college, and intellectual performance the only requirement for graduating. And there was little insistence on these.

Not a few scientists were lured from their frugal old projects by the glitter of grants. It was not avarice, for the money was not for their pockets. It was selfless admiration of the unaccustomed flow of gold. Also it was lust for power. Imaginations were taxed for projects requiring substantial staff, equipment, and computer time. Scientists thus seduced probably gave up inspired projects, in some cases, for contrived ones. Certainly they sacrificed much of their prized research time to their new administrative responsibilities, and much of their scientific writing to the writing of proposals and reports to foundations. Men who in their youth had chosen the austerities of science over the material rewards of a business career were now in business after all, though without those rewards.

Expensive projects became possible. Science is the better for the vast sums that have been poured into it. To deny this would be more than paradoxical; it would be wrong. The paradox is just that such largesse sometimes works adversely.

Universities prospered, and faculty salaries rose a good deal faster than the dollar fell. Teaching loads were lightened with the expanding of faculties. Secretarial aid was provided and reprints were subsidized. Men whose passion for the things of the mind drove them into an academic career were now spared the old penalties. This is good in itself. It has worked also for the progress of science and scholarship, by allowing scientists and scholars more time in which to be creative.

It may be supposed to have worked for the progress of science and scholarship also in another way: by attracting talent. But here we must look out again for paradox. The trouble is that vocation and amenity vary inversely. When academic life is hard, only the dedicated will put up with it. Allay the rigors and you draw men away from other occupations. The academic life, when eased of hardship, has other attractions besides pursuit of truth. It is clean and somewhat prestigious work in pleasant surroundings, and the vacations are long. It is a continuation, even, of one's glorious collegiate youth. Thus it is that the recruitment effected by improved conditions must depress the average level of dedication to science and scholarship. The dedicated are still there, true, undiminished in absolute number; but a sag in the wider average does little for their morale.

Learned journals throve and multiplied. Existing journals thickened, and new ones were subsidized almost as soon as they were said to be needed. Productive scholars had grown more productive, thanks to the lightened teaching load and the provision of secretaries. This accounts for the thickening of existing journals. The new ones, however, are a locus again of paradox. There are other motives for publication besides that of furnishing the profession with needed truths. There is vanity, and there is the widespread notion, sometimes founded, that academic invitations and promotions depend on publication. Certainly, then, new journals were needed: they were needed by authors of articles too poor to be accepted by existing journals. The journals that were thus called into existence met the need to a degree, but they in turn preserved, curiously, certain minimal standards; and so a need was felt for further journals still, to help to accommodate the double rejects. The series invites extrapolation and has had it.

What now of the paradox? Granted the uselessness of the added journals, what harm do they do? Mere waste of money is unparadoxical and beside the point; my paradoxes have to do not with unproductivity but with counter-productivity.

Regrettably, however, the counter-productivity is there. The mass of professional journals is so indigestible and so little worth digesting that the good papers, though more numerous than ever, are increasingly in danger of being overlooked. We cope with the problem partly by ignoring the worst journals and partly by scanning tables of contents for respected names. Since the stratification of the journals from good to bad is imperfect, this procedure will miss an occasional good paper by an unknown author. Even if we can afford the miss, it is rough on the author.

It was in the increased admittance and financial support of students that the new prodigality came its most resounding cropper. Marginal students came on in force, many of them with an eye on the draft, and they soon were as bored with college as they had been with school. In their confusion and restlessness they were easy marks for demagogues, who soon contrived a modest but viable terror. A rather sketchy terror sufficed, in the event, to bring universities to their knees.

This turn of affairs is explained only in part by increased enrollments, and still only in part by a slackening of entrance requirements. There was a third factor, more obscure, and here it is that paradox again intrudes. If in former times a student went through college on highly competitive scholarships, mere pride of achievement would tend to make him prize the college education that he thus achieved. If, again, a student put himself through college on his earnings, he must have been prizing the education for which he was working so hard. And even if a student sailed through on his father's largesse, still he saw himself as privileged and was ready enough to ascribe failures good-humoredly to his own blitheness of spirit. Mass subsidy, on the other hand, soon loses its luster and comes to be looked upon as each man's due, his return for serving society by attending class and learning what society wants him to know.

Good students are perhaps as numerous as ever, in among the bad. But the atmosphere in which they work is the worse for the hostilities and so are the standards of education. The department that I know best has freed its graduate students of the requirement of general examinations, because these were said by student activists to induce anxiety. It has also ceased to require any history of philosophy for the Ph.D. in philosophy.

It's an ill wind that blows no good. The Arab oil embargo spared us thousands of highway fatalities and decelerated the pollution of our air. I shall not venture to say, in a similarly cheerful spirit, that recent curtailments of funds for higher education are apt to hasten the renaissance that prodigality failed to bring. I offer more modest cheer: affluence was in some paradoxical ways counter-productive, and as we mourn its passing we may console ourselves somewhat with that reflection.

25

The Times Atlas

This is a sturdy twelve-pounder and stands a foot and a half high. Between its dedication to the Queen and its terminal list of errata there are, in three numbering systems, a total of 557 sprawling pages. Almost half of these are given over to the maps, and most of the maps are two-page spreads.

Western Europe begins with a double page of Iceland, just Iceland, a full twenty inches from cape to cape, all delicately tinted green and tan for elevations and white for glaciers and surrounded by the blue sea. Other tastefully sea-girt subjects of great two-page spreads are New Guinea, Ireland, northern Scotland. Smaller countries get two-page spreads too; there is one for Belgium, one for Holland, one for Switzerland. On these three the scale soars to nine miles to the inch, and the detail is luxurious.

Even two metropolitan areas come in for double pages: London and Paris, at a mile and two-thirds to the inch. The London map shows a Greater London which, since we last looked, has been officially constituted as such and has superseded the counties of London and Middlesex. Middlesex is no more.

New York is not forgotten. It and lesser cities are given decent coverage on a smaller scale in insets. One of these little insets actually exceeds in scale the London and Paris

---

This review of *The Times Atlas of the World*, Comprehensive Edition, by the Times of London, is reprinted from the *Washington Post* and the *Chicago Tribune* of May 5, 1968.

maps, by a factor of three; but it is not of New York. It is a map of the Kremlin. The book is generous to Americans in the way that matters: in giving fullest treatment to places less familiar to us than America.

The intensity of coverage is impressive. Western Europe is not all accorded the scale of Britain, Belgium, Holland, and Switzerland, but it is in general accorded a scale of around one to a million. An inch stands for about sixteen miles. This is still so big a scale that three of the whacking two-page spreads are needed for France, three for Spain, three for Italy. Some outlying regions are also accorded this generous scale, notably Greece, Israel, northern Egypt, Hawaii, and the portion of America from Washington to Boston. To visualize the scale: Washington and Boston are at diagonally opposite corners of the two big facing pages at one to a million.

Regions thus searchingly depicted are shown again more sweepingly on a scale of one to two and half million. A two-page spread on this scale just suffices to show all of France together, or all of Spain. These maps still show more detail than we find in most atlases. When we move out to eastern Europe, the Middle East, the Caucasus, northeastern India, Japan, Canada, and the United States, this scale becomes the usual medium of fullest treatment. And very adequate it is; apart from our familiar United States the detail in these maps is, for most of us, unprecedented.

Par for the rest of the world is a scale of five million. To visualize the scale: Mexico, corner to corner, just takes a two-page spread at five million. This still means overwhelmingly detailed representation when applied where it is applied: throughout Australia, Indonesia, Africa, South America, China, Central Asia, Siberia. It takes five such two-page spreads to cover Asiatic Russia. Try this on a friend: open the book to the vast two-page map of north central Siberia and put masking tape over the page heading. Despite the deft draftsmanship and delicate tinting and the abundance of place names, he may well be lost.

A scale of five million is thus a feast when you get far out. This book treats the whole inhabited world on those terms, besides treating so much of it more fully. Everything is recapitulated, for perspective, on various smaller scales as well.

As a cake has its frosting, so an atlas has its maps of the polar icecaps. This atlas goes farther and includes maps of the moon. These are in a prefatory section along with climatic and economic maps of the earth and a quantity of material on the earth's core, the stellar universe, and the exploration of space.

In the exuberant detail of this atlas there is no stinting of place names. This is a largesse which, once bestowed, has to be doubled; for the names are indexed. The index, four columns to a page, takes up nearly half the book. If these columns were laid end to end they would reach more than a quarter of a mile; and there are fourteen lines to the inch. This means nearly a quarter of a million lines; and few entries take more than one line.

These hundreds of thousands of locations are specified in the index by map number and by letters and numerals keyed to the margins of the maps. "A valuable addition," we read in the preface, "is that these locations are also given their . . latitude and longitude, a combination which no other world atlas so far incorporates to such an extent." Now latitude and longitude are not only admirable; they are sufficient. The editors would have done well to follow the time-honored example of *Goode's School Atlas* all the way by omitting the key letters and numerals. They could thus have cleared the margins of the maps and eliminated half a million letters and digits from the index. This space in the index would have been better spent on pronunciations or areas or populations.

The quarter-mile index is implemented by a list of convenient abbreviations such as "Utt. Prad." for "Uttar Pradesh" and "Vdkhr." for 'Vodokhranilishche." What is more impressive, there is a glossary explaining some twenty-three hundred terms from forty-seven languages. This is useful in view of the policy of favoring native designations on the maps.

The packing of information into the maps has been aided also by another device, a detached plastic panel summarizing the map conventions of color, abbreviation, and other symbols.

In a disarming gesture of realism the editors have ruled up a back page with many blanks for errata, and have filled in a few. Here are a few more. Hokkaido is listed in the front matter as an island protectorate of Japan; it is simply a component island of Japan. Barbados is represented on the map (but not in the front matter) as "to U.K."; this ceased to be true in 1966. Nova Granada is rendered in the quarter-mile index (but not on the map) as Novo Granada; this puts it in a column where one would not look it up. There may be a further erratum in the fact that the tint of Antarctica does not seem to match anything on the plastic panel.

Curiosity is fired by a tiny inset of San Salvador or Watling Island, whose scale is indicated in cramped quarters as $1:1\frac{1}{4}$ m. Does this mean one to a thousand and a quarter, or an inch to a mile and a quarter? The plastic panel explains "m." as "metre"; that will not do. Some measurements solved the problem: it is one to a million and a quarter.

Most of these maps are from the five six-pound regional *Times* atlases that came out between 1955 and 1959. Nothing has been lost, yet compactness has been gained, and with it some additional maps and other material, along with updating of plates. The maps are an inexhaustible store of lore and an unflagging delight to the eye. Seen in the light of what you can now get with $45 in the supermarket, the book is a good buy.

26

Mencken's American Language

The American Language as I knew it in my callow days was the third edition, 1923, revised and enlarged. It ran to five hundred pages, counting pp. i-x. There have since been a fourth edition, further revised and enlarged, and two supplementary volumes and some magazine pieces. What is now before us is an abridgment of all that, and an abridgment not uncalled for. For all its abridgment, the volume exceeds the 1923 enlarged edition by a factor of 2⅓. (To verify, add xxv and 777 and, all over again, cxxiv in back, and then compare print and format.)

Along with his abridging, the editor has made corrections and, in brackets, judicious supplementations. Between author and editor the 1923 mistakes have dwindled.

Thus in 1923 (p. 164) Mencken reported R. G. White (fl. 1868–1881) as deploring the American *presidential* and favoring *presidental*, "following the example of *incidental, regimental, monumental, governmental, oriental, experimental,* and so on." Mencken failed to observe that four of these six are irrelevant, being built not on Latin participles in *-ens* but on *-mentum*. Also he failed to observe that *presidential,* paralleling *referential,* is impeccable as an adjective for *presidency.* Now the new abridged volume still mentions

Reprinted with permission from *The New York Review of Books*, January 9, 1964. Copyright © 1964 Nyrev, Inc.

that there had been disapproval of *presidential*: it mentions
it six times (as against twice in 1923, which helps explain
why this is 2⅓ times as long as the 1923 edition). But happily
it skips the reasoning.

This may seem to you like sweeping the dirt under the
rug. Similarly for the next case. Take p. 182 of 1923 on *bust*:
"This . . . has come into a dignity that even grammarians
will soon hesitate to question. Who, in America, would dare
to speak of *bursting* a broncho, or of a *trustburster?*" Appreciation that *bust* means *break* would have prevented this
remark. Now in the new abridged volume I still find no
equating of *bust* to *break*. But the remark is gone.

I see it rather as editorial restraint, reluctance to meddle
beyond necessity. My view is encouraged by some passages
containing the technical term *back-formation*. In 1923, p.
190, Mencken misapplied the term to *prof, co-ed, dorm*, and
the like. In this new abridged edition, the mistake persists
(p. 203) and even recurs (p. 213). Yet the editor knows better. In the course of one of his bracketed inserts (p. 205) he
uses the term himself and uses it right.

Many errors are gone. In the 1923 edition *dead* was called
preterite (p. 285), *you* in *How do you do?* was called objective (p. 305), Rainier was called the greatest American peak
south of Alaska (p. 357), the verb *house-clean* was listed
among nouns used as verbs (p. 198), the open *o* sound in
standard *sauce* was misidentified (p. 323), the British
prounuciation *et* for *ate* was taken for distinctive American
(pp. 275, 280, 284), and *rench* was said to be the invariable
American for *rinse* (p. 281). These errors, hence no doubt
also many others, have disappeared.

Cases of mere bad judgment have been eliminated too.
Thus in 1923 Mencken attributed the "raciness" of *Where
are we at?* to "the somewhat absurd text-book prohibition
of terminal prepositions" (p. 187); surely it is due mainly
to the redundancy. He saw the noun *try* as an apocopation of
trial (p. 191); surely it is rather a freshly nominalized verb.
He saw *kindergarden* as of a piece with pardner (p. 325);
surely folk etymology is more to the point. In each case better judgment has now prevailed—not by substitution, just
by deletion of the injudicious passage.

Cases of bad judgment are also preserved. The vernacular *tole* for *told* was lamely explained in the 1923 edition (p. 288) by assimilation of *d* to *l*. "So also, perhaps, in *swole*," Mencken continued, "which is fast displacing *swelled*." It should be evident that standard *told* is (like *sold*) anomalous: it resembles a strong verb in the drastic vowel change from *tell*, but is weak in taking -*d*. The dropping of this -*d* is mere resistance to anomaly. As for *swole*, the fact is that *swell* used to be a strong verb, preterite *swoll*, participle *swollen;* adjectivally this old participle is still going strong; small wonder, then, if there is still a little life in the old preterite. Assimilation indeed. Happily the *swole* tale is missing from the new edition, again by simple curtailment; but the *tole* tale still hangs on (p. 531).

Some strong-verb trouble even emerges since the 1923 edition. Thus in the new edition an Irish pronunciation *ped* of *paid* is cited to illustrate "a tendency . . . toward strong conjugations" (p. 529). It is parallel to standard *said*, and weak. Also in the new edition we read, apropos of a contrary tendency toward weak conjugations, that "even when a compound has as its last member a verb ordinarily strong, it is often weak itself. Thus the preterite of *to joyride* is . . . *joyrided*" (p. 532). This again is no proper illustration; to *joyride* is not a compound of *to ride*, but a compound noun gone verbal, and nouns newly gone verbal always make weak verbs. Here the editor's touch is arrestingly light: he inserts the bracketed remark "and no baseball player ever *flew* out to end the inning; he always *flied* out." This example slyly shows that he has properly in mind the point about nouns gone verbal, and no nonsense about compounds; still he leaves Mencken's remark intact.

Early and late there is a puzzling insensitivity to the orthography of hard and soft *g* and *c*. In 1923 (p. 232) and again in the new abridged edition (pp. 483f), we read: "The superiority of *jail* to *gaol* is manifest by the common mispronunciation of the latter by the Americans who find it in print, making it rhyme with *coal*." What is really glaring about the English *gaol* escapes mention, the soft *g* before *a*. Nor do I find in either edition any notice of the one other example I know: the frequent American pronunciation of

margarine. Correspondingly, where *skeptic* and *sceptic* were
compared (1923, p. 233), the anomaly of hard *c* before *e*
went unmentioned. And in the new edition *Passaicite* and
Quebecer are exhibited (pp. 681f) with obviously no thought
of a soft *c*.

The handling of foreign languages is postpossessing. In
the new edition Mencken speaks of the *sermo vulgus.* Look
who's talking. Read *sermo vulgaris,* or, following Cicero,
vulgi sermo. Between editions mistakes in foreign words
(1923, pp. 256, 338, 358, 364) have been caught, but one
would welcome wider perspective. Thus in the new edition
(pp. 374f) *Polack* and *Chinaman* are given under Terms of
Abuse, and their histories in English are enlarged upon, with
never a hint that *Polak* is the Polish for Pole and *Chinaman*
is a translation of the Chinese term. Or again take *a* as in
He musta been. We read: "The OED describes this reducing
of the OE *habban* (Ger. *haben*) to *a* as the *ne plus ultra* of
the wearing-down tendency among English words" (p. 534).
If we are to dwell on the point, French bears notice for its *a*
from *habet.*

"Mencken always insisted, with what seems to most linguists an excessive modesty, that he was not a scholar himself"—so writes the editor, to everyone's credit. It is a credit
to Mencken to have insisted, a credit to the editor to remark
that he did, and a credit to the hearts of most linguists to
have protested. As for the book, in attainment and in evident aspiration it is less linguistic treatise than fun book.
So be it. *Vive le sport.* And it is less fun book than, if I have
found an adequately neutral word, compendium. It is for all
its abridgment a big compendium of varied material, varied
in entertainment value, varied in degree of inconsequence.
Thanks to its thick index it is admirably suited to sporadic
reading.

It is not primarily a manifesto, but it savors of that too.
The American Language early and late casts an image of its
author as *vulgi defensor,* champion of the low-faluting.
There is an air of indiscriminate forthrightness and no nonsense. It is murky air, and it blankets conflation. Through
it darkly we seem to descry two gathered hosts opposed:
regular fellows on the left and a mealy-mouthed ruck of

schoolmarms, Englishmen, and displaced Latin grammarians on the right.

Now this illusion of a simple contrast is a confusion of five separate contrasts that are pertinent to Mencken's remarks and quotations. One, assuredly, is the contrast between English in the United States and English in the United Kingdom. A second is the contrast between English grammar efficiently described as by Jespersen in expressly devised categories, and English grammar clumsily described in earlier decades in categories inherited from Latin grammarians. A third is the contrast between speech as a basic trait of the human species and writing as a recent derivative cultural quirk. A fourth is the contrast between colloquial and literary style. And a fifth is the contrast between the descriptive and the normative treatment of language.

Mencken quotes E. H. Sturtevant thus. "Whether we think of the history of human speech in general or of the linguistic experience of the individual speaker, spoken language is the primary phenomenon, and writing is only a more or less imperfect reflection of it." (p. 517). In his next sentence Mencken invokes Jespersen, and in the next he quotes H. E. Palmer thus: "[Spoken English is] that variety which is generally used by educated people in the course of ordinary conversation or when writing letters to intimate friends." Now Sturtevant was alluding to the third contrast in my list of five; Palmer was concerned with the fourth, and Jespersen always primarily with the second. Mencken pictured all three linguists joined as in crusade against a common mawkish host.

Whatever it was that Mencken stood for may seem, for all its softness of focus, to have prospered; witness the new permissiveness of the Merriam-Webster dictionary. "*This data* and *like I said* are all right now," the schoolboy protests when his theme is marked down. "The new dictionary says so." That fixes the schoolmarm.

I shall not argue that this is a scene best calculated to have gratified Mencken. But it does suggest that the last in my list of five contrasts is the one that merits most thought: that between descriptive and normative.

Schoolmarmism comes in part from tampering with facts

to accommodate a poor theory. Insofar it is bad. And school-marmism is normative. Scientific linguistics is descriptive, and good. The new permissiveness of the dictionary, a waiving of the normative in favor of the descriptive, is therefore good. So now anything (if it is already going) goes.

Let us sort this out. Scientific linguistics is indeed good. In particular a purely descriptive, nonnormative Merriam-Webster was a good thing to make, if the work was competent and the job had not previously been adequately done, which is as may be. But there is a fallacy in calling the result permissive; if the book is not normative it no more permits than forbids. And it would be a fallacy also to conclude from the virtues of descriptive linguistics and the faults of schoolmarmism that the normative must be bad. This would be a normative conclusion and a false one.

Behind the schoolboy's illusion there is a feeling that nothing in language is wrong save as a rule-book makes it wrong. People fail to reflect that there remain values in language even if all dictionaries go descriptive, and conversely that normative dictionaries and other manuals of good usage when they do exist are purely advisory, like cookbooks. In this capacity they are useful even against bad schoolmarms.

References

Adler, Mortimer. "Has philosophy lost contact with people?" *Newsday*, November 18, 1979, part I, §2, pp. 5, 13.

Armstrong, D. M. "Against 'ostrich' nominalism: reply to Michael Devitt." *Pacific Philosophical Quarterly* 61 (1981), in press.

Austin, J. L. *How to Do Things with Words.* Cambridge, Mass.: Harvard University Press, 1962.

———— "Truth." *Proceedings of the Aristotelian Society* suppl. vol. 24 (1950), 111–128.

Bchmann, Heinrich. "Beiträge zur Algebra der Logik." *Mathematische Annalen* 86 (1922), 163–229.

Boër, S. E., and W. G. Lycan. "Knowing who." *Philosophical Studies* 28 (1975), 299–344.

Boole, George. *An Investigation of the Laws of Thought.* London, 1854.

Carnap, Rudolf. *Physikalische Begriffsbildung.* Karlsruhe, 1926.

———— *Der logische Aufbau der Welt.* Berlin, 1928.

———— *The Logical Syntax of Language.* New York and London, 1937.

Carroll, Lewis. *Symbolic Logic.* Edited by W. W. Bartley III. New York: Potter, 1977.

Church, Alonzo, "A note on the Entscheidungsproblem." *Journal of Symbolic Logic* 1 (1936), 40–41, 101–102.

———— "Ontological commitment." *Journal of Philosophy* 55 (1958), 1008–1014.

———— and W. V. Quine. "Some theorems on definability and decidability." *Journal of Symbolic Logic* 17 (1952), 179–187.

Cohen, P. J. *Set Theory and the Continuum Hypothesis.* New York: Benjamin, 1966.

Davidson, Donald. "The logical form of action sentences." In Rescher, pp. 81–95.

———— "On the very idea of a conceptual scheme." *Proceedings and Addresses of the American Philosophical Association* 47 (1974), 5–20.

———— and Jaakko Hintikka, eds. *Words and Objections.* Dordrecht: Reidel, 1969.

References

De Morgan, Augustus. "On the syllogism, no. iv, and on the logic of relations." *Transactions of the Cambridge Philosophical Society* 10 (1864), 173–230.

Devitt, Michael. " 'Ostrich nominalism' or 'mirage realism'?" *Pacific Philosophical Quarterly* 61 (1981), in press.

Dewey, John. *Experience and Nature.* La Salle, Ill.: Open Court, 1925.

Duhem, Pierre. *La théorie physique: son objet et sa structure.* Paris, 1906.

Dummett, Michael. *Truth and Other Enigmas.* Cambridge, Mass.: Harvard University Press, 1978.

Evans, Gareth, and John McDowell, eds. *Truth and Meaning.* Oxford: Oxford University Press, 1976.

Fann, K. T., ed. *Symposium on J. L. Austin.* London: Routledge, 1969.

Føllesdal, Dagfinn. "Knowledge, identity, and existence." *Theoria* 33 (1967), 1–27.

Frege, Gottlob. *Begriffsschrift.* Halle, 1879.

———— *Funktion und Begriff.* Jena, 1891.

Geach, Peter. *Reference and Generality.* Ithaca: Cornell University Press, 1962.

———— *Logic Matters,* Oxford: Blackwell, 1972.

Gödel, Kurt. *The Consistency of the Continuum Hypothesis.* Princeton: Princeton University Press, 1940.

———— "Die Vollständigkeit der Axiome des logischen Funktionenkalküls." *Monatshefte für Mathematik und Physik* 37 (1930), 349–360.

———— "Ueber formal unentscheidbare Sätze der Principia Mathematica und verwandter Systeme." Ibid., 38 (1931), 173–198.

Goodman, Nelson. *Ways of Worldmaking.* Indianapolis: Hackett, 1978.

———— and W. V. Quine. "Steps toward a constructive nominalism." *Journal of Symbolic Logic* 12 (1947), 97–122.

Hahn, Hans. *Ueberflüssige Wesenheiten.* Vienna, 1930.

Herbrand, Jacques. *Ecrits logiques.* Paris: Presses Universitaires de France, 1968.

Hintikka, Jaakko. *Knowledge and Belief.* Ithaca: Cornell University Press, 1962.

———— *The Intentions of Intentionality and Other New Models for Modality.* Boston: Reidel, 1975.

Humphries, B. M. "Indeterminacy of translation and theory." *Journal of Philosophy* 67 (1970), 167–178.

Jevons, W. S. *Pure Logic.* London, 1864.

Kahr, A. S., E. F. Moore, and Hao Wang. "Entscheidungsproblem reduced to the AEA case." *Proceedings of the National Academy of Sciences* 48 (1962), 365–377.

Kaplan, David. "Quantifying in." In Davidson and Hintikka, pp. 206–242.

Kripke, Saul. "A completeness theorem in modal logic." *Journal of Symbolic Logic* 24 (1959), 1–11.

Löwenheim, Leopold. "Ueber Möglichkeit im Relativkalkül." *Mathematische Annalen* 76 (1915), 447–470.

Macdonald, G. F., ed. *Perception and Identity: Essays Presented to A. J. Ayer.* London: Macmillan, 1979.

Mencken, H. L. *The American Language.* Abridged ed. edited by R. J. McDavid, Jr. New York: Knopf, 1963.

Munitz, M. K., ed. *Identity and Individuation.* New York: New York University Press, 1971.

Nelson, R. J. "On machine expectation." *Synthese* 31 (1975), 129–139.

Ogden, C. K. *Bentham's Theory of Fictions.* London: Routledge, 1932.

Peacocke, Christopher. "An appendix to David Wiggins' 'Note.' " In Evans and McDowell, pp. 313–324.

Peano, Giuseppe. *Formulaire de mathématiques*, vol. 1. Turin, 1895.

Peirce, C. S. *Collected Papers*, vols. 2–4. Cambridge, Mass.: Harvard University Press, 1932–1933.

Quine, W. V. *Mathematical Logic.* New York, 1940. Rev. ed., Cambridge, Mass.: Harvard University Press, 1951.

―――― *From a Logical Point of View.* Cambridge, Mass.: Harvard University Press, 1953. 2d ed., 1961.

―――― *Word and Object.* Cambridge, Mass.: MIT Press, 1960.

―――― *Set Theory and Its Logic.* Cambridge, Mass.: Harvard University Press, 1963. Rev. ed., 1969.

―――― *Selected Logic Papers.* New York: Random House, 1966.

―――― *The Ways of Paradox and Other Essays.* New York, 1966. Enlarged ed., Cambridge, Mass.: Harvard University Press, 1976.

―――― *Ontological Relativity and Other Essays.* New York: Columbia University Press, 1969.

―――― *Methods of Logic.* 3d ed. New York: Holt, 1972.

―――― *The Roots of Reference.* La Salle, Ill.: Open Court, 1974.

―――― "Designation and existence." *Journal of Philosophy* 36 (1939), 701–709.

―――― "On empirically equivalent systems of the world." *Erkenntnis* 9 (1975), 313–328.

Ramsey, F. P. *The Foundations of Mathematics.* London: Routledge, 1931.

―――― "Theories." In *The Foundations of Mathematics*, pp. 212–236.

Rescher, Nicholas, ed. *The Logic of Action and Preference.* Pittsburgh: Pittsburgh University Press, 1967.

Russell, Bertrand. *The Principles of Mathematics.* Cambridge, Eng., 1903.

―――― *The Problems of Philosophy.* New York, 1912.

―――― *Our Knowledge of the External World.* New York and London, 1914.

―――― *Mysticism and Logic and Other Essays.* London, 1918.

―――― *Analysis of Mind.* London, 1921.

―――― *Analysis of Matter.* New York, 1927.

―――― *Inquiry into Meaning and Truth.* New York: Norton, 1940.

——— *Human Knowledge*. New York: Simon and Schuster, 1948.

——— *Logic and Knowledge*. London: Allen and Unwin, 1956.

——— "Meinong's theory of complexes and assumptions." *Mind* 13 (1904), 204–219, 336–354, 509–524.

——— "On denoting." *Mind* 14 (1905), 479–493. Reprinted in *Logic and Knowledge*.

——— "Mathematical logic as based on the theory of types." *American Journal of Mathematics* 30 (1908), 222–262. Reprinted in *Logic and Knowledge*.

——— "The philosophy of logical atomism." *Monist* 28 (1918), 495–527; 29 (1919), 32–63, 190–222, 345–380. Reprinted in *Logic and Knowledge*.

Ryle, Gilbert. *Dilemmas*. Cambridge, Eng., 1954.

Schilpp, P. A., ed. *The Philosophy of Bertrand Russell*. Evanston, 1944, and New York: Harper, 1963.

——— *Albert Einstein: Philosophy-Scientist*. New York: Tudor, 1951.

Schlick, Moritz. *Fragen der Ethik*. Vienna, 1930.

Schröder, Ernst. *Der Operationskreis des Logikkalkuls*. Leipzig, 1877.

Shahan, R., and C. Swoyer, eds. *Essays on the Philosophy of W. V. Quine*. Norman: University of Oklahoma Press, 1979.

Skolem, Thoralf. "Ueber die mathematische Logik." *Norsk Matematisk Tidsskrift* 10 (1928), 125–142.

Sleigh, R. C. "On a proposed system of epistemic logic." *Noûs* 2 (1968), 391–398.

Smart, J. J. C. *Philosophy and Scientific Realism*. London: Routledge, 1964.

——— "The methods of ethics and the methods of science." *Journal of Philosophy* 62 (1965), 344–349.

Tarski, Alfred. *Logic, Semantics, Metamathematics*. Oxford: Clarendon Press, 1956.

Times Atlas of the World. London, 1968.

Tinbergen, Nikolaas. *The Herring Gull's World*. London: Collins, 1953.

Tooke, John Horne. Έπεα πτερόεντα; or, *The Diversions of Purley*, vol. 1. London, 1786. Boston, 1806.

Tracy, David. "Metaphor and religion: the test case of Christian texts." *Critical Inquiry* 5 (1978), 91–106.

Turing, A. M. "On computable numbers." *Proceedings of the London Mathematical Society* 42 (1937), 230–266; 43 (1938), 544f.

Unger, Peter. "I do not exist." In Macdonald, pp. 235–251.

Urmson, J. O. "On Austin's method." In Fann, pp. 76–86.

Venn, John. *Symbolic Logic*. London, 1881, 1894.

Von Neumann, John. "Eine Axiomatisierung der Mengenlehre." *Journal für reine und angewandte Mathematik* 154 (1925), 219–240.

Waismann, Friedrich. "Verifiability." *Proceedings of the Aristotelian Society* suppl. vol. 19 (1945), 119–150.

Whitehead, A. N., and Bertrand Russell. *Principia Mathematica*, vol. 1. Cambridge, Eng., 1910. 2d ed., 1925.

Williams, Bernard. *Morality*. New York: Harper, 1972.

Williams, D. C. *Principles of Empirical Realism*. Springfield, Ill.: Thomas, 1966.

Wittgenstein, Ludwig. *Tractatus Logico-Philosophicus*. New York and London, 1922.

—— *Philosophical Investigations*. Oxford: Blackwell, 1963.

Wright, Crispin. "Language mastery and the sorites paradox." In Evans and McDowell, pp. 223–247.

Index